Praise for
The Pelican Squadron

"Characters right out of Dickens. Their depth makes the story a great read. Very complex and credible villain. Lines and descriptions right out of Hemingway. Reminds me of the WWII RAF veterans I knew while flying sailplanes at the London Gliding Club at Dunstable Downs in the UK. The story set the right atmosphere to bring back those memories. Excellent description, great ending."

—James Wastvedt, English instructor, English School System

"Very moving beginning. Great dialogue. Prose like Fitzgerald but much more interesting. From the beginning of the last part of the novel I could not put it down. The story has verisimilitude. I could believe it actually happened."

—Steven Mason, University of California, Berkeley, post grad instructor, creative writing department

"Sherman manages to tie together the war-torn past and Silicon Valley-present in an effortless way through well-written characters and evocative dialogue. Couldn't put it down once I started, and the ending only left me wanting more."

—Nathaniel Mellor, short story author and fiction editor of the online publication Pigeon Review

"*The Pelican Squadron* captures the excitement, deception, frustration, money, mystery, and even love that imbued Silicon Valley in the 80s and 90s. I know, because I lived through it. It's clear that the author, Harvey Sherman, did too. And even though it's a hefty book, the pace is fast. Be prepared to go inside the iconic communities that birthed so much of the culture that surrounds us today."

—Mark C. Leonard, CARTWRITE PUBLISHING

The Pelican Squadron

HARVEY GENE SHERMAN

Published by
Rusty Pelican Publishing

Print ISBN: 979-8-218-26787-2

This is a work of fiction. No events or persons, living or dead, with the exception of historically and publicly known people, are part of the story.

Note: Duarte's is not as depicted in the novel. I needed a saloon open at night for dancing. Duarte's is repurposed for this. Visit their website for bar hours if you go in the evening: Duarte's Tavern (duartestavern.com). It's a cool place. Photos of the food they serve there make me hungry.

Acknowledgements:
A grateful thank you to the following people, without whose encouragement and assistance this novel would never have been completed:

Don Wollesen, technical consultant - light aircraft
Joan Wollesen
Thor & Donna Thorson
Ann and Dick Tilton
John Butler, Englishness
Nathan Mellor, Editor
Phil Edwards, proofreading

Business, Crime, Suspense, Fiction, Historic Fiction, Mystery, Technology

Interior text printed in Palatino

To Artists and Their Struggles

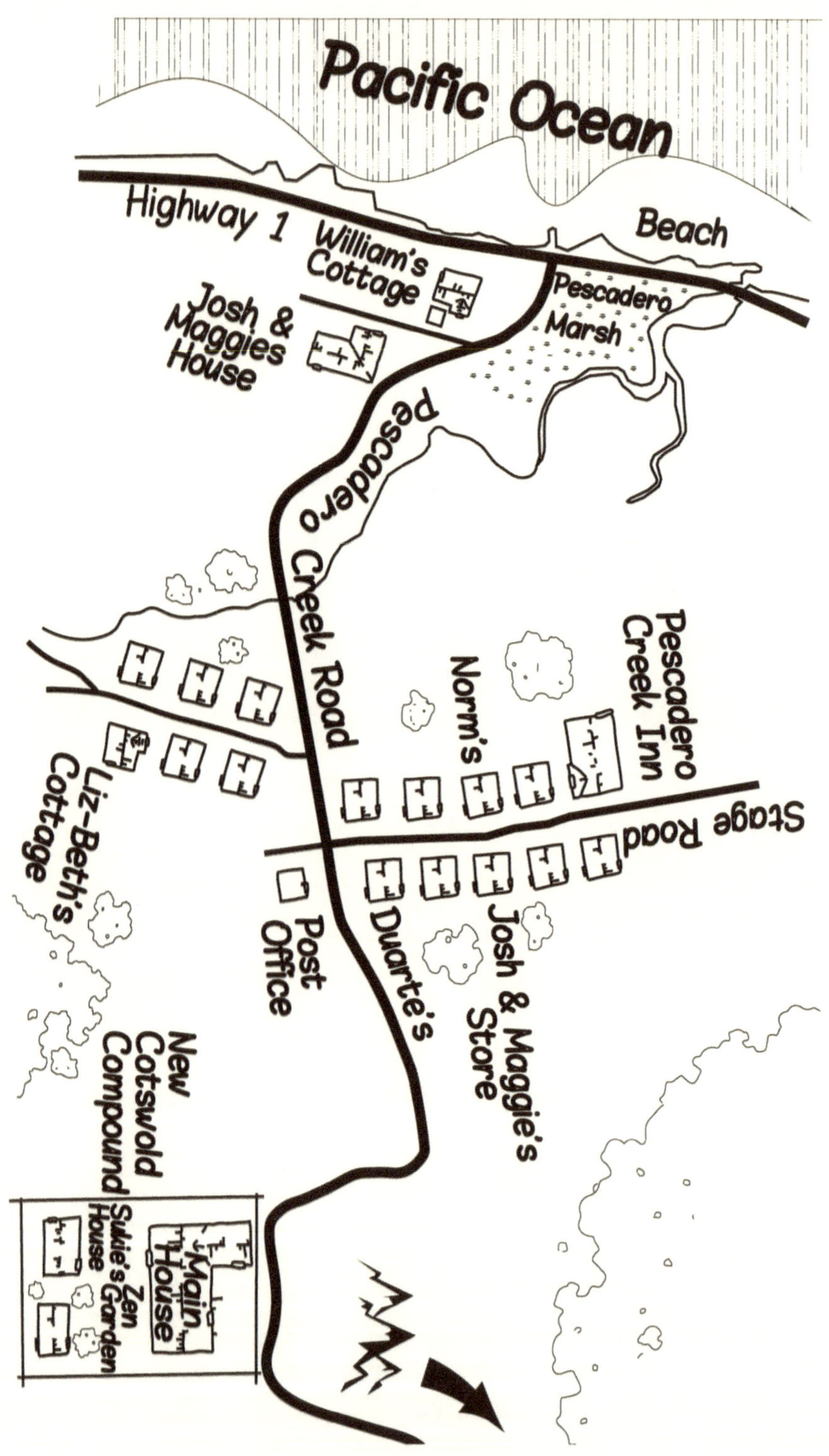

Pacific Ocean
Highway 1
William's Cottage
Beach
Josh & Maggies House
Pescadero Marsh
Pescadero Creek Road
Pescadero Creek Inn
Norm's
Liz-Beth's Cottage
Stage Road
Josh & Maggie's Store
Duarte's
Post Office
New Cotswold Compound
Sukie's Zen Garden House
Main House

Two Theaters One War

It began as a routine mission. Clear weather over Europe, airplane running well, light intermittent flak. Bombs released somewhere near the target, you could never tell exactly. On the return flight the wolves found them when the moon rose.

The impact shook the ravaged plane from end to end. You would have heard a loud dull thud from inside the fuselage when it hit the ground. The structure groaned; its welds and rivets strained to hold it together as it traversed the contours of the field in a final act it had not been designed to perform. A meadow of gentle elevations if you walked or drove across it, felt like a mogul field from inside an aluminum tube skidding to the ending of a horrific flight. Propellers bent, a wingtip caught the edge of a dip, pirouetting the plane in a slow motion death spin while a battered crew held tight to anything at hand. They prayed it would end quickly, and wondered if they could walk out on two good legs to view it as whole men from outside the plane when the horror ended.

Several hours before, the plane labored to rise slowly in twilight, carrying a crew of seven and 14,000 pounds of high explosive bombs. They headed east into hostile skies over occupied Europe in route to German submarine pens on the North Sea coast, one of many protagonists in a hostile flight carrying malice to a malignant enemy. On the return flight they were caught and attacked by everything the Luftwaffe could throw at them.

During the desperate aerial fight for survival, his flight engineer was killed, shot through the head in a harrowing frontal assault. Machine gun and cannon fire smashed the cockpit and blew a gun turret off the plane. Plexiglas broken out, oxygen gone, hydraulic fluid lost, most of the instruments shot out, a healthy man would have difficulty maintaining level flight. Wiggins was no healthy man. Shot through the leg with a 7.92 mm round from a nose gun of an ME 109, the navigator bandaged him as he piloted the plane due west with a tourniquet on his leg. Weak and nearly bled to death, no one else could fly the plane. On a clear night, with a full moon, Wiggins managed to bring his shot-up Lancaster over an abandoned field near Verune, Flanders, saving the remains of his crew and himself, before slumping over the yoke and passing out.

The Lancaster landed itself. Wiggins lost consciousness before the plane reached the ground. The navigator couldn't apply the tourniquet on his leg soon enough to keep him awake. It did save his life. Most of the crew were banged up or shot up, one of them dead from the frontal assault of an ME 109. They spent the rest of the night and the following day hiding in dense woods near enough to hobble to and big enough and far enough from the landing site to avoid detection. The following night they wandered the countryside until the resistance found them. The Belgians patched them up, fed them, smuggled them to the coast, and hid them in the wine cellar of an ancient stone farm house while further transport could be arranged. The wine was good. The weather changed to overcast. The moon cycled to a crescent and the skies darkened for travel. Reaching the coast in the back of a civilian truck, they traveled under cloud cover, transferred to the hold of a fishing boat on a secluded beach, and ferried across the channel. Wiggins might have spent the rest of the war a prisoner in East Prussia. This would be a different story.

Wiggins enlisted in the RAF early in 1939 at age 18, to do his part for King and country in a war he'd anticipated. A bomber pilot who flew England's heavies, Halifaxes and Lancasters. He participated in more than twenty five missions over Western

Europe. Promoted to flight, then squadron commander in his early twenties, on this night in December, 1942, the Germans shot his Lancaster down over occupied Europe.

Rehabilitation in a Sussex hospital left Wiggins with a noticeable limp from a leg wound that would never completely heal. Assigned a staff position, he planned and briefed bombing missions. His crew recovered rapidly. Reassigned, given a new captain, flight engineer and plane, they returned to combat status in time to volunteer to skip-bomb the Mohne Dam in the Ruhr Valley, May 1943. One of half the crews to survive the mission, six months later, they were shot down again over Germany and lost to history.

Wiggins recovered near airbases engaged in the Battle of Britain, when in the early days of the war England fought Germany alone. Now their squadrons took the war to the Germans. After gaining energy and strength, Wiggins ventured into town where he found a pub to his liking. He made it his regular after-hours mission. In the winter of 1944, whilst pounding down pints at *Chequers* he engaged in spirited economics debates with JM Keynes who frequented the pub with his partner. Wiggins caught the eye of young beautiful Elisabeth Victoria Simpson who had by coincidence the same surname as the American woman King Edward VIII abdicated to marry in 1936. A free spirited American, an odd match for the reserved Wiggins, Ms. Simpson came over as a nurse with US 8th Air Force Bomber Command. Thought by a stiff-necked female officer to be flighty for her profession, she reassigned Liz-Beth to the motor pool. Pretty, fun loving, Liz-Beth received a Jeep to chauffeur senior officers. Accustomed to driving farm equipment in America, Liz-Beth drove nimble little short wheelbase Jeeps over narrow English country roads, *con brio*. Ms. Simpson promptly crashed three jeeps before being unofficially classified a threat to the war effort. More importantly a threat to the career of the motor pool CO, a little driving instruction including orders to slow down made it safe for social and recreational transportation. With minor damage and no injuries reported, the accidents provided amusement and moral for the motor pool. Surviving without a scratch earned her the nick name "Lucky Simpson." She became the go-to pub delivery driver. "Get me Lucky" became the code phrase for "Get me to the pub," driven of course, by Ms. Simpson.

On an evening pub run, Ms. Simpson spotted the dashing Wiggins trapped in boring conversation at the bar, eyes darting around the room searching for rescue. After breaking free of three adoring Americans, Liz-Beth crossed the room and attached herself without introduction. With an arm wrapped around his, she beamed at Wiggins and tossed her head toward the other end of the room.

Enchanted by this fearless free spirit, Wiggins made good his escape by allowing Liz-Beth to drag him away. She left him no choice. She had no intention of letting go of his arm until he came along. *No way we lose this war*, Wiggins thought. When Ms. Simpson discovered the tall, decorated Wiggins had the great dry English wit and could cut a rug in spite of a limp, she knew she had her man. From that evening, to the disappointment of many, the charming RAF officer had Liz-Beth to himself.

Wiggins managed assignment as advisor to 8th Air Force Bomber Command. After that he and Liz-Beth were seen together everywhere, and the romance became official. They drove to Brighton and London. They danced, they dined, they attended theater. They carried on for the better part of a year while Ms. Simpson perfected the art of driving a jeep to the pub, back finding excuses to go when Bunny went there to decompress. Wiggins took an occasional milk run with the boys of the 8th in their Fortresses. Liz-Beth learned to corner the little Willys like the Jeep ran on rails. She ran through the gears like Wilber Shaw and slid to a stop like Ty Cobb slid into bases.

Then the war in Europe ended.

* * *

On the other side of the world, Captain John Beckinsdale struggled to keep his plane in the air. Streaks of oil leaked out of holes in the engine cowl where the bullets entered and spread across his windscreen erasing his forward vision. He felt the impacts, the vibrations and sounds of an uneven beat of a damaged engine. He smelled the smoking oil and leaking coolant. He John knew the motor would not last. The doomed plane could not return him to Henderson Field even if it had enough fuel. The patrol and the fight carried him north and west beyond the return range of his airplane as he maneuvered radically on maximum power at the limits of his Wildcat.

Saito Saki marveled at the flying skill of the American he'd heard of and finally met in the air. Saito flew a Zero, a Japanese plane with superior dog fighting capability. The length of time and effort it took to reduce the Wildcat surprised him. In his flying experience over the previous five years with the Japanese Airforce, he'd never encountered a pilot so skilled and determined to survive.

The Wildcat shuddered again as more bullets from the Zero nicked Beckinsdale's shoulder and shattered his instrument cluster. The radio destroyed, his control surfaces barely responsive, John thought these were the last moments of his life. He could only pull back the Plexiglas and hope to parachute to the ocean without being shot.

Saito paused his assault when he saw the nose rise and the Wildcat slow as the American leveled it and opened the canopy. Saito knew he needed to finish it, but couldn't carry out the ending to this magnificent fight. Something noble in his ancestry compelled him to give the pilot a chance to live. *I wish I could offer a wing to walk across and fly him home a prisoner,* Saito thought. He pulled alongside the stricken Wildcat and opened his own cockpit to look at the American. He saw a patch of red stain spread across the pilot's shoulder and could not bring himself to resume the attack on an injured pilot and a crippled plane. He imagined himself in the American's position, hurt and struggling to keep his plane in the air. *What would this man do if our positions were reversed?* Saito wondered. As the American turned his head, Saito saw the grim look on his face, and a grimace of pain. At the maximum range from his base, hundreds of miles to the north, Saito could not linger. He nodded once, tipped a wing, and flew off toward Buin.

Captain Beckinsdale had little time to reflect on the nobility of Saito's act of mercy, how it might end if they encountered each other again. With the Zero flying away, John thought he had enough control to bring the Wildcat down. The flight ended in ocean swells 50 yards from a beach. John saved his .45 and rescued his first aid kit. He swam to the island and dragged himself onto the sand. Exhausted, in pain from his injured shoulder, he watched the wings and fuselage of the Wildcat disappear below the waves and settle on a shallow reef, leaving a few feet of the tail section above the water line. The surf pushed the damaged rudder back and forth as if the plane waved goodbye. John flew 20 missions in the Wildcat he'd named *Miriam*, after a lost love. *It's only metal, plastic, and rubber*, he told himself. Even so, he felt like his best friend just died.

John didn't know his exact location. He crawled into the jungle to clean and bandage his shoulder, to hide and wait. Within the hour two islanders walked toward him along the beach. The men had seen the plane come down and came to investigate. John took a chance. Like many people who lived in the Solomon Islands, the villagers resented the Japanese for enslaving them to build their structures and defenses. They assisted the Australians, now Americans. John took a chance. They led him to their village where they fed him and explained with gestures they needed him to wait. John wondered if they intended to turn him over to the Japanese, if he had to surrender or fight his way out. *Where could I go?* he thought. John knew there were no Americans on any island in the area. He'd heard islanders sometimes brought downed fliers to the attention of Australian coast watchers and returned them to their bases. He could only trust and hope. As afternoon turned to dusk the villagers brought out an outrigger. They beckoned John to join them. Four islanders pulled the boat and a passenger into the surf by moonlight, paddled into the ocean and headed south. When they rounded the island and turned southeast, John understood they were taking him home. The patrol and the flight had taken him 250 miles northwest of Guadalcanal.

Over the next days, they traveled by moonlight along coastlines as much as possible to avoid Japanese patrols. John slept on a bed of palm leaves under a tarp, lulled to sleep by exhaustion and rhythmic paddling synchronized to soothing melodic island songs in a language he didn't know. They beached the boat when the sky began to lighten and hid in the jungle during the day. They lived on fruit and dried fish from a friendly village. John developed a fever from his wound. He lost track of the day of the week and didn't remember arriving at Guadalcanal. He vaguely recalled the sound and flashes of gunfire and explosions from Japanese planes flying over to bomb Henderson Field as the villagers paddled into the bay.

Young in life but old in occupation, the attrition of a tour on *Cactus*, the name the US military gave the island of Guadalcanal, took a toll on John. No longer capable of leading a combat patrol, Captain Beckinsdale's nerves were as shot up as his Wildcat. His CO sent him to the States to teach new pilots the skills he used to survive. After discharge from a Texas base at war's end, he relocated to a suburb of Seattle where he did little but rest between shoreline walks along Lake Washington until he felt ready to return to life.

Beckinsdale found work at Moffitt Naval Air Station in California, testing surveillance and avionics equipment for Lockheed under contract to the Navy. He settled into a modest Mountain View house. In a few years he'd saved enough money to buy a dilapidated cottage with a barn across from the Pacific Ocean, in the small village of Pescadero as a weekend retreat. A nearby airfield made a convenient location to fly in and pick up a surplus

Jeep he parked there. He found the work easy and weekends on the coast pleasing. John enjoyed an occasional low altitude flight up the coast over water, along the beaches to the Farallon Islands where he indulged a lifelong love of flight, spending hours aloft with the island birds. In the early 1960s he took up the hobby of car racing. He stored a car in the barn and towed it to races at Laguna Seca with the Jeep. With the passage of years, his nightmares faded. Captain Beckinsdale left the horrors of war in the South Pacific behind and began a new life.

* * *

Colonel Sukie Nakajima gazed at the Pacific Ocean from a cliff below Mt. Suribachi. He noted the scent of a mixture of Pacific Ocean salt spray and sulfurous soils of the island as he listened to waves crashing on a beach he thought would soon be covered in blood and bodies and equipment of an invasion force and that of the island's defenders on the mountain above him. He imagined a vast American fleet arriving in the morning half-light after several days of enduring its air arm bombing and strafing hopeless defenders. A vision he did not wish to see.

"Colonel Nakajima."

"Please call me Sukie."

"Sukie. I like this name. It is a friendly name. Please call me Saito."

"Thank you Saito."

"You are supervising construction of our island defenses?"

"Yes. An extensive bunker system and a great many locations for hidden artillery with 18 miles of tunnels to connect them. For many of us I have dug their tombs."

"Will you complete this before the Americans arrive?"

"Yes."

"Can we keep the Americans off this island?"

"We have not repelled any American landing. How is it in the air?"

"It is not good. In the beginning we did well. We decimated the first Americans we grappled. We had better planes. They are smart those Americans. They learned how to overcome the deficiencies of their planes, to fight us on their terms when they could win. After that they downed one of us for every one we downed of them. We cannot win such a war. Soon they will bomb the home islands mercilessly if the army cannot hold this place and the next one. Already they bomb us from Guam."

"We cannot, Saito. There are too many. They command the seas. We cannot supply this island and cannot grow food here. The soil is too sulfurous."

"Then we will lose this war. We cannot replace our pilots even if we could make enough planes. We are sending inexperienced pilots to their deaths. The Americans now have superior planes and experienced pilots. Our positions are reversed from the beginning when we could only fight them to a draw. They have many more airfields for training pilots than we have in all of Japan. They send pilots experienced from the fighting to train them. We can spare none. Soon there will be no experienced pilots left to fight them."

"Like you?"

"Like me. I am lucky to be alive. I don't know how much longer. Survival is more difficult now, more luck, more a game of avoiding their guns than engaging them." Saito paused for a moment as his words settled their weight inside him. He shared a pivotal experience.

"I once fought an American, a very brave man, the best pilot I have ever seen. We fought a long duel. He made one mistake. He did not know the capability of my plane. My bullets crippled his. He had to slow and fly straight. I saw his canopy open. He must have thought it was his end. I eased alongside of him and saw he had been injured by my bullets. I saw the blood spread from his shoulder. I felt badly for this brave young man who worked so hard to be the great pilot that he was. An acrobat of the sky. He was an enemy but I thought of him as a fellow pilot. I thought I could have killed him so easily."

"What did you do?"

"He smiled at me through his pain. I could see he did not hate me. That touched me to the bone. I showed him mercy. I let him go. His chances of survival were small. His plane could not stay in the air. Our duel took him too far from his base. I would like to know what happened to this man, if he somehow made it home."

"They have rescue people."

"I know. We do not. We cannot spare the ships and planes. Pilots are precious. We should try."

"What did you do after that?"

"I flew home. When they rearmed my Zero, my ground crew told me I had no bullets left in my guns. The American could not have known this. I could not have killed him. He flew so well, he made me miss so many times. I shot my weapons into the air." Saito paused, turned to Sukie and lowered his voice. "Please don't tell anyone I let him go. I don't know what they would do."

"I will keep your secret." Sukie nodded.

Saito continued from an impassioned heart. "Our brave young men. We are sending them to die. We do not armor our planes so they will be light and maneuverable. They explode from the American's guns. That is the merciful way. Some spiral down into land or sea, in a fireball, like riding a Roman candle. That is the horror way. Soon we will have nothing but Kamikazes and me, the last fighter pilot. There are only 80 of us here. The Americans when they come in the hundreds, they will sweep us from the skies."

"Kamikazes in the air?"

Saito nodded yes. "Piloted flying bombs to crash into ships. We will do great damage but still we will not win."

Sukie looked at Saito in horror. Saito asked him reflectively, painfully. "Why do we fight this war with the Americans?"

"I don't know, Saito. I am a humble builder."

"Where will they send you after this?"

"Singapore."

Saito stared into the sky. "I don't think I will see the end of this war. Tomorrow I will train a group of Kamikaze fliers. Soon we will seek American ships."

Sukie looked into Saito's despairing eyes. "I hope you live past the end, and I too so we can meet in better times."

"I wish to see you too, in Japan at my home where we will toast our survival with Sake."

Saito gave Sukie a headband decorated with a rising sun.

"Keep this for me Sukie to return or remember me."

Sukie showed Saito a photo of his mother and father, his two brothers and a younger sister. "It has our address in Tokyo on the back," he said. Saito took it and turned it over.

"I know this area," he said. "I miss the sights and sounds of happy shoppers in the market, the smell of fresh fish, the taste of Ramen. I will meet you there after the war if I survive."

Sukie saw an officer walking in their direction. "Here comes that sadist Tanaka."

"You know him?"

"Yes, I knew him in China. He is very evil. He committed crimes against women, children, helpless prisoners. Tortures, rapes, killing for sport."

"I heard we did terrible things to Australians and now Americans, to downed fliers, the worst. There are rumors of cannibalism. They will make us suffer for such people after the war."

"Captain, Sakai!"

"Colonel Tanaka."

Saito saluted Sukie, not Tanaka.

"They are waiting for you in headquarters. Come immediately," Tanaka yelled from ten yards away.

"Yes, Colonel." Saito turned to Sukie again and lowered his voice. He shared with earnest eyes what he knew in his heart. "There will be no mercy for Japanese people for what we have done."

Sukie gave Saito a grim look. He too, knew the fate of his country. Saito pulled a strip of paper out of a shirt pocket.

"Please keep this, Sukie-San. I feel I will not survive this war. You may well. If I do not it will be something to remember me by. It is my haiku. I had dreams that are no more. This hideous war has stolen them from me. Perhaps there will be memories of me, of who I was, what I dreamed. They will send me to die for the emperor while he is safe and living in luxury in his Kyoto palace. We can no longer supply these islands. The Americans bypass them and leave us to starve. You have a better chance of survival my friend. They need you to build their defenses for the Americans to destroy, if necessary, all the way to Kyoto. You will survive Colonel Nakajima. Please say you will remember me."

"I will remember you. A brave man who did his duty and was capable of mercy when others were not, but I hope you will be more than a memory."

"Good luck to you, Colonel Nakajima."

"Good luck to you, Captain Sakai."

"Saito, come NOW! General Kuribayashi is waiting for you," Tanaka shouted in impatience and anger. *He is insubordinate,* Tanaka fumed.

"Yes, Colonel."

Saito and Sukie looked into each other's eyes.

"I enjoyed our little talk" Saito said.

"And I too. I hope to see you again."

"At your family home."

Saito bowed and offered a grim smile. He stood and joined Tanaka. They walked away.

His death mask, Sukie thought. *Poor man. I hope he lives.* As he watched Saito walk away he wondered; *Why do we do these things to each other? We are only on this earth a short time. What happens to us, the way we treat each other, they are the only things that matter in this life.*

A Journey to California

One

After V-J Day, now RAF Wing Commander Colonel Wiggins transferred to Singapore as attaché to Lord Mountbatten, Supreme Allied Commander, Southeast Asia Command in time to participate in the victory parade. Before leaving Sussex, he married Miss Simpson to get even he said, for all the Brit birds the Yanks had stolen when they "occupied" England. After her discharge, the now Mrs. Elizabeth Victoria Simpson Harold Bentley-Wiggins followed Harry to Singapore. Sussex motor pool never recovered. Singapore became a crown colony the following year. After 6 months of administration work, Wiggins had enough of RAF life. He decided he had no interest in a career as bureaucrat or politician. Twice war weary in respective generations, deeply in debt, most English citizens struggled with family losses and distressed finances. Churchill was out. The English people no longer tolerated the burden of supporting a million-man army garrisoned in foreign lands. Wiggins didn't wish to participate in dismantling the empire he had risked his life to save. With no appealing future in the RAF, he decided to move on.

Mrs. Wiggins never took to Singapore and didn't want to return to England. Too gloomy, she said. Homesick for America, excited by boundless post-war opportunity, she dragged Wiggins to San Francisco, where they used his considerable contacts in England and Singapore to set up a trading company in 1947.

The "Wiggins Trading Company" operated out of a warehouse in the South of Market neighborhood where they could be close to waterfront piers. Harold and Liz-Beth moved into an apartment on Telegraph Hill. After establishing the business, they purchased a single-family home in Pacific Heights with an expansive view of the San Francisco Bay.

Harold Bentley-Wiggins was an authentic and proper English gentleman born and raised in Berkhamsted, Hertfordshire, the only child of a public school mathematics instructor. Harold was not so academically inclined. Harold's father Alfred taught at Berkhamsted School, founded 1541 by John Incent, Dean of St. Paul's Cathedral. The family lived near the campus in a modest but comfortable home. Harold day-boarded. Novelist Graham Greene, who attended when Harold's father served as headmaster, later wrote he had been "molded in a special way through Berkhamsted." Baroness Clementine Spencer attended. She later married Sir Winston.

Tall and slender, Wiggins sported a thin mustache. He could have been David Niven's brother. His small animated eyes, dark and narrow-set, missed nothing. Wiggins carried himself erect, head up and back, on a long narrow neck. Long slender arms were hard and muscular. He strode with the deliberation of a walking tree, moving gracefully and confidently in spite of the limp, with the momentum of a man who presumed he would have his way.

Harold preferred being called "Wiggins" or Harry by his friends. Mrs. Wiggins called him "Bunny." Athletic, a good footballer, an average student, Harry claimed to be better at both than he was.

Wiggins could sell you the coat on your back and the hair on your head. He dressed and groomed like a diplomat. An upper-class British accent enabled him to glide through doors that didn't open for everyone, and ease though difficult negotiations. He knew how to compromise with grace and say no without burning bridges. He entertained his way through business deals.

Unlike his math whiz father, Wiggins couldn't sum a column and produce the same answer twice. Numbers bored him. The skills that eluded him were a natural gift to Liz-Beth. Their partnership succeeded. Liz-Beth turned out to be a good CFO and a shrewd investor with a cash surplus; talents that enabled them to build significant professional relationships and wealth outside of their trading business. Over the years, the Wiggins Trading Company provided a comfortable life, and the funds to build a generous retirement.

Liz-Beth was a pretty, long haired honey blond from Wisconsin of Scandinavian descent. Her lovely slender arms looked vulnerable in a dress, but she grew up familiar with farm work and possessed an abundance of strength. She ran like a track star and walked weightlessly, gliding so softly her feet seemed to float above the ground. Her large brown eyes and warm smile melted glaciers. Keen wit hid behind a disarming doll-like face but Liz-Beth was no girl.

Liz-Beth adopted an irascible juvenile parrot she found in a San Francisco pet store. The bird belonged to the Telegraph Hill flock that inhabited San Francisco. It showed up on the doorstep one morning and moved in. She named it Mr. Chuckles. The bird "spoke" English and Japanese. Except for intent, he understood neither. He had a large vocabulary for a bird but in the presence of anyone besides Wiggins and Liz-Beth he rarely said anything but "Shut up stupid!" Chuckles cursed in Japanese when something or somebody upset him.

Wiggins resented Chuckles for his habit of interrupting his reading. He had to leave the room to escape the confounded parrot. Wiggins liked the bird in spite of it, found its independence admirable and amusing, qualities he admired in Liz-Beth. "Can you leave me in peace you stupid bird!" he admonished. "I'll feed you to a hawk!"

"Shut-up Stupid, Shut-Up Stupid!" the fearless bird answered, wings flapping, displaying his crown.

"Stop bothering Mr. Chuckles," Liz-Beth would say in amusement. "Stop bothering Mr. Chuckles. Stop bothering Mr. Chuckles," Chuckles repeated. Amused by the predicament of a man who stared down death in a world conflagration but allowed himself to be chased out of his own room by a bird, Wiggins abandoned the space.

Mr. Chuckles liked rum but the birdbrain he was, he didn't know when to quit. Liz-Beth had to cut him off. Chuckles would throw down any brand but he seemed to have a preference for Captain Morgan. A parrot of discriminating taste, he cocked his head and stared if Liz-Beth offered a brand he considered to be substandard. Maybe he liked the pirate on the label or the Morgan Girls. Liz-Beth sometimes gave him enough to make him tipsy, not enough for him to swing to the upside down position. It kept him swaying back and forth quietly. Chuckles liked his buzz. It must have been fun to be a parrot in a spinning room. "If only parrots could smile" thought Liz-Beth. She knew what made him happy. When he didn't need attention Mr. Chuckles perched quietly like a good parrot while Bunny and Liz-Beth read or listened to piano music from the romantic period. Chuckles like romantic piano. It relaxed him. When they entertained, they moved him to a bedroom before the guests arrived to prevent him from disturbing the evening. A cloth over his cage and a few sips of rum kept him quiet. It didn't take him long to figure out what the rum was for and how to obtain it. He made a fuss. The villagers knew him as "The drunken parrot of Pescadero." Yo, ho, ho, Mr. Chuckles! "Yo, ho, ho," squawked Mr. Chuckles but only for Liz-Beth and Wiggins.

Liz-Beth had a fetish for consignment shopping that had little to do with money and everything to do with fun. Co-owner of a trading company, she was a shrewd trader. She dressed her "chauffer" Sukie in a dark suit. He drove her and Mr. Chuckles in a Bentley. Sukie stood by an open rear door in a wide stance, hands clasped in front of him, while Liz-Beth brought the bird inside to model clothing. A cultured parrot, Mr. Chuckles helped Liz-Beth select outfits to trade for clothing she brought in the boot of the Bentley. Chuckles turned away in distain when an outfit failed his standards. He flapped his wings, whistled and made kissing sounds when he approved. A parrot fashionista! More often than not, he had it right.

Neither Liz-Beth nor Sukie shared their thrift shop adventures with Wiggins. Mr. Chuckles knew how to keep a secret too. Wiggins knew Liz-Beth drove off with Chuckles in his cage and Sukie dressed in a suit. He knew she often returned wearing a new and expensive looking outfit while spending hardly any money. Some kind of shopping genius or master shoplifter; Wiggins didn't know and didn't want to know. He liked her taste and enjoyed seeing her well-dressed. Other than spending little to accomplish it she gave him no reason to inquire. He sometimes thought she funded a secret clothing account with profits skimmed from the business. As long as bills were paid, there were no financial surprises, and no arrests, he didn't care how she did it. It didn't surprise him. Liz-Beth managed their financial affairs well.

During a weekend drive down the coast to Santa Cruz, Bunny, Liz-Beth, and Mr. Chuckles stopped in the little village of Pescadero where they fell in love with the rocky beach, the coastal hills, both blocks of downtown, and the quirky local population. After years of summer visits they bought land in the foothills east of the village including an easement with a trailhead to the beach. Some day they thought, they would live there. By 1957, ten years after starting the trading business, they had done well.

Two

Wiggins recruited the venerable Sanshiro Nakajima to maintain his home when they lived in Singapore. "Sukie" could make or repair most anything with a modest set of hand tools. Military-political relationships enabled Wiggins to bring Sukie to America where he maintained the house in San Francisco, later the house where they spent weekends in Pescadero.

Wiggins fished Sukie out of Changi Prison in Singapore after the war ended. Built as a provincial prison by the British in 1936, they used it to house POWs after the war as the Japanese did while they'd occupied it. Changi is an infamous place. Japanese captives suffered and died there. The British held Sukie during war crimes investigations resulting from eight years' service as an officer in the Imperial Japanese Army. Imprisonment may have saved him from revenge killings even though he committed no crimes. The Japanese government conscripted Sukie. He was a pacifist.

Sukie received professional education at Hokkaido University in Sapporo in the Japanese style of architecture and construction before the war. Commercial property experience enabled him to serve his country without participating in the fighting. Late in the war, he'd commanded an engineering unit in Singapore that maintained roads, bridges, and railroads, and managed civilians who kept the water, power and sewer infrastructure functioning. Sukie witnessed atrocities. He did not participate in them. He thought cruelty to POWs and civilians in occupied countries were crimes against humanity, not at all native to Japanese tradition or morality hijacked by militarists in the 1930's. Sukie believed the best part of Japanese culture had been replaced with something evil and self-destructive.

Sukie stood on the opposite side of a prison fence dressed in a once proud now dirty and tattered officer's uniform the first time Wiggins saw him. Years of working in the sun turned Sukie's skin dark and leathery. Physical labor calloused his hands. Though thin from poor wartime nutrition, he stood erect, appeared alert, and vigorous.

Wiggins thought he saw intelligence in Sukie's eyes, composure that transcended the harsh circumstances he lived in. A prisoner, not a criminal, Sukie appeared unbroken. He accepted defeat of his country as a matter of fact. He did not despair of it. Wiggins saw the strength of character he looked for. Sukie saw a British officer who did not look on him disdainfully. Wiggins asked the camp commandant to arrange an interview. They met man to man, not captor to captive. in the commandant's office.

If he hadn't seen worse Wiggins would have cringed at the dismal state of Sukie's tattered uniform. Sukie noted the contrast to Wiggins' freshly washed and pressed Royal military attire.

"Wing Commander Wiggins, Royal Air Force, General Staff, Far East."

"Japanese Imperial Army soldier, Sanshiro Nakajima." Sukie began with the organization he belonged to first and his name last in Japanese tradition. He did not state his rank. He bowed respectfully.

"I am in need of a man to help repair and maintain a rather large home in Singapore. I understand you were responsible for facilities and are skilled in such work."

Sukie presented his qualifications.

"I know you were an officer. I cannot offer you a management position or promise long term employment. I need one man of many skills and experience who is willing to work with his hands. I can offer a small salary, daily meals, your own room, in return for hard work and long hours. I will treat you fairly with as much respect as you earn. You will have a modest, but safe and comfortable place to live, good food, but little more. I don't know for how long, or what may happen in the future. I can get you out of this place if you are willing to provide my wife and myself with the assistance we require. Does this interest you?"

"I would like to leave this place, Wing Commander Wiggins." Sukie spoke in textbook English with little accent. "If you provide as you offer, I will serve you well, and honorably. I will help you make a good home for as long as you want me."

"I will be in contact with you. Please be patient."

Sukie bowed. Wiggins nodded in agreement. He knew he found his man.

Sukie turned out to be a first-class gardener, a magnificent chef of both eastern and western cuisine, and an excellent carpenter, a practitioner of traditional methods of Japanese construction.

After Wiggins bought land in Pescadero, Sukie constructed the equipment shed, greenhouse, and his own humble Japanese style home at the eastern side of the property, near the foothills. Beautifully crafted in the traditional method with Japanese hand tools, a small but comfortable home satisfied a man of simple taste and few possessions. He designed and planted a Japanese garden next to his house. He constructed a Zen Garden for relaxation, meditation, spiritual life. Sukie managed contractors during construction of the manor house for Mr. and Mrs. Wiggins. The workers initially resented a Japanese supervisor. Sukie earned their respect with patience, by demonstrating skill and knowledge.

Quality of life with the Wiggins' exceeded the life Sukie knew when he served Japanese militarists, and as a poor rice farmer's son growing up in Japan. He rewarded kindness and opportunity by performing his duties professionally, with enthusiasm and dedication.

Skeletal when Wiggins discovered him, Sukie ate himself portly in California. In spite of a life of physical activity, by the time he completed his own residence, he resembled a miniature sumo wrestler, a Buddha absent the thick black hair he had at a younger age. Content with a simple life in San Francisco, and later in Pescadero, he dreamed of no other. In time he felt like a family member and was treated as one.

When he met Wiggins at the Changi prison, Sukie knew little more than textbook English. After moving to Pescadero he frequented the public library in Cupertino. There he met the librarian Mrs. Akiko Ito, a third generation American who had been interned with her family in a camp at Manzanar in the Owens Valley during the war. In spite of internment, Mrs. Ito's husband joined the 442nd Infantry Regiment, the Japanese American unit which became the most highly decorated infantry regiment in US Army history. Sadly, Corporal Ito did not survive the war.

Born in America, Mrs. Ito had never visited Japan. She had no friends or relatives there, and spoke no Japanese. A willing student, Sukie instructed her. From this he became proficient in conversational English. Sukie read western history and sociology, keeping what he learned between himself and Mrs. Ito. He subscribed to American and Japanese periodicals. Eventually, he spoke perfect and elegant English, better English than many Americans.

*　*　*

On a trip to London, Wiggins visited his childhood home. He made the pilgrimage to Tewkesbury in The Cotswolds, halfway between the Forest of Dean and Stratford-Upon-Avon where he spotted a large manor house that must have belonged to a man of titles at one time but now looked abandoned and in disrepair. Upon inquiry with a local realtor, he discovered the owner had died and his heirs considered putting it up for sale. Wiggins bought the property. The residents of Cotswolds weren't happy to lose a 500 year old stone manor home and its contents to a crude new-world place like California. Wiggins donated the land to a private boy's school where his father once taught math to placate them. He included enough funds to establish a football field on the site to be called "Alfred Wiggins Field" after his father. Fair Compensation, he said, for removing the house to America. An impulse purchase, he thought it had potential but here it stood in England, far from its intended home. *Our property in Pescadero needs a house,* he thought. *We can use it there on weekends and holidays. Why not move it?* Liz-Beth thought it both a foolish and wonderful idea to relocate a house from England. With the trading company doing well, they could afford the indulgence. It would not be the only stone building moved to Northern California from England. Two pubs had been relocated from England to the Bay Area.

Wiggins made an inquiry at the firm of Fenwick and Partners because they worked internationally and might know a way. The project amused Roger Fenwick. They struck a deal. Fenwick put architect Parker Barfield on the project because of his experience renovating old stone manor homes. He knew how they were constructed, therefore how to deconstruct them, the theory goes.

Barfield thought it would be feasible to disassemble the house from top down, a course at a time, and mark each stone with a code to indicate which wall and course they belonged to so the house could be reassembled accordingly. Down it came, both stories. Wiggins would have to roof and drywall it in California but the ancient oak floors would be usable as were the windows which were crated for shipment.

The stones were stacked on pallets according to floor and room, loaded on lorries, and taken to the nearest port for shipping across the Atlantic, through the Panama Canal, up to San Francisco and transferred to trucks for the drive to Pescadero.

Wiggins hired subcontractors for Sukie to manage, and up the manor house went. Wiggins and Liz-Beth stayed at the local Inn on weekends to join in the work on the property. Liz-Beth thought it proof of insanity, and marvelous. Wiggins spent a month in England planning the project, interviewing vendors and managing it. Horribly expensive, Wiggins thought it was worth it.

Arrival of the caravan stunned the Pescadero villagers. It began as an outrageous project. It ended as a local architectural masterpiece, a source of village pride. The manor home was a magnificent thing; by far the largest house in the village, the only one with stone walls. It had a two-story exposed beam great room across from an open kitchen. It had a long, heavy wooden dining table made from a single ancient plank of oak cut from the heartwood of a great tree. The table seated twenty people. A huge sofa and several large chairs with soft, deep cushions embraced the people who sat in them. A stone fireplace reached the second story ceiling to warm the house in winter and serve as a cooking hearth. It took the chill off cool, foggy summer evenings. Bunny's prized Benelli hung over the mantle. Its bright work and engraving blazed in the house lights. He covered the walls with paintings of fox hunts and hounds, steeple chases and cricket matches that came from the house in England; of English castles, of summering at lakes, of sailboats and rowboats, of picnicking at riverfronts.

Wiggins spent years of weekends and vacations building a three-foot wall of small stones found on the property to surround and mark its boundaries. He planted an English garden irrigated to support plant life native to rainy England. Heirloom roses thrived in abundant sunlight. The butterflies rejoiced. The colors in their delicate wings rivaled the palette of rose petals. Ladybugs took up residence in summer. He stocked a pond with koi where he and Mrs. Wiggins shared tea in the afternoon. They entertained villagers, guests from San Francisco, occasional visitors from across the oceans. They prepared lavish meals, sipped French wines, single malt scotches, and Irish whiskey in the great room. The men smoked cigars and pipes as they listened to music, played bridge, discussed the news of the world. They stared into fireplaces fueled with wood from trees sourced from the property. Wiggins felled, rounded and split them by hand. In summer they retired to the garden for ocean air, moon and star gazing. Sheltered from city light by coastal mountains, skies black as ink were perforated by circulating stars on clear nights. Brilliant moons lit paths across the ocean. Much bigger than any man, woman, dog and parrot needed, to those who thought relocating a stone manor house across an ocean a foolish, uneconomic project, Wiggins asked dryly, "Have you been to the Hearst Castle?"

Three

Harry and Liz-Beth shared an open, expansive, second floor office over the trading company warehouse South of Market, with a wall of windows overlooking the San Francisco Bay. The view included the Bay Bridge, Treasure Island, Alameda, and a mixed marina of private fishing and sail boats. Their twin desks faced north, parallel to the long side of the rectangular space. An east wall of glass framed sunrise and moonrise over the marina. A kitchenette lined the opposing wall. A leather sofa and two arm chairs occupied the center of the room, surrounding a rectangular glass top coffee table with a China tea service, and a brace of daily newspapers and magazines arranged across the surface. A vast, handmade Persian rug that looked like it consumed a lifetime of weaving, covered aged, original oak floors, the color of medium roast coffee. Once a nightclub, they turned the building into warehouse and office. The walls were unpainted red brick. HVAC ducts and water pipes painted black, hung under sixteen foot plaster ceilings with tungsten fixtures to light the room. An eight by ten foot Blaeu map of the world hung on the wall opposite the windows.

The Bay Bridge spanned across Treasure Island to Oakland and glowed romantically at night. Mesmerized by the view, Harry and Liz-Beth stared at lights reflecting off the water when they stayed late to call or fax agents in Asia, manage preparation for a morning shipment, or stroll along the embarcadero to the financial district for dinner. Harry's life, when he didn't travel, tethered him to a telephone handset; Liz-Beth's to the warehouse and the company ledgers.

As the Wiggins Trading Company prospered, the reputation of the owners spread through business circles of San Francisco. Harry and Liz-Beth developed relationships with successful people though private clubs and business associations. A time of population growth and business expansion, they learned of opportunities to invest in growing local companies. One business, a successful manufacturing company from which they acquired commercial audio equipment, caught their attention when it sought capital to design and introduce a consumer product line and expand nationally using noise reduction technology licensed from local audio pioneer Ray Dolby. The owners, Edgar and Evelyn Baldwin, were social friends. Harry and Liz-Beth decided to help them. "Baldwin Audio" did well. The company obtained distribution, built a sales force, increased production, made a profit and paid a dividend. Using Wiggin's contacts, Edgar sourced components from Asia to reduce the cost of systems assembled in South San Francisco. The day before a quarterly dividend distribution, Edgar paid a visit.

Edgar arrived at the Wiggins Trading Company on a gloomy, wet day, a week after Thanksgiving, at the beginning of several weeks of rain Northern California sometimes receives in late fall or winter. The receptionist thought he looked uncharacteristically tired and disheveled. He greeted her and walked upstairs to the executive offices.

Edgar could be described as a man of averages. Average height, average build, average weight. His face lacked distinguishing features. Olive skinned, well dressed, well groomed, Edgar parted his short black hair on the side, and had a full head of it. He wore a single breasted, narrow lapel Nordstrom suit off the rack, medium grey, over a white button-down long sleeve shirt, with a burgundy tie. Varying little day to day, it seemed like Edgar owned only one suit, one shirt, one tie, or a closet of clones. Edgar's shoes were sturdy black lace ups, freshly shined. He looked like any other conservatively dressed businessman. You could pass him in a crowd without noticing him. That afternoon,

Edgar's appearance diverged from convention. His shoes had lost their shine since his previous visit. Under his raincoat, a typically freshly pressed suit was rumpled as if he slept in it. His tie hung uncharacteristically off-center, loose around the soiled collar of a wrinkled shirt.

Edgar poised on the landing to compose himself. He tried to straighten his tie but realized the condition of his clothing made looking crisp, neat, and professional impossible. He fidgeted with his wrinkled collar, pulled on the sleeves of his suit jacket, tried to straighten pant legs that no longer held a crease and gave up. He turned the doorknob. Harry looked up from the phone and waved Edgar in when the door opened. Liz-Beth leapt from her chair and sprang to the door to greet him.

"Let me take your coat, Edgar. It's all wet."

She hung it in a reach-in closet.

"Can I brew tea, Edgar?"

"Yes. I'd like that."

"Have a seat on the sofa. I'll bring it."

Edgar arrived with an uncharacteristic look of despair. A dark shadow covered his face. In mid-afternoon, unshaved since the previous morning, he looked like a hungover Humphrey Bogart. Liz-Beth brought the teapot, poured two cups, and sat next to him.

"Edgar, what's wrong? You aren't your cheerful self."

"I have unpleasant news, Liz-Beth. I'll wait for Harry to join us."

"Is Evelyn okay?"

"Yes, she is," he assured her but offered no more information.

Liz-Beth inspected Edgar's face as he added cream to his tea. It alarmed her. Her stare increased his discomfort. She looked away. Edgar appeared as though he hadn't slept well in weeks. The corners of his eyes were wrinkled, his skin beneath them puffy; ringed faintly in dark crescents. They were red. His cheeks looked sunken. He looked thin.

He held his tea cup with unsteady hands. He looked weak

and vulnerable, not at all the proud, successful businessman Liz-Beth and Harold knew him to be.

Harry ended a call and returned the phone to the receiver. He walked to the sofa and stretched out a hand. Edgar looked up at Harry, shook it without standing, with a grim face and uncharacteristic weakness. Harry noted Edgar's appearance. He smiled warmly, ignoring it. "Edgar old boy, to what do we owe the visit?"

"I hardly know what to say, Harry. My timing is terrible. I should have told you sooner. I lacked the courage."

"Let's have it man. Liz-Beth and I can manage."

Harry sat on the other side of Edgar from Liz-Beth. He put an arm around Edgar's shoulder.

"What is it old man? You're among friends."

"It's just that. We aren't paying the dividend tomorrow."

"That's it? That's all of it?" Harry chuckled. He knew it couldn't be from the appearance of the man sitting next to him.

"We don't care about that. It isn't important to us."

"You're correct without knowing why. The dividend hardly matters. I had to tell you today. I didn't want to surprise you tomorrow."

Harold and Liz-Beth stared.

"I've lost the company. I just failed at the last bank after trying everything and everywhere else. It was my last chance."

"You haven't tried us," Harry said.

"I couldn't take more of your money, not under the circumstances."

Liz-Beth leaned forward in shock. Harry rose and moved to the chair next to Liz-Beth, on the opposite side of the coffee table from Edgar.

"How did this happen?"

"You remember a few years ago we decided to incorporate Dolby's technology into a receiver product line and expand North American distribution?"

"Yes, of course. That's why we invested."

"It went well for a while. Eighteen months ago, our salesman paid a visit to a distributer to find out why orders were declining. He discovered a warehouse stocked with cheap copies of our products."

"Counterfeits?"

"No, Liz-Beth, branded Japanese products in similar designs with cost saving modifications, assembled in Asia. They made cheap copies of our consumer products, sold them for two thirds of our price and took the market."

Liz-Beth held her hand to her forehead. She took a deep breath.

Harry frowned. "Who is it?" he asked.

"That's the worst of it, Harry. Our own parts supplier found the commodity parts business unsatisfying. They knew the company that builds the systems, adds the value, makes the profit. They went into competition with us, without telling us their intentions."

Harry pursed his lips, shook his head and let out a breath. "They blindsided you. What did you do about it?"

"I confronted them in their office. They made no denial. They smiled and said too bad they are more competitive than we are. What we think is unethical, they think is good business. We can't compete with their labor and material cost."

"Oh my God." Liz-Beth set her teacup down. Harry grimaced.

"Three months later they opened a facility in Oakland to expand sales and distribution across North America. They seemed to have unlimited money. A Japanese consumer electronics giant invested in the business. They used the money to fund expansion. I've never seen a company grow as fast in a mature industry. They began labeling and marketing the products under an established brand. It gave them instant brand recognition, perception of quality. Before year end we were competing with a Japanese consumer electronics giant - our own parts supplier, with vast resources and lower costs. We couldn't match the prices. Made in America no longer means anything."

"Oh, Edgar. Why didn't you say something?"

"I didn't want to burden you Liz-Beth, not without a solution, you of all people - personal friends and investors. I don't know what you could have done to help. It was my problem to solve."

"We might have been able to help you."

"You have your own business to look after, Harry. I thought I found a way. Someone introduced me to a private equity company that invests in these situations. They said they could pay off our debt, help move production off-shore, lower costs, gain economy of scale. It sounded promising."

"What's the name of the company?"

"Cousie Capital Investments."

"Jesus Christ, those sleazy bastards? They've screwed more people than Casanova."

"I tried everywhere else first, Harry. The business looked bad on paper. I couldn't sell any plan I could think of, not even to myself."

"You could have tried us, Edgar. They're a financial mafia that breaks people with pen and paper and steals their assets. What happened?"

"I sold them controlling interest on condition they let me run the business unimpeded; their role strictly financial. They came in and took over the board. I had to agree to obtain the money. They paid off our debt and we reduced our prices. Orders spiked. Six months later they applied for a very large loan based on an optimistic forecast, secured by the assets of the company. I told them we couldn't grow fast enough to make the payments. We could increase market share by reducing prices, but more cost cutting would create quality problems and damage the company. I told them we couldn't compete as a small independent firm in the mass market consumer electronics business against a giant Japanese consumer electronics company. They told me they couldn't back out of the loan, to execute the business plan, it was their job to bring in the money and make the strategy, my job to make the strategy work."

Edgar lifted his tea cup. Harry filled his. He stirred in cream while Edgar continued.

"After the funding came in, they paid themselves a giant "special dividend." They pulled their investment out and then some. We paid them a monthly management fee while I ran the company. If we succeeded, they made more, if we failed, they could sell the assets, pocket the proceeds and move on with a profit. Heads they win, tails I lose. I couldn't do anything to stop it. From then on, success or failure of the business no longer mattered to them."

"It never mattered."

Edgar winced. "No, Harry. I guess it didn't. They made their money by purchasing the equity and leveraging it. I had to lay off everyone I could and reduce parts and materials cost. It cut into quality and worked the remaining people harder for less money. It didn't go over very well. Employees made the company work. I needed their support. I told Cousie I couldn't keep it going like this. He offered to sell their interest back, for more than they paid for it of course. A stick in the eye. He knew I couldn't buy them out and it made no financial sense. He said it was fair because they increased the value of the company, that the financing they obtained proved it."

"If he left the money in the company," Harry said.

"I'll never forget the snarky "gotcha" look, the crooked smile on his face. The more we sold, the more we lost, the more capital we burned. Customers complained about quality, employees about pay cuts and hours. I knew it couldn't last. I shopped a plan to try to raise the money to buy Cousie out and restructure the debt. I didn't get anywhere. By then I'd worn out from the stress. I didn't believe in it myself. We carried too much debt and Cousie Capital held too much equity. We could have abandoned the mass market, focused on an upscale niche where customers pay a premium, a segment the Japanese don't care about. That market is too small for us now. If I shrink the business or not, we can't cover the debt payments. We're running out of money and I can't do anything about it."

Edgar looked haggard.

"Our employees. They'll lose their jobs. They don't deserve that. Financial engineers - they don't care about anybody."

"You can't blame yourself, Edgar. It sounds like you had to try something radical."

"You're right Liz-Beth. Well that's it then." Edgar looked defeated.

"Is there nothing we can do to help you?"

"I don't see a way out. I'm tired of it. I don't want to fight it anymore."

"What are you going to do?" Harry asked.

"I don't know. Everything Evelyn and I have is tied up in the business. I leveraged it a long time ago. The Mercedes, the house. I can't make the payments without a good salary. We'll have to sell the furniture and move into the Volvo."

"Jesus, Edgar. Does Evelyn know?"

"Of course she knows. We did it when we renovated the offices and bought new equipment. It needed replacement."

"I mean the urgency."

"Look at me, Harry. How could I hide it?"

"Yes, of course. Stupid of me to ask."

"How is she taking it?"

"Better than I am. She says I can go to work for somebody, she can find a job, we can save up, start over."

"You can, you know," Liz-Beth said. "You're still a young man. We can help you."

"I lost your money, Liz-Beth. I can't let that happen again. It doesn't matter. I don't know what to do. I never worked for anyone else or anywhere else."

"Edgar, don't despair. People have setbacks. They recover. We don't care about the money. We're your friends. Why didn't you tell us sooner?"

"I was ashamed, humiliated. I've lost everything. Our supplier undermined me. I…I didn't think clearly how to manage it. I took the family business in the wrong direction and ruined it."

"It isn't your fault, Edgar. It's force majeure. The Japanese are disrupting many industries."

"I know, Harry. It was my job to find a way."

Liz-Beth thought Edgar was falling to pieces.

"Edgar, stop. Take a breather. Don't go to work tomorrow."

"I can't give them an excuse to fire me. I need the salary as long as I can collect one."

"Go to Napa this weekend. Harry and I will go with you. Don't make any decisions for a few days. If it's over, it's over. If it isn't, you need a break from it. You look awful Edgar, like you haven't slept in days."

"I haven't."

"Why don't you go home, have a good rest. Let the private equity guys deal with the dividend, the employees, and the Japanese. A few days won't matter. You and Evelyn, Liz-Beth and I can drive down the coast for a long weekend. We can stay in a B&B near the beach, stuff ourselves with seafood, hike the hills together."

"I'd like to, Harry. What's left of the company needs me. We have to disappoint shareholders tomorrow, and I brought in their money. Some of the employees are shareholders too. They depend on the dividend, especially since we cut their salaries and we had no money to put in the profit-sharing plan. I can't go off on a mini-vacation and leave it to strangers to tell them."

Edgar paused; eyes glazed in a million-mile stare, into a private abyss, a place only he could visit.

"I must be going."

"Don't leave yet, Edgar. Why don't I call Evelyn? We can go to dinner, take your mind off this at least for an evening."

"No, no. Thank you for the invitation, Liz-Beth. I have to go."

Edgar set his cup down. He retrieved his raincoat from the

closet. Harry and Liz-Beth looked at each other. "Bunny, we can't let him go when he's like this."

"What can we do?"

Liz-Beth followed Edgar to the door, threw her arms around him and hugged him. Edgar's arms were limp.

"It will be alright, Edgar." Liz-Beth tried to sooth him even though she had no solution to offer.

Edgar knew it wouldn't be. His chin wrinkled and he shuddered. He teetered on the edge of a breakdown. Liz-Beth released her grip. She stepped back. She couldn't comfort or hold him.

"I'm sorry about your money."

Edgar turned and walked out the door, down the stairs, past reception, into the rain and the wind.

Four

"We shouldn't have let him leave, Bunny."

"What could we do, wrestle him to the floor?"

"We introduced him to the parts supplier."

"It isn't our fault, Liz-Beth. He asked for a source in Asia."

"If anything happens to him, I'll never forgive myself."

"We tried. He doesn't want us to help him. We have to leave him to his wishes."

Liz-Beth put a hand on her forehead.

"What can we do?"

"You better call Evelyn. See if she's alright."

Evelyn answered the phone.

"Yes, I'm alright, Liz-Beth. Thank you for calling. How did he look?"

"Not so bad."

"Tell me the truth."

"Terrible. He frightened me."

"I'm afraid for him. He's been despondent. I don't know what he might do. His grandfather started the business. He went into it directly from university. It's the only thing he knows. Edgar can live with poverty. He isn't vain. It won't be forever. We can both work. Losing the family business though; employees and friend's money, I don't think he can absorb that. He knows he still has me. It isn't enough. That hurts, Liz-Beth. I don't care so much about the business or the money. I married Edgar for Edgar. He's everything I need, but I'm not enough for him."

"He loves you, Evelyn. You know that. My God. What can Bunny and I do to help you?"

"Nothing if he won't let you. Be friends and wait until he asks. What else can you do?"

"Will you keep in contact with us? Let us know what's happening?"

"Yes. He has to make the dividend announcement, bring employees up to date in an all-hands meeting. Some started with his father. We don't have the money to keep all of them on. He blames himself. It's going to be hard on him."

"It isn't his fault Evelyn. Foreign competition is impacting many American companies."

"He wanted this consumer product line to make it *his* business; to grow it beyond what his father and grandfather left him, to give himself something to be proud of. That's what he believes. If he hadn't done that, we could keep making and selling custom commercial systems and keep the business going forever."

"It's easier to see a falling piano after it hits you. You can still do that in a new business. You can start over. If it's over, you can't look back. You can only make what you can of it and move on to something else."

"I know. I can do that. It's Edgar who has to bear it. I have to make dinner. I'll call you tomorrow."

"Promise?"

"I promise. Thanks for calling Liz-Beth. I love you."

"Love you too, Evelyn. Whatever happens, Bunny and I are your friends."

"I know I can count on you."

Liz-Beth returned the handset to the receiver.

"I can't work anymore today, Bunny. Let's go to dinner."

Five

The Thursday work day came and went. Liz-Beth and Bunny went to the office and tried not to think about Edgar. They found it impossible.

"If she doesn't call soon, I'm going to call her."

"Leave them alone, Liz-Beth. We'll hear from them. It's only afternoon."

When the day ended, they hadn't.

The morning meeting went badly. Shareholders were not happy to lose a dividend. Edgar didn't tell them the full extent of the dire state of the company. That would come later. Employees are not philosophers. They were angry. They blamed Edgar. Defenseless, Edgar took it personally. It hurt him deeply. Edgar had to let some of them go, possibly all of them before it ended. Some his father hired, who came to the house for his funeral. They were a family. In profound sadness he thought, *My father left them in my hands and I failed them.*

Edgar skipped lunch, went into his office, and closed the door. He told reception not to disturb him. He sat at his desk, disconnected the phone, and folded his arms on the desktop. He laid his head on them. He remembered Hemmingway wrote "A man could be destroyed but not defeated." Edgar couldn't see the difference.

Depression makes you doubt who you are, where you are, how you arrived there. Edgar thought people, places, events, take up residence in your mind, set your course, lead you through life to its ending. In the long hours of the afternoon, when Edgar sat alone at his desk, they visited him as he sank deeper into a crushing depression. He felt their weight press down on him with a tonnage that grew exponentially in the imagination of a defeated man. These people, these events that cut and strike and hurt you, come to visit when you're defenseless to remind you of your failures. Their martial skills are multiplied by your weakness and your losses.

Edgar remembered when his father brought him to the office as a child, to see his grandfather who still came to work daily to the business he started. He remembered when he worked there after school, before he went away to college. The thought of losing it trampled him. *What am I going to do?* he asked himself. *It's the only work I've ever known, the only place I ever worked. I don't know how to work for someone else. I don't know how to apply for work. How will I pay the bills? Who will take care of Evelyn? What can I do for the men I have to lay off and their families? They know what's coming. They hate me. The men my father hired, the ones who were here when I came to work in the afternoons, after high school, the ones who taught* **me** *the business.*

Financial engineers, Edgar thought. *They took everything. All I own of it now is what I can carry.*

Edgar waited to the end of the day for everyone to leave. Completely exhausted, when the sun went down, and the office fell into darkness, he slept at his desk, the first deep sleep he experienced in weeks. At 8:00PM he woke, pulled on his raincoat, and stepped into the night. Edgar looked both ways down a lonely street. He stood outside the building entry, leaned against the door, and took a deep breath. He smiled for the first time in weeks; a strange unnatural smile, eyes narrowed and red, cheeks puffy, a furrowed brow. A clenching, pain-infused smile, unrecognizable as his own, disturbing to family or friends, had they been there to see it.

Clouds covered the sky, but two weeks of rain had ended. Reflections of street lamps shimmered in breeze-rippled puddles of standing water. The city looked dark, abandoned. Edgar walked past his Mercedes on Bryant Street, turned the corner on

Second, walked north, and passed under the freeway on a gloomy, eerie night. *The bums must be hiding,* he thought; *a night to be rolled.* He didn't care. He crossed the intersections of Harrison, Folsom, Howard, Mission, the narrow streets and alleys between them. He heard jazz playing faintly in a club through an open doorway beneath a neon sign somewhere down an alley. *The Blind Spot.* The neon sign burned through cool, humid air. A city bus rumbled past and slowed to a stop. Two emotionless faces stared at him through the buss's windows, lonely faces sitting in adjacent rows, illuminated by interior overhead lights. *Wouldn't the ride be better if they sat together,* Edgar wondered? The door opened. No one stepped out. The driver looked to see if Edgar wanted a ride. Edgar shook his head. The door closed. The bus moved on. Edgar thought it the loneliest night he ever witnessed, and this, the loneliest life he could ever know. He clenched his jaw. His neck muscles flexed. He continued walking. When he reached Market Street, he crossed and descended the granite stairs of the Montgomery Street BART Station. BART trains did not pass by Edgar's home.

Six

Harry and Liz-Beth shared a quiet dinner at home. They worried about Edgar but didn't speak of him or call. They watched TV and waited. The call came at 10:00PM.

"I'm sorry," Evelyn said, before Liz-Beth could speak. She sounded shaken.

Liz-Beth placed a hand over her mouth. Expecting the worst, she fell back against the wall.

Evelyn's voice cracked. She stumbled through the words.

"The shareholder meeting went badly. The all hands meeting was worse. They were very hard on Edgar. They blamed him for everything. They don't understand, Liz-Beth. They're just carpenters, metal workers, assembly workers. I'm so sorry, Liz-Beth. Edgar didn't come home tonight. He walked into a BART station and stepped off the platform in front of a train. Edgar is dead."

Evelyn broke down and wept into the receiver.

Liz-Beth bent over and wrapped an arm around her abdomen. She slid to the floor in shock, legs splayed out in front of her. Too stunned to speak, she leaned motionless against the wall, numbed by what she heard.

"The police are here, Liz-Beth. I have to go."

"Evelyn, Evelyn," Liz-Beth called, but Evelyn had hung up the handset.

Seven

In spring 1987, forty years after founding the Wiggins Trading Company, Bunny and Liz-Beth sold out. Sixty-seven years old, Wiggins thought, *We've done enough.* In a few months, Liz-Beth would be sixty. After selling the house in Pacific Heights, they moved into the one they relocated from England to Pescadero to live there year round. A massive home for only two of them, they named it *New Cotswolds.* They added a Brittany Spaniel puppy to the family. Wiggins named the dog *Bentley.* Bunny and Bentley. His companion and responsibility, Wiggins cared for the dog, his best friend after Liz-Beth.

Wiggins bought a fine mid-length hunting coat for winter, a corduroy jacket for spring and fall, mid-calf boots for walking the foothills behind the property with Bentley. He carried his prized Benelli Legacy twelve-gauge shotgun when he and Bentley went birding. Wiggins kept the gun oiled and loaded, but he never fired at anything that drew a breath. Brittany's are active dogs that need daily exercise. So did Wiggins. "Let's chase the birds," Wiggins would say. Bentley jumped and spun around in excitement, vigorously wagging his tail as Wiggins reached for his birding jacket and the Benelli. If he could have spoken, Bentley might have asked Bunny why he never shot the birds. No matter. He knew his job was flushing them out and he reveled in it.

Wiggins liked to shoot but not anything living. He bought a 1980 Berretta over and under 12 gauge to shoot skeet at the gun club in Portola Valley until housing encroached when Palo Alto expanded over the crest of the hill and a newly minted Silicon

Valley technology mogul lobbied to shut the club down so he could live in peace and quiet on an estate near the range. He built his own range underground. After the club closed, Wiggins sold the Berretta, never fired a gun again and never missed it.

Wiggins watched the ocean thrash against miles of coastline from hills above the village. The sound of the redwings, the hawks and shorebirds, the surf and the scent of the ocean soothed his soul. He found a perch to enjoy magnificent late afternoons above mesquite trees and tall grasses. Cattails swayed in breezes above the meadows. Reflecting off breaker and swell, the sun lit sandy beach, grassy lowlands, cappuccino colored earthen cliffs in brilliant contrasting colors. In games of hide and seek between sun and cloud, earth and ocean were spot-lit in magical painted images. Brilliant copper sunsets turned scarlet and faded as the sun melted into the ocean. Cooling rain squalls cleansed the air, leaving rainbows arching.

Standing on cliffs with Bentley beside him, Wiggins smoked his pipe as seabirds chased fishing boats for scraps, whales breached on great migrations, ocean-going ships plodded in the distance. Squadrons of pelicans floated on breezes, surfers caught the last wave. Wiggins sat on a boulder holding Bentley's warm body against his, an arm around his second-best friend. As they watched the sun set behind endless patterns windblown into the ocean's surface, he thought how fortunate he was to survive the war, want for nothing, do the things he wanted, have a wife and dog who adored him, to be, after all the years and adventures, still there, in a favored place, contented among the living. Liz-Beth knew their spot on the cliff. She sometimes swung a telescope to frame them against the evening sky and think about how much she loved them.

Wiggins loved English literature. He sometimes read it aloud while walking around the house with a book in one hand, while gesturing with the other hand as if performing on a stage. He quoted Bacon, Marlowe, Carroll, Dickens, and of course

Shakespeare. A living encyclopedia of their lives and works, he practically memorized their novels and plays from reading them so many times and roleplaying their characters.

Wiggins purchased clothing on visits to England. Made from the best materials and had them expertly tailored to fit his tall narrow frame. Savile Row shirts were made during visits to London. Woolen suits, coats, hats and scarves were purchased at Harrods. He dressed well for San Francisco and for travel, but he hardly needed to in Pescadero where heavy woolen sweaters, casual pants and jackets made in Scotland kept him warm on foggy summer days and cool, windy nights. He bought a fine long hunting coat for cold weather and a corduroy jacket and boots for long walks in the hills with Bentley. With pipe in hand he looked like a university professor or the English country gentleman. He paused nearly anything for afternoon tea. He loved gardening especially caring for roses.

Twice a month, Liz-Beth and Bunny drove to San Francisco in an immaculately maintained pre-war Bentley to visit friends, private clubs, attend cultural and charity events. They drove the coastal highway in a pristine MGTD to Santa Cruz or Monterey, to play a round of golf or visit the aquarium. A dedicated mechanic, Sukie kept the cars in perfect condition. He practically polished the paint off them. Liz-Beth likened driving the Bentley to driving a lorry. She didn't like either. She enjoyed the nimble little MG. It reminded her of Jeeps she drove in England. It stirred memories of wartime life, of good times and old friendships that made her smile. The MG drove left-handed, the Bentley a right hander. Wiggins loved the Bentley.

Liz-Beth and Bunny loved jazz and classical music. During a drive on the coast, they discovered the *Bach Dancing and Dynamite Society*, a non-profit housed in the *Douglass Beach House*, a building with an auditorium at Miramar Beach, El Granada. The organization brought culture to the Northern California coast. After attending a piano concert, they fell in love with the place, became patrons and frequent visitors. They introduced it to friends from San Francisco to show them they hadn't quite become uncultured beach bums, not completely.

Wiggins complained about the idiotic way he thought Americans brew their beer weak and serve it cold. He preferred it strong, warm, fresh or not at all. He kept a supply of authentic Guinness in the house, replenished from private stock smuggled into the country by a business associate. Guinness brewed in Ireland is the Guinness Wiggins craved. Importing it became an adventure. It didn't stand up to long voyages across vast oceans, through the Panama Canal, traversing half way 'round the world. They flew it in. It arrived airfreight in false bottoms of crates filled with pub antiques from Ireland under the eyes of customs agents who looked the other way for a rare bottle of imported single malt. The real thing, Wiggins had to have it.

Wiggins laughed at American whiskey made from corn. He knew what his Scottish friends would have said, "a waste of good corn." Wiggins didn't think service staff should be "entrepreneurs." He paid for food and drink. Liz-Beth did the tipping. "It is their privilege to serve us," Wiggins would say.

Every D-Day, June 6th, Wiggins donned his RAF uniform, wings, battle and service ribbons, medals, cap, and polished boots. He strode proudly into Duarte's with Liz-Beth, to hoist a pint to all the lads who rode landing craft, stormed Normandy beaches, and flew cover above them as he did in a medium bomber. In spite of his injury, he convinced bomber command to let him ride with the Yanks as an observer during the first days of invasion. It made him proud, and not the slightest bit shy of sharing his wartime experiences with an audience mesmerized by romantic stories told in Elizabethan accent and gesture as if performed on stage. He bragged about meeting Air Chief Marshall Sir Hugh Dowding, which he did, and Mr. Churchill, which he did, in RAF headquarters as a young man during the Battle of Brittan, though as a bomber pilot he didn't participate in that phase of the fighting. "If Shakespeare were alive today, it would be Churchill and Dowding he would write of," Wiggins liked to say.

He spoke lovingly of little friends; solid, trustworthy Hurricanes that took down German bombers, fast, graceful Spitfires that flummoxed the German fighters over England. He spoke with reverence of the handful of outnumbered pilots who saved the country in early days when England fought Germany alone. He spoke with admiration of sturdy bombers he flew over occupied France, Belgium, and Germany, how they always brought him home, almost. He spoke of reckless off-base parties that lasted long into the night when bad weather grounded flights and they didn't know who would or would not return from the next mission. His audience wondered how they could celebrate with abandon in desperate circumstances - or how they couldn't.

Wiggins enchanted the crowd. He shared how he met, romanced and won the love of the beautiful Miss Simpson while Liz-Beth sat on a stool beaming beside him. She chose him as she remembered it but never shared her version.

The 6th of June crowd at Duarte's believed everything Wiggins said. He never told them he was shot down, wounded, and returned to service. Asked about the limp, he simply described it as nothing, a minor war injury. He didn't think of himself as a hero. To Wiggins, he only did his duty.

Eight

Liz-Beth watched Bunny rise from his favorite chair in the great room. He moved slowly, more deliberately than in years passed. *He's aging,* she thought. It hurt her to watch him grow old. Wiggins retrieved his vest from the coat closet. He slipped his pipe and pouch in the pockets. He reached for his walking boots. Bentley had grown older too but had not yet caught up with the age of his master. The dog watched and waited for an invitation with his head resting on outstretched legs in the vestibule. Less excited by the routine than he once was, Bentley still enjoyed walking the trails.

"Let's go Bentley. Come on boy," Wiggins said as if the dog needed motivation. Bentley lifted his head, stood and waited obediently, eyes fixed on the elderly man Wiggins had become. Bunny pulled his walking staff from the basket by the door, swung the door open, and stepped into the late air. It smelled fresh and cool. He tasted the salt from the ocean and scent of the beach. The old wound hurt. He limped more than he had a few years earlier but never complained. Bentley assumed his position on the right, a step behind his master as they started up the trail that led to the western foothills.

Liz-Beth watched Harry lumbered up the hill to greet another sunset with foreboding. *He shouldn't be doing this,"* she thought. *I won't stop him. He'll have to arrive at a place where he accepts his limitations.*

Liz-Beth stepped through the kitchen door. She glanced at the thin marine layer lingering offshore. *The sunset will be glorious,* she thought, *a sky on fire, the most sensational of the year.* She smiled at wisps of clouds sailing eastward overhead. Liz-Beth returned to the kitchen. She looked at the trail winding into the hills through a window, in time to glimpse Bunny and Bentley struggle past a bend where man and dog stepped beyond the line of sight behind the trees. *I hope he makes it home tonight* Liz-Beth whispered. Her heart sank. She shuddered. She realized, unless a different event took him from her, some sunset he wouldn't. She felt sadness for this once vibrant man, reduced by age, she loved so dearly. *He's my whole life*, Liz-Beth thought. *What would I do without him?*

Liz-Beth put the thought out of her mind. She cleared the dinner table and loaded the dishwasher. She selected an unfinished book, brought it to a well-lit place in the garden to bask in the glory of the afternoon sun until the outside houselights came on. She worried for the first time for a man who had been strong all his life and now seemed so weak, so vulnerable to things that were until recently no concern at all.

Wiggins reached his favorite outcropping on the ridge, a perch where the ground fell sharply below it toward the ocean. Bentley sat beside him. Their eyes met. They understood each other as well as any two beings could, absent spoken language, an understanding grown over time and experience. Bentley looked at Bunny with all the admiration and unconditional love a dog can offer. Wiggins petted his dog.

Wiggins scanned the sky, the hills, the beaches. He closed his eyes and found himself at the controls of his Lancaster as it breached the clouds. He dreamed he played a game of hide and seek with them among the heavens. He understood what John Magee meant when he penned the last lines of his poem, *High Flight. I put out my hand, and touched the face of God.*

Wiggins thought of his first combat crew, their adventures over occupied Europe. Sadness enveloped him when their names and faces appeared in a daydream; the horror of attack, the scream of pain, the terror of crash-landing. The memory returned when he allowed it to. A tragedy after the experiences they shared, that they didn't survive the war. Wiggins felt survivor's guilt, from memories he wished he could have left in 1940's skies over Europe. He stared into the blue, imagined flying his Lancaster alone, navigating through scattered clouds, accompanied by empty seats of flight engineer, navigator, bomb aimer, wireless operator, gunners long dead. At that moment, Wiggins felt more tired than he ever had. Bentley whimpered. Wiggins closed his eyes. He flew into his dream and faded.

The sun put on a spectacular performance. It turned the clouds and the ocean crimson. Liz-Beth marked the time. She knew the spot where Bunny and Bentley sat on the ridge. She thought she might go to the telescope room, to search for familiar silhouettes against the sky. She decided against it. *I'll leave them in peace*, she decided, even though she knew they couldn't see her watching from the distance.

As the sun melted into ocean and crimson clouds faded with the dying light, Liz-Beth thought, *They'll be returning now*. She smiled. The vision of Bunny and Bentley walking down the hill together made her happy. They would be home with her soon, and safe. The sky darkened. Bunny and Bentley didn't return, and Liz-Beth knew.

Liz-Beth called Joshua and Maggie, owners of the Pescadero general store. They arrived inside New Cotswolds' gates in minutes. They found Liz-Beth stoically sipping tea in the kitchen. Maggie leaned over and wrapped her arms around her. Liz-Beth set her cup down and held Maggie's forearms. They didn't speak. Joshua went to the Japanese tea house for Sukie. For the first time in her life, Liz-Beth surrendered control.

"Sukie and I have flashlights."

"I'm going with you, Joshua." Liz-Beth sounded determined.

"There's no reason for all of us to go."

"He was my soul mate for almost 50 years. I have more reason than you."

"What if he returns a different way?"

"There is only one way" Liz-Beth said to Maggie.

"Then all of us will go."

A solemn procession walked up the east trail; Joshua leading, Sukie at the end of the column. No one spoke. Darkness descended by the time they arrived. They found them on the ridge. Bunny faced the ocean, head back, rested against a boulder. His arm wrapped around Bentley who leaned against him, head buried under a shoulder, as if trying to hold fast to the soul of his master when even a dog knows he can't. Bentley lifted his head. Sad eyes flashed in Maglite beams as he watched four forlorn figures approach.

Joshua tried to pull the dog away. Bentley wouldn't go. Liz-Beth squatted next to Wiggins. He took no breath. They checked his pulse and found none. Eyes closed; the look on his face serene.

"He found his place, Liz-Beth" Joshua said.

Tears streamed down Liz-Beth's face. She held Bunny's arm, and sat at his side opposite Bentley. She buried her face in Bunny's chest and wept.

Maggie wrapped her arms around Liz-Beth. Joshua sat next to Bentley. Sukie sat before them. They remained quiet until Liz-Beth lifted her head and cried out.

The marine layer floated onshore. A breeze brought the fog with an evening chill that descended on the foothills. They decided not to move Wiggins off the ridge at night. They had no cellphone service, nothing to carry him with, insufficient light for traversing a winding dirt trail, steep in some places trail. They could contact the volunteer fire department in the morning. Sukie hiked down the hill to New Cotswolds for something to keep them warm. Halfway down the trail, after a lifetime of hard work and hardship, after standing up to loss and sacrifice that broke the strongest men, Sukie did something he had never done. Beyond earshot of the others, he shut off the flashlight, sat in the middle of the trail, and wept for his savior, his employer, his friend.

Sukie returned with blankets. They wrapped them around the scrum and spent the night thinking about all they remembered and all they did with Harold Bentley-Wiggins. The moon appeared full and bright through a gap in the clouds opened by a breeze, to cast its light on the group and illuminate the face of the soul who often chose this place to spend the evening and came here to his end.

With night almost ended, they slept. All except Liz-Beth, who had more to contemplate and wanted to visit it all. Sukie rose with first light. He walked down the hill and called for help. Four volunteers returned with a stretcher. They carried Wiggins down to lay him to rest.

Since Mr. and Mrs. Wiggins had no children or siblings, two bloodlines ended. It made Liz-Beth sad to think after all they built together, there would be no one to receive the legacy.

Liz-Beth reflected on a good life well lived. She smiled to think Wiggins loved and allowed himself to be loved, lived as a man who did what he wished and it always seemed to turn out well. He served his country and his people. He came with her to America and brought Sukie with them. He built a business that provided honest work for many people. He donated to charities, contributing much in two countries an ocean apart.

Wiggins never took Bentley to England to bird in the English countryside as he said he wished. Liz-Beth convinced him Bentley couldn't miss what he hadn't known and couldn't imagine, and all earth is earth.

After a brief service, Liz-Beth buried Wiggins at the back of the property near the wall he built, inside the estate he built, under the shade of a juniper tree that lived there forever. "You've gone and left me, Bunny," she said. "I hope you're walking the fields and hills with Bentley, where I expect to join you, dear, just not anytime soon if you don't mind."

Nine

With Bunny gone, so were weekend visitors and dinner parties at New Cotswolds. Liz-Beth no longer visited friends in San Francisco. She sometimes missed them but she loved Pescadero and the New Cotswolds property, adjusted to life as a widow, decided to stay on as long as Sukie did. Sukie showed no interest in leaving. After Bunny died, they became closer, less employer-employee, more friend and partner.

A middle-aged dog when Bunny passed, Bentley lived a long life in dog years. He missed Bunny. Liz-Beth and Sukie did their best to keep him distracted. He sniffed the house where Bunny sat, slept, and kept his personal things. They exercised him in the meadows, on beaches where he chased birds energetically and unsuccessfully into canine old age. A sad day when he passed, Liz-Beth and Sukie buried him next to Bunny and wished them good hunting.

Liz-Beth evolved into one of Pescadero's most eccentric characters. She tended the property with Sukie, lived comfortably on conservatively invested proceeds from the sale of the trading company. A major stockholder in San Francisco businesses, Liz-Beth attended shareholder meetings prepared as anyone. She added a tone of sarcasm when she thought management engineered profits, made foolish decisions, misbehaved. She badgered them to donate to her favorite charitable causes. They did; quid pro quo for peace between shareholder meetings. The money supported the arts, the poor, the parks of San Francisco. They contributed funds to develop a state park at Pescadero Beach. San Mateo County received money to help purchase property next to New

Cotswolds including part of the eastern foothills where Bunny and Bentley went hiking. Liz-Beth convinced the county to designate it a nature preserve. Not an altogether altruistic effort, it codified the city greenbelt.

Liz-Beth sometimes faked an upper-class London accent and did it well. Villagers who didn't know, thought her some sort of English lady who grew up in the Midwest, married an Englishman, acquired an accent, lived in a huge house, drove an MG and employed a Japanese gardener who chauffeured her in a Bentley. Exotic stuff for rural San Mateo County.

Liz-Beth quipped of tea in Windsor Castle with Bunny, the Queen, and Mr. Churchill. Hyperbole, a joke. In so charming an accent no one knew or cared if it were fact or fiction. The villagers wanted it to be true. Mr. Churchill was gone. The Queen didn't take phone calls from Pescadero. Who in Pescadero would call to ask?

Liz-Beth took the MG for drives along the coastal highway. She never lost the thrill of speed. She raced through town, all two blocks of it, into the countryside, engine roaring, announcing her coming and going, exhaust pipe assaulting store windows and citizenry. It reminded her of tearing through the English countryside in the Jeep. The villagers tolerated it; only for Liz-Beth.

She decorated her bicycle in wildflowers picked along the trail. She peddled through the village with an umbrella across the handlebars to pitch in the sand on sunny days, when she exercised her way to the beach instead of driving in the MG, or having Sukie drop her in the Bentley. On those days she left Sukie contented to his gardens and himself. She dressed him like a chauffeur in a bowler hat for outings in the Bentley. A short, portly Asian man in chauffer's clothing looks amusing opening a car door for a tall, well dressed, Caucasian lady carrying a parrot in a cage. Sukie thought it ridiculous. He played along because it made Liz-Beth happy.

Liz-Beth sometimes brought Mr. Chuckles to the beach in the MG, or in a basket on her bicycle. She brought him out of the cage so the children could feed him. An avian social magnet, a consummate ham, Chuckles enjoyed attention. He understood "Do you want to go to the beach?" He paced his perch, beaked the bars of his cage, and climbed about it.

Liz-Beth overdressed for Pescadero. She donned floppy hats, brightly colored dresses, costume jewelry. She carried a parasol to shade her porcelain skin and wore white canvas-top tennis shoes. Liz-Beth never left home without makeup. She splashed on enough Houbigant to be noticed. On special occasions she wore Puppy Love from the bottle Wiggins gave her when he brought Bentley home without discussing adoption. Worked for Liz-Beth. She liked Bentley, acquired a new perfume, and appreciated the sensitivity Bunny had for her feelings.

Liz-Beth read trashy novels at the beach to the sound of crashing surf. She enjoyed temperate days when warm sun battles cool breezes to a draw before retiring behind the horizon to relinquish the evening to stars and moon.

Liz-Beth enjoyed Duarte's, the only semblance of nightlife in Pescadero. Like Bunny, she preferred Guinness on tap. If for no other reason, she drank it in Bunny's honor.

Liz-Beth flirted with every man, woman, and beast in town. Only Sukie, Joshua, and Maggie knew what to make of it. She carried candy and cookies for children. She listened respectfully to their thoughts and dreams. The opposite of the reserved and dry Mr. Wiggins, Liz-Beth's quirky, outgoing personality fit life in a California beach town. Inhabitants knew the eccentric lady who rode a bike, drove with her parrot in an MG, or arrived in a chauffeur-driven Bentley, this pretty lady with the colorful summer dresses, and floppy hats, the paperbacks, the newspapers and magazines she read in a beach chair under an umbrella. They enjoyed the smiles and compliments she gave everyone who walked by, how she made the children blush when she told them how smart they were, how beautiful they were, and they could do anything they wanted.

Ten

Sukie's life in America exceeded any he had known when he served Japanese militarists or in his early Spartan years as a farmer's son in Japan. He traced his family history back to a 12th century warlord. His family and their possessions, some of them ancient and priceless antiques disappeared with countless others in the bombings of the home islands. With his history erased, he became the last Nakajima and it haunted him. With no personal ties to return to, he felt fortunate to have the Wiggins family to work for and bring him to America. Coming to a healthy, vibrant America instead of returning to the devastation, poverty and shame of post-war Japan did not make a difficult choice.

Sukie was a small dark skinned man with an oval face and leathery skin. He had strong and calloused hands from years of labor. He never stopped performing physical work, even as an army officer. He did it because he liked it. He had been slender, nearly skeletal from living in the deprivation of wartime Singapore when he met Wiggins. As he grew older he made up for it by eating himself portly, eventually assuming the appearance of a miniature sumo wrestler, a Buddha without the thick hair he grew at a younger age. Contented with a simple life in San Francisco and later In Pescadero, for many years he dreamed of no other. A quiet man, Sukie kept to his work and refrained from engaging in idle conversation. Over time, a professional relationship with Harry and Liz-Beth grew into family. Sukie kept a post office box in Pescadero. He subscribed to American and Japanese periodicals. He eventually became capable of communicating in perfect and elegant English, better English than many Americans.

On a warm spring afternoon, a year after Bentley passed, Sukie asked Liz-Beth if he could sit with her in the garden. *Curious*, she thought. *He knows he doesn't have to ask.* Sukie spoke in a solemn tone she had never heard from him.

"May I sit with you for a moment Mrs. Wiggins?"

"I'm surprised and pleased, Sukie. Please do."

Sukie chose a garden chair facing Liz-Beth. He leaned forward.

With language skills she never imagined he possessed, in a calm methodical voice she never heard from him, he began.

"I must apologize for what I'm about to say."

Liz-Beth looked into Sukie's eyes. She sat at attention. *What is this?* She wondered.

"Mrs. Wiggins, I have worked for you and the late Mr. Wiggins for many years since he rescued me from Changi Prison, a great kindness I could never forget or ever fully repay, at a time when Japanese people were nearly universally hated for terrible things some of us unfortunately did during the war. I will never know; I never *can* know what caused Mr. Wiggins to choose me instead of so many others, or why he chose a Japanese person to work for you. I am sure he rescued me from a difficult life had I survived at all. For that I am forever indebted to his memory and to yourself Mrs. Wiggins, for allowing me to live and work on your property, and I must say, it has been a privilege to serve you."

Liz-Beth froze in apprehension.

"As you may know, many of my countrymen, in their shame, in their love and devotion to our emperor and our country, from their ignorance, from misguided teachings of our military leaders, could not bring themselves to face the things that happened, could not bear to accept that our emperor and our leaders could have been wrong in any way. Some of us could not accept that we lost a war we should not have engaged in. Many of us took their own lives as has sometimes been our way. Some hid in mountainous regions and remote jungles in foreign lands, pretending the war had not ended, wasting their lives on a lost cause. Others suffered poverty and deprivation after the war as Japan slowly recovered. I am so very fortunate to have been brought to this country where I have lived in peace, good health, and comfort; free and safe from retaliation by people who believed they had reason to make all Japanese suffer for reprehensible things a few of us did. I owe a great deal to this country for the good and easy life I have lived here. It is a rare event in human history that one country, having defeated another in war, then helped the people they defeated to recover, instead of plundering and punishing them. America has done this for Japan, first bringing our people out of a dark age of self-imposed isolation and feudalism into the modern world, then freeing us from leaders who brought suffering and shame to our nation."

Where is this going? Liz-Beth wondered.

"Since I have lived with you and Mr. Wiggins, I have never been uncomfortable, fearful or hungry, not for one day. I have enjoyed this wonderful climate in California, with its beautiful hills and beaches, and kind people who live here. I am sorry I never said this to Mr. Wiggins. I tried to do in deeds what I did not say. I am comforted by the belief that he knew I felt this way."

"As a young man, in 1937, when I left Japan to invade China with the army, I saw terrible things. I am an old man now. Not so old, that I can't return to speak about things I've seen and learned, and come to believe, and in some small way help the next generation to understand this must never happen again."

"I am no emperor, no leader of men. I can be a teacher. I know your language, your people, your country well. I have written these things I have thought. I can offer them for others to read. I can explain them. My view of history is not widely believed in Japan. It is, I think, a view worth sharing."

Liz-Beth lowered her head and stared at the patio stones. Sukie continued.

"As contented as I am here in America, it is not my home. It can never be my home or my country, or its people my people. My people are Japanese and my country is Japan. I was born there. My ancestors were born, died, and are buried there. I have thought about this for many years. I think my country and my people need me, and I need them. I need to tell what I have learned and complete my life in telling. I am sorry I must tell you, in the twilight of my life, I wish to go home."

Liz-Beth heard the words she feared and felt the pain conveyed.

"I wish to be in my country with my people again. I wish to live in my ancestral home on Honshu to spend the time I have left in schools, explaining to young people that many in my generation did things we believed were right, but were wrong. In acceptance of this, we can forgive ourselves and be forgiven. I want my people to know America and Americans as much as it is possible, without living among you. I want to help them understand and accept history so they can progress from it, to embrace American people and be welcomed in America. I hope this gift will be received well, and be helpful to as many Japanese people as I can share it with. Then, when I am gone, I wish to spend eternity in peace with my ancestors in my homeland."

Sukie and Liz-Beth stared into each other's eyes for what seemed an eternity. Liz-Beth leaned back in her chair.

"That's the most beautiful thing I ever heard, Sukie." Liz-Beth's eyes watered. She fought and failed to hold back tears. "I had no idea you had such thoughts. Why didn't you tell us? We would have helped you."

"I was not ready."

Liz-Beth sobbed into a handkerchief.

"Please do not cry Mrs. Wiggins. I do not want to hurt you. I will stay as long as you need me to help transition your life. I will stay at least one more year. Then I must go."

Liz-Beth wiped her eyes.

"I'm so sorry, Sukie. I must cry because your feelings are so beautiful. I'm proud of the way you faced the challenges of your life with so much integrity. You educated yourself in our language, discovered what you need to do, and did this with no help from anyone. I never knew this is what you wanted. I'm happy for you, Sukie. I'm also sad because you didn't share this with us, and you didn't ask us to help you. We would have treasured that. I'm sad because I will miss you so very much."

"Mr. Wiggins knew my thoughts. We agreed, when the time came, I could tell you. I am sorry I could not share this sooner. I gave my word."

"I understand, Sukie. You are lucky to know your purpose. Leave me now, please, Mr. Nakajima. You have been so much a part of our lives, Mr. Wiggins' and my own. I need to be alone to absorb this, and I must cry."

"I am so sorry, Liz-Beth. Please continue to call me Sukie. I have grown fond of this name you have given me."

"You've hated this name."

"I am fond of it now."

Liz-Beth managed a tearful smile. She patted her cheeks with the handkerchief.

"I will miss you Sukie. Not as much as I wish you to be happy."

"Thank you, Mrs. Wiggins. It was an honor to serve you."

"Can we have more talks like this one before you leave?"

"I will try Mrs. Wiggins."

Eleven

Within the month, Liz-Beth bought a building lot. She had a modest one-story cottage constructed closer to town, where she thought she would someday need to be. She designed it in Victorian style, of sticks and cedar shakes, resistant to salted wind, sun weathering, infestation, with large picture windows in the living room and dining room facing west toward the sunset, though she could not see the ocean from the house. She planned on painting it white in the tradition of the original Pescadero homes, even though she preferred colorful hues of Victorian San Francisco. The village council suggested painting it yellow pastel as Sukie told them she preferred. She did.

Liz-Beth donated New Cotswolds to San Mateo County. She no longer needed or wanted to live in such a big house or care for it now that Harry, Bentley, and soon Sukie, would be gone. As a condition, she instructed the little Japanese style house Sukie built for himself, its pond and gardens be preserved and maintained as part of the property, and if he returned, for Sukie to have personal use of it at no cost.

The county turned the great stone house into a bed and breakfast, the property into a mini-ranch to be operated as a non-profit for the benefit of local charities, with five percent of the revenue earmarked for the Japanese/American History and Cultural Center in San Francisco, and yearly access for its members and guests as a week-long summer retreat.

Liz-Beth fenced the Juniper tree, the graves of Bunny and Bentley, a plot for herself on the eastern side of the property next to the wildlife reserve. She included a plot for Sukie though she knew he would never use it.

Complete and ready for occupation, Sukie recruited volunteers from the village to move the things Liz-Beth wanted with her into the cottage. They left the rest of the Wiggins' possessions in the English manor house on the New Cotswolds property.

"Will you need help Sukie? I'm sorry I didn't think to ask."

"No, no, Mrs. Wiggins. I saved most of the money you and Mr. Wiggins were so kind to pay me. Transportation costs are paid. I made arrangements with a private school in Japan. They will greet me on arrival and provide me with a place to live."

"We should have paid you more."

"No, no, I have enough. As you know I prefer a few simple, comfortable things. I lived a good life of work and study. What could I have spent money on? I invested half of my compensation in your companies. I did very well!" Sukie beamed the biggest smile Liz-Beth ever witnessed on his face.

"You sly dog. All these years you eavesdropped on our business affairs."

"It is not so hard to know your thoughts when you speak them openly as if I have no interest. I knew all your business secrets."

"How did you know it would turn out so well? You took a big risk with your money."

"I took no risk at all. I know how successful you and Mr. Wiggins were. I lived on this property. I managed the construction of your mansion. I drove a Bentley! There were no Bentleys in Japan!"

Sukie laughed uncontrollably from his seat on the floor. He held his generous belly and rolled on his back, unable to stop laughing, making no effort to. He laughed a child's laugh, the great laugh of his life.

"It was so easy!" he said when he caught his breath. "I knew your business ventures were the source of your wealth. How could investing in them fail?"

Liz-Beth shook her head, joined him in laugher. He's either fool or wise man, she thought. She realized Sukie invested to participate and contribute, not merely profit.

"Sukie, how did you learn to speak English so good?"

"How do I speak English so well, Mrs. Wiggins."

Liz-Beth laughed, "Corrected by a Japanese POW."

"From books and TV. From listening to you and Mr. Wiggins."

"Nooooo." Liz-Beth shook her head.

"From Mrs. Ito."

"Oooooh! The Cupertino librarian? She's a cute one."

Sukie blushed.

"Is Mrs. Ito your girlfriend?"

"No, no, Mrs. Wiggins."

"You can tell me."

Sukie didn't answer. Where is this going? Liz-Beth wondered. She let it go.

"You kept secrets from me, Sukie."

"You do not share everything." Sukie smiled.

When the time came for Sukie to leave, Mrs. Wiggins rode in the Bentley with him to the pier in San Francisco where his ship to Japan docked. She wanted to drive. He prevailed on her to let him drive her and the Bentley one last time. Sukie had booked first class passage, an outside window berth with a balcony. He brought little with them to the ship, as he lived and dressed simply and already shipped the tools and furnishings he made in Pescadero. His notebooks, books purchased from the Half Moon Bay bookstore, fit in the boot of the Bentley. Bookstore employees assumed he bought them for Mr. Wiggins. Books of the English language, of western literature, history, science, a few personal things were already onboard.

"Now I will see how it feels to be served," Sukie said with his chest out and a confident smile.

"Be kind and respectful and it will be their privilege to serve you."

"You and Mr. Wiggins were good teachers and kind employers. I will be as kind and good as you have been to me."

Liz-Beth stepped forward and surprised Sukie by embracing him. She had never done that. She towered over him and it embarrassed him. She pinned his arms to his sides. He didn't know what to do. When she released him he stepped back and bowed. Liz-Beth bowed in return.

"You know Mr. Wiggins loved you, Sukie. He wanted you to be happy."

"Yes, I know. And if you will permit me to say it, I know you loved me too. I will think of you always, and say kind words about how you saved me and helped me have a happy life in California where I learned what I need to do. I loved you both. I will tell the Japanese people."

"You must write about your new life in Japan."

"I will. You must write to me."

Liz-Beth began to cry. "Please do not cry, Mrs. Wiggins," Sukie pleaded. "You will make me cry too." He did the only thing that could prevent it. He turned abruptly, stepped onto the gangway, and climbed rapidly without looking back until he disappeared into the ship. Once inside, he came to the rail. They waved goodbye. Liz-Beth waited for the ship's horn to signal departure and the sailors to untie it from the dock. She watched it depart with a handkerchief to a check. Sukie stood at the rail until Mrs. Wiggins was very small, and she walked to the Bentley to leave.

*　*　*

Liz-Beth drove the Bentley to the dealership where Sukie brought it for service. She no longer had a driver and she didn't like driving such a big car with a big wooden steering wheel on the wrong side. She sold the Bentley to the dealership service manager. She could walk or ride her bike anywhere she wanted, find most anything she needed in the village. She had the MG and a house with closets full of designer clothing that would last a lifetime, even if she had to risk being seen wearing an outfit more than once. She could still visit thrift stores if she wanted to. It would not be not as often or as much fun as when she rode with Mr. Chuckles in his cage in the back seat next to her and Sukie driving the Bentley in a chauffer's uniform with a bowler hat.

Not until that moment did she realize how much her life just changed. She wondered if the service manager at the Bentley dealership could have an employee take her to a store to buy a pair of Levi's, a blouse, and a pair of canvass sided boat shoes she suddenly and inexplicably wanted to wear, wait for her to change into them, buy lunch from a street vendor, and drive her to Pescadero, when it struck her that she just sold Bunny's Bentley, gave away his house, and his property, and life would never be the same. She began to cry. Her tears flowed freely. She cried for the wonderful life it had been, and the unknown future it had just become.

Kicked to the Curb

Twelve

William Beckinsdale was the only child of a journalist mother and a pilot father. His parents came late to having children due to their age at the time of their marriage. They cherished him for the gift of parenthood.

William grew up in Mountain View, Northern California, in the heart of Silicon Valley, too late to invent the personal computer. The two Steve's, Wozniak and Jobs, had already done that. Too late also for the emergence of computer networking, William came of age in time for the merger of voice and data networks to become practical. That was his opportunity. Where there's a business, there's an engineer.

A quiet introspective boy, William possessed self-confidence, a strong will, a strong personality. Attractive, intelligent, a better than average athlete, he preferred the solitude of surfing to team sports. William always had girlfriends but little interest in long term relationships. Like his idol Steve Jobs he enjoyed building electronic gadgets and programming computers. Like his friends in the Hewlett-Packard computer club, William was a nerd.

The public schools William attended, Huff Elementary, Newton Graham Middle School, Mountain View High, were known for good scholarship. Academic achievement earned acceptance to a number of excellent universities. He chose MIT for the quality of their electrical engineering school, and to experience life in Boston.

After graduation, William returned to Northern California to begin a career in Intel's computer networking business. A year later Intel sent him back to Boston for a telephony conference which introduced him to the idea that voice traffic could be carried over data networks, essentially for free. Money spent on less efficient voice specific networks could be saved. Where there's a need there's an engineer. Where there's a need for an engineer there's a business opportunity.

William knew an integrated circuit company like Intel would make semiconductors for switches that routed communications traffic, but would not make the switches. A good place to begin a career, William knew he could never achieve his ambition working there. He returned to school to work on a master's degree in computer engineering at Stanford. The life-changing event that motivated him was the tragedy that took the lives of his parents. Mortality, the lesson that life can end anytime, unexpectedly, focused him on what he needed to do.

William thought he could start a company to design, build, and sell switches that could carry voice over data networks. While still a graduate student he began building prototypes. When demand for voice over data networking blossomed, he left school mid-term to start the "LightSwitch" company, with his inheritance initially. With a working prototype he attracted angel investment. His designs succeeded. Over the next five years the company grew rapidly from a garage operation to a significant business with assembly facilities and offices in Santa Clara. Rapid growth in internet usage transformed the world. Potential for riches attracted abundant capital; easy money that led to extravagance and excess best described by quoting Alan Greenspan who described stock prices at the time as "Irrational Exuberance." A great surge in stock valuation, by as much as 100% in the NAS-DAQ in 1999 alone, floated all boats, seaworthy or not, including LightSwitch, a company that provided infrastructure for internet service providers, until it ended…

Thirteen

William rose as if it were any Monday morning. He showered, soaped his face from a shaving mug, and shaved with a straight razor, a luxury he allowed himself, time permitting. He brushed his short light brown hair, dressed in a freshly laundered white long-sleeved buttoned-down shirt, and khaki colored gabardines; standard Silicon Valley business casual. He laced up a pair of Cole Haan honey brown Oxfords, and strapped on a simple Seiko watch. He glanced at his special occasion watch in a glass top winder, his father's 1942 Breitling slide rule chronometer Type 42. William found no messages on his Blackberry. Odd, he thought, not even from Asian suppliers. Somebody usually had something to say Monday morning. He slid the Blackberry into a shirt pocket.

William walked to the kitchen of his Joe Eichler ranch house, built with the rest of the subdivision in the 1960s. Modest, comfortable, inexpensive, Eichler's signature floor-to-ceiling walls of glass brought the outside in. Well-suited for mild climates and good weather, Eichlers were ubiquitous in Silicon Valley.

William ground an ounce of Peet's Sumatra and brewed a cup in a press. He stored the unused grounds in an airtight container. He drank his coffee black and strong with two slices of whole grain bread from freshly baked loaves bought at Zelda's neighborhood bakery. He toasted and spread them with a layer of plain Philadelphia cream cheese, added a tomato slice, a slice of onion, and sprinkled them with fresh ground pepper. When he had lox, he toasted a bagel instead.

William stepped outside and picked up a copy of the San Jose Mercury News. Nothing in the headlines caught his attention. He finished breakfast, placed the mug, plate and utensils in the dishwasher for the Tuesday maid service. He slid his laptop into a Tumi leather brief, walked to the carport, placed it on the passenger seat of the BMW, and drove to the office in an immaculate, bright silver, late model 5 Series sedan, the quintessential "C-suite" car for young Silicon Valley executives. His college car, the Alfa GTV, occupied the other space in the carport under a cover.

Commercial buildings lined the Bayshore Freeway access roads behind three story sound walls and billboards. Divided by Jersey barriers, nothing about it is appealing. During rush hour, it doesn't work. *They should have named it the Slow Shore Freeway,* William thought. Morning traffic between Mountain View and North San Jose is heavy by 7:30AM. William preferred leaving an hour earlier to avoid the worst of it. This morning he allowed himself the luxury of an extra hour of sleep. He expected a long day because of an afternoon board meeting.

Driving on 101 in either direction in rush hour is frustrating. The radio distracted him from deliberately smashing into the Suburban crawling ahead of him. Creeping south on Highway 101 enabled him to come up to speed on the morning business news, he rationalized, as he passed through Sunnyvale. NAS-DAQ up, Cisco bought another of more than 140 companies they would eventually acquire in a decade. Another competitor taken out of the market in exchange for a container load of Cisco stock. New products for Cisco to build, market and sell. Another batch of newly minted paper millionaires in the neighborhood; a regular monthly story. William squeezed the rim of the steering wheel, took a deep breath, and sighed at the speedometer hovering marginally above zero. *Good thing the BMW has an automatic transmission,* he thought. *This would be miserable with a clutch.*

William arrived at the office parking lot at 8:15AM. It took forty-five minutes to drive thirteen miles. If he left a little earlier he could have peddled his Cannondale, taken a quick shower in the gym across the parking lot, walked to the office, and dropped in the chair behind his desk. He'd pedal to work daily if he didn't sometimes need a car during the day. Maybe, he thought, he should leave a car at the office and peddle. William parked at the back of the lot. The space he preferred near the building entry is never available past his usual 7:00AM arrival.

William gazed at the hills across the bay above the city of Fremont. A steep climb, they rose three thousand feet above the water. He hiked them on weekends and weekday evenings for exercise and views of San Francisco, though most days an ugly brown layer of pollution obscured the city. Cattle are found grazing at higher elevations above subdivisions that end below the Fremont peaks. So tame they behave like big dogs when they introduce their newborn calves to two legged visitors.

The morning air felt cool and crisp as William preferred it, this last week of February in the year 2000. Verdant from winter rains, the east hills appeared lush and lustrous as they do a few months of the year before spring rains end. By the beginning of summer they'll be brown. It rained Sunday morning turning them a shade deeper. *The view will be wonderful from the seventeenth floor*, William thought, from the board room and his corner of the executive offices.

Fourteen

O sgood Dunn, one of LightSwitch's board members, greeted William when he exited the elevator as if he stood there waiting for him. Curious, William thought. How long was he standing there?

"Ozzie, how are you this morning?"

"Doing well, William, thank you."

A middle-aged professional investor, Osgood managed a private equity company founded with family money made on the Chicago Board of Trade in the 1800s. He made angel investments on his own, and later stage investments as a partner in the venture capital fund "Dunn & Cousie." Osgood arrived early for a monthly afternoon board meeting.

Portly, balding, grey haired, in his mid-50s, Dunn had pale, clammy skin in spite of a Northern California address. He lived in the San Francisco fog basin, north of Market Street, the financial district. Osgood's pumpkin-shaped head, blotchy, pock-marked face, and thick layer of fat around his neck made it impossible to look good in a tie, even in custom made shirts, and his weren't. His small piercing light blue eyes were set wide. They protruded frog-like from a clean-shaven face that could be improved with a neatly trimmed beard or a moustache but Osgood could never be attractive. His pupils always looked pinned as if he were drugged, but never in his life had he used drugs. They straddled a clump of a nose that looked like a mutated strawberry and vaguely matched it in color. William thought Osgood would look more appealing in a gas mask.

Five foot eight, Dunn stood two inches shorter than William.

He leaned back to balance a protruding belly. Resembling W.C. Fields in brown, Osgood wore an ill-fitted, off-the-shelf, two-piece suit over a white and brown striped shirt as if he needed stripes to make him look heavier. He left his collar open Silicon Valley business style. A dark brown tie draped over the passenger seat of his new black S Class Mercedes for business meetings in the San Francisco financial district where Dunn & Cousie leased offices. The best you could say for Osgood's appearance is his clothes were freshly laundered.

"What brings you in so early, Ozzie?"

"What brings you in so late, William?" Osgood answered through a grin. "You usually arrive before 7:00 AM."

"I asked you first," William said warmly, to one of his early investors. "Shall we go to the board room?"

"No, that's… what I want to talk to you about, the reason I'm here early. Can we go to your office instead?"

"Sure."

William noticed a change in Osgood's tone.

"Let's enjoy the view of the hills together while we can, Ozzie. Bottled water? Can I get you coffee?"

"Thanks. I've had some. I'll wait for you."

William walked the hall to the coffee counter. VK Prakash, LightSwitch's VP of Engineering, sipped a cup of Darjeeling by the hot water dispenser. He didn't notice William approaching. *"In a trance,"* William thought. The look on VK's face appeared focused and serious.

"Wrestling a technical problem VK?"

"Oh hi, William." VK escaped his thoughts.

"What's on the plate today?"

"Nothing. I have to go to a meeting. See you later." VK pivoted and walked down the hallway.

That's odd, William thought. *VK likes to chat up a morning.*

William returned to his office. He found Osgood gazing at the east hills through floor-to-ceiling windows as the morning sun warmed the room.

William sat behind his desk. Osgood sat in the arm chair across from him.

"About the board meeting. The board decided to postpone it."

"Oh? That's odd. To when?"

"Not sure. I'm here to discuss something with you, for the board I mean."

William came to attention. Dunn fidgeted. William thought he detected a glint of moisture on Osgood's forehead. The serious expression, the body language, the consolatory tone of Dunn's voice concerned him. William hadn't expected what came next.

"The board came to agreement over the weekend. We can no longer allow you to run the company. You have to give up your position as CEO."

"*What?* Shouldn't we discuss this together?"

"I'm afraid not."

"It's a final decision?"

"Yes."

"For what reason?"

"The way things are going."

"Excuse me, Osgood, didn't we agree last month a soft quarter caught the company at a bad time. Surprised the entire board except me. It isn't a management problem."

"Yes, I know."

"Then tell me again why you're removing me."

"We've been arguing over strategy since the summer."

"I argued to stop expanding when Intel told us their book to bill analysis forecasted slowdown. I had it right."

"Yes, but we can only move forward as one voice, and we've been divided." Dunn waved his hand over the desk, pursed his lips and shook his head.

"We agree *now*, don't we? Excuse me Osgood, Intel told Cisco the same thing they told us. Cisco is firing eighty-five hundred people they hired last summer and throwing $2.5 *billion dollars'* worth of obsolete inventory in a dumpster. Why hasn't Cisco's board fired John Chambers?"

"Don't compare yourself with John Chambers, William. Not many people can run a technology company the size of Cisco, and this isn't about that. It's our fiduciary duty to act, William. You know that."

"Duty to whom, Osgood? This is a private company. I founded and brought you into it. Between myself and the board, we own almost all of it."

"We're going to take care of you, William."

"What job do I have?"

"I'm afraid none."

William felt his face burn with anger. He stood. He trembled. He leaned his weight forward, and placed his fists on the table.

"You're throwing me out of the company I founded to cover up your own incompetence; *YOU*, my first outside investor!"

"We're buying you out."

"And the difference is?"

Dunn opened a leather brief and removed a manila envelope.

"We would like to make what we feel is a generous offer to tender your shares."

"I bet it's generous." William sat down. "I don't want to sell my share of the company."

"You can no longer run it, and we want to buy it from you."

"Who is *we*?"

"Board members, mainly."

William shook his head. "When I invited you to invest in this company I didn't think you were a vulture capitalist. I thought we were in this together for the long term. That's what you said."

"At the time, we were. Now the order book is falling off a cliff. There are debtors, lienholders, suppliers coming after us, a landlord and employees to pay, too much capital equipment, facilities are too big, a staff that's too big, product development projects we can't afford, not enough capital to carry us through this soft patch."

"Yes, I know. And this is because?"

Osgood didn't answer.

"Your solution to this stupidity contest is to blame it on the one board member who argued against expanding, so you and the rest of the inmates can run your asylum."

"That's an example of belligerence we can't have. The arguing, this blame game has to stop."

"No problem. You and your buddies get out of the way and give me a chance to fix it."

"That isn't going to happen."

"*Oh…Oh,*" William raised his arms with his palms up in frustration. "It's OK for you to blame *me*. No blame for *you*? You said, 'Don't worry about it. We have lots of resources if we need them.' Where *are* those resources? Bring them now."

"Give it up, William. You aren't going to get anywhere making the same argument over and over. It hasn't worked in the months you've been trying to float it. This is the problem the board has with you."

"A red herring. You, not I, created the problem and are in the way of finding a solution. You don't have all the shares either."

"No, but you can't run the company without consent from the board, because you no longer have a majority. You don't have board support either. What matters is who has the ability to execute a solution."

"Execution is the right word. You need somebody who *has* a solution."

"I'm the messenger. One of the executioners if you have to see it that way."

"Who else is in on this?"

"The decision was unanimous."

"I have no friends, no supporters on the board? Nobody wanted to do anything differently? Nobody wanted to keep me in *any* capacity?"

"This isn't personal. We don't hate you. We just need to salvage what we can of our investment. It's a business decision."

"You morons cratered the company. You're scapegoating me."

"We're removing you because we can't work with you."

"*Bullshit!* You're removing me because I didn't *agree* with you. Now you can't have me around because I know you wrecked the company."

"See it however you wish. We could have sent you email. We could have called you. We could have locked you out. I convinced the board members we could have a civilized face-to-face discussion. If you control yourself we can. If not I'll walk out of here right now. There will be no further discussion, no severance package, no tender. You'll be out with two weeks' pay, accrued benefits, and we can pick over the remains of your company."

"I need clarification of that. What about the tender?"

"We can downsize the company. You know it needs capital. Right now, no unprofitable private company can raise money. We could sell the business to a bigger company that can use the technology, the patents, the engineering staff. To do this, we have to engineer a massive equity dilution, have a reverse split, create a lot of new shares. We can't give you any. Your stake in the company would be reduced to next to nothing. You would probably still become unemployed. It's the worst possible outcome for you. Even if we could find a way to keep you on, you would have little more than a job."

Son-of-a-bitch is playing me, William thought. "You want me out so you can play financial engineering."

"There's potential management conflict with an acquiring company. You may be unable to adjust. How can we convince the management team of another company you're going to be happy with this arrangement when we don't believe it ourselves? Most of the employees and everything else will probably have to go. Do you want to stick around for that? You'll be out in a year anyway. Under the circumstances an acquiring company will want a leadership change."

"We can't think of employment to offer that isn't insulting. Do you want to be demoted? Report to another CEO? Rather than that, we decided to offer to buy your shares for more than they're worth so you have funds to move on. We might even back you in another venture. We aren't monsters, William. We just don't see another way."

William stood. He walked to the window to gaze at the east hills while Dunn waited quietly.

Fait accompli, William thought. *Not like I didn't see it coming. It would be hell to continue working with these guys, after this presentation, with reduced responsibilities under another management team. Dunn's right about this. It couldn't last.*

What else could I have done? Quit? Hand over the business for them to plunder? Hose down the people I hired? Lay everyone off when they don't deserve to lose their jobs? Carry on with the company crippled, devoid of the resources it needs to get back on its feet? What difference would it have made? They want me out anyway. They had to rush this goddamn expansion and blame me when it didn't work. Behind my back. Those fuckers! How can I build a company with a board like this one? A horrible ending, but I can't dig us out when every day I have to fight them and their cross purposes. I hate being kicked to the curb. I hate their plan. What can I do about it? I'll be happy to be rid of them.

"Who are you selling the company to?"

It's going our way, Dunn thought. "We don't have a prospect yet. We have to start shopping."

"CEO's get a rich package when they exit."

"When they leave rich companies. I'm afraid we can't do that. We can give you half a year's salary, accumulated entitlements, prepaid healthcare through the year."

"It's done then?"

"Yes. I'm glad you're coming to closure."

Dunn offered an envelope. "I have documents for you. I'd rather hand them to you than email them. Considering your history, your position with the company, we're willing to let you take them home for review. I suggest you sign and send the originals back ASAP before any of it can be withdrawn. We can compensate you quickly."

William took the envelope. "I'll read it now."

"I'm afraid you can't do that. I have to ask you to leave the building."

"Are you kidding me? This is still my company and my office!"

"No William. You were terminated at 6:30AM this morning. I would appreciate it if you leave your laptop, your Blackberry, any company property. I'll have your personal things packed and sent to your house."

"I'll leave when I'm ready."

"You can't stay here. I have to have security walk you out if you don't leave now. Please don't make me do that."

"You fucking assholes."

William gritted his teeth. He grimaced. He placed his Blackberry on the desk.

"The laptop is in the trunk of the car. You can come and get it."

"Drop it off at the front desk or send it in."

Dunn stood and backed away from the desk. He didn't offer his hand, didn't think William would take it. He guessed right.

William picked "Dusty" off the table by the window. He walked past Dunn and out the door without so much as a glance at him. He ignored employees standing in the hallway when he walked to the elevator. They milled about heads down, eyes cast on the floor to avoid him.

They all know, William thought. *I'm the last one to find out. Not one of them has the balls to speak to me. Cowards. All of them.*

William stepped out of the elevator into the lobby. He left the building without speaking to anyone. When he looked over his shoulder, he saw Dunn followed him in the other elevator. *That bastard*, he thought. *Did he think I would steal a painting or bomb the building?*

When William passed through the lobby, Osgood Dunn returned to the elevator, punched in floor 17 and walked down the hall to the boardroom.

When William reached the parking lot, VK called him.

"William. Please wait up."

William turned around. "What is it, VK?"

"I'm really sorry about this. I asked them to let you stay on, said we were all behind you. I felt so helpless. I couldn't do anything to help you."

"Why the fuck didn't you call me over the weekend?"

"Ruin your weekend? What good would that have done?"

William took a deep breath. *VK's right*, he thought. *I wouldn't have slept for two days and two nights. No, I would have called Dunn argued with him and the other board members. Nothing I could have done would have altered the outcome. The board dropped a piano on me. I'm glad it's over. I can't put it on VK. He's been a great partner from the day I hired him.*

"How long have you known?"

"They called me into an afterhours meeting Friday. Alesha and I felt terrible all weekend. They've been discussing it for a while, I guess. They complained about disagreements. I told them you know what you're doing, you could get us out of this. I couldn't do any more than that or they would have turned on me. I didn't know it had gone this far until Friday."

"Who called you in?"

"Dunn, and somebody I didn't recognize."

"I didn't even know they were here Friday. You could have said something."

"I couldn't. They told me not to discuss it with you."

"They threatened you?"

"A veiled threat." VK waved his arms in frustration like John Madden did on gridiron sidelines.

"They said people who demonstrated they were team players could stay on. I have a family. My daughter wants to go to Harvard. The tuition is outrageous. I'm sorry about what happened. I don't know what I could have done to help you."

"You couldn't do anything, VK. It *was* a threat."

"How bad was it?

"How do you think it feels to be ambushed and assassinated? Do you know if all of them wanted to do this?"

"Oh no, I'm sure they disagreed."

Dunn lied. That SOB, William thought.

"How do you know this?"

"Their Friday meeting."

"You attended this meeting?"

"No, from the hall. I heard them through the doorway. I met Lupe there. We needed the board room for an engineering meeting."

"Do you know who was on which side?"

"No. I heard voices, just barely."

VK took a deep breath. He looked down at the parking lot. He shook his head.

"Dunn saw me *leaving* at the end of the day. He asked me in. He told me to come in early this morning, shut your Blackberry down, forward your email, your text messages and voice mail to him, and reset your passwords. Tell only whoever needed to know, and tell them not to tell anyone. That worked for a nanosecond. Then he told me what they were going to do and not to tell you or anyone else."

What a surprise, William thought. *Impossible to keep this a secret.*

"What plans did they share with you?"

"Just you were moving on."

"Nothing about what they were planning to do with the company? Acquisition or merger plans?"

"Nothing like that."

The two friends paused.

"Nobody said a word to me. Nobody approached me on the way out of the building. That hurts." William's stomach contracted. His heart rose into his throat. "I hired, I worked with most of those people. They were my friends. Now I'm a pariah."

"We're all in shock. Don't hate them. They don't despise you. They don't know what to say or how to say it. I'm struggling and we've been close from the beginning. Some of them hardly know you. What do they say to a CEO they hardly know after he's just been sacked?"

"Now I know how the Roman Generals felt when the senate no longer needed them, and sent them off to be murdered."

"It's isn't like that, not with the employees. Look," VK said, raising his arms in exasperation, "I… we had a great relationship. We did good things together. I know none of this is your fault; or *my* fault. If there's ever a chance for us to work together again I'd love that. I want you to believe this. I hope you feel the same way."

"I'm not angry at you. I'm upset and confused. I don't know what to say or think about anything."

"I understand. Thank you. What are you going to do? Do you have any plans?"

"I have no idea. I've just been decapitated."

"Whatever you do, I wish you the very best. You were a great leader, very supportive when things were tough. I enjoyed working through problems with you. I wish we could work our way through this one."

"I prefer to think of us as partners. Hey, what are you smiling at?"

"The pelican."

"You didn't think I would leave Dusty with them, did you?"

"No disrespect, I didn't think it was important."

"You know Dusty and I go back a long way. I need all the friends I can get."

VK chuckled. "I didn't mean anything by it. I know he's your pal."

"Apologize to Dusty."

"Apologize to a stuffed pelican?'

"I'll let it go one time."

"I'll try to be more respectful," VK said. He laughed and shook his head. "If there's anything I can do to help, please ask."

"Thanks, VK. I will. I can't think of anything off the top of my head… Ah…" William raised a hand.

"Can you please give my best to everyone? Tell them they all did great work. I wish I could thank them in person. They threw my ass out of the building!" William chuckled. "I feel like a pirate forced to walk the plank."

"I'll make sure word gets around. It will be appreciated. None of us wanted to see you go. Good luck, William. Do something good, and call me when you get it started, will you?"

"Can you let me know what's going on with the company?"

"There are some things I won't be able to discuss. I'll share what I can."

"Oh, one more thing. Dunn said he would have someone ship my personal things. Could you go to my office and do that right away, do it personally? I'd rather not have anyone else do it."

"I'd be honored."

"You better go now before you get in trouble for talking to me."

"Some things are worth being in trouble for. God, William. I can't work for a gestapo."

"All the best, VK."

"Goodbye William." A man in a dark suit stood menacingly beside Osgood Dunn at a boardroom window. They watched the two friends say goodbye. "Gentlemen," Dunn announced, "the board meeting of the LightSwitch Company has just started."

Fifteen

Traffic died down by the time William left the office park. He chose a leafy suburban route instead of the freeway for whatever comfort he could derive from it. He drove west on Montague to the Central Expressway where he merged with traffic in the northbound direction. He continued through Santa Clara and Sunnyvale. He exited at West Middlefield Road, drove to his house in the north end of Mountain View. When he reached the house, he parked the BMW in the carport, went inside, and flopped on a couch. When he tore open the envelope Osgood Dunn gave him, and read the documents, he learned why Osgood wanted him out of the building.

William had never been so infuriated. He stood, lost his breath and balance. His heart skipped a beat. He grabbed his chest. For a moment he thought he might have a heart attack.

Those bastards. Those fucking bastards, he said out loud. He sank into the couch. The board offered him less than the sum of his own money he used to start the company and take it to the first round of funding. William felt he earned most of the credit for making LightSwitch into a functional business. He knew he deserved better. After multiple funding rounds he still owned a significant share. If he had to accept this offer they were buying him out for a nothing-burger. His recent wages were less than he earned in his last year at Intel. He drew no compensation for the first year of full-time work at LightSwitch, nothing for the part time hours he put in while he attended classes and built the prototypes, nothing for all the evening and weekend overtime. Financially, he would have been better off if he never started the company.

William could live with financial reversal. Losing the company he quit school to start with his inheritance, all the things he hoped to achieve with it hurt much more. *All that time and effort,* he thought, *half a decade and more, and I have to give it up. What a terrible waste.*

William walked to the kitchen, opened the refrigerator and retrieved a bottle of Odwalla. He returned to the great room and sprawled on the couch. His eyes glazed over as he sipped the drink, documents of defeat in hand. A personal Dunkirk. His mind turned to puree. An hour and a half later his pragmatic side prodded him into a decision he needed to make. William knew the computer industry already entered recession. He could do nothing about that. Long-term future didn't seem to matter. William had to deal with *now.* William glanced at his watch. *Almost 11:00 AM. The board meeting, if they held one, probably ended.* He called Osgood.

"William," Osgood answered firmly.

You could have heard a pin drop in the boardroom.

"Is the board meeting over?"

"Yes."

Osgood lied. They moved it up, William noted.

"I read the documents."

"And…"

"This is hideous, Osgood. You have to do better."

"Hold on a minute." Dunn excused himself to locate an empty office.

"Sorry. I had to find a private room… I can't."

"I've never known you to take a position without wiggle room."

"I mean the board can't. We could be skewered by investors. They could sue and hamstring the company."

"Bullshit. You know this is outrageous."

"It isn't. It's your share and more. The company isn't worth what you think."

"You know what this offer means."

"Yes, I do and I'm sorry."

"Let me keep the equity if the shares have so little value."

"Our issues are unresolved if you have voting shares."

"Create a class of non-voting shares, a tracking stock."

"No."

"Increase the separation amount. It's based on income concessions I made this year. Base it on what I earned last year. It should be 30% higher."

"We can't use last year's compensation."

"The board can do anything it wants."

"It can bite us when we try to secure financing."

"Who's going to dig that far into this and care about it? I'm not asking for the moon. Extend it to a year."

"We made you the best, last, and only offer. You have to decide if you want this or nearly nothing when the shares are diluted. Look, I know you probably hate my guts right now. You probably hate all of us. We aren't happy about it. We're professional investors and board members. We make business decisions, not personal decisions. It's part of the business of starting and guiding companies. I know it's ugly for you. It isn't any fun for us either."

"Thank you for not saying it hurts you more than it does me."

"You must know we prefer expanding, making acquisitions, mergers, taking companies public. You might think the board is stealing the company from you. I wouldn't blame you for thinking such a thing. In time you'll see it isn't what we're doing."

The son-of-a-bitch is playing me again, William thought. *They end up with the company and all the assets, I get half a year's income at reduced rate, accrued benefits, less cash than I invested.*

"If there's anything left of our relationship that can permit you to believe what I tell you please consider we are doing what we have to do, exactly for the reasons stated. We are not evil. We are not trying to screw you. I don't have to take all this time to explain it. We're trying the only thing we can come up with to save our own asses. I'll admit to that. We're also trying to get you out of this with something, just not what you think you deserve. It could be worse. We could let the money run out, shutter the place, let the value of your equity drop to zero, sell the remains. We won't get much but we'll get nearly all of it. You'll get a few shares of a company in chapter 7. Believe what you want about fault, responsibility, fairness. We have no better option. If you can believe that or if you can't I suggest getting out of this clean with cash in your pocket is better than no cash, and equity worth the square root of ZERO."

William sat quietly in the sofa while Osgood continued.

"I repeat. Your employment is *terminated*. Take some money and do something good with it. I can't spend the rest of my life explaining this. Take a couple days to think it over. Under the circumstances I can get the board to live with that. I prefer you make a decision and get on with it. In any case, unless you have something new and significant to add, this discussion needs to end *now*."

"You're always closing aren't you Osgood," William thought. William knew he could go no further. Dunn had all the cards. He wanted to be done with it and horrible that it is, put this part of his life behind him. He needed no time to think about that. For six months company problems consumed him. It ruined his personal life, isolated him from most of the people he cared about. When it would end and how; they were the only things he didn't know before today. He had to choose between the parachute or being thrown out without one as the plane spiraled into the ground. He could think of no alternative.

"If I agree to this, I want one thing that isn't in here. I never want to hear about this again."

"Pardon the pun. Done," Osgood said.

"If I sign and fax this to you, when can I expect a check for the value of the shares?"

"I'll send it by courier out of the Dunn & Cousie account."

"Why Dunn & Cousie? The company has no position in LightSwitch."

"I want it on the books as a loan to preserve what little cash LightSwitch has left. What difference does it make to you? Dunn & Cousie will buy your shares. You'll have your money. The result would be the same if you sold them to LightSwitch or the man-in-the-moon."

What the hell are they doing? William wondered. *Dunn & Cousie, not LightSwitch, is buying my equity. To flip my shares to another investor or a company when they sell LightSwitch? Do they think they are worth more than they offered me? What do they have in the pipeline? Whatever it is, I can't do a thing about it.*

"The severance check?"

"I'll have the company cut a check and mail it to you."

"OK Osgood. I'll sign and fax. Not right this minute. I have to normalize this."

"At-a-boy, William. In time, you will see this was your best course of action. The pragmatist always wins. I have no doubt you will land on your feet somewhere. If you need an early stage investor, I would be pleased to take a call from you. I mean it."

What chutzpa this guy has! William thought. "If I'm not here for the courier have him leave it under the mat. I might have to get out of here for a while to avoid losing it. I have to go vomit."

"Godspeed, William."

Osgood returned to the board room.

"William agrees, will sign and fax, probably today."

"What a relief."

"You have a talent for this, Osgood."

"First time he was sacked. Took some talking down," Osgood said.

"Thanks for handling it, Ozzie."

"Now he can't cause trouble. We can get our deal moving. Let me introduce my candidate for new board member and co-chairman, my partner at Dunn & Cousie, Mr. Robert Cousie."

Sixteen

William brewed a pot of Zen. He heated half a Quiche Lorraine in a toaster oven, and carried them with a mug to the back yard. He placed them on a teak table and sat in a chair. The branches of his delicate Japanese maples were bare, a metaphor for his life. The leaves were brown, down, left on the ground to desiccate over the winter. The patio resembled a stained, discarded carpet. No birds landed; no squirrels hung from empty feeders. *Opportunists,* William thought. They left months ago for neighboring yards where food is plentiful. The bushes grew wild and needed pruning. Sporadic watering over the summer left bare spots in the grass. Flower pots were empty of life. Outdoor furniture hadn't been cleaned. Painted frames faded and peeled. Flagstone hadn't been pressure washed. The yard looked desolate, abandoned. The way William felt.

William had no visitors in the months since his girlfriend moved out. In his misery, he didn't think he could do a thing about it. He couldn't remember if she left in September or October, nor did he think it mattered. LightSwitch was gone forever. As far as he knew, so was the girlfriend he ran off. His friends were still friends, but he spent little time with them since the middle of last summer when the company began to unravel. William felt lonely and alone.

William took a deep breath, looked around the barren yard, and asked himself, *Why am I here?*

He carried the mug and the half-eaten quiche to the kitchen. He found room in the dishwasher for the mug and plate, dropped the quiche in a plastic bag, and placed it in the garbage. He left the kitchen, but abruptly returned and retrieved the quiche. *I'll leave it in the Sub-Zero for the housekeeper*, he thought.

William reached in a hall closet, pulled out his luggage and threw it on the bed. He stuffed the bags with all the clothing they could hold, four seasons of it, leaving only enough slack to zipper them. He filled a toiletry bag with daily necessities, zipped it into a plastic bag with his shaving kit, and stowed it with the luggage in the trunk of the BMW.

He retrieved the monthly bills from a file cabinet in the home office and slipped them into a pouch in his back pack. He took his credit and frequent flyer cards, passport, personal Blackberry, and $180 in cash he kept in a hidden desk compartment. *I'll leave the Dyson*, he thought, a poor attempt at gallows humor.

He took the title to the BMW and a digital camera. He took a mini flashlight, a combination compass / GPS, a pair of Bushnell 16X50 binoculars, and a chronograph with a woven nylon band he hiked with. He packed a portable backup drive, and a flash-card reader.

William remembered the company laptop in the trunk. *Screw the board*, he thought. *They can come and get it. I need one.* If they pressed him, he could send it back and replace it. Not today. Today he wanted to get the hell out of Mountain View and Silicon Valley.

William packed little else; no photos, no other artifacts of his life, his parent's lives, or his ex-girlfriend's. Not his exercise equipment, downhill skis, or his new Cannondale bicycle. He took little more than what he could wear, what he needed to groom himself, a Hanukah candelabra purchased on vacation from a street vendor in Israel, two Yahrzeit candles taped with dates to remind him when to light them for his parents, and Dusty.

William forwarded the land line to his cellphone, left a living room light, the heat and power on, set the thermostat to 45. His neighbors and service vendors would soon realize he left, but nothing could be done on short notice to protect the property. *Screw it, he thought. It's the least of my problems.* A safe deposit box at the downtown Mountain View branch of the Bank of America had everything else important.

Most of William's money went into the company. A lot less came out. When the house is empty the monthly cost is nominal. With no mortgage, property tax is the biggest expense. William had enough money to last two years if he managed it carefully.

William left a note in the kitchen for the cleaning service, and one on an outside hose bib for the lawn service. "I'll be gone for a while. Please continue to maintain the property. I'll mail you a check monthly." To the cleaning service note he added, "Please take any food you wish from the refrigerator and throw the rest away."

William threw an armload of coats and jackets and his hiking boots in the back seat of the BMW. He addressed a cover letter, signed and faxed the documents Osgood gave him to LightSwitch, and placed copies in the file cabinet. He locked the house and left for the post office to forward the mail.

William left the downtown Mountain View post office appropriately located at 211 Hope Street. Noting the address, *I could use a basket of this*, he said to himself. He drove to Palo Alto on the Central Expressway where the name changed to Alma and the expressway ended. He continued to Page Mill Road where he turned west.

William drove past the Hanover Street and Porter Drive entrances to Hewlett Packard across from the south side of the Stanford University Campus. *So much history in those two campuses*, he thought. He took the northbound ramp onto Highway 280, a broad, scenic, divided freeway, lined by large hilly parcels of well cared for landscapes and stands of mature trees. Private estates, contemporary commercial properties and the Stanford campus set well back from the road made for a pleasant drive. No billboards line Highway 280, beauty to the 101 beast.

William drove north past Sand Hill Road. Some of the largest venture capital partnerships in Silicon Valley, and the world, maintain offices on Sand Hill, in office parks arrayed along two and a half miles of road, dividing West Menlo Park and the north side of the Stanford Campus. William spent a good deal of time on Sand Hill raising money for his company. This day he traveled west, in the opposite direction of money. Not so distant on a map, Palo Alto and Menlo Park were a world away from his destination. *Appropriate*, he thought, *to leave where the journey began.*

William exited Highway 280 onto Woodside Road, drove west through picturesque Woodside to where it turned into La Honda Road and continued winding to the top of the hill; to the ridge where it crosses Skyline Drive at Sky Londa.

Sky Londa is little more than an address at the crossroads of La Honda Road and Skyline Boulevard on the backbone of the Santa Cruz Mountains halfway between San Francisco and San Jose. Both beautiful winding roads with smooth well-engineered surfaces, La Honda Road runs east/west and passes through the tiny hamlet of La Honda and not much else as it winds its way to the Pacific Ocean.

Skyline Boulevard runs north/south. The canopy above it is dense enough to block the sun. The road can be dangerous in heavy fog when it lingers in trees overhanging a damp highway. It soaks the canopy so thoroughly on foggy days, droplets fall to ground as if it's raining. William drove through clear skies and warm temperatures.

There's a little strip mall with a gas station at Sky Londa on the northeast corner of Skyline Boulevard at La Honda Road. The Mountain Terrace restaurant, Skywood Trading Post, Sky Londa Realty and two gas pumps are located on the parking lot where motorcycles line up by the dozens on weekends and weekday evenings in summer when daylight lingers for an evening ride. It's one of the few places in America where Ducatis outnumber Harleys five-to-one. A gas station on the northwest corner called Alice's Station stood between a motorcycle repair shop and Alice's Restaurant. Not the one of Arlo Guthrie fame. It's a good stop anyway. This being California you can probably get anything you want there too. If you saw officer Obie he'd be in a rocking chair by then, faded like the memory of the movie. William parked the car. He didn't want to be a rebel. He just wanted a beer.

Alice's is a rustic place, a cabin in a clearing at a crossroads. Without a tarmac parking lot it would look frontier. William wondered if horses were ever hitched to the railing when two female riders came around the corner of Alice's, dismounted, hitched up and walked inside. Alice's has an expansive outdoor deck, good casual food and cold beer, exactly what William thought he needed.

William chose a table where he could watch his car, loaded in plain view with his wardrobe on the back seat.

When the waitress arrived, he ordered a Smuttynose Robust Porter, an east coast craft beer because he liked the name, and a blue cheese mushroom burger, medium rare, side salad. He rarely drank alcohol before happy hour. Getting sacked for the first time from his own company is a special occasion.

A young, svelte waitress, a local green-eyed, long wavy-haired redhead beauty took his order. Freckles splattered the pale skin of her face, and arms exposed beneath a white short-sleeve cotton blouse, tucked into painted-on Levi's cutoffs. She stood on legs of a track star. She tied a red bandana around her neck and wore a pair of white canvas sided Sperry Topsiders with no socks. *Miss Daisy of California*, William thought. *Oh my. I'm feelin' better already.*

The waitress looked aloof and self-absorbed as if she thought herself the only attractive cheerleader at a Friday night football game. Miss perky walked a bouncy bossanova, swiveling hips and swinging body parts around a narrow waist as if Alice's played Stan Getz on a turntable and she danced to it.

What isn't classic about this?" William asked himself.

"How are you on this beautiful winter day?" the not-real-shy waitress asked.

"Great. I got sacked this morning so I ran away from home."

William forced a smile. Why did I say that, he wondered? Did I expect hugs and kisses?

"Oh, I'm so sorry," the waitress answered insincerely. *Another one* she said to herself, *It's an epidemic.* She tilted her head and pouted.

"It's no big thing. I started the company."

"You fired yourself?"

"No, my board of directors decided they could run it better."

"That's terrible. Maybe food will make you feel better."

"I won't be hungry."

The waitress and her magnificent hair bounced back to the kitchen. *Pleasant enough,* William thought. *No interest in me or my story.*

William moved lunch to the deck in the mid-day sun. He ate his blue cheese mushroom burger medium rare, side salad on a potato bun. He preferred a Kaiser roll. *In this too,* he thought, *not my day.* He sipped the Smuttynose. "Another?" the waitress asked. Third of a pint left, William declined. He watched motorcycles stop at the intersection, cross over, and accelerate westward down the hill on La Honda Road. *All riding in the same direction,* William thought. *My direction. Downhill."*

One by one the riders opened the throttle, leaned into the turn, and accelerated off the mountaintop. "*Music,*" William thought. Ducati riders wore full face helmets and riding suits like Grand Prix racers. Harley riders rode casual. Some wore yarmulke size black helmets. D.O.T. legal, they protected nothing. "*Blue collar guys*" William guessed. He guessed wrong. Many were small business owners or technology company executives who liked riding Harleys and looking *outlaw.*

William preferred the look and feel of a Ducati, the "naked" Monster model in particular. He admired Harleys too, that "bad boy" look the bikes and riders all have in some degree. Most of them rode with contented expressions, living a life, he imagined, far different from the one he just left, where it seems you have to please everybody except yourself to succeed.

On a midday winter Monday, unencumbered by balance sheets and creditors, board members and investors, production and delivery schedules, William envied them before remembering as of this morning, he was unencumbered too.

William wondered if they fantasized riding with a certain redheaded waitress wrapped around and behind them. Maybe they preferred it exactly as he imagined they rode. Alone, riding to anywhere and nowhere, whenever and wherever they wanted. *Freedom. The open road*, William thought. He longed for it.

William grinned as he contemplated trading the BMW with all his worldly possessions contained therein for a Harley Shovelhead. He didn't care if the trade was fair or not, only that he felt the impulse, and he could. A thing of beauty, an act of defiance. That made it fair, he reasoned. He daydreamed trading straight across with the guy fueling his bike after retrieving it from the motorcycle shop next door. Then, in the dream, William pulled on a fringe suede jacket, threw a leg over the bike, fired it up, and listened to it lope under him – potato, potato, potato, and with bedroll secure, atlas of the world between the handlebars, saddle bags bursting with provisions, he would ride off into winding road glory, never to look in the rearview mirror. He could do it. He had the title to the BMW in the glovebox.

The redheaded waitress saw William lost in reverie, a cheek resting on a palm supported by an elbow on the table, a vacant stare into an almost empty parking lot. She dropped the check off without disturbing him. William had that silly-happy look on his face when the body is in one time and place, the mind in another. Burger and salad gone, the glass held the last two ounces of beer. He snapped out of his dream and threw down the rest of the porter.

William left a $20 bill on the table for a $12 lunch. He took a long lingering look at the redheaded waitress serving a middle-aged couple at a nearby table. She ignored him and took their order with a self-satisfied grin. "Nice bandana," he whispered loud enough for her to hear it. She smiled. *A man could lose himself in that head of hair,* William thought to himself. A little afternoon delight would have been nice. It wasn't gonna happen.

William returned to the BMW, smiled at the deeply tanned, long haired Harley rider in the brown fringed suede jacket, returning the hose to the gas pump. *Right out of Easy Rider*, William thought. He placed the BMW transmission in neutral and turned the ignition key to unlock the steering column. He coasted down the gently sloping parking lot to the other side of the pump and braked to a stop. He pulled out a credit card, slid it in the card reader, and selected premium to top the tank off. He shoved the hose in the filler neck and squeezed the handle.

"Trade you straight across."

"No thanks." The Harley rider smiled.

"Got a laptop in the trunk," William offered with a nod and a wink.

"Nooooo," the Harley rider shook his head and chuckled.

"Didn't think so."

The rider threw a leg over the Harley, kicked the starter and roared off toward downtown Woodside.

With the BMW tank full, William returned the hose to the pump, started the car and turned down La Honda Road.

Seventeen

Anyone who drives west on La Honda road from Skyline Drive knows how relaxing it is if you know your car and you don't test the limit of adhesion. The surface is smooth, the curves varied, well-engineered and many. The drive from Sky Londa to the Pacific Ocean is almost all downhill. You can ease into a rhythm; let the car drive itself through the forest, down the hills, across flat open terrain where you find it. It will take you to a place where your mind drifts from events that torment you.

William drove past the little hamlet of La Honda. Too small to support anything resembling downtown, if not for the biker bar on the south side of the road you could easily miss it. A couple of one-story commercial buildings, a few residential streets behind the bar, an elementary school a hundred yards to the north on Sears Ranch Road is all of it.

William had the road to himself all the way to the coast through the unincorporated town of San Gregorio near Highway 1, Cabrillo Highway, the road that runs along the Pacific Ocean.

San Gregorio, population two hundred and fifty, has an address but isn't a town. It's an intersection with a country store and post office in the center of an agricultural community. The most exciting thing in San Gregorio is fresh fertilizer. The next most exciting thing was the prostitute that left on a stagecoach when the hotel closed. William passed through uneventfully.

When he reached Cabrillo Highway, William turned south. He drove a few miles along the ocean to Pescadero Creek Road where he turned left and drove two hundred yards east to a gravel driveway on the south side of the road. William turned up the driveway and stopped at the end, at the top of a knoll overlooking Pescadero Beach where his father bought a tiny one-bedroom cottage a few years before William was born there. His parents used the cottage more than he did, as their summer vacation home, and weekend retreat.

William retrieved the keys from a locally fired red clay flower pot by the back door purchased by his girlfriend last summer at the "Luna Sea" gift shop. He unlocked the cottage door and swung it open. He threw his bags on the double bed, hung his coats and jackets in a hall closet where he dropped his boots and shoes, and left unpacking for later. He placed his laptop, the external backup drive, and the camera on a sturdy well-worn antique secretary made in the mid-west that belonged to his grandfather.

He set Dusty next to the binoculars and compass, on a shallow wooden table under a great room picture window facing the ocean. He could see the surf, rocks and beach from the window. The old Honeywell thermostat read 52 degrees. He turned the electric radiant heat on, and set the temperature to 65.

William took inventory in the kitchen. Equipped from a visit last year to the Mountain View Crate & Barrel, he found a Rubirosa of a peppermill, a GE toaster oven and a coffee press. A vintage hand crank coffee bean mill rested next to cookie and coffee jars on the counter. "Gotta have my cookies and coffee," he said out loud.

He found a two-liter bottle of water in the ancient white enamel refrigerator, and an ice cube tray in the freezer. The gas range worked. It needed something to cook. He took a long pull from the water bottle as he walked into the bathroom where he found a stack of neatly folded clean towels, a floor mat on a shelf above a hamper, a bar of local craft-made "Beach Linen" scented glycerin soap in a dish on the sink and a bottle of 365 Shampoo on a ledge in the corner shower. He toggled the light and fan switches. They worked. The fixtures ran hot and cold and didn't leak. The cottage had no room for a bathtub but William had a clean and functional bathroom, kitchen, and climate control. *Lap of luxury*, he told himself. *It'll do.*

William returned to the great room. A rosewood glass window-top humidor sat on a writing desk with an assortment from "Holt's Cigars," a mail order house in Philadelphia. The humidor belonged to his father. William never saw his father smoke. The cigars, William guessed, might be as old as he is. The favorite dog-eared paperbacks William owned forever and occasionally re-read were stacked next to the humidor. *The Adventures of Tom Sawyer, Moby-Dick, A tale of Two Cities, The Great Gatsby, The Moon is Down, To Kill a Mockingbird, The Count of Montecristo*, and *The Old Man and the Sea.* He purchased six more last year to add to the cottage library. *The Prince of Tides, A River Runs Through It, All the Pretty Horses, The Green Mile, The Endurance*, and one he thought most appropriate; *Jonathon Livingston Seagull.*

A miniature American flag flew from a stand in a heavy onyx bookend. The other bookend flew the flag of Israel. He stored his father's Model 1911 Colt .45 semiautomatic in a drawer with half a box of hollow point rounds.

A photo of his parents standing in front of their Cessna 210 Turbo at the Half Moon Bay Airport hung on the wall next to the picture window. The only photo of them in the cottage, William chose this one because they looked so happy. Local black and white landscapes mounted in simple black frames hung on white wallboard. William thought he would take a few of his own. The cottage had no photos of William's his friends or girlfriend. He displayed one his mother liked of him at 12 years old next to a princess phone on a nightstand. On one knee in a wetsuit, arm around a surf board with an end planted in the sand at Pillar Point, Mavericks Beach, site of the annual "big wave" surfing competition. Local surfer Jeff Clark stood behind him with a hand on William's shoulder. Clark founded the world-famous competition in 1999, long after William learned to surf there.

An ivory chess set carved by an unknown artist and an unopened pack of playing cards rested on a small wooden dining table next to a baseball glove wrapped around a hard ball. A leather football sat next to the glove in the unlikely event of sporting company.

William picked up a landline handset. Dial tone. Good thing. Cellular service is spotty on the coast. *These old rotary phones are a pain in the ass,* he thought. *How did people put up with this?* Maybe because after more than 40 years they still work. He spun the dial to listen to it spin back. *Phones should have voice response and computer menus,* William thought. *Somebody will do it.*

William called his childhood friend Andy Solomon. Last summer Andy told him he wanted the BMW for his wife when William replaced it. Andy bought it over the phone. William asked him to check the NADA book value online. They agreed on a number in the middle of the range. William knew the car would bring high retail. He didn't care to squeeze every penny out of a friend. He only wanted the car gone. Friends since junior high, Andy needed a solid, moderately priced automobile his wife could use to commute to a teaching job at a Santa Clara elementary school. Andy agreed to swing by the Mountain View house, bring a check for the BMW, the courier package from LightSwitch if he found it there. William told him to look for the key fobs in the flower pot by the front door, the title under the mat, William at the beach if he didn't find him at the cottage. The cottage needed provisions. William wanted to visit the beach and walk two miles to Norm's bakery in downtown Pescadero, to buy something for breakfast. He knew he might not return in time to meet Andy.

There isn't much to do in Pescadero. As far as William knew no peers lived there. *What would they do here?* he wondered. You can farm the land, milk a goat, shovel rocks and dirt around, clean up the yard, go to the beach. William thought he could take up surfing or running again. He could hike the hills, read a book, start a photography hobby or a garden.

The Pescadero Creek Inn anchored the north end of two blocks the villagers called downtown. A pub called Duarte's opened at the south end on the corner of Stage and Pescadero

Road not long after the 7th cavalry roamed the west. Owned and operated by descendants of the founders, Duarte's offered all the nightlife found in Pescadero. The bakery, general store, gift shop, a custom furniture shop, an antique shop, a two-story town hall with a few rented offices, and not much else, filled in the street between Duarte's and the Inn. The post office put up a shack on the south side of Pescadero Creek Road before the civil war. A retirement planning business occupied one of the offices in the town hall building. William wondered why anyone in Pescadero needed retirement planning. It seemed to him, if you lived there, you already were retired.

In the last census six hundred and fifty people claimed Pescadero home. William wondered how they assembled enough students to field a high school football team, a band, and a cheerleading section at the same time, but compared with San Gregorio, Pescadero was a metropolis.

Half Moon Bay is the closest city to Pescadero. It's much more populous and developed. You can walk there in half a day. William thought he might hike it sometime. He could take Stage Road, a pretty country road with views of the coastal hills and the ocean. He could run to Half Moon Bay if he conditioned for it, a half-marathon in each direction. The idea of running a marathon to eat lunch in Half Moon Bay amused him. Not enough to make him want to do it.

That's everything to know about Pescadero. Except for a pit stop in Davenport, civilization began forty miles south in Santa Cruz, or nineteen miles north at Half Moon Bay. Pescadero feels small, remote, isolated. When the marine layer rolls in, it's also foggy, bleak and lonely.

William needed an internet connection. Probably narrow-band dialup service he thought, slow compared with broadband in Silicon Valley, maybe unreliable. Email would work well enough. The general store might sell paperbacks. When he finished Johnathon Livingston Seagull he could order more. A one-hundred-page appetizer of a novel, it wouldn't take long. *Amazing* he thought, *more than a million copies sold two years after publication. Maybe I could write the sequel, Johnathon Livingston Seafood.* William laughed out loud.

Locked in the barn, his father's old sports car hadn't been on the road since his parents died. A weekend hobby, the last time sunlight fell on it, his father raced it at Laguna Seca. The car needed total restoration. William had the skills for much of the work, tools and equipment on site, all the time in the world. After five years of designing data switches for phone companies he welcomed the idea of working on something analogue and simple with his hands.

William changed into a pair of Khakis, a windbreaker, and a long sleeve blue denim shirt. He laced up his hiking boots, walked outside and searched the BMW to make sure he unloaded it completely. He locked the car, dropped the key fobs in the flower pot, slid the title in an envelope, placed it under the welcome mat, and closed the car door behind him.

William's father had built the cottage on the eastern third of a five-acre parcel that sloped gently toward the ocean. A seasonal marsh that dried out in summer bordered the south side of the property where a two and a half mile long foot and bike path connected Cabrillo Highway with downtown Pescadero. The property ended at Pescadero Creek Road to the north, Cabrillo Highway to the west, Josh and Maggie Wertheimer's property to the east. The Wertheimer's owned the Pescadero general store. William knew them. Soon, he would know them better. They built their house on the other side of an easement to a shared gravel driveway William's father sold them for a dollar. Other than the Wertheimer's, William hadn't seen anyone near the cottage besides the letter carrier who delivered mail to a box on Pescadero Creek Road. William left the cottage door unlocked. *What is there to steal?* he thought. *Robbers would think the owner so poor they might leave something. A six-pack would be nice,* he mused. *Maybe I should post a note on the fridge. Dear robbers, sorry I have nothing for you. Could you please leave a six-pack? Any brand of porter. Leave the front door open. Thanks! I'm a talented, unemployed CEO. If you need a part-ner, I can drive the getaway car if you have one I can borrow.*

William laughed out loud, relieved after everything that happened the last six months, that he still had a sense of humor. *Maybe there's hope for me*, he thought.

William decided to see what had to be done to restore his father's car. He brought a Maglite, a yellow pad and pencil, the key to the lock on the barn door. He walked across the gravel, keyed the lock, unhooked the latch and stepped inside. The barn smelled musty. He switched on a pair of overhead florescent lights. The poster size photo of his dad racing the car through the "Corkscrew" at Laguna Seca was the first thing he saw.

William pulled the cover off the car, folded it and placed it on a shelf. The car looked sad resting on flat tires with a cracked windshield in thirty-five-year-old red paint under a layer of dust deep enough to choke a hog. William could live with rough appearance. This paint was too far gone. He thought it a shame to remove the patina but felt he had to. *It will look new again*, William thought, even though he liked as it was.

The car wore number 33, his father's club racing number from early days of vintage racing. It would be sanded off, painted over, gone forever with restoration and conversion to a street car. It made William sad to think he had to erase his father's number. It didn't change his mind about what he felt he needed to do. He looked at the name painted on the driver's side door. Driver: John Beckinsdale. William's eyes teared. *I miss you dad*, he whispered.

The once blood red paint had faded to a blotchy, thin pink in places. Scratches and cracks covered the body. The nose and lower flanks looked like a rock chip farm. Bent, cracked, mis-aligned; panels needed repair and straightening. A dent the size and shape of a man's butt cratered an aluminum fender where he guessed an inconsiderate race fan rested his weight in a paddock. It made William angry.

William unfolded the Haartz cloth top he found on a shelf. Worn, torn in places, it could be taken apart and used as a template to cut and sew a replacement. He inspected the chrome bumpers, windshield pillars, a painted roll bar. Not too bad he thought. He might be able to leave some of it unrestored.

He peered into the cockpit. The dash looked decent. Smith's gauges probably needed rebuilding. So did both seats. Originally black, the carpet faded to a mottled greenish orange where the sun burned it. A once lustrous finish on the handmade walnut steering wheel had been sun and weather beaten into dull and lifeless. It could be restored.

William opened the driver's door and illuminated the foot well with the flashlight. Rodents chewed the wiring and left a smelly pile of droppings on the carpet. He'd replace the carpet and rewire the car.

William jacked the car up and positioned ramps under the tires. He set the handbrake. *I wish dad had put a lift in here,* he thought. He rolled under the car on a creeper, inspected the drivetrain, suspension, steering rack, the frame from end to end. He discovered rust where the paint had been scraped. It looked superficial.

The brake calipers needed rebuilding since it had been so long since the car had been driven. He would replace the entire system from pedal to wheel. It looked like the car leaked from everywhere. He wondered about the condition of the motor, transmission, and differential. If bolt and clamp tightening didn't seal the leaks, he had to pull it all apart and replace the gaskets. "Better do it anyway" he thought, to make it reliable.

William rolled out from under the car, leaned over a fender, turned the latches and lifted the hood. All the components were in place. The radiator held clear fluid. The passages were not plugged. He found only light corrosion. *I can use it. I'll flush it and change the hoses.*

The carburetors were dried out. They needed rebuilding. He pulled out the dipstick. Oil, not cappuccino. It's what he hoped for. The motor might be usable for street driving. He had to crank it to find out.

William hadn't run the motor in a year. He crossed his fingers. He reached for the key and turned. Nothing. He remembered the disconnect switch. He found it next to the driver's seat, threw it to engage the battery. He turned the key again. Still nothing. He switched on the headlights to see if the starter circuit failed. No lights. Mice probably crippled everything; battery likely dead, too old anyway.

William checked the cell phone signal strength. Two bars. He called Andy Solomon, "Solly" again. The call went into voicemail. "Solly, this is William. Sorry to bother you again. I need a battery for dad's car. Can you swing by NAPA on the way down? It will save me a trip to Half Moon Bay. Thanks bud, sorry to trouble you."

William squatted to inspect the wire wheels. He found rust where spokes attach to hubs and rims. He had to send them to a vendor for restoration.

William picked a yellow pad and pencil off the bench. "Needs everything" he wrote across the page in big letters, underlined it and drew a big smiley face to match his own. A list served no purpose. He would restore the car system by system, doing the work he enjoyed, farming the rest out to vendors. He took a deep breath. *"Six to eight months,"* he whispered. *Needs upholstery too.* A lot of work but he wanted to drive it. Even if he didn't, he didn't want to sell or leave it in this condition. *Great opportunity to do this while I have time,* he thought.

William lowered the hood and replaced the car cover. He leaned the creeper against a wall, rolled the jack under a bench, left the car on ramps and switched the lights off. He left the barn, locked the door behind him.

By 4:30 PM the sun worked its way toward the horizon. William no longer had time to walk to Norm's Market and return before sunset. He knew he could knock on Josh and Maggie's door, needed to let them know he arrived, tell them he'd be staying. He didn't have to worry about dinner. They wouldn't let him leave without feeding him. Living across the driveway would be handy. He could hitch a ride when they open the store in the morning, ask Josh for help if he needed it, grab a ride somewhere, call if the car fell on him while he worked on it. William decided to walk to the beach for sunset. Provisions could wait until morning.

William walked down the gravel driveway, turned left at Pescadero Creek Road and walked to Cabrillo Highway. He crossed to the beach, picked up a stone, walked to water's edge and skipped it across the cove. He slouched against a boulder, boots in the sand, hands in his pockets, jacket collar turned up against an ocean breeze. The sun warmed his face. Sea lions rested quietly, lounging across boulders still warm from a day in the sun. A flock of pelicans dove in the surf. Shore birds scampered, skirting the surf, pecking a meal out of the sand. William watched the ocean swells and felt the tension melt away. He felt as serene as he had been, as far back as he could remember.

William's mind faded to white, idling to keep his body functioning. When the sun turned the sky orange and disappeared into the ocean, the time to leave arrived. Suddenly alert, he rose, took a lingering look at the surf, the rocks, the wisps of orange clouds, and returned to the cottage.

The BMW was gone. He found a package from LightSwitch, a handwritten note and a personal check in an envelope under the doormat.

Sorry I missed you, William. I heard what happened. Sandy and I are so sorry. I missed your call. I'd like to buy you a beer at Duarte's, go to Half Moon Bay for a battery, but I have to get home for dinner. If there's anything Sandy and I can do, please call us. Thank you for being a great friend, for giving us such a good deal on the car. Sandy says she'll take good care of it. You can borrow it anytime. All the best, William. We know you'll get through this and return stronger. Give your girlfriend a break and call her. She loves you (stupid). Love, Solly and Sandy.

Shit, William thought. *Everyone knows already.*

William stepped into the cottage. He placed the note, the package and the check on the secretary. He wanted to read the note over and over but he needed a fire. He brought a suede firewood carrier and his father's leather gloves to the wood pile under a lean-to on the landward side of the cottage. He stacked the fireplace and lit a fire. He walked across the great room to the kitchen, retrieved the water bottle from the fridge and sat in the chair behind the desk under the picture window. He rested his feet on the desk and leaned back to watch the sky darken over the ocean.

The fire came up and took the chill off the cottage. It felt like the long day it had been. William drank half the remaining water and thought at first how miserable he was, then how he shouldn't be. *I'm in better shape than most people*, he told himself. *I just need to start over.*

Eighteen

Joshua and Maggie closed the general store and drove home.

"Looks like William's here, Maggie."

"How do you know, Josh? I don't see his car."

"The lights are on. I smell smoke from the chimney."

"On a weekday. How odd. Want to invite him for dinner?"

"We can see him tomorrow."

"I'd like to know who's there."

"Okay, Maggie, I'll knock on his door."

William saw the pickup headlights when Joshua turned into the driveway. He heard the crunch of boots on gravel. William opened the door before Joshua knocked. He caught Joshua with his fist in the air.

"Hi, Josh. I expected you to drop by."

"Are ya hungry? Maggie's fixing chicken. We have plenty."

"Have I ever said no to food?"

"Nope."

"Do I have time for a shower?"

"Sure, come over when you're ready. I'll open a bottle of wine."

"See you soon, Josh. Thanks for the invitation."

Joshua asked Maggie to make dinner for three, to expect William in an hour.

William threw two more logs on the fire and closed the fireplace doors. It enabled him to leave it unattended and dampened with vents that moderate airflow to make it burn slower and longer. The fire would keep the cottage warm through dinner. The furnace would have worked. He preferred the fireplace. He showered, dressed in jeans, a white long sleeve button-down shirt and the navy-blue cotton cable sweater his girlfriend bought him in San Francisco for his birthday. He missed her. It saddened him to think of it, but he didn't want to forget the day. She sometimes wore the sweater. He imagined her standing there in the great room wearing it. William held the sweater to his face and thought he smelled her perfume.

William laced up a pair of tennis shoes and walked across the driveway. Maggie met him with a hug at the front door. Joshua handed him a glass of Bonny Doon Syrah. William and Joshua sat in the great room while Maggie finished making dinner.

"None of my business William, but we share a driveway. It's a little odd for you to show up on a Monday with no car. Did you walk from Mountain View?"

"You have a right to ask about the strange behavior of your neighbor."

Joshua listened with concern as William shared his day. He excused himself, went to the kitchen and asked Maggie not to bring it up during dinner. "William had a business disaster, Maggie. Don't ask about it unless he broaches the subject. I'll give you the details later."

The three of them shared a somber dinner. William didn't stay long after they finished. "Can I borrow a little coffee for tomorrow morning, Maggie?"

"I'll get you some. How about a croissant?"

"Sure."

Maggie returned from the pantry with an eight ounce bag of coffee and a butter croissant in a bag.

"Keep the coffee William. We own the store."

"Thanks, Maggie. Please excuse me for leaving early. I'm exhausted. I need a good night's sleep." He wondered if he could sleep at all. "Thank you for dinner."

"That's okay, William. We'll have lots of opportunities to spend time together," Maggie slipped before she caught the gaffe. The look on William's face made her wish she hadn't said it.

Right about that, William thought. "Can you give me a lift into town in the morning? I need to pick up a few things."

"Sure, we leave the house at six forty-five. You can borrow the truck if you need it."

"Thanks. I need it. Goodnight Josh, Maggie."

William hugged Maggie and shook Joshua's hand. After he left, Joshua shared what he learned from William. "That poor boy, Josh. What he went through the last year. Enough stress for a lifetime."

"It isn't all pain, Maggie. He had successes, already did more than most people ever do, and on his own too. He has a lot to be proud of."

"He doesn't look proud."

"Would we? He has the force. He's young. He has talent, brains, education. He can bounce back."

"He looks terrible. Like you did when I made you quit."

"I was older and I wasn't well."

"It's a high ledge he fell from."

"It isn't the fall that kills you. It's the landing if you don't bounce."

The fire burned itself out before William returned to the cottage. He left the damper open when he found it smoldering. He turned the light out, went into the bedroom, undressed to his underwear and rolled into bed. *My new life starts tomorrow*, he thought. *Hope I like it*.

William's mind didn't shut down until the sun brightened the morning sky, not long before Joshua and Maggie left for the store without him. They thought it better not to wake him.

Nineteen

William rose at 9:30AM. He pulled a pair of black sweats out of a duffel bag and slipped into them. He turned up the thermostat, brewed a mug of coffee, dropped into the chair behind the great room desk and bit into the croissant. *I need to order newspaper delivery*, he thought.

William reviewed the events of a year. In a spring full of potential, orders ramping, in the middle of a product refresh and a funding event, William accelerated hiring. He had little time for anything but work. In the middle of summer, business hit a wall. Life nosed over into a spiral and crashed to pieces. *What a difference a few months made*, he thought. Pressure mounted. By fall he became impossible to live with. He abandoned his friends. His girlfriend moved out. A few months later he lost the business.

William had a modest amount of money and no debt. He had a roof over his head; two roofs, actually. Not where he wanted to be, far from expectations. Success is cumulative. Recovery would be hard, but he had many years to accomplish it. What next? Get a job? Start another company? Do nothing for a while?

William had no immediate family. He hadn't seen his girl-friend in months, didn't know if he still had one. He hadn't seen his friends either. He thought he could count on them if he needed them. Not what he wanted. William lived independently, capable of taking care of himself since his parents died. That's how he preferred it.

William watched the Silicon Valley technology business implode. He thought contraction would be severe, but temporary. Demand for services would catch up with overbuilt infrastructure.

Service providers would start buying equipment again. Dotcom companies had to find a way to generate revenue or burn through their money and go out of business. Tens of thousands of people had been attracted to an industry that for now no longer needed them. Some were new to the Bay Area, lured by the promise of riches like gold rushes of the previous century. Many had limited technology background. Companies desperate for bodies needed anything they could contribute and paid them well. *They would be hurt the most,* William thought. *Tech workers with advanced skills and experience would struggle too. The next few years wouldn't be fun for anybody. This is a good time to take a rest,* William thought. *Observe the shakeout; see what to make from it.*

What a Monday, William told himself. *Thrown out of the company I founded in the morning. Packed my clothes, shut my house down. Went to the post office on Hope Street. Drove to Sky Londa, bought lunch from a freckled redhead, offered to swap the car, laptop and wardrobe for a Harley, my Silicon Valley executive life for a biker life on the road. That would have been unfair to the biker!* William chuckled.

Maybe I should have done it. I did the next best thing. I moved here where nobody can find me, a place where there's nothing to do and no one to do it with. I have no transportation, just a broken-down old race car. What an idiot. It didn't occur to me to throw my bike rack on the car and bring the Cannondale.

I have a project, a car restoration that will take too long and cost too much. If I succeed, at least I can say I accomplished something. What do I do with my life after that?" he asked himself. *"Congratulations William. You're pretty fucked.*

He watched the pelicans diving for breakfast through the picture window. "Don't you wish you were flying with them?" he asked Dusty. "It's just you and me now, old friend."

Twenty

William stood on the western side of his property at the edge of the knoll overlooking the ocean. A rare sunny 60 degree winter day felt like summer. He watched the surf crash over the rocks. A breeze blew in from the ocean. The sun warmed his face. By noon it would be t-shirt, or no-shirt weather.

William watched the lady in the floppy hat peddle her bicycle along a path next to the highway. A bright yellow dress and white canvas top tennis shoes completed her ensemble. A woven basket clamped to the handlebars held a paperback, a brown lunch bag, a beach towel, and a collapsed beach umbrella strapped across the top. She crossed the coastal highway, walked the bike onto the beach and set up a reading station. She smiled serenely at the beauty of the cove, the glory of the morning. She paused for a breath of salt air, spread the beach towel and pitched the umbrella in the sand. She settled herself under it, picked up the book and began reading.

Two months had gone by since William moved into the cottage. He hadn't conversed with a soul in the village besides Joshua and Maggie. A curious thing since he avoided everyone else in Pescadero, he felt an impulse to join the lady with the floppy hat as he watched her peddle to the beach. It didn't take long to decide the worst that could happen was not much at all, to shrug his shoulders and begin walking.

William descended the knoll and crossed the highway. He vectored straight to the umbrella. He looked down at a smiling lady in a yellow dress. All he could think of was "Hi."

"Good morning, young man."

"My name is William."

"My name is Elizabeth Victoria Simpson Harold Bentley-Wiggins. You can call me Liz-Beth."

"You're the nutty lady of Pescadero."

Liz-Beth laughed. "I'm not nutty. I'm a free spirit. You're a well-mannered, brilliant conversationalist, highly skilled in social graces."

Ashamed of his clumsy introduction, William raised a hand. He shook his head. "Mea culpa. I didn't mean to offend you. Please accept my apology."

"Apology accepted. I've been called worse by worse people. You must be the hermit of Pescadero."

"I'm not a hermit. I wouldn't be here talking to you. I prefer the company of eccentric people. I meant it as a compliment."

"Shall we call it even and begin again?"

William offered a hand. Liz-Beth shook it hard once.

"Even," Liz-Beth said. "You've come to the right place. Why don't you have a seat. I won't have to strain my neck to be eccentric with you."

"Thanks for the invitation, and a second chance."

"You're welcome."

William sat next to Liz-Beth on her blanket.

"I couldn't see much of you hiding up on the knoll. You're a nice-looking young man. It isn't every day I get this lucky."

William blushed.

"You're a lovely lady."

"Thank you. If I were a few decades younger I'd be on you like peanut butter on jelly."

William grinned. "It would be an honor to be spread. Have you been spying on me?"

"Sure. Have you been spying on me?"

"I wouldn't call it that. I've seen you come to the beach."

The conversation reached an impasse. Liz-Beth thought she might resume reading. That would be rude.

"Do you like it here William?"

"Sure, wind, sand, ocean. What's not to like?"

"Fog."

"I don't mind it. I watch it from the window sometimes."

"You do that too much."

"How do you know that?"

"Our mutual friends, the Wertheimer's."

"Oh, you know Josh and Maggie."

"Forever. Everybody knows everybody around here. There aren't any secrets in Pescadero."

"Have to talk to them about that."

"They meant no harm. What do you like the most about the beach, William?"

"Cool air, warm sun and warm sand."

"Then you like it in winter."

"Yes. Best of all on sunny days like this one. No crowds, the beach to myself, almost."

"Would you like me to leave?" Liz-Beth smiled.

"No, no. Please stay."

"I prefer summer. I like people, activity. A beach is depressing without people. It looks unloved. It must be sad and lonely on a beautiful day like this one if no one comes to enjoy it. Sorry. I'm a little melancholy. I miss Bunny."

"Bunny?"

"My lover, my friend, my husband for fifty years. He passed away."

"I'm sorry."

"What are you doing in Pescadero, William?"

"I came here to figure out what I need to do."

"Do you have a girlfriend?"

"Not sure. I had one. Tell me about you."

"I grew up in the Midwest, lived in England, Asia, married a wonderful man. We lived there together. They were nice places. We were happy. An Englishman who grew up when they still had an empire. The poor fools thought they were men of the world and they owned it. Bunny could have lived anywhere. I'm an American girl. I grew up in America and you know, we don't think that way. We think America is the center of the universe, there's no better place and no other place matters."

"You came home."

"Yes. My man came with me. He knew he could be happy anywhere as long as we were together."

"Do not urge me to leave you or turn back from following you; for where you go, I will go, and where you lodge, I will lodge."

"You read the bible."

"I did." William nodded.

"Where you die, I will die, and there I will be buried. Thus, may the Lord do to me, and worse, if anything but death parts you and me."

"Beautiful words, Liz-Beth."

"Bunny knew I wouldn't stay in England. That hopeless fool used the quote in his proposal. I loved him for it. A sentimental man."

"A romantic. You succeeded in business, could do whatever you wanted, live wherever you wanted. You lived in New Cotswolds."

"We had a modest amount to start with. We made more with it. We built New Cotswolds from a rocky meadow. It doesn't matter what you have. It doesn't matter what you do. It matters who you share your life with."

Liz-Beth continued. "You know the house we lived in is quite magnificent."

"New Cotswolds."

"Did anyone ever tell you how it arrived here?"

William looked at Liz-Beth with curiosity. "Arrived here?"

"Bunny visited an old friend in Cotswolds on a business trip to England. It's a tourist area of cute little towns. Winston and Clementine are buried there. The area has a lot of old stone homes. He drove by one with a for-sale sign in the yard. He had to have it. The woman who lived there died. Her children left it in disrepair and didn't want it. The price was right and they threw in the furnishings we wanted. We owned the property here but hadn't built anything on it yet. He wanted to bring it over."

"Are you serious? You shipped the house from England?"

"I thought it was crazy but he said everything around here is built out of sticks. We make things to use up and replace. In Europe they build forever."

"Some of the homes in northeast are built of stone."

"I know but where would we find that kind of stone around here? We had to ship it anyway."

"Not across the ocean."

"Two oceans. It came through the Panama Canal. We unloaded it in San Francisco and trucked it down. The villagers thought we were nuts."

"I'll bet."

"We could have built a smaller house but after we moved in we loved it. You should tour it sometime. I'll take you."

Liz-Beth paused to think about the house.

They sat quietly, gazing into the ocean. Liz-Beth continued.

"I've known lots of people, paupers to kings, Bunny the closest of course. I hardly knew one of the people I spent the most time with, did the most things with. Sukie, our gardener and caretaker. He worked for us for many years. I didn't know him until the day he told me he was returning to Japan. We brought him here from Asia to work for us. We gave him a place to live, work to do. He groomed his sand, tended his rocks and found himself. Here, he discovered what *he* needed to do."

"Groomed his sand and tended rocks?"

"A Japanese Zen garden. He made and groomed it, meticulously raking soothing patterns in the sand around the rocks. An art form. Different every time I saw it. He said it made the garden happy and tending garden made him happy."

"A happy garden."

"A happy gardener. What do you do when you aren't watching me?"

"I'm restoring a car my father left me. It suffered a great deal of neglect."

"Your Zen garden. I have a little sports car. Bunny brought it over."

"What is it?"

"An MG. Sukie maintained it. Kept it running like a top. Maybe you could help me with it."

"What's wrong with it?"

"It's grumpy sometimes. Bunny said they need to be driven. I don't drive it enough. Maybe you can give it a little exercise."

"I'd be happy to."

Liz-Beth gestured to the east hills. "What happened over there?"

"How did you know about that?"

"Josh and Maggie."

"I'm going to have to talk to them."

"I asked them."

"A digital gold rush. Pulled them in by the thousands. Every kind of person. Every background. It's changing the world. Not fast enough to support all the people who jumped in, all the companies that started. Most of them didn't make any money. It collapsed when the money ran out."

"1637. Dutch Tulip Bubble."

"I guess in a way. In the valuations of internet companies. This is about new technology. It isn't a fantasy."

"Every so many years, in one form or another, at one scale or another, in some place or another, in some business or another."

"This was a big one."

"They're all big, honey, when you're in it. It isn't the end of the world. It's a chapter we keep repeating because we keep trying. That's a good thing. You get over it, move on, do something else. Seems like you didn't do so badly."

"I did well for a while. I have to start over."

"It doesn't matter. You don't have to be Buffett or Gates. Don't compare yourself."

"You don't know me very well."

"I know enough. I was fourteen years old when the war started. I was sixteen when I went to Europe, seventeen when I got married, nineteen when I dragged Bunny to San Francisco and we started our trading company, grew it, sold it and retired here forty years later."

Liz-Beth paused to think about what an adventure life had been.

"Except for visiting Josh and Maggie, this is one of the two most intelligent conversations I've had since Bunny died. The other one was with Sukie on the day he told me he was leaving. You walled yourself off on the knoll but you left a window open. I peeked inside, didn't I?"

"Yeah, you did."

"You know what Rockefeller said about it?"

"No."

"In 1909, after becoming very rich, he said; '*The novelty of being able to purchase anything one wants soon passes. What people want most cannot be bought with money.*' Not long after that, he started giving it away. Established a nation of libraries, gave the world of books to millions of people."

"Do you think it made him happy?"

"I didn't get a chance to ask him. I suppose he found it satisfying. He could have stopped anytime. I guess he preferred it to counting and recounting his money. There's a big difference between enjoying a little solitude and putting yourself under long term quarantine."

"You're about the age my mother would have been. She was a war correspondent."

Liz-Beth held out a hand and William took it. "You miss her, don't you?"

"Yeah, my dad too."

"You don't get over it. You can get used to it. Bunny's gone. Makes me sad to think about him. We had a wonderful life together. The memories keep me going. I'd do it again. I wouldn't change any of it except to make it last longer, and one other thing, a friend who left this earth too soon."

Liz-Beth gazed far into the ocean.

"I'm sorry, Liz-Beth."

"Don't be. You know that Wordsworth poem, honey? – *Nothing can bring back the hour of the splendor in the grass, of glory in the flower.*"

"*We will grieve not, rather find strength in what remains behind,*" William added.

Liz-Beth nodded. "You need to do something. Find somebody to do it with. Here, have half a sandwich."

They shared lunch as the sun passed overhead. They watched the seal cows tussle for position, bulls watch over their harems, gulls and pelicans put on an aerial performance. Liz-Beth glanced at her watch.

"It's been a wonderful day and I've enjoyed meeting you. I have to pick up a few things in the village. My friend Maria is making dinner. Would you like to join us?"

"No, thank you. Some other time, though. I'm going to stay here and think about what I might find in a rock and sand garden."

"Don't think too much about it. It's simple unless you hunt for something that isn't there. Do you mean it about joining us for dinner?"

"Sure."

"I live in the yellow cottage at the south end of Stage Road, at the trail head. Why don't you stop over some afternoon, have a look at the MG, stay for dinner?"

"Sounds like fun."

William lifted Liz-Beth's bicycle. Liz-Beth closed the umbrella and collapsed the shaft. She folded the beach towel and placed it in the basket with the book. She placed the floppy hat on her head, bungeed the umbrella to the basket and stepped over the bike frame while William held it upright.

William looked grim. He wished Liz-Beth would stay longer. Liz-Beth pulled him down by an arm and kissed him on the cheek.

"Chin up, William. It will get better. I promise. Practice Zen on your car like Sukie did in his garden. You'll learn what you're supposed to do. Will you promise to come by the house, look at the MG, stay for dinner?"

"I promise."

"When would you like to?"

"Later in the week. Should I call you?"

"Just knock on the door. We aren't formal around here. Nice meeting you, William."

"Nice meeting you Liz-Beth."

Liz-Beth walked the bike across the beach, coasted across the highway and peddled to her cottage. *"What a screwed-up kid,"* she thought. *"He's a sweetie though. Maybe I can help him."*

William watched Liz-Beth peddle down the road, turn east on the trail, and pass behind the knoll where he couldn't see her. He spent the rest of the afternoon thinking about rocks, and sand, and Zen while he waited for the sun to disappear behind the marine layer.

Twenty-One

A few days after meeting Liz-Beth, William ran out of excuses. When he reached a good place to pause work on the car, he decided to visit the following afternoon.

The general store stocked locally grown flowers in a refrigerated case. William called Joshua to ask if he could drop off a bouquet to bring with him. Joshua delivered it with a bottle of Pinot Noir. He knew Liz-Beth hadn't been the cheerful lady she could be. Except for visits to the beach, she hadn't been out much or received many visitors after Bunny died. William lived like a hermit since arriving in Pescadero. Joshua thought they could use each other's company. He offered to drive William to Liz-Beth's. William wanted to walk the trail Liz-Beth took to the beach.

William felt uncomfortable visiting unannounced. He called the number Joshua gave him. Liz-Beth suggested a 4PM arrival so he could look at the MG before dinner.

William left the cottage at three. He dressed in hiking boots, blue jeans, and, his father's copper colored suede car coat over a long sleeve shirt and a knitted vest. The scent and the texture of the suede reminded William of his father. He enjoyed wearing it as he had as a boy when it hung shapelessly on him like a tent or when he snuggled up to his father in the car when his dad wore it on a drive.

Tall grasses on the knoll brushed against William's pant legs as he made his way to the southern edge of the property where it sloped abruptly to the trail. Acres of late winter wildflowers blanketed the meadows to the south beneath the foothills. Water pooled in marshes flooded by winter runoff. Red wing black birds called their mates from perches on the stalks of cattails. William turned east on the trail. He paused where foothills and sky reflected in pools left by morning rain. He turned and lingered where the trail rose high enough to see the ocean behind him.

The temperature dropped into the forties when broken clouds covered the sky. William liked clouds and cool weather. He found endless days of perfectly blue skies of Silicon Valley summers monotonous. Sometimes he hoped for rain to break the heat. Coastal weather suited him. Liz-Beth met William at the cottage door, thanked him for the wine and flowers.

"Come in and meet Maria. She's prepping for dinner. I'm sure she would like to meet you. Hope you like chicken."

William stepped into the house.

Middle-aged, oval faced, petite, demure, Maria followed her family to America from their ancestral home in Hermosillo, Mexico. She lived with her two teenage children and her husband in a modest Half Moon Bay rental house owned by her older brother. Her brother migrated a decade before her to work in the building trade. Maria's husband worked for her brother in his tile contracting business in San Carlos.

Maria helped Liz-Beth keep the cottage clean and did most of the cooking. Cooking didn't appear on Liz-Beth's fun list. Bunny enjoyed it. Between he and Chef Sukie, the only thing Liz-Beth had to do with food was eat it. Queen of New Cotswolds, Bunny called her. Since Sukie left and she hired Maria, Liz-Beth discovered she enjoyed cooking, but only with Maria.

"Maria, come and meet Mr. Beckinsdale."

"Hello Mr. Beck-in-dale. It's nice to meet you."

"It's a pleasure meeting you, Maria. Please call me William."

"William, why don't you have a look at the MG while Maria and I prepare dinner? Here's the garage door opener. The keys are in the ignition."

William found a pristine MGTD behind the garage door. Medium-grey, not the British Racing Green he expected, it had a mauve color soft top, cut down doors that hinged at the back in the "suicide design," a luggage rack, a spare wheel and tire hung on the boot. It had stamped steel wheels instead of wire wheels early MGs are known for, and red interior leather matching the painted grill. "Must be the luxury model," William thought. It amused him as luxury is not part of the brand.

William circled the car. He couldn't find a scratch or a paint chip. He unlatched and lifted the bonnet. "My God," he said out loud. "It looks like it's never been driven."

William opened a door. He looked at the odometer in the varnished walnut dash. *Just under twelve thousand miles! What a barn-find this is*, he thought. William returned to the cottage.

"Liz-Beth, it's like a new car."

"We had a Bentley when we lived in San Francisco. We walked to the office from our first home, didn't drive the MG much. After moving here we took the Bentley when we visited the city. Bunny and I used the MG when we felt sporting. I miss our drives in it to Santa Cruz and Carmel."

"This car is 50 years old. You put less than 250 miles a year on it!"

"Yes, too bad. We loved it, just didn't have much use for it. Sukie drove it to Half Moon Bay and back once a month to keep it in good condition and the battery charged."

"Is it running now?"

"I started it yesterday. Why don't you take it for a drive? Dinner won't be ready for an hour."

"Love to."

"Turn the ignition switch, pull out the choke, and pull the starter handle."

"Starter handle? You better show me."

Liz-Beth laughed. "Computer scientist. Doesn't know how to start an old car. Do you think Martians left it?"

"An Englishman designed it. Is there a difference?"

The MG started easily and idled smoothly for four cylinders. William backed it out of the garage. *"A little jewel,"* he thought. Liz-Beth showed him where to store the windows.

"Why don't you drive up Stage Road to La Honda Road and come back on Highway One? It's a good way to get a feel for it," Liz-Beth suggested.

William drove through town with his arm over the cut-down door and an ear-to-ear grin. He waved at people who turned their heads when he drove by. When he passed the Pescadero Creek Inn, he honked the horn at diners sitting on the patio. They waved. He drove across the bridge, over the creek, into the countryside.

Stage Road is twisty and narrow. There are places where the drop-off is steep and there are no shoulders or guardrails. Embankments you could bury a car in line the inside of turns. William drove carefully down hills, through blind turns, over gentle rises with views of the ocean and foothills. His eyes focused on the tarmac ahead of a long grey hood as he adjusted to an unfamiliar car on an unfamiliar road.

Doesn't have a lot of power, he thought. *It might beat a school bus in a drag race. It might not.* The steering felt quick and responsive. It gripped the road in spite of narrow tires. *"Doesn't weight much,"* William thought. The sight of the road a few feet from the cut-down door, the roar of the engine, the rush of the wind made it seem faster than it was. A stiff suspension on a light car transmitted every road imperfection. The most fun William thought, you could have in a car under 50 miles per hour.

William reached La Honda Road, twenty miles north of Pescadero. He turned west to Highway 1 to return along the ocean. The car cruised comfortably at fifty-five miles an hour. He grinned as he turned on Pescadero Creek Road and drove up his driveway to see if Joshua and Maggie were home before realizing they wouldn't have closed the store yet. He turned the car around, drove downtown, pulled up in front of the general store and sat in the car with the motor idling until one of them noticed. Maggie saw him first. She called Joshua as she passed through the front door.

"Where'd you steal this?" Maggie winked.

"I borrowed it. I'm thinking of stealing it. It's a blast!"

"Looks like fun" Josh said. "Liz-Beth enjoys it."

"Most fun I had in a car in years. Dinner's probably ready, though. I better go."

"See ya."

"Good to see him having fun, Josh. First time I saw a smile on his face since he moved here."

"Like a teenager with his first car."

William returned the car to Liz-Beth's garage. She met him at the door with a glass of wine.

"What do you think?"

"It drives great. It's fun."

"I miss driving down the coast in it with Bunny."

"You're a devious woman, Mrs. Wiggins. I guess I'm the new chauffeur."

"Men are so easy. Loan them a toy and they're yours. I give you credit, William. Bunny didn't get it for years."

"Maybe he did, and he liked it."

"If I fooled him or I didn't it was wonderful."

Maria joined them at the dinner table. "Liz-Beth told me you were in the computer business."

"Yes, before I moved here."

"My nephew is in the computer business in Santa Clara."

"Really? What does he do?"

"He's an engineer. He works for a company with a funny name. Light Box or something."

"LightSwitch?"

"Yes. LightSwitch. You know this company?"

"What's your nephew's name?"

"Guadalupe."

"Lupe? Lupe Garcia?"

"Yes. Guadalupe Garcia. You know him?"

"Yes, we hired him as an intern." William contemplated the coincidence.

"When you see him, tell him I wish him well."

"Thank you, I will."

When they finished dinner Liz-Beth brought another bottle of Pinot Noir to the living room.

"Why don't you introduce William to Senior Chuckles?"

"Good idea, Maria. Can you bring him in?"

Maria returned from the spare bedroom with a stand and Mr. Chuckles in his cage.

Mr. Chuckles looked sad, like he felt abandoned. Liz-Beth approached the cage. "Ahhhh, Mr. Chuckles. We were so inconsiderate to leave you in your bedroom while we ate dinner, weren't we?"

"Liz-Beth."

"No need for sarcasm, William. Birds have feelings. They're smarter than you think."

Mr. Chuckles become alert and animated when he saw William. He raised his wings, extended his neck, and swayed back and forth on his perch, raising one foot, then the other. He seemed to be dancing.

"That's my happy Chuckles."

"Look, Mrs. Wiggins, he's staring at William."

"How strange, Maria. He can't take his eyes off you, William."

Liz-Beth opened the door to the cage and brought Chuckles out on a wrist. "Hold out your arm, William."

Chuckles hopped on William's wrist.

"Amazing. I've never seen him do that with a stranger. He never did it with Sukie."

"He likes Mr. Beck-in-dale."

William wrinkled his brow, leaned his head forward and bent his elbow to bring the bird closer. William and Mr. Chuckles had a bird-person moment.

"He's happy, Maria. I wish I had this on camera."

When William moved his hand away, Chuckles walked up his arm to his shoulder and started grooming him.

Liz-Beth's jaw dropped. "He's only done that with Bunny."

"William has a new friend, Liz-Beth. You must be a nice person, William. Birds can tell this."

William sat in a chair. Chuckles stood contentedly on his shoulder as if they were old friends. Chuckles bobbed his head. He made happy parrot noises.

"He babbles, Liz-Beth."

"It's like baby sounds, William. He does that when he's happy. Sometimes he talks to himself. He knows a few phrases. He whistles, he learns songs, sings them off-key. It's pretty funny."

"Really."

"You won't like it if something scares him. He shrieks like a banshee; an icepick in your ear. Don't make him angry. He knows how to get to us."

"Thanks for the advice."

"Sukie made a big mistake. He started vacuuming with Chuckles in the room. Chuckles hates the vacuum cleaner. He flew off his perch and chased Sukie out of the room. Chuckles never forgave him. He tries to bite Sukie if he gets close. He can do a lot of damage with that beak."

"I'll try not to get on his bad side."

"I have to pick up a painting in Capitola in a few days, in a gallery in the mall by the beach. Would it be too much trouble to make it an outing? I don't like driving down the coast alone. If you don't have an appointment..."

"Who's being sarcastic?"

Liz-Beth smiled.

William smirked. "Here we go."

"We can take the MG, stop for lunch someplace. My treat."

"Ah *ha*, bet you used this one on Bunny."

"Yep, in England. With a Jeep."

"In that case I'd be honored...I think."

"The strategy still works. Shall we say Saturday morning, 10-ish?"

"Saturday, it is."

The headlights of a dusty late model Camry stopped in front of the cottage. A short, stout man rang the bell.

"That must be Maria's husband, Guillermo."

Liz-Beth greeted him. Covered in tile dust and mortar, Guill-ermo declined to enter the house.

"Leave the dishes Maria. I'll take care of them."

Maria said goodbye and left with Guillermo.

"It's dark, William. Why don't you take the MG home?"

"Keep it overnight?"

"I'm not going anywhere. You can bring it back Saturday. I hardly drive anyway. It might as well stay at your house."

"I'm sinking deeper. You're a crafty lady, Liz-Beth."

"I'll take that as a compliment. I'll take Chuckles. See you Saturday morning, William.

* * *

Joshua and Maggie shared the San Francisco Chronicle in the living room. Joshua sipped a single malt scotch. Maggie poured a glass of white wine as William turned into the gravel driveway.

"What would you like to bet that's Liz-Beth's new chauffeur in the MG?"

"Not a dollar, Josh. You win."

Twenty-Two

The fog moved in Friday afternoon. It blanketed the coast like a sheer, translucent, linen shroud. It hung in the air overnight, dampening exposed surfaces, rendering them cold to the touch. On nights like this one, William appreciated the fireplace.

William woke late Saturday, threw down toast and coffee, scanned the headlines in the San Jose Mercury News. He pulled on his father's car coat, pushed the MG out of the barn where he parked it behind his father's car and drove to Liz-Beth's.

Liz-Beth rose early and waited for him.

"What do you do with Chuckles when you're gone?"

"Worried about your new friend, William?"

"We can't leave him alone all day."

"Maria's coming to clean. She'll feed him and keep him company. I use to take him in the car sometimes. He can be a pain. He stays here today."

"Can I see him?"

"Miss him already?"

"Yeah, I do."

"I would have had Maria wake him. Let's go in his room."

Liz-Beth pulled the cover off the cage. Chuckles opened his eyes, looked at Liz-Beth and William and waited. William brought him out on a wrist. The bird climbed on his shoulder.

"Ever think of getting him a girlfriend?"

"Heavens, no. I don't want a flock of them. Put him back, William. He has food and water in the cage. Let's get on the road. Maria will be here soon."

The MG cruises comfortably, though not quietly at the

Highway 1 limit. William wouldn't have chosen a car with a raucous engine, soft top, and plastic side curtains for a meeting, but he quickly adjusted to the sound of the engine, the wind, the fluttering of the top and windows.

The cabin is cozy. A passenger could doze off on a long ride in spite of the noise. William loved the car. Liz-Beth slid down in the seat and rode contentedly. *Just like me and Bunny*, she thought. *Good to be on the road again.*

They drove past Bean Hollow and Pidgeon Point beaches where the lighthouse and the hostel are, Gazos Creek, Año Nuevo where they parked to watch elephant seals lounging atop boulders in the surf. As many as 10,000 come in the spring to mate and give birth. They drove past Waddell Creek at Rancho del Oso. They stopped for lunch at the Davenport Café across from Waddell Beach, past the entrance to Big Basin, California's oldest state park where the largest contiguous stand of Giant Sequoias is found south of San Francisco.

The fog lifted while they ate lunch. They walked across the highway. A hundred yards south, they crossed railroad tracks and continued to the edge of a cliff to look out on a horseshoe shaped cove. Several hundred feet high, a steep trail led from the edge of the cliff to the beach. A flat-top haystack fifty yards in diameter rose to eye level in the center of the cove like an ocean mesa. William wondered how many millennia were needed for the ocean to carve out the cove. Swells drove waves through a natural arch at the base of the haystack to lap the shore. Children played on the beach. William hiked to the water to photograph them while Liz-Beth waited at the top of the cliff. He thought black and white photos would look good on white cottage walls. They did.

William and Liz-Beth walked around the cliff on the south side of the cove to look for whales. Too early for the humpback migration, they didn't see any. When they returned to the MG William removed the windows and stowed them to keep the cockpit from overheating in the sun. They drove south past the road that leads to the Bonny Doon Winery, continued to the outskirts of Santa

Cruz where they turned west to Natural Bridges State Beach and picked up West Cliff Drive to tour the neighborhoods that line the ocean until they reached the Santa Cruz boardwalk. They crossed the bridge over the San Lorenzo River and continued on East Cliff Drive to Capitola.

Pastel colored stucco walls of the beachfront Venetian Hotel line the downhill slope to a strip of restaurants on the north side of the mouth of the Soquel River which flows so slowly it looks like a cove. You could paddle up the Soquel with a spoon. Capitola is as cute and cheerful a beach town as you will find on the Central California coast.

William dropped Liz-Beth off at the entrance of the mall. He drove up the hill on the south side of town and found a space in the municipal parking lot overlooking the beach and the pier. He descended a long cement staircase built into the hill and entered the mall where he found Liz-Beth inspecting beach bags in an open-air stall inside a mall that resembled a Middle Eastern bazaar.

"I'm going to be here for a while. Why don't you climb the hill to the south? Walk the cliff above the cement ship if you don't feel like shopping. If I'm not here when you return, I'll be on the deck of one of the beachfront restaurants."

"The car's in the lot above the town. Give you an hour?"

"That's optimistic. If you haven't returned, I can spend the afternoon sipping wine and being happy."

William walked two blocks through town and crossed the street. He climbed the ten-story concrete staircase to the top of the cliff on the south side of the cove. He lingered to admire the view of the beach, the pier, the pastel walls of the Capitola Venetian and the homes above it, their lawns manicured to the edge of the cliff. He walked along the cliff and sat on a bench overlooking the cement ship. He watched flights of pelicans riding breezes. "They're everywhere along the coast," he thought. He walked through the neighborhood, a mixture of cliff-top mansions overlooking the ocean and modest bungalows across the road until he reached the Monarch Cove Inn where he brought high school dates when butterflies migrated from Mexico and covered the grounds like a quilt with their delicate colorful wings. His girlfriends swooned at the sight and fell in love with him for the weekend, so he believed.

William turned back when he reached New Brighton Beach. *This is a place I could live*, he told himself. He took a deep breath of ocean air and smelled the salt. *I haven't felt this good in a year*, he said to himself. He returned to the mall in time to carry a beach bag of packages for Liz-Beth.

"What's in the bag?"

"Scented candles, soaps, a painting by a local artist, things I need for kitchen and bath."

They crossed the street and chose a seafood restaurant with a deck over the water. The hostess showed them to a table on the deck. They ordered a bottle of wine, a salad and a shrimp cocktail to share. They watched the sun descend toward the ocean, the kids play in the sand.

"Liz-Beth, tell me about Bunny."

"You don't really want to hear about that do you?"

"Sure I do."

"Bunny loved English literature. He read it aloud, wandered the house with a book in one hand, gesturing as if he had an audience. He quoted Bacon, Marlowe, Carroll, Kipling, Dickens, of course Shakespeare, some of it memorized from studying it at university. He bought clothing made of the best materials on visits to England. He looked great in suits on his long, narrow frame. So distinguished in a pencil moustache. He could have been a clothing model. They were tailored from wool cloth purchased at Liberty's. In London, where he bought his shirts. He liked tweed jackets, and vests, an occasional tie in a traditional Windsor knot or a cravat when we entertained at home. He looked like a university professor or a country gentleman. He smoked a pipe. He liked Dunhill cherry and walnut Cavendish. I liked the scent of it in the house. So masculine. He smoked it in a Tsuge Ikebana pipe imported from Japan. I bought it for him for his 60th birthday. He lit it with a Dunhill lighter and wrote letters with their fountain pens. We took them to the post before you tech people invented email."

"I'm not that young," William smirked.

"He wrote in beautiful longhand penmanship on a modest desk crafted from the finest mahogany. He thought artistic qualities of a fine pen enabled him to add emphasis to his handwriting. He never wrote a letter without one."

"A lost art."

"He preferred Breitling timepieces. He owned several; his favorite an analogue Montbrilliant chronograph on a dark brown leather band."

"I have my father's."

"Bunny rarely missed afternoon tea. He loved gardening and enjoyed caring for roses. You can remove an Englishman from England, but you can't remove England from an Englishman. Except for tipping, the "fake" Guinness we have here, and driving on the wrong side of the road, Bunny slid right to life in America, without becoming American."

"We had fun with Chuckles. He drank rum, but the birdbrain didn't know when to quit. I had to cut him off. He'd drink any brand but preferred Captain Morgan. Bunny joked he liked the pirate image on the label or the Morgan girls. Sometimes it made Chuckles tipsy, not enough to swing upside down, but enough to put him to sleep or keep him quiet as he swayed back and forth on his perch. Chuckles liked his buzz. It didn't take him long to figure out how to get one. He made a fuss. It must have been fun to be a parrot in a spinning room. *If only parrots could smile,* Liz-Beth thought. Chuckles stared off into space, gently rocking to music. He seemed to enjoy romantic piano. Chopin and a tablespoon of rum pacified him. He liked rock too. He dipped and danced to anything with rhythm. The villagers knew him as "The drunken parrot of Pescadero.""

"He doesn't seem to need it now."

"No, he's older now. He was a real pain in adolescence. We had to pacify him."

William smiled at the vision of his avian friend as a teenager throwing a tantrum.

"We had a hunting dog we named Bentley. Bunny used to take him in the hills to chase birds."

"He went hunting in Pescadero?"

"No William, just hiking. Bunny never fired the gun. He spent weekends and vacations marking the "New Cotswolds" boundary with that three-foot wall made of stones found on the property. Kept him busy for years. He and Sukie planted and irrigated a garden with native plants from rainy old England."

"I've seen it from the road. It's awesome."

"It took years for those heirloom roses to grow into hedges. They thrive in California sun. Sukie stocked the pond with koi where we had afternoon tea. We entertained weekend guests from San Francisco and visitors from across the oceans. We served lavish meals, drank great French wines, sipped single malt scotches and Irish whiskey. The men smoked cigars and pipes. We listened to music, played bridge, discussed the news of the world. We stared into flames dancing in the fireplace. Bunny stacked wood sourced from the property. He felled the trees, rounded and split them by hand."

"He must have been strong, Liz-Beth."

"Abe Lincoln strong, William. We spent summer evenings in the garden. We made fires on the beach at night. Full moon at the beach is brilliant. It lights a path across the ocean as it travels across the sky."

"Wow, Liz-Beth. You had a great life here."

"I'm glad you asked, William. I enjoyed sharing it with you. You wanna tell me about life in Silicon Valley?"

"Not much to tell, Liz-Beth. It's just suburban sprawl and work."

"What happened in business?"

"I'd rather not talk about that."

"I understand. Your girlfriend?"

"She was terrific, really. We had fun. I was so busy with work. Liz-Beth, I really don't want to get into this now. Can we talk about it another time?"

"Sure, sometime when you feel like it."

William fetched the car when they finished the wine. He parked in front of the restaurant, stored the beach bag in the boot, and they left.

On the drive back they stopped to watch the sunset behind Pidgeon Point Lighthouse. When the sun reached the horizon, refraction through a light haze turned the world a brilliant orange. William took the photo, removed the windows and the top from behind boot and installed them to keep the cabin warm as the air cooled after the sun retired into the ocean. A westerly breeze pushed the marine layer toward shore. The moon rose from the east, over the foothills, as William dropped Liz-Beth at her cottage.

"Thanks so much for driving, William."

"I enjoyed the company and the MG."

"I haven't been anywhere in a while. What a treat. Would you like to come in?"

"No, thanks. I need to get home, get to bed and up early. I'm glad you dragged me out, Liz-Beth. This is the nicest day I've had since I came here. All I've done is work on the car, eat and sleep. I need to get the car done, get on with my life and enjoy more days like this one."

"Time heals all wounds, William. It will get better. You'll know what to do when you're ready. Anytime you want to go somewhere, please consider taking me along if you will, won't you?"

"Sure. Can I take the MG home?"

"Of course." She kissed him on the cheek, said good night, and stepped into the house.

William returned to the cottage no longer despondent as he had been when he arrived in Pescadero.

Twenty-Three

Roberto, Marco, and Sergio, brought the car to the cottage on a flatbed Friday evening.

"This is a special car, William. I hope you enjoy driving it."

"I have no doubt I will, Roberto. It look's great. Thanks for the great work, for letting me do some of the mechanical work at your place, and for finishing so quickly."

"It was a pleasure working with you. Bring it back sometime. We'll polish it some more."

"Thanks, Roberto. I don't think it needs more polishing. It needs driving."

"We don't care. We like having it in the shop like we did when we painted it for your father, don't we boys?"

"Like old times," Marco nodded.

"We liked your father," Sergio added. "Come by when you're in Half Moon Bay, William. We want to see it on the road again. Let's go, boys."

Team "Alonso and Son's" returned to the flatbed. They waved as they started down the gravel driveway.

Joshua heard the flatbed diesel engine compression-braking. He came to see who visited William. He walked around the car, viewing it with admiration.

"The car looks great. Is it finished?"

"Thanks, Josh. I *think* it is. I have to test drive it."

Maggie joined them. "Is it the same car?"

"You're sweet Maggie."

"What a transformation. I didn't expect to see it done yet. Sooner than expected, isn't it?"

"It is, Josh. The paint shop helped out. Some customers waited."

"It looked like it needed a lot of work" Maggie said.

"It looked worse than it was. Metal and paint work can take forever. I didn't want a museum piece. I needed a decent job done quickly."

"Too bad you had to take John's name off the door."

"I had to."

"How does it sound?"

"Awesome."

"Are you gonna take it for a drive?" Josh asked.

"It's getting late. I'll push it in the barn, celebrate over dinner at Duarte's, drive it in the morning. Would you like to join me at Duarte's? My treat."

"How nice of you, William. Sure, love to."

"I couldn't have done it without your encouragement, and your pickup truck."

"We were happy to help out, William. Liz-Beth would probably like to join us. Okay with you?"

"Sure, Maggie."

"Let's pick her up on the way to Duarte's, Josh. I'll call and invite her."

"It'll be nice to hear her run, see her rolling down the road again. Your father used to wake us up when he left for Laguna Seca before sunrise" Josh said.

"Hope you didn't mind."

"Not at all. We loved having him and the car here. Like having Paul Newman or Steve McQueen for a neighbor. Your dad was an American hero William, but for real."

"Nice of you to say that, Maggie. I remember. Mom and I stayed overnight to load it in the trailer and get an early start in the morning. We met him at the track before that, when I was too young to help out. Those were good times. I miss them."

Twenty-Four

Four months had passed since William had fled Silicon Valley for Pescadero. In early spring, the summer tourist hoard had not yet claimed the beaches and clogged the coastal highway with motorcycles, cars and land-yachts.

William slept well and rose before the sun. He stood, stretched, pulled on a pair of jeans, a white t-shirt, and the denim shirt he draped over a chair the previous evening. He walked into the great room thinking he didn't need the wall that divided the cottage, considered removing it, transforming the cottage into a studio with a sleeping nook.

William stepped into the tiny kitchen. He loaded a press with coffee while water heated in a metal tea kettle on a two-burner gas stove installed when Truman was president. The white enamel on the stove scratched and chipped with time, but the flame burned clean. It cooked his food as well as any gas stove would and William liked patina.

William gazed through the picture window his father installed in the front wall, at the vacuous blackness of sky and ocean across the from the highway. He leaned on a well-worn butcher block counter and waited for boiling water. It occurred to him the intersection of Pescadero Creek Road and Cabrillo Highway needed a street lamp but he preferred the knoll dark at night. He thought someone might die at the intersection someday like James Dean did in 1955 on the same highway near Paso Robles.

William sipped coffee at the desk beneath the picture window. His mind idled as first light filtered through a haze. The coffee tasted rich, and strong, and good. It warmed him inside.

An outline of rocks appeared in the surf through a shroud of light fog. Birds began to stir and contemplate breakfast. Seals would soon slip into the water to go fishing, birds take to the skies. He heard the surf though the window. William loved the peaceful knoll, the mesmerizing view in early hours, more than any other place he knew.

The sun brightened the sky as it rose behind the coastal mountains. It burned off the fog, turned wisps of clouds pink, and lit the ocean an inch at a time as sunbeams crept over surf, and rocks, and sand, and the western end of the knoll, covered in curious tube-shaped plants that only live in sandy soil of coastal lowlands.

William emptied the mug and laced a pair of canvass top boat shoes retrieved from beneath the desk. He lifted his father's jacket from a hook near the back door, pulled it on and draped a white scarf around his neck.

He crossed the gravel to the barn, keyed the padlock and disengaged the latch. The doors swung open on creaking rusty hinges. He reached down, released the doorstops and heeled them into the ground. Attached to a car parked in the middle of the garage a new license plate read "PELICAN 1." William peered into dim light. He stood outside for a moment with a hand resting on a door jamb. He stepped in, threw a light switch and walked around the gleaming car, admiring every angle. He never tired of the silhouette, even though it had been in the family longer than himself, and is one of his oldest memories. He favored the rear three quarter view from the passenger side. From that angle chrome ringed Smith's gauges in a center cluster are unobstructed by a beautifully crafted wooden rim steering wheel. The curve of the fender arches over the wheels, the mound of the hood between them, the leather covered dash, the rake of the windshield. He imagined it hurtling out of a LeRoy Niemen painting. William loved the symmetry of the nose, the polished aluminum egg crate grill framed by a simple chrome hoop attached to over-riders set between two headlights. It looked graceful, fast, vulnerable, seductively feminine, all at the same time. *If a human could love a car,* William thought. He loved this one and everything it meant.

He turned the latches, opened the hood, and set the prop rod in place to begin the ritual to the God of starting. He inspected the engine compartment, checking for dried fluid stains, exhaust leak carbon. He inspected fuses, wiring harness, plug wires, hoses, water pump / alternator belt tension. He checked the accelerator linkage. He pondered the miracle of compressed air, fuel, and electricity that come together at the precise instant needed to start and run a motor that revolves as fast as 100 times a second. He lowered the hood but didn't latch it.

William opened the door and dropped into the driver's seat. He stabbed a firm brake pedal. He threw the battery switch, flashed headlights and parking lights. They lit Liz-Beth's MG parked in front of him.

He pulled the choke cable halfway out, pressed the gas pedal once to the floor, and turned the ignition key. The starter turned the motor over. The pistons compressed air and fuel. The coil fired. The fuel ignited. Dual exhaust pipes, exiting ahead of the rear tires on opposite sides of the car, battered the barn with staccato explosions that bounced off walls, ceiling, and ground, in four channel stereo, as if the car tried to blow the building up and knock it off its foundation.

The motor strained against its mounts and shook the car. The driver's side exhaust pipe below his ear tried to deafen him.

William moved the transmission lever into reverse, let the clutch out, fed the motor a little gas and backed the car out of the barn. He shifted to neutral, set the parking brake and stepped out to wait until the motor came up to operating temperature. He lifted the hood to look for fuel and water leaks. Oil pressure and voltage gauges read normal. The motor sounded crisp and healthy. He walked around the car listening to exhaust notes like concert lovers savor concertos; music to William, like rapid, rhythmic beating of bass drums. When the electric radiator fan switched on William knew the coolant reached operating temperature. He closed the choke. The motor slowed to a lope.

As morning half-light gave way to daylight, William stored the prop rod, lowered the hood and secured the latches. He pulled on his driving gloves and snapped the buttons closed against the backs of his hands. He dropped into the driver's seat and switched on the headlights. He turned on the heater fan to warm the cockpit under the tonneau cover and feed defroster vents to keep the windshield clear. He backed around to point the car to the road, and idled down the gravel driveway, stopping at the tarmac to look for cross traffic. He turned left onto Pescadero Creek Road and drove to Cabrillo Highway, listening to exhaust pipes playing scales between gear changes.

No traffic appeared on Highway 1 when William turned right for the drive to Half Moon Bay. He drove the speed limit, warming the car's systems, savoring a relaxing morning drive as the sun climbed above the coastal mountains. A clear, crisp winter day, air still, except for the wake of car and driver penetrating it. William sighted no vehicles, heard no sounds, of anyone else on the highway. He motored north to a deep mellow exhaust system drone. Scarf zipped inside his jacket, his straight brown hair blew in the wind. Engine heat passed though firewall and heater ducts warming his feet, legs, and body. Head, neck, and shoulders bathed in sunlight, tanning his skin, highlighting his hair. He scanned the foothills, the beaches, the ocean. He glanced at birds in flight and thought when he has the road to himself on a clear Saturday morning there is nothing in the world he would rather do. The sound of the car carried for miles in damp coastal air that hovered over lowlands near the ocean and echoed off the foothills.

"There he goes, Josh."

"I love the sound of that car, Maggie."

"Let's get going. We need to open in a couple of hours. Somebody is going to need something."

"No need to send the business to San Gregorio."

It took twenty minutes to reach the outskirts of Half Moon Bay. William veered right on a street intersecting the coastal highway at a thirty-five-degree angle. He drove a mile through downtown to highway 92.

Downtown Half Moon Bay is a mile of two story commercial buildings several streets deep east and west of main street. William parked in a corner lot in front of an auto parts store. A handful of residents and tourists walked by on the sidewalk to one of the breakfast cafes. William stepped out and lifted the hood while the motor idled. He looked under the car for leaks, listened for unwanted sounds and didn't find any. He lowered the hood and latched it. The auto parts store in the strip mall emptied into the parking lot. A few people crossed the street from the gas station.

"Isn't this the car Alonso painted?"

"It is."

"I heard about this car, wondered if I'd see it on the road."

"What do you think?"

"It looks great and sounds awesome! I remember when your father stopped here for parts and bought aviation gas at the airport."

William smiled. After fielding a dozen questions, he listened patiently to stories about how somebody knew somebody who has one, could have had one, or used to have one, a million years ago, and wished they bought it or hadn't sold it. William excused himself as politely as possible and returned to the driver's seat. He waved at the store owner standing in the doorway. Over the last few months William bought a crate full of parts there. Gus returned the wave. *He got it on the road,* Gus thought. "Keep the shiny side up, William," he whispered.

William exited the lot onto Highway 92 and drove a few blocks to the intersection at Cabrillo Highway. When the light turned green he turned south.

William cruised out of town at the limit under clear skies on a damp cool morning. He had the morning and the road to himself. When he reached a long flat straight stretch where he could see several miles ahead, William disengaged the clutch, stabbed the gas pedal to match engine RPM to the speed of a lower gear, shifted the transmission, let out the clutch and mashed the gas pedal. The carburetor butterflies sprung open. The accelerator pumps shot a load of fuel into throttle bodies. The motor delivered a surge of power releasing the wrath of Satan as the rear tires broke loose and struggled for grip. The car snapped a fishtail on the cold damp highway. William turned the steering wheel to straighten the car. The motor spun up quickly. Exhaust pipes bellowed and the car shot forward in a rush of acceleration. Reaching the RPM limit quickly, William shifted into the next gear at over 100 miles an hour, held the gas pedal down and watched the tachometer and speedometer needles climb. The car ate up the highway as it accelerated over 130 miles an hour where he backed off the gas pedal, shifted into 4th gear and held the speed steady as he checked the gauges and felt the power of the motor push the car through the atmosphere. William pumped an arm in the air and let out a great *Wahoo!* He barely heard himself over the buffeting wind and the sound of the motor. A smile spread across his face. He marveled at how stable, how capable the car felt of a great deal more speed as it cruised comfortably in high gear. He glanced at hills and mountains, the beach and ocean flying by as he came to the last 1000 yards of highway before it rose and crested and turned left into a blind curve carved through a hill and he had to back down near the speed limit to avoid scarring the bejesus out of anyone coming from the opposite direction and in the event they were on his side of the road when they met. The headlights are bright but not that bright. The horn is loud but not loud enough to save him.

William completed the rest of the drive at a leisurely pace, listening and sensing for physical and aural feedback of anything unwanted. He heard none. The car rolled down the road as smoothly, he thought, as a 12-cylinder Packard. He knew it didn't but enjoyed the fantasy. He turned off Cabrillo Highway at Pescadero Creek Road and slowed to a stop at twin mailboxes where Joshua read his mail in anticipation of William's arrival. Joshua glanced at his watch. Right on time, he thought.

"How'd it go?"

"Road test complete. It runs great!"

William switched off the lights and the motor.

"Don't turn it off," Joshua pleaded. "I love the sound of it."

"I'd like to be able to hear you, Josh. I'm not going to push it up the driveway. I'll start it for that."

"Clean the carburetor out?"

"Oh, yeah. Have to use up the winter gas. No good mixing it with spring gas."

"I wouldn't do that to my lawnmower. Nice drive?"

"Yeah."

"Do anything interesting?"

"Na, just a morning drive."

Sure it was, Joshua thought. *I heard it.*

"All the times I saw your father come and go in this car I never thought to ask. What is it, William?"

"It's an AC."

"Sorry, I'm not a car guy. What's an AC?"

"An English car made by a very old company."

"Sounds like an American engine."

"It is."

"Is this the car Carroll Shelby built?"

"Shelby didn't build it, Josh. He bought them from AC, installed a Ford engine and made it a winner."

"Didn't he call it a Cobra?"

"Yeah, he did."

"Is it fast?"

"You know I wouldn't exceed the speed limit" William said with a wink.

"Sure you wouldn't. I heard it."

"Yeah, it's fast" William said.

"I want a ride I it."

Joshua leaned over the door and looked into the cockpit.

"The top of my head might be higher than the windshield" he said.

"We can take the seat out." William scratched his head. "Not sure where to put your legs."

William pointed at his mailbox. "Anything for me?"

Joshua opened William's box. "Junk mail. I'll toss it for you. I have to take Maggie to the store before she banishes me to the couch."

"I doubt that will happen."

William started the car, nodded at Josh, rumbled across the street, up the driveway.

Joshua lingered to listen. *If he gets himself arrested one morning it will be worth it*, he thought. *I'll bail him out.* Joshua walked to the house.

William stopped outside the barn. He set the handbrake and stepped out. He lifted the hood and set the prop rod to look in the engine compartment. No leaks. The motor sounded smooth and crisp. He did a quick walk-around inspection, lowered the hood, cut the motor, released the handbrake and pushed the car into the barn. He turned off the heater fan, threw the battery disconnect switch, reset the hand brake.

William stood outside the open barn doors listening to the exhaust system ticking as it cooled. *That was great*, he thought. *Dad would've been proud.* He pulled up the doorstops, swung the doors closed and snapped on the padlock.

William passed through the cottage door and hung up his scarf and jacket. He poured a half mug of coffee from the French press and warmed it in the microwave while he turned on the computer and sat down to check email and voicemail. He carried the mug to the picture window and sat at the desk to gaze at the ocean. William felt better than he had in a long time. *No wonder my father loved that car*, he thought. For the first time since arriving in Pescadero William felt pretty good about the future.

William watched his favorite birds through the picture window; pelicans diving for brunch. He thought their ridiculous bills made them look like a pterodactyl. He marveled at these large whimsical birds. Ungainly on land, graceful in flight, riding the breezes with their necks bent upward and back, that huge beak pointed into the airstream. As comical as it makes them look on the ground or thrashing in the struggle to swallow a fish, the beak is part of the airfoil in flight, like a phallus parting the sky for the body.

He looked up the name in an online dictionary. From the ancient Greek *pelekan* he learned, from the word *pelekys* which means axe. "The axe that flies through the sky. That's what you are Dusty," William said to his companion; "a flying axe."

How can they track fish while coasting above a churning ocean? Do they think like a fish? Is that how they catch them? William never tired of watching them fold their wings, rollover into an inverted dive, stretch out their legs and neck, pierce the water like an Olympic diver and come up with a fish nearly every dive. *Nature's perfect fisherman,* William thought. *Great fisherman who surf the breezes over Pescadero beach, a place where fish live.*

Twenty-Five

When a fog that blocks the brightest stars on a moonless night descends on the coastline, the intersection of Cabrillo Highway and Pescadero Creek Road is as dark as a coal mine. You can't see the ground beneath your feet, or your hands in front of your face.

A limousine rolled down Highway 1 from the north, turned left on Pescadero Creek Road and stopped at William's driveway. William saw the headlights illuminate the tarmac, briefly pass behind the berm, and stop below his line of sight. From the cottage he couldn't see the end of his driveway where it met Pescadero Road. When the road went dark he assumed the car moved on. From their house east of the driveway, Joshua and Maggie saw the headlights too. From their living room window, they can see where William's driveway intersects Pescadero Creek Road.

The driver's door opened. A large, well-groomed, dark suited man stepped out. He walked around the back of the car and opened a passenger door. A pair of red flats at the end of slender legs in skin tight stove pipe blue jeans swung out of the back of the limo. A petite young woman stepped lightly on the tarmac as the driver popped the truck lid, removed two large rolling bags and a carry-on, and set them behind the car. The woman handed him a credit card. She zipped a black leather jacket against the night chill, pulled a Giants cap over her head and looped a pony tail through the portal made by the band. The limo driver reached for a credit card slide. The woman sighed, took the receipt and the credit card, put them in a wallet and slipped the wallet in a handbag.

"Hell of a dark night."

She nodded.

"Man, its quiet around here. Want me to pull your bags up the driveway?"

"No, I can manage."

"Are you sure?"

"Yeah, I'm sure. Thanks for driving all the way down here."

"That's OK. It was good to get out of the city, get on the highway. Can you take it from here?"

"Yeah, I got it. Thanks for being so kind."

"You take care. Here's my card. Call if you need a ride back or you need one when you come in the city."

"I talk too much, don't I? Thanks for listening."

"No worries. I hope things work out for you."

"I feel like we made friends on the ride."

"We did. Call me in the city if you need me."

"Thanks. I will. Careful driving back."

"I'm always careful."

With no street light to penetrate the fog, Joshua barely made out the black limo. It looked like a pair of lights suspended in space, with a man, a woman, and three bags on the ground in front of them.

"William has company, Maggie, and he doesn't have a sister."

"*Oh*? What's this Josh?"

The driver turned the limo around, flashed his high beams, drove to Cabrillo Highway and turned north. The woman shielded her eyes as he passed. She watched him leave as she and her bags disappeared into the night.

"Shouldn't you go down there, Josh?"

"No, it's William's business. Let him handle it."

"I don't think he knows he has company."

"Let it go, Maggie. Whatever it is. Let it happen."

"She might need help. It's dark out there."

"I'll keep an eye out in case they need us."

The woman switched on a penlight she removed from her

handbag. She pulled the strap of the carry-on bag over her shoulder, reached for the handle of one of the roll-ons and struggled up the gravel driveway. Halfway to the cottage, she dropped the handle of the roll-on bag and worked her way through the darkness toward the outside light by the cottage door. When she reached the door she saw Williams' shadow cast across the deck by the reading light behind him. She knocked on the door.

Who in the world could it be this late? Josh? Maggie? They'd call, William thought. He contemplated reaching for the .45 in the desk drawer. *"I won't let this place make me paranoid,"* he thought. He opened the door.

"Natalie!"

"Surprised to see me?"

"Yeah, I am."

They stared at each other.

"Would you like to ask me in?"

"Ah…sure, please come in. I'm sorry, you surprised me."

"Are you glad to see me?"

"Yeah, I am."

Natalie realized she had to take control. She rested the shoulder bag on the floor and threw her arms around William. She nuzzled William's neck. She sighed and hugged him. William though he sensed a little desperation. He wrapped himself around her like a cocoon.

"I left a bag in the driveway and one on the road. Could you get them for me?"

"Of course."

Natalie set her handbag down next to her shoulder bag and washed her face in the bathroom. William took his Mag light, pulled her bags up the driveway, into the cottage. Natalie leaned on the sink, looked in the mirror and pondered what to say after a week of rehearsing. She removed the baseball cap and let her hair out of the pony tail. Dark brown with natural highlights, it spread across her shoulders; wavy, silky, shiny, thick, luxurious. William returned with the bags, entered the cottage and paused to gaze at her through the open bathroom door as she dried her face with a towel. *Still under any circumstance, the prettiest girl I ever saw.*

"Looks like you might be staying for a while."

"I'd like to."

William rolled the bags into the bedroom and left them on the floor next to the bed. He joined Natalie in the great room.

"What's going on, Natalie?"

"I missed you."

"I missed you too. It's late. Why didn't you call?"

"I didn't want to talk on the phone. I wanted to see you."

"We broke up, didn't we?"

"Not exactly. I moved out. We never spoke about it."

William took a deep breath. "I was humiliated. I didn't want to talk to anybody."

"Not even me?"

"I felt like a failure."

"You aren't a failure. Your friends care about you. They worry about you. I worried about you. You should have called me."

"You're right. I should have."

"That hurt, William. You moved here and didn't even tell me. I had to hear it from Sandy. It's like you ran away and didn't want to have anything to do with me."

"I didn't want to put you through this."

"I was supposed to go through this. I was your girlfriend. We were supposed to work things out together."

"What else? You didn't stop by to say hello."

"Let's sit down."

They sat on the love seat.

"I quit my job."

"Ah Natalie, why'd you do that?"

"I got sick of the office politics. They treated me like an intern. I needed to move on."

"Do you have a job lined up?"

"No."

"What are you going to do?"

"I'll go back to work. I just need a break from it."

"How much of a break?"

"I don't know. Enough."

"We're a couple of unemployed beach bums."

"We aren't bums. We're just unemployed."

"Can I get you something to drink?"

"Do you have any white wine?"

William opened a bottle of Pinot Gris. He brought two glasses from the kitchen.

"I was such a jerk."

"I forgive you, William. I can't stay mad at you."

"You know about the company?"

"I heard about it. I'm really sorry."

"Let's not talk about it now."

"What are you going to do?"

"I don't know, Natalie. Nothing for a while."

"Can I do nothing with you?"

"Sure Nat. I missed you."

"I missed you too."

William put his glass down, took Natalie's, set it the coffee table. "Do you know what I want to do now?"

"Yeah, the same thing I want to do."

Twenty-Six

Natalie rose at first light. She hopped out of bed, walked into the great room with a bounce in her step she didn't have the last year of her young life. She felt as happy as she could remember. She looked into the bedroom at William sleeping face down like the dead. *Guess I wore him out last night*, she said to herself with a giggle. She padded across the hardwood on bare feet to brew the morning coffee and see what they had for breakfast. She tugged the tail of Williams' shirt. It covered her to mid-thigh. She felt a draft in the cabin, but nothing penetrated the warmth she felt inside. She crossed a tanned leg, opened the refrigerator, found a bag of Norm's bagels and lox spread and learned she had to go food shopping to avoid malnutrition and scurvy.

Impervious to the morning chill, Natalie opened the door and stepped on the deck. She leaned on a rail and watched her breath dissipate when she exhaled. The fog lifted during the night. It would be bright, sunny, a lovely warm winter day on the beach. She heard William stirring though the open doorway. She drank her coffee, set the mug on the table, ran into the bedroom and jumped on him. William rolled over and pinned her to the bed. They rose, went to the bathroom and squeezed into the corner shower. They dressed in beach clothes and sat on the loveseat to munch bagels and spread.

"What do you want to do today, Natalie?"

"Let's go to the beach."

They tossed a football. They chased each other and fell in a pile in the sand. They sat William's camera on a boulder, set the timer to 10 seconds and took a stack of hugging, kissing, silly face photos; William with Natalie on his back, on his shoulders, until holding her over his head to exhaustion, they collapsed in the sand and laughed until their sides hurt. They stretched out on the beach, caught their breath, laid on their backs and watched the wind blow the clouds overhead. They listened to the surf, the gulls, the seals barking; they fell asleep in each other's arms, rolled up in a beach blanket. They woke at noon.

"Why didn't you drive down?"

"I sold the Honda."

"What'd you do that for?"

"I paid for parking and hardly used it. Cabs are easier than driving and parking in the city. I took trains to the peninsula. Somebody picked me up at the station or I walked. I thought it was better to have the money in the bank in case I needed it."

"For a car."

"For whatever."

"What did you do with your apartment?"

"I paid five months in advance, to the end of the lease. We can use it if we go to the city. We have no space here. I need a place for my things. If I moved out, I would have spent it on moving expenses and storage. I didn't know if I could stay here. Can I try?"

"We can make it five months."

Natalie smiled. She hugged William. "What do we need a car for?"

"We don't. We can start a farm, live off the land. We need a tractor."

"Come on."

"I borrowed one from a neighbor. I can use it whenever I need it. We have two cars. I…. *we* have dad's old car in the barn."

"That beat up old thing?"

"I cleaned it up a little. It isn't so bad. Come on. Let me show it to you."

Great, Natalie thought. *It would be better to haul it off to the dump to make room for something better.*

They picked up the football, camera, and blanket, and walked to the barn. William keyed the lock, swung the doors open, and pushed the MG into the sunlight.

"What's this? It's cute."

"It's a 1955 MG, belongs to a neighbor."

"I want a ride in it."

"Later, let me show you dad's car."

When William pushed his father's car out of the barn, Natalie's jaw dropped to her navel. She walked around it, eyes wide, mouth open.

"Oh, my God, William. What did you do to it?"

"Do you like it?"

"It's beautiful. I can't believe this is the same car."

"Wanna go for a ride?"

"Sure!"

William started the car. It idled with a distinctive rumble. He opened the driver's door and gestured for Natalie to step in.

"You want me to drive?"

"Sure, it's just a car."

"It sounds like a BEAST."

"No, No. I detuned it to make it easier to drive. Give it a try. It won't bite you."

Natalie gathered her hair into a ponytail and stepped in while William went to the house for her baseball cap.

"Take it easy. It's still powerful."

Natalie slipped on the cap, pulled her pony tail through the hole above the strap in the back, let the clutch out and stalled the engine. She looked at William and smirked. "You better drive it."

"You can do it, Natalie. You need to learn in case you have to. Just give it a little gas first. Let the clutch out slowly until you feel it engage and the car starts moving. You'll get used to it."

Natalie restarted the car. This time she started it rolling. She waved at William as she rumbled down the driveway. William waved back with a big smile on his face.

Natalie turned right on Pescadero Creek Road, left at Duarte's, drove through town, turned around at the cemetery on Stage Road. William waited on the front deck with the morning paper. *This is too much fun to stop*, Natalie thought, as she returned and drove past William's driveway. William smiled when he heard her drive by. *I knew she would do that*, he thought.

Natalie turned right at Cabrillo Highway, drove up Highway 1 to San Gregorio where she turned around and returned to the cottage.

She parked on the grass in front of the house.

"What do you think?"

"It drives nice. What did you do to it?"

"I made it into a street car."

"So powerful. I hardly touched the gas pedal."

"Be careful. You can lose control. "Did you get any looks?"

"Are you kidding? I could have been married five times. You guys. So frog-eyed I thought their eyeballs were going to fall out."

William smiled. "That's enough food for the ego for one day. Let me put it away. We need a daily driver. Why don't we drive up to Mountain View and bring back the Alfa? A hard top and roll up windows will be handy when it's cold and rainy. The back seat will come in handy if there's more than two of us."

"Do you want to go now?"

"No, just sometime soon."

"What's wrong with the MG? It has a top and windows."

"Nothing, it just isn't my car. I don't want to take responsibility when I have one of my own. I promised to drive MG occasionally to keep it in good condition. One of us will drive it sometimes."

"What happened to the BMW?"

"I sold it to Solley. He wanted it for Sandy. I thought she told you everything."

"Not everything. What did you do that for? That was a nice car."

"I wanted to be rid of anything that reminded me of Silicon Valley. What did I need an expensive luxury car for? A board meeting? A night at the opera? I didn't want the lease payments when I no longer needed the car. Let's say hello to Joshua and Maggie."

William pushed his father's car into the barn, pulled the barn doors closed, and locked them. They drove the MG to town and parked it in front of the general store.

"I like this, William. It's cute" Natalie said.

"You can drive it. I'll take the Alfa."

Joshua, William, and Natalie sat at a window table while Maggie waited on customers. The phone behind the counter rang.

"For you, William" Maggie said.

"How could it be for me? Who is it?"

"Who do you think it is?"

"Liz-Beth"

"Who's Liz-Beth?"

"Don't get excited, Natalie. She's old enough to be your grandmother."

"And rich, attractive and single."

"Thanks, Josh. Maybe Natalie *should* worry."

"About grandma?"

"Wait until you meet her. She's wonderful. You'll like her."

"Hello, Liz-Beth. Can't a man visit his friends?"

"In Pescadero, William? You must be kidding."

"How did you know?"

"Spoke to Maggie this morning."

"What can I do for you, Liz-Beth?"

"Your girlfriend is driving all over town in your car, and you dumped me. I want to meet her. Why don't you bring her over for dinner unless you have other plans, something better to eat than yesterday's bagel."

"You know me too well. What time?"

"Dinner time. You know we aren't formal."

"Okay, we'll see you around four o'clock. Red or white wine?"

"Red. Maria is making some kind of a Montezuma meat dish."

"As long as it isn't his revenge. See Ya later."

This is a pleasant surprise, Liz-Beth thought. *Maybe he does have a life.*

"We better get moving, Natalie."

"Nice meeting you, Josh, Maggie."

"We're coming too, Natalie. It's a welcoming dinner, since you'll be staying for a while."

"How did you know that, Josh?"

"Saw the bags."

"There are no secrets in Pescadero." William said.

"We're happy to have you here Natalie," Maggie said. "Welcome to the family. We have to keep the store open. See you at Liz-Beth's around seven."

William and Natalie returned to the cottage, stored the MG in the barn, walked to the beach to sun in the sand until the time came to go to Liz-Beth's for dinner. When they left the store, Joshua looked at Maggie.

"Don't say it," she said.

"Sorry Maggie."

"Don't be sorry. I know I'm handsome."

"That's the prettiest girl I've ever seen in my life."

"I knew you were going to say that. Every pretty girl is the prettiest you've ever seen. She's the prettiest girl I've ever seen. It's nice having young people around."

"Sure is. Can I be in love with two girls?"

"You mean three girls."

"Yeah, Maggie. All three of you."

"You can be, and you have my permission."

Twenty-Seven

Winter passes slowly on the central California coast. The year 2000 began by toggling between foggy and sunny days, with little excitement to break the monotony between "Mavericks," the surfing competition in January, and the "California Dream Machines" show at Half Moon Bay airport in April.

Natalie squeezed into the cottage. She and William explored the restaurants from Montara Beach to Capitola. They discovered live music at the *Bach Dynamite Dancing Society* in Half Moon Bay. They drove the MG to the *Bonny Doon* winery just to be on the road. They loved the little car like Liz-Beth did. They visited Liz-Beth twice a week, once when Maria made dinner mid-week, once when they brought brunch on the weekend. Natalie and Liz-Beth became best friends. William tinkered with his father's car though it only needed driving. He improved the cottage and the landscaping. He and Natalie planted a vegetable garden.

* * *

Liz-Beth invited Natalie to luxuriate in her tub. She knew Natalie and William didn't have one. Liz-Beth wanted to get to know Natalie when William wasn't with them. She wanted to ask about William and his parents. They chose Sunday afternoon, a day when the general store closed early and Joshua planned on driving William to Mountain View to bring back the Alfa.

The cottage phone rang at 8:00AM. "Who is it?" William answered, a bit annoyed and not quit awake yet.

"Who do you think?"

"Liz-Beth? Is something wrong? Why are you calling so early?"

"I wanted to catch you before you had breakfast, see if you want to eat here."

"Now?"

"Yes."

"I have to find you a boyfriend, Liz-Beth."

"Do you think you can make it before noon?"

"For breakfast?"

"For the boyfriend."

William chuckled.

"I'll get Natalie up."

"Does she wake up beautiful?"

"I'll ask her."

"Do you wake up beautiful Nat?"

"Of course I do."

"She says she does"

"I thought so. I do to. Get over here."

William hung up the phone.

"Do I have to ask who that was?" Natalie asked.

"The woman's a piece of work" William answered. "Let's go, resistance is futile."

They showered, dressed and arrived at 9:30AM after a 20 minute walk. Liz-Beth served coffee and biscuits.

"What kind of breakfast is this? Is this what you got me up at 8:00AM for?" William asked. "You said you were cooking breakfast."

"I said I was *fixing* breakfast. You know I only cook with Maria. I can't believe you fell for that one."

"I was half asleep."

"Watch out for old age and treachery, William. Maria will be here this evening. She'll cook us a great Spanish dinner. Good morning Natalie. You *do* wake up beautiful like I do. What makes you glow so early on Sunday morning?"

Natalie blushed.

"Never mind."

Joshua pulled up in the pickup truck. "Biscuit special, Liz-Beth?"

"You know me, Josh."

Joshua and William left within the hour.

"What's all this about?" Natalie asked.

"I needed to get him out of the house so we can have some girl talk."

"If you don't mind I'm going have that bath you promised."

After an hour of bliss in the bathroom sanctuary Natalie joined Liz-Beth and Mr. Chuckles in the great room. Natalie approached the cage.

"What's wrong with Mr. Chuckles today? He's sulking."

"He looks sad sometimes, Nat. A visit from William seems to be the only thing that perks him up on gloomy days like this one. I think he misses Bunny. He's been much quieter since Bunny passed away."

"You miss him too, don't you? …Sorry, Liz-Beth."

"That's okay, dear. I'll never get over it, but I've learned to live with it."

"Does he know Bunny's gone?"

"I think he does. Birds have memories. They understand the passing of time. I think they understand aging. They read our emotions. Chuckles knows I'm not as happy since Bunny passed. He probably feels the same way for the same reason. He's reading *your* emotions. See how he's watching you?"

"How long do they live?"

"Chuckles is a cockatoo. They can live as long as we do."

"How old is he?"

"I'm not sure. I didn't raise him from a chick. I think he was young when I brought him home."

"Not a chick like we are."

Liz-Beth chuckled. "No, not chicks like us. He might be around longer than me. He could be with you in middle age."

"Can birds cry?"

"Yeah, they can cry. Not with tears. They have feelings. Sometimes I think Chuckles would shed tears if he had them."

They moved to the dining table when Liz-Beth brewed a pot of tea.

"I'm glad we have this chance to talk, Natalie"

"Me too."

"Natalie, I need to ask you about something. I understand if you don't want to discuss it."

"About what?"

"About William. He's your boyfriend. He's also my friend. I care about him, about both of you. Do you mind telling me what's going on with him? Why isn't he doing anything with his life? I know about the business. That isn't forever. He's smart, educated, young. He has a beautiful, wonderful girlfriend. He isn't rich but he can pay the bills for a while. He should be the happiest guy in the world. Pardon me for saying so, you're wasting your lives here. Does he have any ambition?"

"It's okay to ask. I'll share it with you if you promise to keep it between us."

"I promise."

"I have to tell you about his parents."

"John and Miriam."

"Do you know about them?"

"Their photo's hanging on the wall at Duarte's."

"Did you meet them?"

"Everybody in town knew them. They came here two weeks in summer, two in winter, a few weekends during the rest of the year. Everyone ends up at Duarte's. They were a beautiful couple. John celebrated D-Day with Bunny. He was sweet to listen to Bunny go on about the RAF when John was a pilot himself. John was quiet, reserved, sort of mysterious. He didn't share wartime experiences. Bunny talked about them all the time. Miriam was a lovely woman. Very intelligent. Well educated. Much more outgoing than John. I wish I could have spent more time with them."

"What else do you know about them?"

"We knew Miriam was a journalist. We read her articles. She was brilliant. We knew John was an aviator. We knew he worked for Lockheed, not what he did there. Some sort of consulting we thought. We knew he was a flier in the war. Quite a guy from stories I heard about him."

"It can't be overstated."

"Bunny flew in the war too. I met him in England when I went over as a nurse. I wasn't much of a nurse. They made me a Jeep driver. I drove the officers around, smashed up a few Jeeps before I got the hang of it. I was wild. That's how I met Bunny. Driving RAF officers to pubs near London."

Liz-Beth laughed. "I'm a farm girl. I learned to drive a tractor at age 12, drove a Jeep like it could run over everything like a tractor, and so fast. I was a menace on narrow English roads."

"Must have been fun."

"It was."

"How well did you know John?"

"Not well. We heard about some of his experiences when his buddies met him at Duarte's. Somebody named Jason who worked with him at Lockheed in Sunnyvale visited sometimes. A mechanic named Eddie. Miriam shared some. There were newspaper clippings, photographs. That's always the way with the brave ones. They think it's just doing their job. Bunny was outspoken about the RAF. He loved the men he flew with. He never spoke about his own adventures. They were rich and extensive. He said they didn't want to go to war. When they had to, they wanted to win. They didn't want to let anyone down, especially not each other. Some experiences must have been terrifying. Memories were difficult. Sadness for lost friends, the horror of it. They saved the world."

"From the beginning?"

"The beginning. I want to know it all."

"William's father grew up in the Midwest, somewhere in Nebraska I think. His people farmed; small family farms. Some were in dry goods. His father owned a mercantile store. When he was little, John saw an airplane at a state fair. He was hooked. After high school he joined the Navy to learn to fly. He trained at Hampton Roads, Norfolk, Virginia. He and one of the cadets became friends. Guy named Cohen. From New York City."

"A farm kid and a city boy. Odd couple. From a banking family?"

"Yeah. How did you know that?"

"I didn't."

"The family had a summer home in the Hamptons, on Long Island. A waterfront mansion. Like something out of Gatsby. Cohen invited John to a summer weekend party on a four-day leave. John's eyes landed on Miriam. She attracted him like a magnet to a compass needle."

"I can understand that. She was beautiful, wasn't she?"

"Yes, and exotic to a farm boy. He approached her and it was magic. She was intelligent, educated. He was so Midwest Norman Rockwell, dashing in his uniform."

"Like Bunny. They were quite a couple, weren't they?"

"They lit the room, Liz-Beth." Natalie paused to think about them.

"Was she a Cohen too?"

"No. Family friend from private school. A high school senior in love with a handsome naval aviator, in love with an intelligent exotic East Coast beauty. He visited whenever he could get there. They were popular. It made people happy to be around them. Miriam was accepted to Syracuse University School of Journalism. Classes began in the fall. They didn't want to separate, but Syracuse was too far and too difficult to get to in those days. John knew he had to ask her to wait or marry him. The Hamptons were a dream world to him. He didn't think he could give her anything like it. It didn't matter to her. She believed in him, knew he would succeed at something. She didn't need to be rich. She wanted a career of her own. He made a terrible mistake."

"He broke up with her?"

"Worse. He let it wither. When he earned his wings the navy stationed him in Coronado, San Diego. The other end of the world. She might have changed her plans and gone with him, attended another school if he asked her. He didn't know he mattered more to her than life in New York."

"Foolish boy. I followed Bunny to Singapore. He followed me to San Francisco. You make the life you want together. It isn't where you live. It's who you live with."

"John thought he didn't deserve her. He was afraid she would break his heart. He broke it himself and hers with it."

"How foolish to give up something so special so easily. How did she take it?"

"She was deeply disappointed. He went to San Diego, promised to visit, but never did. Eventually they stopped writing. After a while she started dating."

"How did John take it?"

"He suffered loneliness, depression. He left the military after his tour. Joined a flying circus to do the things he saw them do the first time he saw an airplane. When his parents died, he sold the store and bought a biplane. He lived like a flying hobo who owned the transportation. A tumbleweed with no permanent address. He flew around the country wherever the wind blew him, performing at county fairs, selling rides to rich people. He landed in fields, stayed with friends. When war broke out he sold the plane and rejoined the Navy. Because of his age and experience they made him a flight instructor. He wanted to get into the fighting. The following year he transferred to the Pacific, ended up at Henderson Field on Guadalcanal, one of the first flights to land on the island from a carrier after marines captured the airport."

"In the Cactus Air Force? They had a terrible time. Bunny told me about it."

"Miserable living conditions. Temporary shelters, hot, humid, daily rain, bad food, mosquitoes, disease. A high percentages of them were always sick. I don't know how they flew in those conditions. The Japanese bombed the airfield every night. The Marines fought in the jungle next to the runway. The Japanese Army had not been beaten anywhere yet. They might have lost the field and the island. Some of the pilots he knew didn't make it home. John was a natural, a phenomenal flier from the experience before the war. Skills and confidence brought with him probably saved him. He became a legend."

"Bunny told me the Japanese had better planes."

"In the beginning, that's what I understand. We shot down some of their best pilots before Guadalcanal, at the battles of the Coral Sea and Midway, some of the ones who bombed Pearl Harbor. The air war was pretty much an even fight. By the following year we had better planes. After that it became easier. John flew through the tough period."

"How do you know so much about this?"

"You mean how does a girl know history? Have you read Barbara Tuchman?"

"I'm ashamed of myself."

"They called John's unit the Pelican Squadron."

"What a story. What happened to Miriam?"

"After graduation, she found a job at the New York Times. She moved to the city, married a guy who turned out to be a jackass. Would you like to guess?"

"Cohen?"

"Yep," Natalie nodded with contempt. "Robert Cohen. William's father was Miriam's second husband."

"Why did she do that?"

"She couldn't find what she had with John. Robert hadn't channeled his inner jackass yet. He looked like a good catch. She wanted to marry and start a family. Friends and family pushed them together. John was her man but he left. She never stopped loving him, but she didn't want to spend the rest of her life pining over him. Robert didn't love anybody but Robert. He was all about ambition and money. He cheated on her from the beginning. He wanted someone who could help him with his career."

"Why didn't she divorce him?"

"She wanted to make it work long after she knew she couldn't. Robert followed the family into the banking business. He married a career, not a woman. He didn't let it get in the way of his philandering hobby. Miriam stayed busy with The Times. Her uncle was another banker. After the war started, he moved to Washington to work for the Roosevelt administration. He helped the Pentagon negotiate military contracts, expand production, supply war material. Miriam wanted to cover the war from as close to a war zone as possible and as far away from Robert as possible. She used her uncle's influence to obtain an assignment in Darwin, Australia. Robert stayed in New York and took a mistress. Miriam was happy to be on the other side of the world."

"I think I know where this is going."

"Yep. The Japanese withdrew from Guadalcanal in 1943. When immediate danger passed, Miriam flew over in a transport plane to research an article. She stepped off the plane and walked right into John."

"Oh, God. I knew it. She didn't know he was there?"

"No idea. They had no contact in years."

"In war, the unusual is usual. What happened after that?"

"The romance picked up where it ended. John visited her in Darwin. They had quite an adventure. He took her up in a two-seat reconnaissance plane. They were in the air when he spotted Japanese planes flying in to bomb the city. The Japanese made a mess of Darwin. The flight might have saved her life. John radioed it in and flew out of harm's way. The Zeros came after them. Their plane was too fast. They got away. Robert rejoined the Navy after Miriam moved to Australia. He expected to be drafted anyway. He heard about the affair. He used the same influence Miriam did to have himself posted there. Miriam couldn't stop him. She did the next best thing. She used her uncle's military contacts to post him to John's squadron. She knew John would look after him."

"She used John's love for her, and his friendship with Robert to protect her no-good husband?"

"Yeah."

"What a terrible thing to do."

"It was. But Robert was her husband even if he wasn't a good one. She felt as long as they were married she had to do what she could to get him through the war. Would you do something like that for Bunny?"

"For Bunny, anything. For a jackass, nothing."

"She told John before Robert arrived. He took it badly. He agreed to look after his friend. Then he stopped talking to her. She was very hurt. She didn't expect that. As before, she couldn't get through to him."

"How did this turn out?"

"Robert was full of undeserved bravado, a mediocre flyer, a big cockup. He flew for glory, took stupid chances, put fellow pilots at risk. John wouldn't have put up with it for anyone but Miriam. Robert ignored protocol. On patrol he broke formation, went after a Jap plane on his own he thought was an easy kill, flew into an ambush. The rest of the flight followed to save him, got a in a vicious dogfight with the Japanese, lost a couple of planes. The rest returned low on fuel, their planes shot up, lucky to return at all. John put on a flying clinic. They still talk about it. He drew off the Japanese planes, shot down a couple of them before they damaged his. His buddies couldn't match his maneuvers. They couldn't follow to protect him. He almost sacrificed himself. John flew into the clouds to lead the Japanese fliers away. He earned the Navy Cross. "

"Commendable and foolish. What happened to Robert?"

"He dove and ran."

"The coward."

"The Japanese planes returned to base. John lost his radio. Nobody knew his situation or location. He was wounded. His plane was finished. He ditched in the ocean near a deserted island, swam to the beach, hid in the jungle. A coast watcher saw the plane come down. He sent local fishermen to retrieve him. They spent a few nights island hopping in a small boat, hiding him under fishing gear in case a Japanese patrol stopped them. They stayed in the jungles during the day until they returned him. The base was shocked. They thought he was dead. The coast watcher didn't tell anyone to prevent the Japanese from looking for him."

"He's lucky the natives didn't eat him."

"He worried about that. Miriam was in Darwin when she learned about it. She felt guilty, ashamed. She didn't expect anything like that to happen. Robert never thanked him."

"What did they do about him?"

"They transferred him to Australia, promoted him to a desk job. He never put a bullet in a Japanese plane, but he claimed to. He knew his career in Asia was over. He transferred back to the States, spent the rest of the war at the Pentagon, made a career out of frontline experience with anybody who didn't know the truth."

"What happened to John?"

"Combat fatigue. So many fights. The near-death experience shattered his nerves. He lost focus. Miriam was too close to avoid thinking about her. It tortured him. He needed her, but didn't want to see her. Losing her twice was too much. He spiraled down, became a liability, couldn't lead anymore, couldn't fight anymore. His commander had to remove him. John accepted transfer to Corpus Christi Naval Air Station. He spent the rest of the war teaching combat tactics to intermediate fliers. George Bush was a student."

"George Bush the President?"

"The same. A sad ending to a promising career. His flying reputation remained intact. They still talk about him."

"What happened to Miriam?"

"John left without a word. She heard about it from the other fliers. She wrote to him in Corpus Christi, told him how sorry she was, apologized for pushing Robert on him. There were several beautiful letters unopened and unanswered. John saved them. William opened them, read them and shared them with me after his parents were gone. He keeps them in a box in a closet in

Mountain View. I cried when I read them. She loved him so much, Liz-Beth."

Liz-Beth's brow furrowed. "It makes me want to cry too."

"Miriam stayed in Darwin until the war ended. She moved to Japan for two years to cover the occupation. Robert returned to New York."

"Bunny and I were living in Singapore."

"When Miriam returned to New York, she and Robert talked it out. They had a lot to discuss, so much hurt. They blamed it all on the war. Robert claimed he reformed. They decided to make a fresh start."

"Tigers rarely change their stripes."

"Miriam was excessively loyal, foolish maybe. They moved to San Francisco. He opened a banking office to raise money for Silicon Valley companies. She went to work as a world affairs editor for the San Francisco Examiner. Didn't take long for Robert to backpedal into old habits."

"He sounds like Tom Buchanan in *The Great Gatsby*."

"Exactly, but Miriam was no Daisy. She deserved better."

"What happened to John?"

"He needed a quiet place to recover. A mechanic at the air field in Texas, someone he knew from Guadalcanal, told him about a welder named Mersman he knew at the Boeing bomber plant in Renton, Washington. He lived alone in a cabin on vacation property on the east side of Lake Washington owned by a wealthy Seattle logging family. They hadn't used the property in a generation. They rented it for almost nothing just to have someone living on it. A stream along a trail in a ravine on 35 secluded, heavily wooded acres fanned into a delta where it reached the lake. You could see Mt. Rainier and Mt. St. Helens from the waterfront."

"Sounds lovely."

"And peaceful. A quarter mile long dirt access road crossed a concrete foot bridge over the stream. It was impassible by car, steep, narrow, muddy half the year. Mersman parked a pickup truck on the street at the top of the hill to commute to work in.

A second cabin was unoccupied. Tiny, sparsely furnished, two rooms, with no TV or phone service, a small kitchen and bath, not unlike the one William and I live in. The way John described it our shack is better."

John's friend wrote to Seattle. John rented it sight unseen, picked up his pay, and said goodbye to the Navy. He hitched a ride to Seattle from a friend who flew cargo. He took a taxi to the property, walked down the hill with his duffle bag and moved in. John said it saved him. A quiet cabin in a park, where nobody knew him or the part of his life he needed to forget. Just what he needed.

Fall and winter were wet and gloomy. John laid on a musty old couch in his uniform with a blanket over him for the first ten days listening to steady soothing rainfall on the cabin roof. Mersman did the shopping and cooking for both of them. John said his mind played a feature film of his life across a screen behind his eyelids. He tried to make sense of it as he melted into the couch. After that, he wandered the property for days when he didn't fall in and out of a light sleep, eating little, drinking gallons of iced tea to avoid dehydration. Mersman was very kind. He brought what little mail came to John's postal box, a letter or two forwarded from people John knew in the service, government correspondence left unopened, nothing from Miriam. She gave up when he left Corpus Christi and didn't know where he went.

In spring it ended. John snapped out of it one weekend morning and sprang off the couch. He borrowed the keys to the truck, hiked up the muddy hill, and drove around the lake past the Boeing plant in Renton where they built B-17 and B-29 bombers. He stopped for a meal in a lakefront town named Bellevue. After lunch, he returned to the cabin and followed the trail to the waterfront. He walked along the stream to the delta where he sat on a log. A single engine seaplane banked over Sand Point and glided down toward Kenmore Floatplane Harbor. Engine idling, the plane skimmed the water 20 yards from shore. John saw the sun reflect off the pilot's Ray-Bans. They saluted each other. Like the first time he saw an airplane, John knew what he needed to do."

"That's inspiring. How do you know all this?"

"Family legend. John shared memories of Mersman and Seattle. Miriam filled in the rest."

"He must have been a great story teller."

"He was. I had Dickens for an uncle, but the stories were non-fiction. We made him tell us over and over."

"You must have loved him."

"Oh, yeah. We all adored Uncle John." Natalie sobbed. She wiped her eyes and continued.

"When he returned to the cabin, John asked Mersman if he thought he could find work at Boeing. They went to Renton together. Mersman introduced him to managers who knew John's reputation from fliers who served in the Pacific. They offered him a job testing some hot new plane they were prototyping, the first jet bomber. John turned it down. He thought piloting a bomber, no matter how hot, was like bus driving compared with sports car racing. John was a fighter pilot. The Boeing people had Lockheed contacts. John flew down to Moffett Field in California and accepted work testing single seat airplanes and avionics. It worked for him. The following year he bought a house in Mountain View."

"*The* house in Mountain View?"

"The very one, and later *the* cottage in Pescadero."

"Of course. God, what a story." Liz-Beth looked away for a moment.

"I'm taking so long to tell this. Do you mind?"

"Are you kidding? This is fascinating, a movie script. You're a wonderful story teller."

"Can I use your bathroom?"

"Sure. Like crumpets? I have cheese and tomato."

"Sure."

So many stories, Liz-Beth thought. *The war made them. Same time Bunny and I moved to San Francisco and opened the trading company.* She toasted the crumpets and brought them to the dining room.

Natalie leaned over the sink and stared in the mirror. *I never shared this story, not all of it with anyone,* she thought. *I needed to. I'm so lucky to have a friend like Liz-Beth.*

Liz-Beth sat patiently. She sipped her tea and waited for Natalie to return. Chuckles sat quietly on his perch, watching and listening respectfully as if he understood the meaning of the words.

"There's a lot more. Are you sure you don't want me to stop here?"

"Heavens no."

"Several years later, late one evening he answered a knock on the cottage door. Miriam stood in the doorway."

Liz-Beth smiled. "The same cottage. Just like you did."

"Yeah. Like I did. It was different for them. Robert couldn't keep his fly zippered. She finally left him."

"Why doesn't this surprise me? How did she know how to find John?"

"In the newspaper business they can find anybody. They have an auto and airplane show at the Half Moon Bay Airport every April."

"Pacific Coast Dream Machines."

"That's it. John flew aerobatic demonstrations. His name appeared in articles in Bay Area papers. The famous fighter pilot from the Pacific Theater. Miriam referenced one of them. His address was easy."

"She never stopped loving him."

"No, she never did."

"What a courageous woman. He could have turned her away. What happened next?"

"He invited her in. They talked it through like they should have before he left Norfolk and she went to college. She told him she would have made a life with him no matter what, that she didn't care about the family money or lifestyle, that they could make their own money, enough to be happy. She told him she loved him and still did. She never returned to San Francisco. She filed for divorce, didn't ask for anything. Robert didn't object. He was done with her. Miriam and John had a simple wedding outside the cottage on the knoll in Pescadero with a justice of the peace. Joshua and Maggie attended, the owners of Duarte's, a few of John's friends from work, two friends of Miriam's from the Chronicle. They had a lot of life to catch up on. William came along years later."

"She must have been middle aged."

"They took a chance. William was born in 1969. Miriam was in her early forties."

Liz-Beth rested her elbows on the table, her face in her hands.

"Natalie, I know I asked. How do you know so much about this?"

"Miriam was my aunt."

Liz-Beth's mouth fell open. "You're sleeping with your cousin?"

Natalie laughed. "That's always a shocker. William and I are cousins by marriage. Miriam's brother, Milton Blumenthal, is my step father, my mother's second husband."

"I might have fainted."

Natalie chuckled. "William and I can have children, if he wants them, if he asks me to marry him, if a family can live in a two-room shack."

"Natalie Blumenthal. I hadn't heard that before. Such a lovely name."

"Thank you. I love my name. I'm not giving it up. When we were kids we were always after Aunt Miriam to tell us about her and John. We knew it was quite a love story and John would never tell it. One afternoon when we gathered in Mountain View, men outside tossing a football, women in the house, she gave in, sat us down, told us all of it. She pulled out the letters, the photos, showed us medals, uniforms, newspaper clippings, an afternoon of it, the whole story. Can you imagine the cousins, not much more than little girls at the time hearing this great family love story? It was better than any movie."

"Do you know what happened to William's parents?"

"I'd rather not talk about that. Can't we stop here, with a happy ending?"

"Please. I need to know what happened."

Natalie glanced at Chuckles as if the bird could coach her. "We don't know. They kept a small plane at the Half Moon Bay airport. Sometimes John commuted in it. They flew it on weekends when William was old enough to spend the day with friends. They flew up and down the coast, as far as Napa or Sonoma, just to be in the air together."

"Like father, like son."

"What do you mean?"

"The car."

"Oh, yeah. Never thought of that. He does love driving that car. More than me" she said with sadness in her voice.

"Not more than you. Please go on."

"Something happened on the last flight. The plane must have gone into the ocean. It could be anywhere between here and San Francisco, further north maybe, or down to Santa Barbara or San Diego. Nobody knows. No one knew they were missing until the following day. A search turned up nothing. They were assumed drowned or killed in an ocean crash. That was it. No bodies, no plane."

"So sad. How did William take it?"

"Very hard. He loved his parents. We all did. They deserved long happy lives after what they went through. The service was very sad. No bodies, Liz-Beth. I wasn't prepared for that. It's harder when you don't know where they are or what happened to them. William moved out of his dorm room and into the Mountain View house. He wanted to close up the cottage. I wouldn't let him. He hated coming here. He wanted to burn it down. It made him think about his parents but it also made him think about what he wanted to do with himself. He started a company in his dorm room after his parents died. He built a prototype as a class project. He recruited grad students to help. He didn't have money for salaries or office space. He paid them with stock. They turned the Mountain View house into an engineering lab, filled it with tables and racks of electronic equipment, parts and components. I don't know how he could live in it. A friend at Intel tested their product on their network. It worked. I remember how exciting that was. They gave him an order and invested enough money in the company to lease office space and hire full time employees. They introduced him to additional investors who brought in more money. They used it to hire people and expand. The internet went crazy. The company grew so fast. Some of the investors wanted to go for a large funding round to expand the company. It scared William. His friends at Intel thought the bubble was going to burst."

"That would make it about mid-1999?"

"Yes. His friends at Intel told him something called their 'book-to-bill forecast' showed orders declining. It's some kind of business forecasting system. They make giant investments, billions of dollars in new factory equipment. It takes years. They get crushed if business declines. He told his friends what the board wanted him to do. They said they were advising customers to cut back their orders. The carriers had built up too much capacity. They had miles of something they called 'dark fiber' in the ground and no customers for it."

"What were they doing? They were professionally managed companies."

"William told me the phone company shareholders were screaming at them to keep building out infrastructure to make the stock prices go up. They were looking at the internet companies, all the money people were making – for a while. They threatened to sell the shares if management didn't participate."

"What a crazy business. Bunny and I bought something for a dollar and sold it for two dollars. We liked that better. We couldn't get rich overnight but we did well enough. It was steady and easy to manage. It worked for us."

"I like that better too. You don't live in the middle of a gold rush where people lose their minds. I remember William said when the music is playing, you have to get up and dance."

"How do you know about this?"

"It started when I studied fine art at UCSF. I dated William and stayed with him in Mountain View on weekends. They were possessed. They practically worked 24/7. They set the lab up on the other side of our bedroom wall. They lived on Coke and pizza. I saw it all."

"What happened after that?"

"Business slowed down. William argued with investors over what to do about it."

"What did the board say?"

"They *were* the board."

"*Oh.*"

"They thought the slowdown was temporary. They wanted to raise more money and expand. William wanted to cut back and conserve what they had. Business kept slowing while they argued. Customers cancelled orders. Pretty soon the company was in financial trouble. The board blamed William. It made him very angry. He told me they might have sailed through it if they hadn't expanded."

Liz-Beth took a deep breath. "Then they told him he was out."

"One of them said they wanted to buy his shares even though the company had little value."

"For pennies I bet."

"Less than he invested to start it."

"The other board members?"

"They were in on it."

"This is smelly. I bet somebody bought them. He who has the gold makes the rules."

"We know who did it."

"Who?"

"Robert."

Liz-Beth's eyes widened. "*Robert?* Miriam's first husband?"

"Yes."

"How did he get involved in this?

"He was a partner of one of William's early investors."

"Robert Cohen?" Liz-Beth asked in disbelief.

"Robert Cousie."

Liz-Beth shuddered. Her heart skipped a beat. *"Robert…Robert Cousie?* Please… I'm confused. Are there two Roberts?"

"No. I didn't mean to confuse you. He got into trouble with the SEC over some stock transaction. After that he changed his name from Cohen to Cousie."

"Miriam's first husband is *Robert Cousie?"*

"You know him?"

The blood drained out of Liz-Beth's face.

"What's wrong, Liz-Beth. Are you OK?"

"Give me a minute."

Liz-Beth covered her mouth with a hand, staggered to the kitchen, filled a glass from the faucet and drank. She wiped her mouth, leaned on a counter, and stared out the kitchen window. *Oh my God,* she thought. *Robert Cousie.*

Natalie called into the kitchen. "Are you OK, Liz-Beth?" *Why did Liz-Beth react like that?* She wondered.

"Give me a minute, Natalie."

Liz-Beth whispered to herself. *Miriam's first husband, John's friend who introduced them, invested in William's business, forced William out and bought his equity at a loss to William. How do I get my head around this?*

Liz-Beth composed herself and returned to the dining room. She stared across the table at Natalie. "That's quite story for a little old lady to hear all at one time."

"You aren't so old or little."

"Thank you," Liz-Beth said while she regained her composure.

"Do you know Robert Cousie?"

"Oh, yes. I know him. Twenty-five years ago he squeezed a business associate, a friend of Bunny's and mine, out of *his* company."

"What happened?"

Liz-Beth hesitated, decided Natalie deserved to know, not all of it.

"The poor man lost everything."

"He did it again. To William, and *Me*. My own uncle. How could he do that? How could Aunt Miriam have married such a man?"

"He's a sociopath, Natalie. It's his business."

"Why hasn't anybody caught up with him?"

"Somebody will."

That bastard, Liz-Beth thought. *John and Miriam were dead. Not enough for him, he went after their son.*

"I know the rest. Pescadero is William's self-imposed exile. He blames himself for losing the company, no longer trusts anybody, doesn't want go back and do it again. Right out of Alexandre Dumas except he hasn't tried a comeback."

"This isn't fiction, Liz-Beth. It's our lives." Natalie's chin trembled. She fought hard not to burst into tears. "We were happy before this."

"What did William do about it?"

"He sold his shares and left. He had to. He put his inheritance, all that work, everything he had in that company."

"This is hideous. Did he speak to anyone about it?"

"No, he thought the board…They were all he had."

"Did he confront Robert?"

"Robert was a silent partner of one of the investors. William discovered it later. He thought the board lost confidence in him and wanted him out. Not all of them did. William thinks Robert and his partner swayed the others."

"William came here after that?"

"Yes. The business decline last summer frustrated him, made him impossible to live with. He became short tempered, mean to his friends, mean to *me*. I tried. I couldn't stay with him in Mountain View. I couldn't fix his company. I told him it didn't matter. He could do something else if it didn't work. We could make it together. He wouldn't listen. He grew cold, verbally abusive. I felt degraded. I told him I needed a break, wanted to stay in the city for a while. He didn't even ask me to stay or try discuss it. He let me walk out without trying to hold on to me. That hurt so much. It's terrible, but not the end of the world. We weren't broke. We could have taken time off, gone on vacation, someplace where there are no engineers, no technology, no investors. He wouldn't give it a chance, Liz-Beth. He didn't want me."

Natalie burst into tears. Liz-Beth walked around the table and put an arm around her. Natalie buried her face in Liz-Beth's chest.

"He wanted you, Natalie. The world imploded on him. He couldn't bear it."

"I don't know what I'm going to do. I'm glad we're back together, but I can't live here doing nothing in that shack for the rest of my life. I feel like I threw my career under a bus for nothing. We've known each other since we were kids. We dated for years. My parents lived in Sunnyvale, not far from the Beckinsdales'. We grew up together. I loved him forever. We went to high school together. For years we were just friends, but I adored him. I never lost hope. I kept trying. Finally, we were a couple, but I never felt needed."

"He needs you like he needed oxygen. He just didn't know it."

"All he cared about was computers. He's such a nerd. He only wanted to play with his transistors. What am I going to do? I can't spend my life in a shack with a man who doesn't give a crap about me. I don't want another man. I want William."

"This is nonsense. Some men don't know how to tell a woman they love and need them. Some of them don't even know they do. Any fool can see William needs and loves you. A man can't spend his life living in a closet with a woman he doesn't love. You're a couple, Natalie. I doubt either of you could be happy without the other."

"Why doesn't he act like it? Why do I always have to be the one to hold us together?"

"He may be an idiot, but he's your idiot."

"Do you think he would notice if I slashed my wrists?"

"Good. Say something ridiculous. Here, dry your eyes. Don't flood my house."

Liz-Beth handed Natalie a handkerchief.

"He loves that goddamn car and that ratty stuffed pelican more than me."

"No he doesn't. Think about everything both of you have gone through. If your love for each other hadn't been so strong, you wouldn't be together. You're living a low-grade nightmare. If not for that you would be the happiest couple on earth. It won't last. Stick with it a while longer."

Natalie stopped sobbing.

"When I met William on the beach one morning, he was the most lost, most depressed young man I ever met. That changed when you arrived. He's pulling himself together. I see the progress. In spite of all of it, he's happy and it's because of you."

Natalie blotted her cheeks and looked at Liz-Beth.

"There are 1,000 months in a lifetime. You can spare a few more. Keep the MG. Get out of the cottage. Go to San Francisco. Drive to Santa Cruz, Carmel. Visit the Hearst Castle. If you have to go, you'll always have this time together. You will know you gave it your best. Can there be another love of your life?"

"No that's impossible."

"Would you settle for second best? God forbid, someone who turns out like Robert. I don't want to think about it. Promise me you won't leave. If you feel like leaving, you'll come here and talk to me."

"Ok, I'll try. You're a wonderful friend, Liz-Beth. Thank you."

"You haven't been here that long. Something good will happen."

"He'll get a job and we'll build an addition?" Natalie managed a smile.

"That's my girl."

A red Alfa pulled into the driveway.

"Oh my God. It's four o'clock. It seems like we've been talking for hours."

"You better fix yourself up. Your man is here."

Natalie rushed to the hall bathroom.

William came through the door wearing a big smile.

"It sat for half a year and started right up."

Mr. Chuckles paced back and forth on his perch when William stepped into the house. He clamped his beak on the door of the cage, swung his claws to the bars, and bobbed his head.

Liz-Beth laughed. "You better say hello to your friend before he breaks out of prison."

William opened the cage and brought Chuckles out on a wrist. Chuckles touched his beak to William's nose, walked up his arm, and perched contentedly on a shoulder. Chuckles swayed, bobbed his head and made happy parrot noises.

"Maybe he should move in with you."

"I prefer visiting."

"Maria and I clean his cage and feed him. You have all the fun."

"Works for me. Where's Natalie?"

Natalie burst out of the bathroom. She threw her arms around William and kissed him. Chuckles scrambled around William's back to get out of the way. Liz-Beth went to the pantry to bring Chuckles a treat.

"Whoa, girl, I've only been gone a few hours. Did Liz-Beth have you locked in the bathroom?"

"I missed you."

Liz-Beth's eyes rolled around in their sockets. "Are you two hungry?" she asked. "Should I make dinner, or do you want to borrow a room?"

"Both. I'm starving. Eat now, room later. Rum for Mr. Chuckles." William said. "Yo, ho, ho, Miss Natalie," Mr. Chuckles said.

Twenty-Eight

William and Natalie left after dinner. Liz-Beth made herself a very dry martini. She sipped it in a trance in the great room while she thought about what Natalie shared with her. Chuckles sensed she wanted to be alone with her thoughts. He stood quietly on his perch and watched like a sentinel.

Liz-Beth knew she would never forget the afternoon conversation with Natalie. She let the story float through an alcohol-numbed mind. When she finished the martini she kissed Mr. Chuckles and returned him to his cage. Chuckles paced. He swayed on his perch trying to hold Liz-Beth's attention as if he thought she needed distraction, though he couldn't know why. Liz-Beth's mood, something to do with Natalie is as far as a parrot can reach.

Liz-Beth decided on a walk. She pulled on a suede jacket, slipped on a pair of walking shoes, and donned a hat. A cool winter evening, the sun had gone down, the day given way to dusk. A light fog blanketed the coast forecasting an eerie night. It would soon be dark. Liz-Beth walked from her cottage on Cloverdale to Pescadero Creek Road where she turned left and continued toward the ocean. She paused for a moment at the post office, crossed and walked north on Stage Road past the open door of Duarte's tavern. No sounds emerged from inside. The village looked deserted. She continued past the First National Bank branch building, Maggie and Joshua's general store, Norm's market. Somebody's dog trotted toward her from the north end of the village on the opposite side of the street. Large and black, the dog glanced in her direction before passing disinterested under a street lamp, and disappearing into an alley.

Liz-Beth crossed the bridge at North Street where the Pescadero Creek Inn occupied the corner property at Stage Road. The lights of the Inn illuminated guests sitting at dining room tables next to picture windows. Locals maybe, she may have known them. She continued along Stage Road past the last lamp where the street turned into an unlit county road. The sky grew darker. A three-quarter moon penetrated the fog and outlined the path. Liz-Beth took the west trail past Willow Farm, through Pescadero Marsh, the land she and Bunny traded the county for the wildlife buffer behind New Cotswolds.

Liz-Beth walked across Cabrillo Highway onto Pescadero State Beach. She removed her shoes and continued to the water's edge. The beach still held warmth from the sun's rays. When she reached the ocean she stood in the sand and let the waves lap her ankles. She gazed into the darkness and breathed in the salt air as she listened to the surf crash over the rocks. Sea lions slept on boulders still warm from the afternoon sun. Birds nested for the night. Liz-Beth folded her arms across her chest. She turned and swayed with the waves. She thought about what she had learned in the afternoon. She wondered what the rocks could tell her if they could speak. *Sukie would know,* she thought, *and Bunny. I wish you were here Bunny*, she whispered to a breeze. She wanted him back if only once to ask him what she should do.

Liz-Beth turned and retraced her steps. She crossed a deserted highway, walked back through the park, along Stage Road, across the bridge that arched over Pescadero Creek. Past the Inn, past Norm's, the General Store, the bank building, to the intersection where Duarte's and the post office building stood across from one another, unchanged in a hundred years. While she walked to the beach the locals came out for the evening, as much as inhabitants of Pescadero do. She heard music and laughter from inside Duarte's, through the open door. She didn't look in. A group of people she might have known passed through the entry. She lowered her head so the brim of her hat shadowed her face. No one recognized her in the dim light. Casting eyes at the sidewalk, she continued as they passed.

Liz-Beth turned left at Pescadero Creek Road. She crossed when she reached Cloverdale and turned down the street to her cottage. She entered the house, picked up Mr. Chuckles' cage and carried the bird to her bedroom. He stared at her.

"I need you to sleep in here tonight, Chuckles," she told the bird.

Mr. Chuckles made a parrot noise. He looked into Liz-Beth's eyes as if he understood. He shifted his weight from one foot to the other. He bowed and cocked his head, watching her as long as he could, until she lowered the shroud over his cage.

Liz-Beth returned to the great room. She sat on a sofa in the dark. She thought about Edgar and Evelyn. She thought about John and Miriam. She thought about William and Natalie, the things that happened to them, the challenges ahead, how her life with Bunny had been rich and easy. How lucky she had been. *Life can be so unfair,* she thought. Liz-Beth felt guilty for her good fortune and sadness for her friends. She dropped her head in her hands and cried for William and Natalie. She wondered how she could help her new friends.

Twenty-Nine

Liz-Beth called the general store.

"Can we meet for dinner, Maggie?"

"Sure. What's up Liz-Beth?"

"I'd rather wait until I see you."

"Everything OK?"

"Yeah, fine. Tell you about it at dinner."

"Should I bring Josh?"

"That would be good."

"Do you want us to pick you up?"

"No, I'll walk. Can we meet at Duarte's?"

"We can be there around seven."

"See you then."

Duarte's is the town tavern. Opened in 1894 as a saloon and barbershop, it closed during prohibition, survived flooding, bar fights and drunken cooks. Operated by the fourth generation of the founders, they source daily catch from the Half Moon Bay fishing fleet, serve grass-fed beef and free-range chicken bought from coastal ranches. They cook with herbs and vegetables grown in the tavern garden.

Unchanged since fire consumed most of Pescadero in the late 1920's, Duarte's is a fixture on the coast. The walls are decorated in photos of famous locals; surfers and aviators, farmers and store owners, artists and veterans of foreign wars, bootleggers and fisherman, heroes accumulated over a hundred years. Near the corner of Stage Road and Pescadero Creek Road, everyone in Pescadero eventually wanders into Duarte's. Like the tavern motto, it's "Where Friends Meet."

Liz-Beth read the San Francisco Chronicle while she nursed a pint of Guinness and waited for Joshua and Maggie. She chose the booth below a photo of Bunny in his RAF uniform dated June 6th, 1964, the twentieth anniversary of the allied invasion of Normandy. It reminds her of Bunny leaning on the bar, foot on a rail, lifting a glass in a toast. Liz-Beth sat on the bar next to him, her own glass in an outstretched arm celebrating with the crowd. Liz-Beth always chose this booth. It sometimes made her melancholy, but she liked reminiscing. She felt honored that Duarte's hung the photo.

Joshua and Maggie knew where to find her. They ordered two draughts and three bowls of chowder.

"What's the news, Liz-Beth?" Joshua asked.

Liz-Beth summarized her conversation with Natalie.

"I see why you need to talk."

"Those kids mean a lot to me, Maggie. I knew Bunny wouldn't live forever. I thought I prepared for that. I guess I couldn't be. Then Sukie left. I thought I'd cry myself to death. I miss the old mooncalf. Maria is a good friend. I have you two. My friends in San Francisco have their own lives. I don't drive to the city anymore. They never leave. Chuckles is my constant companion. As much as I love him you run out of things to discuss with a bird. Bunny and I were busy enjoying our lives. We never thought about children. I have no family to comfort me or carry on. It troubled me. Then William and Natalie came into my life and I'm no longer lonely. I've fallen for them. They saved me, Maggie. They're the children I never had. If I can help them though this, it will give my life purpose and meaning. I love that boy as if he were my own. I knew it the day I met him on the beach when he called me the nutty lady of Pescadero."

"They had a tough time."

"They're having a tough time, Maggie. We need to help them."

"What do you mean Liz-Beth?"

"Takes a village" Liz-Beth said.

"We can be friends but they aren't our children."

"They aren't, but they're villagers. William needs a team in his corner."

"What do you have in mind, Liz-Beth?"

Maggie glared at Joshua.

"William started LightSwitch, Josh. He spent five years of his life building it. He needs it back."

"I don't like where this is going, Liz-Beth. I care about them too but Josh is retired. I don't want him in a bar fight."

"Hear her out, Maggie."

"Jesus, Josh" Maggie said.

"I'm not asking Josh to get involved. I need advice."

"Why don't you help William start another business?"

"I thought about that Josh. I'm afraid he may never get over having LightSwitch stolen from him. Even if he succeeds at something else, if he doesn't confront and resolve this, it could haunt him."

"Do you want to start a brawl at your age? How old are you Liz-Beth? Seventy-two, seventy-three?"

"None of your damn business, Maggie."

"Hey, you two. Let's not have our own war."

"I feel like I have one more fight in me, Josh. I want to make it a good one."

"Your mind's made up?"

"It is."

"You would do it without me?"

"Yes."

"Do you really want to take on a couple of professional white collar criminals?"

"Not by myself."

"You're too old for this, Josh. You retired because it's too stressful."

"She can't do it herself, Maggie. These guys are predators."

"What do you know about startup technology companies, Liz-Beth?"

"Not a damn thing, Maggie. I know William went diving in a shark tank without a cage and they tore him to pieces. This is wrong Maggie, very wrong."

"You're gonna level the playing field for him?"

"If I can."

"William has to decide for himself if he wants to get off the mat. Even if he does, how in the world can you possibly help him get his business back?"

"That's what I need Josh to tell me."

"If Dunn and Cousie saw an opportunity to make a good deal for themselves there's nothing illegal about that. If they committed fraud, maybe. Fraud is hard to prove."

"Can't an agreement be voided if it's excessively one-sided?" Liz-Beth asked.

"How do you prove they knew the shares were worth vastly more than they paid William at the time they bought them?"

"Are the two of you seriously thinking about taking these guys on? 'Scuse me Liz-Beth, you've been retired for years. Josh, you're a general store keeper."

"Just a minute, Maggie. You know I ran an international trading company. I invested in successful businesses and served on their boards. Joshua was as fine a corporate attorney as I ever knew."

Maggie fumed. "I can't listen to any more of this. I'm going to the ladies' room. You two go ahead and plan Armageddon."

"She'll come around, Liz-Beth. She needs to let us talk it through."

"If you were going to go about this how would you do it?"

"I wouldn't. If I did, I'm not doing anything without Maggie's blessing."

Liz-Beth nodded. "I understand."

"If I agree to help you, I'm not going to do much, just provide contacts; give you advice when you need it. I'm not a trial lawyer."

"Fair enough."

"A board can fire a CEO. William has no wrongful termination argument for nonperformance or business disagreement. He may have left with more than he would have if he hadn't been forced out and the business collapsed. They gave him something for his shares. He might have lost it all."

"You mean Dunn and Cousie helped him?"

"Maybe they did, even if they didn't intend to."

"You sound like you're arguing for them."

"I'm trying to show you how they might spin it."

"How could they have harmed him?"

"In a way William could unwind the deal? I don't know. We don't know much about this."

"Try something on me."

"They could have intentionally concealed or misrepresented something to convince him the shares were worth less than they knew they were."

"If they did that, could William contest the transaction?"

"Yes."

"Would it be illegal?"

"I don't know, Liz-Beth. This is hypothetical."

"Attorneys are all alike."

"Retired attorney. If you mean we don't want to say something is true or false when we don't know anything about it yes. I'll stick with my answer."

"I apologize."

"I forgive you. It would be easier to bring a civil case. The burden of proof is easier, the chance of success higher. He can sue to unwind the transaction, receive back pay and entitlements and demand punitive damages. If they think they can lose and the company has value they might pay William to go away. It could be less expensive than fighting him. They can't recover their expenses if they win. They can only avoid paying you. William, I mean."

"I like this game, Josh. If they intentionally caused William to fail, or made it look like he failed so they could fire him, isn't that wrongful termination?"

"It could be," Josh said, in a way that sounded like yes.

"How do we build a case?"

"You mean how do you find out if there is one."

"Yes of course."

Joshua didn't answer.

"If William came to you, if you were still practicing, if he asked you to help, what would you say?"

"I'd tell him to start another company."

"Why?"

"It's easier and has a higher probability of success."

Maggie returned to the booth. "Have the two of you decided how to wage World War Three yet?"

"We're discussing it" Joshua said. "We haven't decided anything." Joshua continued. "You have to find a smoking gun with somebody's prints on it. Right now, you don't even know where to look, what to look for, if there's anything to discover. William got a crappy deal? He can't do anything about that."

"Come on Josh. You know Cousie went after him because Miriam left him for his father."

"It looks that way to us. We know Cousie did something despicable in the past and got away with it. It won't do us any good in court. A good defense attorney might make a plausible argument that Cousie invested in the business to *help* his deceased ex-wife's son, or because he thought it was a good opportunity he learned about consequentially from his partner. He could argue William lost his job because he didn't perform, grabbed some cash on the way out and later decided he didn't get a good enough deal. Now he wants a better one from a company struggling for survival. William could look like a coddled, greedy, disgruntled ex-CEO. Dunn and Cousie might look like angels for handing him a parachute. They didn't have to buy his shares. They could have just terminated him."

"If the company wasn't worth anything, why did they want his shares?"

"How would we know? Even if you convince a jury they committed fraud, you still have to prove damages."

"No harm, no foul."

"That's right, Liz-Beth. There is nothing to contest if William received fair value for his equity or if they didn't know it was worth more than they paid him."

"If there *is* any evidence of wrong doing how do you find it?"

"You're a bulldog, Liz-Beth… You investigate."

"Do you know a good investigator?"

Joshua paused.

"You don't know if they cheated William. It could be a waste of time and money."

"I know it in my *bones*, Josh."

Joshua sighed. "You need someone who specializes in business fraud cases, an expert who performs this work for law firms, or white-collar crime prosecutors."

"Do you know such a person?"

"I do."

"Tell me about him."

"Ex-navy, ex-FBI. Criminal justice degree, investigated corporate criminals at the Bureau. Fearless, honest, smart as hell, hates white collar criminals. Rolodex of government and law enforcement contacts, businessmen he helped over the years. As good as anybody."

"I'd like to know what he can find. What would be the best way to contact him?"

"I'll call him. See if he's available, have him contact you if he's interested. There isn't much appeal to this. Investors take over failing company. Friends think founder might be cheated, no evidence. He likes meaty cases. Maybe for a friend of the family. Leave William out of it for now."

"Why?"

"Snoop around first. If it has legs, you can pull him into it. If it doesn't, it will just give him false hope. Use the money to help him start a new business, Liz-Beth. This is going to be difficult. You'll probably fail."

"I can live with failure, Josh. I can't live without trying."

Joshua frowned.

"I can coach from the sidelines. What do you say, Maggie?"

"You are not, under any circumstances stepping into a courtroom again. You can advise."

"Thanks Maggie. Change of heart?"

"I needed adjustment to the concept."

"She knows it's a lost cause," Joshua added.

"I wanna help," Maggie said.

Liz-Beth held Maggie's hand. "Thank you, Maggie."

"I have to talk to Erik."

"Erik?"

"Your investigator if it interests him."

Liz-Beth smiled.

"We're all agreed, then?"

"Just one thing, Josh. If you do this, I want you to *win* this time."

"I'll try, Maggie."

The three of them glanced at each other.

Joshua turned to Maggie and smiled. "Back in the saddle."

Maggie smirked. "OK, Roy Rogers. Be nice to Trigger."

Josh held his hand over the table. Liz-Beth and Maggie placed theirs on top of his.

"Three Musketeers," Josh said.

Liz-Beth smiled at her friends. "No, Josh. The Pelican Squadron."

Thirty

Liz-Beth opened a handwritten letter left on the dining room table two weeks ago. Postmark Japan. Sukie shared snippets of his life as a modern history teacher at Azabu High School in Tokyo where he attended as a boy. Having achieved accreditation in 1895, Azabu is the oldest of the three most prestigious prep schools in Japan. Sukie chose teaching at Azabu for exposure to a large student body and the influence he could wield working at a revered institution.

Liz-Beth's eyes darted across the last words of the last line. She read them several times. "Oh, my!"

"What's wrong. Liz-Beth? You look like you've seen a ghost."

"Nothing, Natalie. This is wonderful news. Sukie's coming!"

"Your cook and gardener, Sukie?"

"Not just cook and gardener. An old and dear friend."

"Why are you so surprised?"

"I've forgotten to read the letter. Sukie arrives *today!*" Liz-Beth held her hand to her forehead. "This afternoon! I have to ask you to excuse me, Natalie. I have to fix myself up."

"For your gardener?"

"Sukie isn't an ordinary gardener, Natalie. He attended an elite university in Japan. He was an architect and an engineer. I don't intend to look like *I've* been doing the gardening."

"You are doing the gardening."

"I don't have time to explain. Why don't you come back this afternoon? I'll introduce you. What's William doing?"

"Polishing his sockets, probably."

"So busy. Tell Prince William his company is requested. He can swivel his rivets or whatever he does with them another day."

"How do you dress for gardeners?" Natalie giggled.

"Any way you want. Informally, like you would any house guest."

Natalie laughed. "Let me know when his majesty the king of landscape arrives."

"Don't be a smartass. You'll like him."

Oh, dear, Liz-Beth said to herself. *I have to straighten the house. What do I wear? I want to look good, like nothing's changed. Nothing has changed; a nice dress, hair, makeup. A good scent, not overpowering.*

A call came from the San Francisco Airport.

"Liz-Beth?"

"It's good to hear your voice, Sukie."

"It's good to hear yours, Liz-Beth. Did my letter reach you before I did?"

"Yes, of course. Thanks for the warning. I cancelled my spa visit."

"You are welcome."

"Will you stay for dinner?"

"Yes."

"Is there anything special you would like?"

"I will make dinner."

"You're a guest. I'll make dinner."

"I do not wish to offend you, Mrs. Wiggins. My cooking is better. I will go to Fisherman's Wharf."

"Will you please call me Liz-Beth?"

"I will call you Liz-Beth, Mrs. Wiggins." Sukie laughed into the phone.

"*You little Chibi,*" Liz-Beth whispered the Japanese word for runt so Sukie didn't hear it.

"Can I come and get you?"

"No, I have a car, a Bentley."

"A Bentley?"

"Noooo, you are so much fun, Liz-Beth. You believe anything."

"You enjoy making fun of me don't you?"

"Yes."

"At least you called me Liz-Beth. I prefer that."

"Thank you, Mrs. Wiggins."

Liz-Beth removed the handset from her ear. She stared at the speaker. *Exasperating little man,* she thought. *He thinks I'm Abbot and he's Costello.*

"May I invite someone?"

"Your boyfriend?"

"New friends and neighbors."

"Too bad it is not a boyfriend. I will bring food for an army."

"See you soon, Sukie."

"See you, Liz-Beth."

Oh shit, two hours. Liz-Beth called Natalie. "Can you be here in two hours, Nat?"

"Sure."

"Can William come?"

"He's taking apart his gearbox."

"He better be here in two hours, with or without his gearbox."

Sukie arrived with two companions and a car full of grocery bags. A young man and a woman, both Japanese, walked at his side a half step behind him.

Caught up in her emotions, Liz-Beth forgot herself. She threw her arms around Sukie. Sukie never acquired the custom of shaking hands or hugging. He stood with limp arms at his sides as Liz-Beth squeezed the breath out of him. She did it partly to embarrass him and partly from the genuine desire to hug him. Liz-Beth released him and stepped back. She bowed.

Sukie looked stunned. *Why does she do this to me?* he asked himself. When he regained composure he returned the bow.

"You have less hair, Sukie."

"You are too skinny, Liz-Beth. You are starving without my cooking."

"Mrs. Ito! How nice to see you! What brings you here besides Chef Nakajima's world-renowned culinary skills?"

Akiko and Sukie smiled at each other.

"I am Mrs. Nakajima."

"Oooooh! I thought there was something besides reading going on at the library. You said Akiko wasn't your girlfriend, Sukie."

"Not girlfriend. Engaged."

"You devil! What a lovely surprise. I didn't think Sukie spent all that time at the library reading. You would have run out of books."

"He read them all. We ordered more."

Sukie beamed.

"I'm so glad you discovered each other. Let me present you with my new friends, Natalie Blumenthal and William Beckinsdale."

"A pleasure to meet you." Sukie and Akiko bowed.

"A pleasure to meet you, Mr. and Mrs. Nakajima." Natalie offered a tentative hand, withdrew it, and bowed with William.

"We heard good things about you, Sukie. We look forward to your cooking," William said.

"You will soon see, Mr. Beckinsdale."

"Please call us William and Natalie."

"Natalie and William are neighbors. They live in the cottage overlooking Cabrillo Highway."

"I know."

"How do you know that, Sukie?"

"What is it I do not know? May I present with greatest pride, my son, Ichiro Nakajima."

"You work fast," Liz-Beth said. "They grow up fast in Japan. Ichiro must be on the Godzilla Diet."

Akiko giggled. "He is our adopted son."

"A pleasure to meet you, Ichiro." Liz-Beth bowed.

"A pleasure to meet you Mrs. Wiggins." Ichiro returned the bow.

"Please call me Liz-Beth."

"Please call me Charles."

"Ichiro will attend Stanford in the spring," Sukie said. He drew his belly in, threw his shoulders back, and stood erect, all five feet, two inches of him. "Ichiro will be studying computer science to earn a graduate degree."

"I studied computer science at Stanford," William said.

"We will have a lot to discuss, William. I have not visited the campus yet."

"I can show you around, introduce you to some of the faculty."

"I would enjoy that."

"Ichiro is from Kyoto," Sukie added.

"A beautiful city from the photos. I have not been there," William answered.

"Your English is good."

"Ichiro speaks English *well*, Mrs. Wiggins."

Akiko giggled.

"Thank you for correcting me, Nakajima–san." *Someday I'll smack the little bugger,* Liz-Beth thought. She knew she wouldn't.

Sukie nodded.

"Where is that evil bird?"

Liz-Beth laughed. "Be nice to Mr. Chuckles, Sukie. He missed you."

"He wants to bite my nose off," Sukie growled.

"You have to make peace with him if you want to stay here. What's for dinner? Not that horrible squid liver soup I hope."

"I make that because I know you can't eat it. My joke on Americans"

Liz-Beth pointed a finger at him. "Squid liver is no joke, Sukie. Shall we bring the groceries into the house?"

The sight of Sukie agitated Mr. Chuckles even though the bird hadn't seen him in years. Chuckles flapped his wings and bobbed his head. He unleashed a menacing torrent of degrading invective in Japanese.

"Hekoki!, Hekoki!" the bird screamed.

Sukie raised a fist. "Kusattare! Kutabure, buka! Crazy bird!"

"Yakamashi Sukie. Yakamashi Sukie."

"That bird is saitei manuke yowamushi, Liz-Beth."

"Sukie Chibi!" the bird screamed.

The violent exchange shocked Charles and Akiko. Liz-Beth, William and Natalie erupted in laughter.

"What are they saying, Liz-Beth?" Natalie asked.

"Chuckles called Sukie a farter. Sukie called Chuckles a shit-drip." Liz-Beth doubled over from laugher. She paused to catch her breath.

"Chuckles told Sukie to shut up. Sukie called Chuckles an idiot and told him to drop dead. He called Sukie a runt. Sukie says Chuckles is a rotten, clueless coward."

Sukie steamed with anger while everyone else laughed.

"I did nothing to provoke that, Liz-Beth."

"You didn't have to answer him, Sukie. You two are like children in a school yard."

"Do you understand Japanese, Liz-Beth?"

"Only a few words, William."

"How did Chuckles learn Japanese? Oh, let me guess."

"He doesn't understand the meaning, Natalie, only the intent."

"That is enough." Sukie added.

Mr. Chuckles quieted down when William approached the perch. The bird hopped on a wrist, walked up an arm and perched on William's shoulder. Chuckles looked contented. He kept one eye on Sukie.

"What got into him?"

"He hates me, Natalie. What kind of way is that to greet an old friend you haven't seen in years? I cleaned the poop from your cage! I fed you, you ungrateful raptor. You could be begging for gruel in a zoo!"

"He knows you never liked him, Sukie."

"I don't dislike him and I did nothing to make him dislike me."

Sukie stepped closer to William. Chuckles raised his wings and his crest. He lunged as if he wanted to tear out an eye. Sukie raised an arm and ducked his head under it to protect his face, though he was out of reach. Chuckles let out a bloodcurdling scream. William threw a forearm in front of Mr. Chuckles, placing a hand over a wing. The bird quieted down.

"Why don't you take him to the bedroom, William?"

"He hates missing a good dinner party, Natalie. He'll put up a fuss until we bring him back. I'll put him in the cage."

Liz-Beth and Sukie joined their guests in the great room after prepping for dinner.

"How long will you stay in America, Sukie?"

"At least through the summer, Natalie."

"How wonderful to be able to spend a summer here, and to have you as guests."

"We are teachers. I teach 20th century history. Akiko teaches English as a second language. We do not work in summer."

"Will you stay at New Cotswolds?" Natalie asked.

"Most of the time."

"William is, I mean was, in the computer business, Charles. He had his own company."

"What kind of computers?"

"Computer networking."

"My specialty."

"We will have a great deal to talk about."

"William's father flew fighter planes in the South Pacific. Oh, I…hope I haven't opened a wound."

"It is OK, Natalie. We all serve our countries in time of war. We don't have to be enemies because our governments disagree."

Sukie and Liz-Beth exchanged glances.

"I teach this in school, Natalie."

"Do your students agree with your teachings?"

"Nationalism is strong in Japan. Many wish to forget history or re-write it. It is misguided. It must be resisted. I am afraid it will never be extinguished."

"William, why don't you and Natalie take Charles to the beach for the sunset?" Liz-Beth suggested.

"I'm sure you and Sukie have a lot to catch up on," William said. "Natalie?"

Natalie went to the powder room. "Meet you outside."

Bored by all this talking, Chuckles closed his eyes. He looked like he could sleep through the night. William carried the cage to the spare bedroom and covered it with a shroud.

An evening with this many nuts will put any bird to sleep, Chuckles thought. Advanced thinking for a bird.

William said goodnight to Sukie and Akiko. He walked outside, leaned on the Alfa, and warmed his face in the sun.

"William is lucky, mother. Natalie has beautiful eyes. That dark brown hair. So thick and silky."

"I thought you were in love with Hiromi."

"Why do you tease me, mother?"

"Because I like to."

"Ichiro is very fickle," Sukie said. "When he learned Keiko Matsui was too old for him he fell in love with Hiromi. Yes, Natalie is very beautiful. She is also William's girlfriend, and he is twice as big as you. There are many nice beautiful Japanese girls in California to choose from."

Natalie returned from the powder room and said good night. She and Charles left for the beach with William.

"How are things going at the school, Sukie?"

"I am a miserable failure."

Akiko interrupted. "No, you aren't. His expectations were too high, Liz-Beth. He thought he could change Japan overnight."

"It changes very slowly, Akiko."

"Then you must have a very long life."

"I cannot live so long."

"You will live long enough to make a difference. There are people who listen, Liz-Beth."

"Japanese people resent you because you are American, Akiko."

"I am not bothered by this. It is their problem."

Liz-Beth interrupted. "Sukie, I have to talk to you about William."

"Yes?"

"I want you to speak with him."

"What do you want me to speak about?"

"You will know."

"I know about William. He is the man who lives in the cottage on the knoll. His parents died. He lost his business in the technology bubble. He came here to be alone. His spirit did not die but it is badly wounded. He is slowly wasting."

"Then you know what to say."

"I have a son. I do not wish to have another."

"He has no father, Sukie. He needs a mentor. He'll respect you. Somebody has to inspire him or he's going to waste his life here and Natalie's too. I would consider it a personal favor if you would try."

"He loves her?"

"Yes, and she loves him."

"A blind man could see it through a granite mountain."

"Will you talk to him?"

"Yes."

"Thank you, Sukie. Take him to your rock garden. Teach him to be serene and unconquerable."

"I will try, Liz-Beth."

"We should toast to a long life so you may complete your mission in Japan. Would you like sake?"

"Do you surf in California?"

Thirty-One

If you turn around on the trail from Cabrillo Highway you can see the Pacific Ocean when you crest gentle rises. The county grooms and gravels the path year-round so the rains, when they come, leave no ruts or pot holes and the trail is always passable for foot and bike traffic.

Joshua and William walked to the end of Reservoir Road, turned east on the trail, past marshes of cattails, meadows of tall grasses, over hills covered in mesquite trees, on the way to New Cotswolds.

"You're receiving visitors this afternoon, Sukie."

"You are visiting, Liz-Beth?"

"William and Josh will join you for tea."

"I have not invited them."

"I invited them for you."

"How did you know I would be here?"

"Where else would you be?"

"Akiko is in Cupertino introducing Ichiro to her cousins."

"Exactly. You can have a meeting of the minions."

"What are you scheming, Liz-Beth?"

"Natalie, Maggie, and I are going shopping. This is a good time for you to get to know William."

"You want me to babysit two grown men while you are shopping."

"Yes."

"I resigned my position when I went to Japan. I am no longer your employee."

"Just this one time, Sukie."

"I am a free man on summer vacation."

"And a good friend. Now be a dear and share some of your vacation with Josh and William."

"What do you want me to say to William?"

"You will know."

Nothing has changed, Sukie thought. "You are a devious woman, Liz-Beth Wiggins."

"And a dangerous and beautiful one."

"Defiantly dangerous. Someone is ringing my chimes," Sukie said.

"Someone besides me?"

"My door chimes."

"It's for a good cause, Sukie."

"I hoped for a peaceful day to myself."

Liz-Beth giggled. *He's a good sport*, she thought.

That woman can make me do anything, Sukie said to himself.

I can get him to do anything, Liz-Beth thought. "Have fun with your guests, Sukie."

Sukie growled into the receiver.

Thirty-Two

Sukie answered the door in a gorgeous handmade blue silk kimono with a dragon embroidered on the back in white, red, and gold thread. He wore simple wooden sandals with traditional white tabi socks. Joshua and William bowed. They removed their shoes and entered the house.

"Welcome to my humble home, American friends. Here I am a traditional Japanese man and it is as if you have entered Japan."

"Thank you for inviting us, Sukie."

"You are welcome, Joshua."

I must get even with Liz-Beth, Sukie thought. *We will never be even.*

"Your kimono is very beautiful. I have not seen this one."

"Akiko made it for me, Joshua. She has great artistic skill. I am very proud of her."

"Is she here?"

"No, Joshua. She is in Cupertino with Ichiro. They will have dinner there."

Joshua and William followed Sukie through the house to the Zen garden.

"Please wait here," Sukie said.

Sukie retrieved a three-legged wooden stool and two rakes from the shed. He placed the stool on the flagstone patio, handed one rake to William, one to Joshua, removed his socks and stepped into the symmetrical perfection of the Zen garden. Sukie walked around the boulders leaving foot prints in narrow rows of sand.

William looked at Joshua. Joshua shrugged.

Sukie sat on the stool. "Now you can enjoy the serenity of the garden and honor yourselves as guests."

Sukie leaned forward, placed his hands on his knees and waited. William and Joshua held their rakes. Sukie raised a hand and nodded, a gesture to begin.

"What is this, rake-on, rake-off?"

"Exactly, William. It is so."

"I'm a grasshopper?"

"Noooo. You must demonstrate you are worthy of the title. The garden is disrupted. It must be repaired. Please begin."

William looked at Joshua. Joshua chuckled, removed his socks, stepped into the sand and began raking. William followed.

"You are Zen gardeners," Sukie growled, arms folded across his chest, his face a grimace. "If you perform well, you may gain entry into Sukie's school of samurai rake-masters. Someday you will achieve great rakeness!"

"You mean rake greatness?"

"Yes, William."

"I think he's been into the sake, William."

"It's only 11:30 AM, Joshua. If I fail, do I have to kill myself, Sukie?"

"If you dishonor yourself, you must decide. Up to you, William"

The three of them laughed.

"How long have you been doing this, Josh?"

"Twenty years."

"Still a student?"

"I'm progressing."

Sukie nodded.

"Sukie has more ranks than grains of sand in his garden. Your rank does not matter. Striving to advance is its own reward."

"You have learned well, Joshua."

"Thank you, Sensei."

"Joshua is a good student. Among the best I have taught. You have potential William, but bad attitude. You must improve. If you do, you have a great future in Zen gardening."

"Thank you...I think."

"Outside you are William the technology entrepreneur, Joshua the store keeper. Here everyone is a simple gardener. The object of gardening… is gardening! It is not to finish gardening. It is to garden, to keep gardening, to never stop gardening. Rake the sand, William. You will achieve balance and happiness."

William and Joshua raked until no footprints could be found in the sand. Symmetry and serenity returned to the garden.

"How do you feel, William?"

"Good…I, I feel calm, relaxed. How often do you do this, Josh?"

"When I come here."

William and Joshua returned their rakes to the shed. Sukie brewed and brought tea on a delicate service, placed it on a low, square, teak table. They crossed legs and sat on tatami mats. Sukie poured the tea, raised a cup and proclaimed:

"I am Shogun of New Cotswolds. You are my honorable gardeners."

William and Joshua raised their cups. Sukie pronounced; "It's good to be the Shogun!"

"This has Liz-Beth's perfume all over it."

"You are a wise man, Joshua."

William looked puzzled.

"I gave you an easy assignment, William. You had only to clear the rows of footprints. Next time there will be no footprints. You will make your own patterns."

"I will do my best for the Shogun. Did you really have a samurai school, Sukie?"

"Of course not. Americans are so gullible. You think every Japanese man in a kimono is a ruthless samurai warrior, a crazy man ready to cut his belly if he dishonors himself, willing to die for his master, or his emperor. Japanese are all tiny, nearsighted, buck tooth, square head fanatics? Do you see my swords? One to cut off your head? One to cut my belly? I wear no sword, no suicide dagger. How could I be samurai?"

Sukie is right, William thought. Stereotypes are stupid. "Do you teach Ichiro?"

"No, William. He is not *interested* in Zen gardening. He wants to listen to rock music, play video games, drive fast cars, have many girlfriends. He wants to be *American*!"

"Did you teach Mr. Wiggins?"

"No, William. I was his prisoner. He rescued me after the war, provided me with honorable work, food to make me healthy, a safe place to live. I could never be his sensei."

Sukie refilled their teacups.

"Josh, you and Maggie have been married a long time. Sukie, for a few years. Do you ever have problems?"

"You have trouble with Miss Natalie, William?" Sukie asked.

"We get along most of the time."

"William wants to learn what we *think* we know about living with women" Joshua said. Maggie and I married young, William. We had our differences. At times we were angry with each other. Sometimes we couldn't remember what we fought over. Stupid things, unworthy of disagreement. It usually ended when one of us realized this and gave in. I learned the best thing to do is let Maggie have her way. The things we argued over mattered so little compared with what we meant to each other. I asked myself which is more important. Winning an argument or making Maggie happy? Always an easy choice, she loved me for it. Marriage became easier after that."

"If you are lucky, you will marry Miss Natalie and share a life together," Sukie added. "She will care for you in old age. You must give her children to care for her, if you leave this earth before her. Do not leave her by herself."

Like Liz-Beth, William thought.

"Children may bring you great joy, comfort, honor, or they may make you suffer. It is one of life's great gambles. You cannot know before meeting them. Too late for us to have children of our own, Akiko and I adapted Ichiro. He is a good son. Sons carry on the family name. If you have two, they will battle. I had a brother. It hurt my mother when we fought. Daughters will bring you much joy. You will love spoiling them. You will never completely understand them. I had a sister. She could make her brothers do anything for her. You should wish for one strong, kind son, and a house full of beautiful daughters!"

"How many daughters, Sukie?"

"You will know when one more will be too many. Women care about family, your western philosopher Sartre wrote. *Love is the entire story of a woman's life but only a chapter in the life of a man."*

"Romance is important," Joshua added. "Family is more important. You provide and protect. They nurture. In your generation roles can crossover unlike Sukie's and mine when fewer women had professional careers. Generally it hasn't changed. Women helped their men from the beginning of time. They're motivated by family, to make and preserve them, to perpetuate them. A relationship can't be all fun and sex."

"They're my favorites, Josh."

"Mine too." Joshua chuckled. "Physical attraction is important. Woman like Maggie, who do not as a priority seek wealth, look for potential since most of us start with very little. I had nothing but debts when we married. She wanted to make a life. We lived in an apartment over a garage in San Francisco. We started with a lamp, an alarm clock, a double bed. She knew we would have money one day. It doesn't matter what you have when you marry. Success is sweeter if you achieve it together."

"I've seen Natalie crying alone in the bedroom. I made her cry."

"Young woman can be fragile, William" Sukie said. "Do not be insensitive. Before you do or say something hurtful, ask yourself if it's so important that you still want to."

"I ran her off once, Josh. I didn't mean to. I was frustrated, angry, not at her. She didn't deserve the way I treated her."

"You are lucky she returned," Sukie said. "Young woman like Natalie. Intelligent, attractive, she can have anybody she wants.

She wants you, William, in spite of your troubles. Do not take that lightly."

"It's hard for Natalie to live here, Sukie. I wiped her tears and felt her tremble. I feel like such a failure."

"You aren't a failure," Joshua said. "You accepted responsibility when you let her move in with you. She may be unhappy here, but some of her tears are for *you*. For what happened to your company. She doesn't want you to waste your life. You have to pick yourself up for both of you. You have to let her help you."

"You should discuss this with miss Natalie," Sukie added. "She would welcome this conversation, to know you care about her needs. You have a good one in Natalie. Do not disappoint her. If you want to keep her, you must express your love. It should not be difficult."

Sukie's words hovered in the air. William stared into the Zen garden.

"That's how it was with Liz-Beth and Harry," Sukie said.

"Harry?"

Sukie smiled. His eyes focused somewhere back in time. "Yes, Mr. Wiggins. His friends called him Harry. My employer and my friend. Out of respect I always called him Mr. Wiggins."

"What a guy Harry was, William. You would have liked him. Isn't that right, Sukie?"

"Yes. A very special man, Joshua. Warrior and humanitarian."

"Harry and Liz-Beth had different interests, William," Joshua said. "He let Liz-Beth have her way. She let him do anything he wanted, no matter how odd-ball."

"Odd-ball?"

"Mr. Wiggins built New Cotswolds," Sukie said. "An insane project Liz-Beth thought. She did not criticize. She let him indulge himself. She discovered she liked it when we completed it. No two people need a home that big. Look where she lives now."

"*Sukie* built New Cotswolds, William" Joshua explained.

"*You* built New Cotswolds, Sukie?"

"I helped."

"Sukie is very modest, William. He's a trained architect, an experienced builder. He managed *Harry's Folly*. That's what we called it. A white elephant we thought they would never finish. Harry and Sukie fooled us. It's the best house in Pescadero." Joshua waved an arm in the direction of the manor house. "Harry's vision, William. Sukie built it."

Sukie bowed his head in modesty.

"You can't deny the craftsmanship in *this* house, Sukie."

"Please stop, Joshua."

"Sukie designed and built this Japanese style house, William. Look around. You won't find a single nail in it. He built a wooden house without nails using Japanese hand tools."

William scanned the house. "Amazing."

"Joshua is Takumi, William, the Japanese name for artesian."

"No, Joshua. I am not Takumi. 50,000 hours of training under a master are required to become Takumi, nearly half a lifetime working exclusively with one tool or one craft. 25 years of instruction and practice. It can be a wood saw, a chisel, or by cutting large and intricate designs out of a single sheet of paper, by cooking a specific style of food. I could not be Takumi of even one tool or craft. Joshua was a great business attorney."

"Successful, William. Not great. Maggie made me give it up. She had other ideas for what she wanted us to do."

"The stress was killing you, Joshua. It is white collar warfare, William."

"But if you were good at it…"

Joshua interrupted.

"I lost an important case. Someone I cared for suffered. After that, the passion for it left me. Litigation can be intense, demanding. I miss it sometimes. I'd go back though, for one more good contest."

Sukie glanced at Joshua. When their eyes met Sukie learned Joshua decided to return to the war of words.

"We lived on a ranch east of here. Maggie convinced me to sell it to buy the store and build the house. A venture capitalist who lived nearby bought our property. Already much larger than ours, he added it to his. Sukie drove Liz-Beth to thrift shops all over the Bay Area. Sometimes she brought Mr. Chuckles."

"Liz-Beth bought clothes at thrift shops?"

"Yes, William." Sukie chuckled. "I stood by the car in a black suit, the Oriental chauffeur. Feet planted, hands together in front of me, a scowl on my face. Like kabuki theater. I pretended I did not understand English. Sometimes I spoke Japanese in a deep hostile voice. I enjoyed scaring white people."

"That was mean," William frowned.

"I should not have done this. You might not think so if you saw the way they looked at me. Like Asian is subhuman, an enemy even after the war ended. Some Americans in your father's generation hated all Japanese people. Now they buy televisions, cars, cameras made in Japan. The government interred Akiko's family in Manzanar, a polite way to say imprisoned. She was *born* here. A *child* who lived behind wire fences in her own country. A prison camp for old people, for children who could do no harm while family members were wounded and killed serving in the American military. They were loyal Americans. They did not wish Japan to make war on America."

"I didn't mean to recall painful memories."

"It is OK, William. It is to know and not be forgotten."

"Did Liz-Beth have no money for clothes?" To William, it seemed incredulous.

"Nooooo. She could buy the stores! I drove her in a Bentley! She did this for fun, an eccentric hobby. She thought it was silly to spend so much for new things; then give them away after hardly wearing them. She enjoyed buying and wearing thrift things. She sold them back to stores, sometimes for more than she paid for them. A game, like a board game and she could win!"

"She owned a fabulous wardrobe," Joshua added. "You should have seen how well she dressed herself. It cost her almost nothing."

"She's teaching Natalie right now."

"How do you know, Sukie?"

"We know Liz-Beth. She doesn't shop at Neiman Marcus. Did they take Mr. Chuckles?"

"I think…Natalie said they did."

Sukie slapped his thighs and laughed. "They went thrift shopping with Mr. Chuckles! If Natalie is as good at this as Liz-Beth, she'll practically dress for life for free. You will wonder where all the expensive clothes came from. Like Mr. Wiggins did. You will need a bigger house, William! You will have to move into New Cotswolds!" Sukie laughed.

"I need a bigger house now, Sukie. Does Maggie do this, Josh?"

"No, William. Maggie doesn't care about fashion. She likes her clothing simple. She is happy in a nice apron. These silly things are what I meant. It doesn't have to make sense. It just has to make them happy. It has to make *you* happy to see them happy."

"Is it this way with you and Akiko?"

"Yes William. It is better to be like our pets. They can't understand what we say or do, but they learn our feelings and emotions. They give us a sniff, figure out what we want them to do, and do it. Harry had a dog named Bentley. Bentley knew what Harry wanted. He did it, and they were best friends."

"Sometimes I feel like Natalie's pet."

"You're getting it William," Joshua said. "Think like Bentley, a wise and happy dog."

"What does Natalie see in me?"

"It's hard to know what's in a young woman's heart. I'm not sure any of us ever will completely."

"Have I fallen into the abyss?"

"No, William. Sukie is Samurai. He traced his family back to the 12th century."

"Stop, Joshua."

"He needs to hear this, Sukie."

Sukie frowned.

"Sukie fought a war he didn't believe in, William. His side lost. He became a prisoner. He lost everything. Home, belongings, career, family, friends. Harry found him starving in a prisoner of war camp. Now he has a home in Japan. He's a respected scholar, a teacher in one of Japan's finest schools where he once studied. He has a fine wife and son. You can pull yourself up from anything, William."

"The bottom can be as good a place to start as any. From the bottom," Sukie added, "you can only rise. There is goodness in your life, William. You are not the circumstances you find yourself in. You are William."

"You're the master of your fate, William, the Captain of your soul," Joshua added.

"*Invictus.*"

"Yes, William. Do not allow yourself to be conquered."

"Oh, I get it, Sukie. *See* your future… *Be* your future."

"Who said that?"

"Chevy Chase."

"Who is honorable Chevy Chase?"

"Caddy Shack."

"I do not know this Caddy Shack."

"It's a movie, Sukie. Never mind. Stick with Henley."

"Honorable guests. This has been a most stimulating discussion. It has grown long and serious. The time has come for *sake*."

"I thought you'd never offer, Sukie."

"You knew I would, Joshua."

"Sukie is a sake connoisseur, William. You're in for a treat."

"Thank you for listening, both of you, and for your advice."

"Thank you for sharing, William," Joshua said.

"Kokuryu Ryu, a Daiginjo Sake. Verrrry good! From Fukui Prefecture, on the Sea of Japan. Brewed by Buddhist monks, it cannot be purchased outside of Japan. I brought it when I returned from self-imposed exile from Pescadero."

"Do you realize what you just said?"

"Yes, Joshua. I am conflicted. I know what I want right now. Kokuryu Ryu will make us unimaginably happy."

Thirty-Three

A red Alfa carrying three women, three shopping bags and one irascible cockatoo traveled south on Cabrillo highway approaching Pescadero Creek Road.

"It's four o'clock. Do you want to drop in on the boys before dinner?"

"Why not Natalie, we might catch them telling dirty jokes, wearing lampshades and comparing biceps."

"I doubt it, Liz-Beth," Maggie chimed in. "Josh has no biceps. If I know Sukie, he and Josh are sleeping off a bottle of Sake and William is as polluted as they are."

"You mean Josh and Sukie are a bad influence on my man and you deliberately left him with them?"

"Yes!" Liz-Beth and Maggie shouted in unison. Natalie swerved the car onto the shoulder and almost lost control. Mr. Chuckles shrieked and started a laughing session.

"Maybe William can learn to be more fun."

"From those two?" Liz-Beth said. "William can teach *them.*"

"I hope Josh pays attention," Maggie added.

"Let's go to Half Moon Bay, have a look at the fresh catch."

"Shouldn't we ask them what they want, Liz-Beth?"

"If I know Sukie, they're into the Sake cabinet by now. Even if they can think that far ahead they're probably in no condition to suggest anything I want to participate in. They'll wander home like little lambs when they get hungry."

"Oh, come on, let's sneak up on them," Natalie insisted.

They parked the car near the entrance of New Cotswolds and walked along the stone wall until they reached the Zen garden.

In various stages of inebriated slumber, Sukie slumped over the table with his face in a pillow and his hands beside him face up. Joshua sat with the back of his head against a wall, snoring with his mouth open. William curled in a fetal position on a tatami mat. An empty sake bottle laid on its side on the table, surrounded by three empty cups.

The women covered their mouths and giggled like teenagers. Liz-Beth bent over laughing until her sides hurt.

Maggie pointed at Josh. "Look at that doofus. They turned it into a frat house. I bet he led them in a few choruses of the *Ant Song*."

Natalie laughed. "*High Hopes*. That's your husband, Maggie. Should we wake them?"

"No Natalie, let them sleep it off," Liz-Beth said. "Let's go to Fisherman's Pier. We'll call them when we get to my house. What do you think, Maggie?"

"They'll be hungry by then. Nothing like hunger to sober a man up and get him moving."

Liz-Beth called two hours later. The phone rang ten times before Sukie rose to answer. The women giggled around the kitchen island. Sukie stumbled across the patio and into the house on unsteady legs.

"You are disturbing honorable gardening class."

"Oh? Did you enjoy the sake?"

Sukie grunted.

"You and your friends better get over here if you want to be fed. Maggie, Natalie and I went to the fish market. We're making dinner."

"Your English is improving," Sukie mumbled, his mind in a fog.

"Thank."

"Wait! Don't start until I get there!" Sukie blurted out.

"Be here in ten minutes."

"We cannot be there in ten minutes."

"Dinner preparation begins in ten minutes."

"Wait, wait. We will be there."

I love it when I do that, Liz-Beth thought. She fed Mr. Chuckles from a handful of peanuts and carried him into the guest room.

Sukie roused Joshua and William. Half-awake, They rushed to Liz-Beth's cottage half awake, for what emergency, they didn't know.

"Did Sukie treat you to sake, William?" Natalie asked.

"Ah…yeah."

"Did you bring some for us?" Liz-Beth asked.

Sukie, Joshua and William looked at each other.

"I'll go back for it."

"That's OK, William. We're drinking white wine."

Maggie and Natalie glanced at each other and giggled.

Sukie insisted on preparing dinner. He put on another clinic.

"Sukie, you could make black beans taste like caviar."

"Thank you Maggie." Sukie beamed.

"What do you think, Liz-Beth?"

"I would have kicked him out by 1950 if he couldn't."

"What would you eat after that?" Sukie asked.

"Chinese food."

Sukie scowled. "Disgusting."

William and Natalie, Joshua and Maggie went home after dinner. Sukie walked to his house in the New Cotswolds compound to wait for Akiko and Ichiro.

Natalie slept like the dead. A procession of thoughts paraded through William's mind. It woke him after midnight. When he rose, Natalie turned over, unaware he left the bedroom.

William stared at the ocean through the great room window. He watched a half-moon sail across a clear sky. Moonlight reflected off the swells. William poured a tumbler of bourbon, sat in a chair and rested his feet on the writing desk. He no longer had to tell himself life would be better. It already was. He chuckled at the thought of the enigmatic Sukie, the amazing experiences he had, how wise they made him. William doubted he would ever understand Sukie. He thought about Charles, how smart and ambitious he is, how much he reminded William of a younger version of himself. He thought he and Charles, and VK, if he could poach him from LightSwitch, could create something significant together.

It's all been about me, William thought. *I'm going to change that,* he promised himself. *I owe them a great deal.* He thought about Natalie sleeping in the bedroom, what a fool he had been. What a lucky one. *More than a girlfriend, Natalie is my partner. Like Liz-Beth and Bunny, like Maggie and Joshua, like Akiko and Sukie. They would not have accomplished as much without each other.* They were happy, William realized, because they had each other.

Mea Culpa, Natalie. Mea Culpa. Why do you stay with me? If not for Natalie, he could drift like a jellyfish on the tide, float through the oceans of life. He could sell the Mountain View house, live on the coast, take up surfing again, never work again. It isn't what he wanted. *What would my parents want of me? My friends would be disappointed. Even that isn't enough, if not for Natalie. I owe her something better*, William thought.

"What do you think, Dusty? Is it time to get off the bench? It's 2AM and I'm talking to a stuffed pelican." William smirked.

Natalie rolled over to drape an arm around a man who wasn't there. It woke her. "What are you doing out there, William? Don't you want to come to bed?"

William swallowed the last sip of bourbon. "Yeah, Natalie. I very much do."

William looked at Dusty. If he believed it possible, he would have sworn the pelican winked.

Thirty-Four

Liz-Beth had just completed a chapter in the novel *Cold Mountain* she borrowed from William. A civil war story, in the text, Inman had just reached the South Carolina border on his journey on foot from a hospital bed in Atlanta. Liz-Beth wondered if her journey to help William would be as long and difficult as the one Inman began when he started for home from the war. William, not she, Liz-Beth decided, had the longer, more difficult journey. Liz-Beth set the book down to answer the phone.

"Mrs. Wiggins?"

"I don't recognize the area code."

"Henderson, Nevada. This is Erik Mason. Did Joshua tell you I'd call?"

"He did."

"Then you know why I called."

"Yes."

"I don't usually take cases like this one. I agreed to have a look for Josh."

"Thank you for that."

"I can commit to preliminary investigation, just enough to see if there's any reason to continue."

"He told me that might be the case."

"Mrs. Wiggins."

"Please call me Liz-Beth."

"Call me Erik."

"Can you help us, Erik?"

"I don't know. There isn't much to go on."

"I understand."

"It would help if I could talk to the client."

"I'm the client. Did Joshua explain why we have to do it this way?"

"He did. Doesn't make it easier."

"Find out what you can. We can go from there. Joshua tells me you're a resourceful man. There's another matter I need help with. We have to keep this one between you and I. *Nobody else*, not even Joshua, can know about it."

"This is getting complicated, Liz-Beth. I don't like secrets. Makes me think it's something I shouldn't be doing."

"I need to find a missing airplane. One that disappeared a long time ago. I have no idea where to start. I only know it belonged to William's parents. They took off from Half Moon Bay and disappeared. Nobody knows what happened to them."

"That's a lot more interesting than a business fraud case."

"Do you perform this kind of investigation?"

"It's more to my liking."

"What does this sort of thing cost?"

"Don't know until I get into it. Search for a plane, recovery if I find it. More than a down payment on a Ferrari, less than a stealth bomber."

"That narrows it down. How do we proceed?"

"I'll include a proposal with my standard contract and mail it to you."

"Address it to my box in the Pescadero Post Office. Liz-Beth 94060 is all they need."

"Will do. I need all the information you can give me. Can I meet you?"

"Do you visit the Bay Area?"

"I do."

"On your next visit?"

"Haven't seen Josh and Maggie in a while. I have to speak to Josh about the LightSwitch business. I'll fly in."

"Do you need a retainer?"

"Friend of Josh and Maggie's is retainer enough."

"If you don't mind me asking, why do you live in Las Vegas? Aren't most of your clients here?"

"Brand mystique."

"Sure it is."

Josh is right, the woman is no dummy, Mason thought. "I like the desert, proximity to national parks."

"An outdoorsman."

"I like deserts and mountains more than people."

"Tell me the real reason."

"My wife would dice me if I told her I considered relocating. My kids would feed me to the cat. I like kitty. Not enough to be turned into cat food."

"I can see how that would discourage you."

"Cathy's a lizard. She loves the desert. I love my wife. She's the only woman in the world who would put up with me."

"Doesn't distance make the work difficult?"

"You would be surprised how much you can learn on the internet. It's the encyclopedia of everything. With a laptop, it's always with you."

"I might like having a computer."

"It would be a pleasure to show you how to use one. Email comes in handy."

"How do you travel to the Bay Area?"

"I keep a Mooney at Henderson Executive Airport, a car at San Carlos Airport. I can get to San Carlos under three hours in the Mooney. In an emergency, I can borrow a Pilatus turbo prop and be there in two."

"Isn't that expensive?"

"I try to keep the travel down."

"I think I'm gonna like working with you, Erik."

"Josh told me I'd find you interesting. I'm not disappointed."

"I don't play cavalier games. I'm confident this is not a waste of time and I intend to succeed."

"No offense intended."

"None taken."

"Would you mind telling me *why* you're doing this, Liz-Beth?"

"Let's just say for good friends, old and new. Sorry, Erik, I like calling you Mr. Mason. Makes our relationship sound professional."

"May I call you Mrs. Wiggins?"

"In our professional discussions, you may. Do you believe in chivalry, Mr. Mason?"

"Always when escorting a lady."

"Mason and Wiggins; I like the sound of that. A lot like a TV show isn't it?"

"Yeah, it is." Mason smiled to himself. "Let's hope it's one of those where the good guys get the bad guys."

"We will, Mr. Mason. We will."

Thirty-Five

Natalie and Charles squeezed into the back of the Alfa, Liz-Beth in the front seat with William. Liz-Beth left a key with Maggie so she could look in on Mr. Chuckles. They left in the morning, drove to San Gregorio on Highway 1, turned east on Highway 84, continued to Woodside. William dropped Natalie and Liz-Beth off on University Avenue in Palo Alto. He drove Charles through the Stanford campus where they stopped at the computer science building to meet Professor Perloff, one of the instructors William studied under. Perloff helped him start LightSwitch and introduced him to angel investors.

The three of them discussed Charles's ideas for improving price/performance of internet protocol switches. They sketched their ideas on a whiteboard and agreed to build prototypes to test in the Stanford Computer Science lab. William left Charles with Perloff to tour the campus together. He walked a mile to Hobee's to meet VK for lunch. They chose a table at the back of the restaurant.

"Are you afraid of being seen with me, VK?"

"I can't afford to lose my job, but I won't work for a company that thinks I can't meet old friends. Are we plotting against the company?"

"I wish I had a plot."

"What have you been doing with yourself?"

"I restored dad's car, fixed up the cottage, made new friends, visited beaches, drove up and down the coast."

"Sounds nice. Not real productive."

"I needed to vegetate a bit."

"Do you like living in Pescadero?"

"It's nice when the sun's out. It's damp and foggy a lot of the time."

"Not much to do, is there? It would drive me crazy."

"Enough for Gordon Moore."

"Intel Gordon Moore?"

"The same. He was born in San Francisco, raised in Pescadero."

"I didn't know that. I guess he had lots of time to think about semiconductors. Something in the water? Hope you're drinking it."

"Smartass. Natalie moved in with me."

"That's wonderful! I'm glad you're back together. How is she?"

"She's great; doing great. I didn't know what we had until she left, how good it could be until she knocked on the door unannounced one night."

"Natalie's good for you, William. Don't let her go again."

"I'm not going to."

"How can both of you live in such a tiny place?"

"It's temporary."

"Why don't you move back into the Mountain View house?"

"We planted roots in Pescadero, made a life there. We might move back eventually. Right now I need the house for something else. How are things with you?"

"Great. My daughter will be home from school for the summer. She and my wife cook like a tsunami. We want her to marry well. They think the best way to catch a man is to fill up his stomach."

"Looks like they've been experimenting on you."

"Thanks a lot. I'm trying to work off a few pounds on the squash court."

"Great. Let's play for money!"

"Very funny. I have to play with my daughter's tuition money. I don't have any."

"What's going on at the company?"

"It's pretty depressing. Business is terrible. Osgood took over as interim CEO."

"Are they looking for a permanent replacement?"

"If they are, they've been quiet about it. We'd love to have you back, William."

"It didn't seem that way the day they sacked me."

"That creeped everybody out. Do you still take it personally?"

"No, I'm over it. I shouldn't have said that."

"Being led by Osgood is like following the generals who ordered the Charge of the Light Brigade. He knows as much about running a technology company as they knew about leading cavalry. Whatever we tell him we can do he doubles down and gives us half the time and resources. When I tell him we can't do it he pressures us to work harder. We're living in a Scott Adams cartoon strip. Dilbert's boss is running LightSwitch."

"Must be difficult."

"It is but Osgood's so ignorant. We learned to admit to half of what we can do. A stupid game. I hate being dishonest. It's the only way we can work with him."

"How does he manage the company?"

"He's a part time CEO. He shows up once or twice a week for staff meetings to throw bombs at us. He thinks he's doing a good job, like we can't live without him. Makes me nauseous."

"Interesting management style."

"Osgood's a money guy with no operations experience. We laid off a third of the staff, subleased some of the office and manufacturing space, sold off fixtures, equipment. We collected so little for it we should have kept it. It seems like all the management team does is plan cuts. We don't talk about how to float the ship, just how to slow the sinking. We're re-arranging deck chairs until we have to toss them over."

What irony, William thought. *They fired me because I didn't want to staff up. Now they're firing the people I didn't want to hire.* William let it go.

"What happened to the product development projects?"

"Postponed, cancelled."

"That'll make it worse. You can't keep polishing turds."

"How can it get worse? There are no buyers. We get a few capacity and replacement orders. We're trying to live on service contracts. You read the papers, don't you?"

"I'd like to hear it from you."

"The dotcoms are collapsing. Many of them never generated revenue, have no idea how. They were great at blowing money. They won't be buying anything from us. They wish they could send our equipment back. We have a name for them. We call them *dot bombs*."

William thought it amusing until he remembered they were his customers.

"The market value of some of these companies declined 95%. Some of the employees borrowed against their stock options because they couldn't exercise and sell the shares during the lock-out period."

"They must be bankrupt."

"Some are, on paper."

"They should have waited."

"They were in a hurry to buy houses, cars and boats. The Ferrari dealer sold out. Now they wish they could take it all back."

"What are the VCs doing?"

"They've gone dormant. The IPO window closed. They can't raise new funds. They're doing triage; conserving cash to feed the companies that have a chance of surviving. Data networks have too much capacity. They laid miles of fiber optic cable nobody needs. Dark fiber. No point in lighting it until they need it. The carriers have to give the bandwidth away. They aren't buying equipment. They stopped making acquisitions too."

"They'll use up the surplus infrastructure."

"In how long? Who will survive? It's a nuclear winter, William. Have you seen the NASDAQ?"

"Yeah, I've seen it. How is it affecting the valley?"

"I've seen job loss estimates at two hundred thousand in the South Bay."

"Holy shit."

"North San Jose has a lot of new office space coming online and no tenants. Exteriors are finished. Interiors and parking lots are empty. There are entire office parks of see-through buildings along Highway 237."

"My God, VK. That will gut the local economy. It must be the same on Route 128 in Boston. We could have a recession with the stock market down so much, and all the high-income job losses. People will lose their homes."

"Some of them are refinancing or taking out home equity loans for money to live on."

"How can they do that with no job?"

"They call themselves consultants."

"No income qualification? The banks have lost their minds. This has to end badly. What else can you tell me about LightSwitch?"

"Morale is down, I can't motivate anybody. I can't motivate myself. We're walking dead, William; bunch of zombies. No plan, no idea how to lift ourselves out of this."

"It used to be fun to work there."

"Everybody's looking around. There aren't any jobs to apply for."

"What's the word on the sale?"

"What sale? We haven't heard a thing about it since Dunn mentioned it the day you left."

"They probably can't find a buyer. Have you thought about joining another startup?"

"With what funding, William? The VCs are hibernating."

"It won't last forever."

"You think so?"

"I know so. There will always be a need for new technology; faster, cheaper, better. The infrastructure will fill up and expand again. I'm certain of it."

"Nobody knows how to make money on the internet."

"All those people using it. Somebody will figure it out."

"I have to stay where I am as long as possible. The crappy job I have is better than no job."

"I met this engineer. Young guy, starting a graduate program at Stanford in the fall. He's been working on solutions to problems we wrestled with. If they work we can leapfrog the competition. We have no legacy products to integrate. We can try fresh ideas with the newest components, build prototypes with samples."

"Sure, you can call Gordon Moore since you were almost neighbors."

"I'm serious, VK. We met with Perloff this morning. He offered help. Nothing like sample parts and student labor to get something started."

"You picked a tough time to start a company."

"I had a nice sabbatical in Pescadero. If I stay too long I'll fizzle. If it were just me, I could take up surfing again, spend the rest of my life looking for the perfect wave. I'm not letting go of Natalie. If I want to hold on to her I have to restart my career, show her some kind of future that would make her happy. I'll get started somehow."

"All grown up with somebody to care about. Interns will work part-time for experience, something to put on a resume. I did it."

"You can do it again!" William laughed.

"I'm so looking for such an opportunity."

"I'm gonna set up the lab in the Mountain View house again. Why don't you have a look at what we're doing."

"I can come by after-hours if you aren't afraid I'll take your ideas with me."

"You can't be serious. You aren't going to take anything to that mess you're working in. To your buddy Osgood and his partners who treat you so well? What would you do with it with no R&D budget?"

"I still work at LightSwitch. I have to improve our products if I can."

"I can't accomplish anything if I don't trust anybody. You aren't going to give Osgood anything, not that he would know what to do with it."

"Remember I told you I would love to work with you again?"

"I remember. And me with you."

"OK, William. If I come by, I expect to be well fed."

"Work for food, eh? Your wife and daughter have you figured out."

"That's how it is, William. From my hand, to the tax man, the wife and daughter and her tuition, the mortgage company, the car lease company, the credit card company, the phone company, the utility company, the gardener, the house cleaners, the insurance company, the gas station. I *am* working for food."

"I can't promise anything that compares with what you're eating at home. You might lose a few pounds if you stay away from the pizza."

"Screw you, William. I'll take your squash money. Just make sure you have vegan and curry."

"I have your order, sir."

"Do you still have that ridiculous stuffed pelican?"

"Dusty wants to get back into action."

VK chuckled at the memory of the pelican standing watch over William's office. "That's what's wrong with the company, William. It hasn't been the same since Dusty left." VK laughed at the thought of Dusty leading the company. "See you at the lab, William."

"The lab will be waiting."

Thirty-Six

The taxi dropped Natalie and Liz-Beth off at William's house in Mountain View. The landscape company had the front yard looking good. The back yard had grown into a weed farm. Inside, the house looked like a Midwest dust bowl.

"I can get the house cleaned up and ready in a weekend, Liz-Beth. I want to move back in here."

"I'll miss you terribly, Natalie. Why is everybody always leaving me?"

"I'm not leaving you. I want to go back to work. I can be here four nights a week, three in Pescadero, in the city when I have to be. You can stay here sometimes if you want to."

"Like grandma. What are you going to do for transportation? William needs the Alfa."

"We'll figure something out."

"Use the MG until you can buy a car. I haven't driven it in ages. If I have to go someplace I can't reach by bike or foot, Josh and Maggie will help out."

"Thanks Liz-Beth. I like the MG. I'll drive you around when I'm in Pescadero. Would you like to see the family photos?"

"I'd love to."

"They're in the dining room."

"This is a nice little house, Natalie."

"It's just a simple rambler."

"It isn't how grand it is. It's how you make it your own."

"William and I were comfortable."

"That crazy Englishman I married thought he had to live in a castle. New Cotswolds is an insanely big house for two people.

I enjoyed it, though. I'd live in a sewer pipe if I could have him with me. Him and that pain-in-the ass dog, Bentley. That dog was the only living thing that could steal time from me and Bunny."

"I'm sorry, Liz-Beth."

"That's OK, Natalie. I learned to live with it."

"These are William's parents when they were young."

"What a handsome couple. They looked so happy."

"After all they went though, they finally were."

"Such a tragedy."

Liz-Beth held the photo of John in his uniform. "Reminds me of wartime. Horrible and wonderful at the same time."

Liz-Beth wiped an eye with a handkerchief.

"Don't cry, Liz-Beth. You'll get me started. I don't want to cry today."

"I want to remember. William looks like his father. So handsome in his uniform. He would have given Bunny a run for his money."

"We could have been rivals."

"I might have shared him with you," Liz-Beth said with a gleam in her eye. The two of them giggled.

"This is me as a kid. This is William."

"Such beautiful children. How did Bunny and I miss out on that one?"

"How did you?"

"We were busy enjoying life, growing a company. Too late after we sold the business."

"We're too old to be kids but William and I can be your children. You can spank William when he deserves it."

"Haha. That sounds like fun. You hold him. You don't speak much about your parents, Natalie. Tell me about them."

"They're busy with their life in Philadelphia. We're there for each other if we're needed. My older sister lives there."

"What do they do there?"

"Dad's a city manager. Mom works for the Art Museum. They live in Society Hill."

"Where's that?"

"It's the old part of the city. They live in a townhouse near the Delaware River. They don't have a view but the River Drives along the Schuylkill River and Fairmont Park aren't far. The Art Museum is on the river at the end of the Ben Franklin Parkway near the university boat houses. It's very nice. A lot of our national history is there."

"I visited once before deploying to England on a hospital ship out of New York. I thought it was quaint. I saw Betsy Ross's house, Ben Franklin's house, Convention Hall, the Liberty Bell, Elfereth's Alley. I love the history. It gave me a sense of what we were fighting for."

"Did you see Elfereth?"

"I'm not that old!"

"Come with me when I visit my parents."

"I'd love to."

* * *

VK returned to LightSwitch. William drove past the Mountain View post office on Hope Street. He stopped at the Farmer's Market before joining Liz-Beth and Natalie.

"Charles is exploring the Stanford campus. Why don't we pick him up later and take him to MacArthur Park for dinner?"

"Great idea, William. We haven't been there in a while."

"Thank you for bringing me along, William."

"We always enjoy your company, Liz-Beth."

"Maria's making dinner at my house tomorrow night. Why don't the two of you join us?"

"I'd like that. I'm returning the following morning to work with Charles for a few days. We need to visit my friends at Intel. I'm gonna set up the lab again."

"Here we go again. If you don't mind I'll stay in Pescadero with Liz-Beth, if it's OK with you, Liz-Beth."

"Stay as long as you like. I love the company."

"I thought we could move back in here, William."

"I'd like to Natalie, but we need a place to work. I can't afford an office right now. I'd rather not live in the lab like we did the last time."

Natalie pouted. "I'm disappointed. We have no room in Pescadero."

William changed the subject. "VK says hello."

"How's he doing?"

"Great. Better if he had a good employer. He says he'll leave his wife for you if I dump you."

"That's sweet. I'll dump *you* if we don't move back into this house."

William let it go.

"Are you guys getting together again?"

"Maybe, Nat."

"Don't screw it up this time." Natalie smiled and shook a fist.

"We're all behind you William," Liz-Beth added. "Natalie, Josh, Maggie, myself, and Mr. Chuckles."

Thirty-Seven

Mason called Liz-Beth two weeks after their initial conversation. "What can you tell me?"

"Of the LightSwitch investigation, lots of smoke, no gun. Dunn and Cousie don't have many friends, do they?"

"None that I know of."

"They left a bloody trail of maimed and dead bodies over the years but they're Teflon coated, experts at camouflage and obfuscation."

"Sounds like the Dunn and Cousie I know. Did you speak with Evelyn?"

"I did. She couldn't offer much help. It's a painful subject. I don't think she knew much of her late husband's business dealings."

"The poor woman. We were close friends. We had theater tickets for the weekend after her husband killed himself. I wish I hadn't suggested speaking with her."

"I made it as easy as I could, bought her lunch in San Francisco. She needed someone to talk to. She needs a friend, Liz-Beth."

"I should have spent more time with her. I have to see her when I get to the city."

"Rumor in the financial community is Dunn & Cousie are strung out. They were aggressive about deploying capital into dotcoms late in the cycle. They have a mediocre portfolio of small companies in various stages of development, all technology, all bleeding cash, some promising but nothing nearing breakout. Typical for small venture capital firms. The top tier players hoover up the best opportunities."

"Did you hear anything LightSwitch specific?"

"Some kind of merger or acquisition activity. Sounds like they're trying to bundle LightSwitch with a portfolio of dogs to sell to a telecom company. It's hard to get information. The buyer is a public company that can't talk about it on the record. Could be Lucent, Alacatel, maybe Nortel, any of them. This is all second and third hand."

"Do you think it's reliable?"

"Reliable, but vague. I sense desperation. Like it's dragging out too long. I think they're coming to the financial brink."

"Where do you go from here?"

"There aren't many places left to look. I don't think I'm going to learn a lot more on my own. I would have sniffed out a smoking gun by now. I haven't heard anything that sounds fraudulent or illegal."

"What do you suggest?"

"I need to talk to William. He can give me a list of doors to knock on, questions for employees, executives, board members who might need something off their chest. Something Dunn and Cousie need to keep locked in the basement. I need him to point me in a direction."

"You can't go any further without speaking to William?"

"I don't think so."

"Think this has any potential?"

"I don't know yet. Maybe you can buy the company from them if they can't sell it. They may be under contract. If it were up to me I'd talk to a few company executives or board members. If nothing pops out I'd think about letting it go."

"OK, Erik. I need to speak to William first. He still doesn't know I retained you."

"I understand."

"How do you want to meet him?"

"I'll fly in, stay with Josh and Maggie. Let me know when to call him."

"What about our other project?"

"Complete mystery."

"Do you think you can solve it?"

"Don't know. I'll get over to Moffett when I come to town, speak with the Lockheed people who scheduled the flights and maintained the plane. See what they know."

"I'll let you know when to contact William."

Thirty-Eight

Liz-Beth drove to William and Natalie's cottage with Mr. Chuckles in his cage on the passenger seat of the MG.

"What a nice surprise! Liz-Beth and Chuckles are here, William."

"To what do we owe this treat, Liz-Beth?"

"Mr. Chuckles misses his friend and needs a visit."

"I'm his friend too."

"Friends; sorry, Natalie."

Liz-Beth opened the door of the cage. She brought Mr. Chuckles out on her hand. Chuckles spread his wings and stretched his neck in William's direction. When Liz-Beth handed him off, Chuckles walked up William's arm to his shoulder. He turned his head to stare at the ocean.

"He likes the view, William. We don't have one at our house."

"We like it too," Natalie said.

Natalie fed Mr. Chuckles out of a jar of nuts Liz-Beth handed her.

"Why can't I have a pet?" She rolled her lower lip into a frown.

William looked at Natalie in disapproval.

"I'm your pet."

Natalie let it go.

"What do you need to talk about, Liz-Beth?"

"You're getting smarter, William."

"I've been hanging around you."

Liz-Beth told William about Erik.

"I wish you hadn't done that."

"I was afraid you might feel that way. We needed to know this is going somewhere before bringing you into it."

"I don't want you getting involved."

"You're moving your life forward, but losing the company still bothers you."

"I can let it go, Liz-Beth. I can't reimburse your expenses."

"I won't take your money for this. This is for my friends Edgar and Evelyn; myself too. Bunny and I invested in their company. We lost our money. Joshua and I took Cousie to court. We were unsuccessful. Edgar is dead. Evelyn's life is ruined. I'm *in* it. Can't you indulge an elderly widow? Just enough to see if something can be done? If not, I'll drop it."

"It isn't your crusade, Liz-Beth. You should let somebody else deal with it."

"I'll quit if we hit a dead end. You can call it off any time you want to."

"Why don't you go along, William?" Natalie added. "It's important to her. It can't do any harm."

William sat at his desk. Mr. Chuckles stared through the picture window as if he never saw the ocean.

"OK, Liz-Beth. I'll talk to Mason. If I'm not comfortable with this it has to stop."

"That's all I'm asking. I'll have Erik get in touch with you."

Thirty-Nine

William spent Mondays through Thursdays in Mountain View, Fridays through Sundays in Pescadero. He worked in the lab in the Mountain View house, shuttled back and forth between Intel and Stanford. Natalie found a job with Young and Rubicam in San Francisco, worked from Pescadero when she could, stayed overnight with the friend she sublet her apartment to when she had to be in the city. Charles started classes. He lived in student housing near the Stanford campus, bought a used Honda Civic to drive to the lab in Mountain View. VK joined them evenings during the week. They made slow but steady progress. William enjoyed starting over. It reminded him of when he invented LightSwitch in his dorm room, one of the happiest times he remembered. Natalie couldn't have been happier unless she lived full time in the Mountain View house and William moved the lab to an office building.

Charles met a Japanese American student on the Stanford campus. They began dating to the delight of his parents. Hiromi was so yesterday. Akiko laughed and teased him about it. If Sukie's chest expanded any further it would have exploded.

* * *

Mason flew into San Carlos in the Mooney. He picked up his sun-faded dark brown ten-year-old Ford Taurus at the airport and drove to Josh and Maggie's. He parked on the south side of Josh and Maggie's house, behind the line of sight from Pescadero Creek Road. He used the key Joshua left him to enter the house and take a shower. Mason dressed, logged into his laptop, checked email, put his cell phone on vibrate and settled in with the San Francisco Chronicle he found in the living room. Josh joined him within the hour. When William and Natalie returned to the cottage, Joshua walked "Mace" across the driveway to introduce him and returned to his house.

A cross between organized crime enforcer and paramilitary, Erik Mason cut an imposing figure. He looked solid as a linebacker, moved with enough athleticism to play the position. Everything about him was big. Six foot one, you wouldn't call him tall. You could call him barrel chested. Thick, hard everywhere, his arms and legs were heavily muscled. A bull's neck connected a large head to a broad pair of shoulders. He looked like he could stop a bus or push one past Sisyphus, right up the side of a mountain.

Clean shaven, intelligent, Mason had short black hair, a deep voice, a Nevada desert tan. He dressed unremarkably in sandals, cargo shorts and a nondescript t-shirt. If not for bulk and fitness, he looked like everyman. A stainless-steel Breitling Navitimer exposed his persona, the one luxury item he wore that revealed an appreciation for quality and indicated he had money. Like the government agencies that trained him, Mason held his cards close to his vest. You couldn't know what he thought, but meeting him left an impression you could believe in. He feared nothing.

Mason shared the progress of his inquiry with Joshua and William. During the hour they spent together William shared the history of LightSwitch from the time Osgood invested in the company and joined the board. Impressed by Mason's presence and Joshua's endorsement, William agreed to email names and contact information of board members he thought might help or could be intimidated.

"I'm gonna start contacting them tomorrow." Mason said. "I don't expect them to make a case for us but the conversations will go right to Dunn and Cousie. If they think they're safe we won't hear anything. If they react it means they have something to fear. You might hear from them."

"Do you really think they'll contact me?"

"They'll think you hired me."

"What if I do hear from them?"

"Volunteer nothing. Don't answer any question that makes you uncomfortable, and don't lie. They'll use everything you say against you. You didn't hire me. If they ask, we met when I visited Josh and Maggie. You don't have to tell them what we discussed. Agree to nothing and try to remember everything."

"I'll do the best I can."

"The better you do, the more it will help. Hope they contact you."

"What about Liz-Beth?"

"I'll keep her out of it as long as possible. If this goes anywhere, she'll be involved. She wants to be. If they ask about her, or Josh and Maggie, you know them as friends and neighbors. Keep them talking and remember what they say. Say as little as possible. Answer questions in one word, one syllable, a grunt if you can, yes or no whenever possible."

"This is like a detective show."

"It isn't like any show. It's your life."

"What do you think is going to come of this?"

"Probably nothing. If somebody doesn't drop a bomb we won't have anything to run with. We cut expenses and move on. Thieves sometimes get away with it. People get screwed. That's how it often ends. Liz-Beth wants to give it a try. Once in a while something pops out that Josh can burn them with."

"I never know what's in the washer until I start agitating. I'm not surprised by any of it no matter how incredible. It's what keeps me doing this. Someday I'll tell you how smart people trip themselves up in ways you think are so stupid you can't believe they did it. Some of them are head cases who want to get caught and don't realize it. Some get away with it too many times, convince themselves they're invincible, get sloppy. It's a game to some people, to see how far they can go. Professional career criminals are the worst. They're ruthless, cautious, they don't want to get caught."

"What are we dealing with?"

"Career criminals. It's very difficult to get hard evidence on them. It's usually circumstantial, not enough to meet the legal standard of proof of fraud. Irritate them as much as you like, but don't push too hard. These guys have significant financial pressure on them. Back down and walk away if it gets confrontational."

"I don't want any trouble. I wouldn't mind if you dropped the whole thing."

"Liz-Beth wouldn't be happy with either of us if I did that."

Mason smiled at William, put a hand on his shoulder. *Like being petted by a bear*, William thought.

"I'm not trying to scare you, William. You have to protect yourself. If these guys are caught committing fraud it's going to cost them a fortune. They can go to prison. At their age it's game over."

"You expect them to contact me, don't you?"

"Yes I do. I think these guys are dirty. If I'm right, when I talk to the board, it's going to scare the hell out of them. They might try to get you to back off. They might be aggressive. I want you to be prepared. Can you handle that, William?"

"Do I have a choice?"

"Not unless Liz-Beth changes her mind. If you hear from them call me on my cell phone while it's fresh in your mind. Don't wait. Don't do anything or talk to anyone else before you talk to me."

"Sure. Any time?"

"24-7. I need to be the first person you speak to."

"Isn't this a little melodramatic?"

"No. It isn't."

Forty

The birds went after the berries in the New Cotswolds garden when Bentley roamed the property. Now they fear red tail hawks and owls. Rabbits and mice aren't safe or brave, nor is the occasional snake. They know escape works better than fighting. When attacked, all living things have to decide between fight and flight.

William and Natalie started a vegetable garden. The property was perfect for it. Mild climate, cool, foggy summers deliver moisture and shield it from heat. Sandy ground needed top soil and fertilization. Easy enough to find in a farming community. They planted lettuce, cilantro, arugula, onions and carrots. They planted pumpkin, zucchini, artichokes and tomatoes. Sukie helped them cover the plants with netting to protect them from pests.

Two weeks passed since Mason visited. He didn't learn anything significant from contact with board members but he sensed anxiety through the phone line as he punched though the list William gave him. William rose early to weed the garden. Natalie tossed a salad for lunch. Late in the morning a black late model S Class Mercedes sedan turned onto Pescadero Creek Road from Highway One, rolled down the street, idled up William's driveway. Joshua watched it stop next to William's cottage while he washed his truck. He dropped the sponge in the soap bucket and sat on a stool where he could see William's garden. William heard tires rolling over gravel. He looked up, saw the car and continued weeding. The driver's door of the Mercedes opened. A stout man in his early-70's with a full head of grey flowing hair stepped out. He dressed smartly in a white button-down long sleeve shirt, black pants and black Gucci loafers. He walked up to William and offered his hand.

"Hello, William. Remember me? I'm Robert Cousie."

William froze. He paused to recall what Mason told him. He shook Cousie's hand.

"Hello Robert. How did you find me here?"

"You aren't hard to find. Are you going to ask me in?"

William thought about Natalie. He heard the radio playing faintly through the doorway. Natalie stood at the kitchen counter with her back to the window. William hoped she wouldn't see or hear the Mercedes, and Cousie would be gone before she knew he came there.

"We can talk here. Why did you come here?"

William glanced at the long handle weeder in his hand. It made a fearsome weapon. Cousie noticed him tighten his grip.

"Not a friendly way to greet somebody. Thinking of using that thing on me?" Cousie flashed a crooked smile of artificially whitened teeth.

William relaxed his grip. He didn't put the weeder down.

"I know you're Dunn's partner. I moved on. I have no interest in getting even."

"Even for what?"

"I'm not getting into that, Robert. It's over."

"Is it?"

"Yeah, as far as I'm concerned."

"Why is this Las Vegas creep calling my board members?"

God, this guy has balls to come here, William thought. *Remember what Mason told you. Stay cool. Give him nothing. Don't lie.*

"I didn't send him after you."

"How did you know it was a man?"

Shit, I gave it away already, William thought.

"I can guess who did. The witch down the road."

"What makes you think so?"

"You know who I'm talking about don't you? I don't believe in coincidences."

"What coincidences?"

"She hired Mason. The two of you just happen to live in this tiny place of six hundred people. You met her after you lost your job and moved here."

Damn, he knows everything, William thought.

"You think you have the right to interfere in my business?"

"Why would I interfere in your business?"

"You deny it?"

William didn't answer.

"Why did you come here, Cousie? Dropped by on the way to Santa Cruz? Need help with your computer network? Just like it here in Pescadero and wanted to visit? What do you want?"

"I want you to get the hell out of my business. We bought your shares. You no longer work at LightSwitch and have no further interest in it. Call off your attack dog."

"I didn't send anyone after you."

"OK. Let's try this another way. What would it take to make you stop?"

"Make me stop what?"

"Don't fuck with me William. I know what you're doing. You could come back to work. Not as CEO. That would be hard to explain. In some advisory capacity. Osgood needs somebody who knows the business. We can give you some of your shares back as options, a consulting contract. We can't pay you much. You don't have to do much. Join the advisory committee. Come to a few meetings, give us your opinion."

"Is the acquisition proceeding?"

"I can't talk about that. Are you trying to derail it?"

"I'm not trying to do anything about it."

"You can work on it."

"I don't think so."

"You could be part of something bigger."

"What do you mean?"

"Come on. Osgood told you about it."

"He was vague. How's it going?"

"It's progressing."

"I need to know more about it. With what company, on what terms, what are the future plans?"

"I can't share that until you come on board."

"I can't agree to anything, conditioned on something I know nothing about."

"You can quit if you don't like it. What's it worth to you?"

"To rejoin the company?"

"To stop looking up my asshole!"

"I'm not coming after you. I moved on to something else. I no longer care what happens to LightSwitch. I'm not climbing back into that bed. It was pretty ugly for me. I wish you would just leave me alone and let me get on with my life."

"You little snot-nose son-of-a-bitch."

"This is between you and me. I'd appreciate it if you left my mother out of it. Unlike you, I still miss her."

"You sneaky, conniving punk. You're just like your father."

"Thanks for the compliment."

"That's no compliment. Your father was a self-righteous prick."

William tried to laugh it off. He knew Cousie baited him. He slid toward the limit of control. *Remember what Mason said,* he told himself.

"My father was twice the man you are." As soon as the words came out of his mouth, William knew he shouldn't have said them. "I didn't mean that. He brought you through the war."

Cousie knew he found a soft spot.

"You don't know a goddamn thing about what happened in the war. I got into it to stop your father from fucking my wife."

"Be careful what you say about my mother. I know how much you cheated on her."

"It's different when a man has other women. Your father kicked me out of the squadron to get me out of the way. They planned it. Your mother was a slut!"

William turned red. He felt anger boiling over. He squeezed

the handle of the weeder. *Don't let him get to you, William*, he said to himself. *He's trying to provoke you.*

William pulled a cell phone out of a pants pocket.

"I have to take this. I'll be right back."

He didn't have a call. He walked to the cottage with the weeder. *I'll wait this prick out. I'll make him snap.* Cousie thought.

William sat under the great room picture window with the phone at his ear where Cousie could see it. He opened the bottom desk drawer and stared at his father's 1911 model Colt .45.

I can shoot him in the head, drag the body around the side of the house, cover it with a tarp, and bury him in the meadow tonight. Nobody will find him, William thought. *We hear guns go off in the hills sometimes. If nobody sees me, I can get away with it.*

Natalie heard William enter the house. She looked out the window. She shuddered when she saw her uncle standing in the garden. She saw the Colt in the open drawer with William sitting in front of it. She rushed the desk, grabbed the gun and wrapped it in a dishtowel. She ran out the door, across the driveway, past Joshua sitting on the stool with a glass of ice tea in one hand, a remote phone in the other. Joshua rushed into the house after her.

"What's going on over there?"

"That's Robert Cousie having it out with William."

"Shit! It's been so long I didn't recognize him." Joshua put a hand on Natalie's shoulder. She shoved the dishcloth at him. He unwrapped it.

"What the hell is this?"

"William's father's gun. You have to hide it from him. I think he was going to shoot Robert."

"Jesus Christ. I didn't think they were getting married. I didn't know they were arguing either."

Maggie arrived from the kitchen. She saw Natalie and Joshua with the gun. "Take Natalie in the kitchen, Maggie."

Natalie protested. Maggie made her sit at the kitchen table while Joshua walked outside. She poured a glass of water. Natalie's hands shook, spilling water as she drank.

"Joshua will take care of it, Natalie."

Joshua returned to the driveway and hid the Colt in a potted plant.

What the hell am I doing? William thought. *If I walked out there with that thing I might have used it.*

William returned to the garden with the weeder.

"Screwing my niece, huh?"

"What we do is our business."

"Then you know the difference between your business and my business. Why don't you stay out of mine, and I'll stay out of yours?"

"You just asked me to come back to LightSwitch."

"Tell you what, punk, you get that hag friend of yours to lay off us. Get the prick from Las Vegas to stop calling board members and I'll call it even. You won't see me again."

"You have no business here, Cousie. I want you to leave."

"Agree to tell Liz-Beth to get off my back."

"Get out of here now."

"Are you going to leave us alone?"

"If you don't leave, I'll call the sheriff."

"He probably owes me."

"You can stand there until tomorrow if it takes that long for the sheriff to get here. I know what you're trying to do. I'm done talking to you."

"Leave us alone," Cousie said as he back-stepped to the car.

"Or what?" William asked after him.

Cousie stepped into the car, spun the tires in the gravel and raced down the driveway. The car skidded to a rolling stop at Pescadero Road. William walked to the edge of the knoll. He watched the Mercedes turn north and speed up Cabrillo Highway.

Leaving is the first intelligent thing he did, William thought.

Joshua retrieved the Colt from the planter, brought it in the house and hid it where it couldn't be found.

Forty-One

William followed Natalie to Josh and Maggie's house after Cousie's Mercedes disappeared over a distant hill. He found the three of them at the kitchen table. Natalie hunched over in a chair, glass of water in hand. Maggie held her other hand. Joshua stood behind her with his hands on her shoulders.

Joshua straightened up when William entered the room. "What the hell was that about?"

William ignored him, leaned down, put his arms around Natalie. She set the glass down, stood and threw her arms around his back.

"Are you okay?"

Natalie looked up at him. "No, I'm not okay. What was that bastard doing here?"

"Mason said they might contact me. I didn't think he would come here."

"I don't want him here. What were you doing with that gun? Were you going to shoot him?"

"I'm not going to shoot anybody. Where is it?"

"I have it."

"Hold on to it, Josh. It belonged to my father."

Natalie sat down. "I don't want that thing in the house."

"It's in a safe place." Joshua said. "What did Cousie want, William?"

"He wants us to back off."

"What did he say?"

"He offered me a consulting job with the company. What

bullshit. They never listened to me. He just wants to buy me off or get me to say I sent Mason after him."

"What did you tell him?"

"Not interested."

"Did you tell him anything about what we're doing?"

"I denied it but he knows."

"He knows what?"

"Liz-Beth is behind it."

"Shit. You better tell her and Mace."

"As soon as Natalie and I go home."

"How did it get so heated?"

"He went after my parents."

"He's trying to get you to do or say something he can use against you."

"He wouldn't get anything but shot if I had the gun with me." He glanced at Natalie. "I didn't mean that. I said things I shouldn't have. I didn't give him anything. I just let him see me get angry."

"Did he threaten you, William?"

"No."

"You need to think about getting an injunction."

Natalie jumped in. "He isn't crazy, Josh. He just thinks he can fix everything with a confrontation. He thinks intimidation is a hobby."

"Driving unannounced up somebody's driveway and starting a confrontation isn't normal behavior, Natalie. It's pretty aggressive. You can ask a judge to tell him to stay away from you and your property."

"I don't think he'll be back, Josh. I'm not afraid of him. He's lucky I didn't cleave his head with the hoe."

"Watch what you say, William. Your words can come back to haunt you. Are you feeling better Natalie?"

"I am now that he's gone. Let's go home, William."

Forty-Two

Mason took the call from a houseboat on Lake Mead.

"You handled it well."

"We don't know any more than we did yesterday."

"Yes we do, William. We learned two things. LightSwitch board members are nervous. They take us seriously. So does Cousie. They feel threatened or they wouldn't have told Cousie I contacted them. He wouldn't have showed up at your house. If we didn't get their attention we could quit now. Since we did, I think we should keep pressuring them. Cousie is either hiding something or we're causing some kind of trouble by asking around."

"Are we any closer to a smoking gun?"

"We learned there's a good chance there is one. That's thing number two."

Forty-Three

Cousie called Liz-Beth that evening. She read his name on caller ID.

"Well, hello, Mr. Cousie. How nice to hear from you."

"Bullshit, Elizabeth. You know why I'm calling."

"OK if you want it that way, Robert. Why don't we at least start by being civil to one another?"

"Get off my back, Elizabeth."

"Whatever do you mean?"

"Same old evasive bitch."

"Be specific. I might answer your questions. I'll end the call if you have nothing of substance to say."

"You hired that creep Mason to harass my board. I want it stopped."

"There's nothing illegal about asking questions."

"It's harassment, interference with a business relationship."

"They don't have to take the call if they don't want to. What are you afraid of?"

"You know a company can't let an outside agitator harass its board. Ask me whatever you want."

"Really. Not so long ago, you wouldn't take a call from me. I guess I didn't have anything you needed."

"You don't need me to explain this to you, Elizabeth. Stop screwing with me! I don't know why I called you."

"I don't know either. I already know what you want. Didn't you talk to William?"

"I know you're working together. That piece of shit. He's just like his father."

"Lucky for him he isn't your son."

"Think you can take me on, Elizabeth? I beat you once, you and your cornpone lawyer, what's his name?"

"Joshua."

"Yeah, Mr. Bean Pole. Mr. Green Jeans." Cousie laughed.

"I haven't forgotten what you did to Evelyn and her husband."

"Oh, you're still pissed about that. Think you can get even. Is that it?"

"No, Robert. That can't be evened. Make you happy, did it?"

"I didn't know her and I didn't kill him. It was business."

"What did you take from them?"

"Did you prove I stole anything?"

"To Joshua, Evelyn and myself."

"That's been decided. You can't try that case again."

"You're a career criminal."

"What makes you feel like you have to crusade for other people?"

"I care about people. You should give it a try."

"Do you think they would do this for you?"

"I hope so."

"What is it going to take to get you to stop?"

"What if I don't want to stop? What if I want to have this contest?"

"For that wimp Edgar? That coward? For that asshole who stole my wife, and the opportunity to serve my country? You think I haven't lost anything? You think I'm not a victim? I was a good provider, a great flier, a combat fighter pilot. Do you think John was a moral man when he stole my wife? Do you think he served his country when he chained me to a supply desk?"

"The way I heard it, you couldn't fly a balsawood model. You burned up a warehouse full of engines, set the world record for ground loops. Where did you get your wings, Robert? Woolworth's? Sears and Roebuck? Which side were you fighting for? The Japanese would have given you medals! Edgar and Evelyn were lovely people. They weren't vicious cutthroats like you are.

Miriam's only flaw was she married *you*. John was shot down saving you when half the squadron was almost wiped out trying to help you. Did you thank him? You dove out to save yourself. Who's the coward? Now you're going after John's son and your niece because she's in the way. What did they ever do to you?"

"I dated Miriam before John did. I introduced them! She was in love with him her entire life even though he dumped her and ran off to San Diego. I married her! She never loved me. She ruined *my* life. Better women would have married me. It cost me a fortune to get myself assigned to Asia so I could try to hold on to her. I had to bribe half the Pentagon. I wanted to serve my country. John held me back. I had to get in it anyway I could. Living with Miriam was like living with an iceberg. John didn't do a goddamn thing for her. He couldn't support her on Navy pay. She dreamed of him every day of her life while we were married. She whispered his name in her sleep. She used me while she dreamed about him. I was nothing to her but financial support and a roof over her head. Don't you think I have feelings?"

"Miriam was brilliant, Robert. She had her own career and didn't need anything from you. She broke off their affair the day you arrived in Australia. If she loved him as much as you say she did, and broke up with him to save you, does that sound like she used you? She sacrificed the love of her life to get you into his squadron so he could look after you. Don't you know that? She asked him to get you through the war. Do you know how hard that must have been? In spite of how terrible it had to be for John, he *did* it. It ruined his career, his chances for a life with her. You know he was almost killed saving you. How can you speak about them like this?"

"Saint John and Saint Miriam. That's what you think?"

I wish I could see his face, Liz-Beth thought. *I just wish I could see his face.* If you cared about her, you should have let her go."

"She was my wife, Liz-Beth, and I loved her."

Cousie's voice cracked. Liz-Beth never heard pain in his

voice, or feeling expressed for another human being. *"Maybe he is human,"* she thought. Is this what's made him so twisted?

"Did you ever tell her?"

"Tell her what?"

"You loved her."

Cousie didn't answer.

"Your wife in name only, Robert. On a piece of paper. A contract, nothing more. How much philandering did you do? How many mistresses did you have?"

"Was I supposed to be celibate, Liz-Beth? A married monk? I'm a man. I have needs. I loved her, Elizabeth. She never cared about me. She used me. Why won't anybody admit it? Why does everyone believe she was a saint and I was Satan?"

"They're dead, Robert. Let the living live. Make something good out of what's left of your life. Think I hate you, Robert? I don't. I pity you. We all love and lose, and love again. We're all hurt. It's how you deal with it, Robert. Get help. Talk it out with a professional."

"Fuck off, Elizabeth. There's nothing wrong with me."

"The whole world's wrong, you're right, everybody's against you. That's normal? Why can't you make an honest living, Robert? Even if what you told me about John and Miriam is true, you're still a thief and a liar. Do you think being hurt entitles you to punish everyone you meet? To steal their property? You went after your own family. You turned this into a vendetta against a dead man's son, somebody who had nothing to do with any of it. You're a MONSTER!"

"You fucking hag. You think I'm made of granite? Why is it always about the suffering I caused, never about *my* suffering?"

"I'm done debating the past, Robert. Sell William back his equity. You and the fat guy…"

"Osgood."

"Osgood Dunn. Sell your shares, give up your board seats, agree to have nothing else to do with William, Natalie, and LightSwitch and I'll stop asking questions."

Cousie laughed into the phone.

"Are you going to let me finish?"

"There's more?"

"Apologize to Evelyn. Compensate her for stealing the family business and driving her husband to suicide."

"Go to hell, Elizabeth! I don't owe Evelyn anything. That was decided in court."

"I'll consider any offer, Robert. I'm not walking away empty-handed."

"You're fishing. If you had something it would be on the table. I'm not going to pay extortion money to get you to stop harassing me. When you have something, call me."

"Why did you go to Williams' house? Why did you call me?"

"Let me know if you ever have anything to bargain with. Until then, get off my back, you cunt-face bitch."

Cousie slammed the phone down.

Liz-Beth heard a click when Joshua placed his handset on the receiver. He joined her in the great room.

"What do you think of that, Josh?"

"That's one pissed off guy, Liz-Beth. I don't remember him being so emotional."

"How did you know he would call tonight, Joshua?"

Joshua cocked his head and raised an eyebrow.

Forty-Four

Liz-Beth, William, Natalie and Maria made chicken quesadillas at Liz-Beth's cottage. William and Natalie started a food fight that ended in a laughing contest after Liz-Beth and Maria joined in. They wrecked Liz-Beth's kitchen. Mr. Chuckles didn't know what to think. *Crazy people. What would they do to me if I did this?*

Maria seemed uncomfortable around William when she served dessert.

"Is there something you want to say, Maria?"

"Yes Mr. Beckensale."

"William. Please call me William,"

"Yes William. You remember my nephew Lupe?"

"Guadalupe? Yeah, we spoke about him. Does he still work at LightSwitch?"

"He has something to tell you."

William looked up from his flan.

"What about?"

"I cannot say. He wants to talk to you in person."

Maria removed a note from an apron pocket. She handed it to William. Liz-Beth and Natalie paused.

"Do you know anything about this, Liz-Beth?"

"No."

William unfolded the note. He found a handwritten message. "Hi, William. I wish to speak to you in private. It's important. Please do not call me at work. Please use this cellphone number in the evening. Lupe."

William looked at his watch. Still early. "Please excuse me." He rose from the table and stepped outside.

"Lupe? You need to speak to me?"

"Yes."

"Can you tell me what this is about?"

"I prefer to tell you in person."

"Has something bad happened?"

"No. I have something to show you."

"Do you want to meet near the office?"

"Can we meet someplace away from the valley?"

"Here, in Pescadero?"

"It would take too long to get there and back. I'd like to meet over lunch."

"You know where Alice's Restaurant is?"

"Yes. I stop there sometimes when I visit Aunt Maria."

"You know the red headed waitress?"

"Yes. Everyone is in love with the red head waitress. Her heart belongs to someone else."

"It belongs to herself."

"I know this is short notice, William. Can we meet there tomorrow?"

"I can be there tomorrow. How 'bout noon?"

"See you then. Thank you, William."

"It will be good to see you, Lupe."

"And you, William."

William called VK and Charles. He told them he would not come to Mountain View the following day. He stepped inside and sat down to his flan.

"This is good. Thanks for a great dinner, Maria."

"I am glad you like it. Thank you for speaking to Lupe."

"You don't need to thank me for that, but you're welcome."

"What was that all about?"

"I don't know, Natalie. He wants to meet tomorrow. Do you need the Alfa?"

"I can use the MG if I need to. I like driving it."

The conversation with Lupe kept William awake. *It had to be about LightSwitch, but what? Lupe's leaving and needs a reference? It can't be personal. We weren't that close. What's going on at LightSwitch?* William wondered. *Something I need to see. He can't tell me on the phone.* William looked at Natalie. She sailed into dreamland halfway between awake and asleep. William gave up thinking about the phone call, kissed Natalie's cheek to make her smile and fell asleep.

William woke at sunrise and went for a run on the beach. Natalie slept in. She had breakfast ready for him when he returned.

"You'll make me fat from all this food."

"Get out and run more. I'm not living with a fat man or a flabby one and I like spoiling you."

"Keep cooking. I'll run more."

William logged into email, scanned the Mercury News, showered, dressed in a tee shirt, sneakers and jeans, pulled on a sweater and kissed Natalie.

"Imposter; you look like Harrison Ford. Not your geeky self." She pushed the sweater sleeves up to his elbows. "Are your sure you're a computer nerd?"

"Pretty sure. Don't do anything without me," William said. He raised an eyebrow.

Natalie blushed.

"Gotcha."

William put on his Ray-ban aviators, a baseball cap and stepped out the back door.

The Alfa isn't powerful like his father's car but it's quick and nimble. It fit William like a glove. After all the miles he put on it he drove it like an extension of himself. William flew up the hill on Highway 84, taking the corners as fast as he dared. The Alfa handled predictably. It tracked through turns as if it rode on rails. William shifted through the gears, keeping the motor in the RPM range were the power is. The little four-cylinder was high spirited and well-tuned. The exhaust system resonated a crisp dramatic tone. *Driving this car will always be fun,* he thought.

I wonder if Red's working today? William asked himself. He hadn't been to Alice's since the day Osgood sacked him. The thought of returning brought memories of a pretty, bouncy red head, the Harley rider, the Ducatis. William smiled. He remembered every mile of the drive to the cottage, the sunset on the beach. Not his favorite memory. It hasn't turned out so bad, not bad enough to spoil his mood this morning. Driving a sports car up Highway 84 always put him in a good mood.

William arrived early. He parked across from the motorcycle repair shop, stepped into Alice's, took a booth in the back to watch for Lupe. A red-headed waitress bounced out of the kitchen and approached the table.

Déjà vu, William thought. "Red" strolled to his table with pad, pencil and a smug look. She slouched, waited for William to speak, smirked at him, ready to parry if he made a pass. Scarlet waves cascaded over her shoulders. Tight faded blue denim shorts, freshly pressed white short-sleeve blouse, freckles, Coppertone tan, narrow waist, legs, attitude. Scented like she came from the spa.

Stunning, William thought. *Daisy of the west.*

"May I have a coffee?"

"Sure. Here for lunch?"

"Yeah, somebody's joining me. Last time I ate here I was pointed in the other direction."

"I remember. Get yourself fired again?"

"No," William laughed. "Stayed fired. I like the food."

Red smiled. "How's it working for Ya?"

"After a difficult start, pretty well. I don't recommend it."

"I'll keep working on my PhD."

William laughed. "Where are you studying?"

"Stanford."

"Really?"

"Girl has to support herself. Where did you think I learned how to take an order?"

"No rich technology boyfriend?'

"None I discuss with customers."

"What's your major?"

"Anthropology. I like studying men."

William laughed. "You're an expert."

"Are you flirting with me?"

"Of course. How 'bout a few extra fries."

"I'll see what I can do."

"Don't get yourself in trouble."

"The cook will do anything for me."

"I bet he will. He probably has a crush on you."

"What do you mean *probably*?"

"I'm William. May I ask your name?"

"Alice."

"Nooooo," William shook his head.

"I can see you graduated cum laude." She laughed and went for coffee.

William watched "Alice" walk to the kitchen, shook his head and sighed. *"Natalie would kill me."*

Lupe stepped through the entry and glanced around the restaurant.

William stood and waved. Lupe walked to the table. They shook hands.

"Good to see you Lupe. How are you?"

"I'm well, William. Good to see you too."

Lupe greeted William with a warm, genuine smile, but he looked uncomfortable. His eyes darted around the room.

"How's work?"

"Not fun like it used to be."

"Please sit down. I ordered coffee."

"Sorry I couldn't say anything on the phone."

Lupe removed a manila folder from a pouch in his lap top case.

"This is the reason I needed to meet you."

William's eyes widened when Lupe opened the folder, pulled out a set of documents and showed him the title page.

"Yellow tabs mark the important pages. Maybe you'd like to read a little."

"I *would*."

"Is Red here?"

"Yeah, serving up attitude."

"I love this place."

"She says her name is Alice."

Lupe laughed. "She tells everyone that. I bet she told you she has a degree in anthropology. I wish she would study me a little closer."

"Here she comes. Could be your lucky day."

"Not with you here, gringo. She pays no attention to me."

"You two cowboys ready to order? How about you, Mr. Brando?"

"I've been ready since the fall of the Roman Empire."

"That was Mr. Heston, but I'll go with it. Let me guess. You're a Centurion."

"A Hebrew prince, betrayed, sent into slavery by a childhood Roman friend. Trained as a chariot driver. This is my mentor, Sheik Ilderim."

"I saw that one, Mr. Ben-Hur. If you want to eat you better order. Your race starts in half an hour."

William and Lupe laughed and ordered lunch.

"She loves me, Lupe. She doesn't want me to die in the arena."

"Alice" smirked and left for the kitchen.

"She loves everybody in pantalones, William, especially if they fall in love with her, which is just about everybody; man, women and beast."

"You're such a cynic. No wonder you're looking around like a spook."

"I don't want anybody in the company to see me here."

"Where the hell did you get the LightSwitch business plan?"

"Somebody left it on a table in the conference room after the board meeting ended, the day they sacked you."

"Holly crap, Lupe. Is it on the company servers or the email system?"

"No, I looked. I'm gonna wash my hands." Lupe left for the restroom.

Holy shit! William said to himself, as he thumbed through the pages. He touched a hand to his head. "Somebody doodled on it."

Lupe returned. William pointed at the doodles.

"Did you do this?"

"No."

"These letters, RC. What do they mean?"

"I don't know, William."

"VK told me about the meeting."

"I arrived before he did."

"Did you hear them?"

"I heard some of it. They aren't real careful about what they say in front of a dumb Mexican."

"What were they talking about?"

"Business talk. It didn't interest me. I'm an engineer."

"Are you sure? It might be important."

"There was something about selling LightSwitch to another company. I don't know much, really."

"That *is* important. Did you hear the name of the company they want to sell to?"

"If I did, I don't remember."

"Come on, Lupe."

"I *don't*, William."

"Who was in the meeting?"

"I don't know those guys. Does it matter? You have the plan."

"Yeah it matters. They can say they didn't know anything about this."

"I don't know who brought it in or who wrote it. Hey, can you leave me out of this? They can say I stole intellectual property and gave it to somebody outside the company."

"I don't know. Why didn't you give this to me sooner?"

"I didn't know it mattered. When Maria told me you and Liz-Beth were trying to do something with the company I read through it and thought you could use it."

"You knew it was important. You kept it."

"That's exactly what they're going to say if they find out. I stole it and I'm a conspirator. You might get your company back. The best I can hope for is I keep my job. I don't have money to hire fancy lawyers. Are you going to pay my legal expenses?"

"I can't pay my own legal expenses. They won't bother you. They know they can't get money out of you if you don't have it."

"Don't you know I'm an illegal immigrant?"

William blanched. "We didn't hire illegal immigrants. How did you get a social security number? You don't have a green card?"

"How could you be unaware of this, William? You were the CEO."

"I don't ask people if they have the right to be here, Lupe. We had an HR department for that. Why didn't you do something about this? NAFTA made it easy."

"You don't qualify under NAFTA if you're already here illegally. My parents brought me across as a kid. What was I supposed to do? Go back to Mexico and ask for a visa? It would have been denied. Do you think I should work as a gardener? Hang around the Home Depot parking lot and look for day work for eighty dollars a day? I'm the first member of my family to go to college. My parents worked like dogs in low wage service jobs to save money to send me. I worked hard in school. I earned a BSE. I deserve better and so do they."

"Lupe, this isn't a big deal. If I get the company back, we can sponsor you."

"Tell the government you want to hire an illegal alien? If they find out I worked for you on a fake social security number they'll arrest both of us. If you *don't* get the company back? Say you want to start one and sponsor somebody who's here illegally? Don't you know anything about this?"

"It's all new to me. There aren't that many deportations."

"Are you naïve, William? Proposition 187 almost passed. A lot of Californians don't want us here. Look what these people did to you. Aunt Maria and her husband, Jose and his wife. My whole family is here illegally. Can you sponsor all of them? You can't even sponsor me!"

"They won't be dragged into this. I'm not going to tell anybody."

"*William!* If someone investigates me, they'll discover it. Those guys who screwed you are company directors. All they have to do is call the INS and tell them they learned they have an illegal immigrant working at the company, to come get him. When they find out I'm not supposed to be here, they'll ask where my parents are and how they got here. They'll find the rest of the family. They can threaten to have us all deported. They didn't hire me, William. You did. They'll use it against you."

"Lupe, if this goes anywhere, somebody is going to ask me where I got this."

"Tell them you found it."

"In my box at the Mountain View Post Office? I kept it to myself all this time? Who's going to believe that? They put you under oath in depositions. I could go to jail for perjury."

"My entire family can be *deported*! I could be convicted of a felony. I would never be able to reenter the country legally. William! Do you care about anybody besides yourself? Do you think about the consequences to other people? I'm trying to help you! Maybe you should give the business plan back. I'll destroy it and forget I ever saw it."

"Lupe, please don't raise your voice. We don't know who's in here. Look, I appreciate what you're doing for me."

"*Bullshit*, William. Nobody has to know where you got this."

"I might need you to say you found it in the board room during the meeting, maybe identify who was in there. I'm not asking you to lie."

"You're asking me to risk my ass. It doesn't help you. It doesn't prove who wrote it. You're going to tell them I took it and gave it to you? *Fuck you William.* They'll put me under oath too. Do you want to share a cell? How can you pressure me like this when I'm risking my family to help you?"

"I'm sorry, Lupe. This is all new to me. I apologize for not realizing…. Look, we have a problem. You know how important it is for me to get the company back. It matters to you too. I don't want to cause trouble for your family. I might have to prove who knew about this and who wrote it. I don't know how to do it without your help, or for you to help without exposing yourself. I appreciate what you did. It might not be enough. We have to find a way. Let's not argue over this. We like each other too much. Maria is Liz-Beth's friend. I don't want anything to happen to her or her family."

"Alice" interrupted with lunch. She saw the conversation turned serious and moved to the next table. William and Lupe ate without speaking. Lupe broke the silence when they finished.

"Can't you just say you found the plan on the way out of the building?"

William took a deep breath.

"I don't know, Lupe. If I need your help, I have to ask."

"I can't promise to help you any further."

William clenched his teeth. He rubbed the back of his neck. "What would you like from me Lupe?"

"I want you to promise to keep me out of anything you do to get the company back. If you succeed, I want to keep working at LightSwitch. American citizens deceived you, stole your company. An illegal alien tried to help you get it back because it's the right thing to do. I want you to remember that."

"You do quality work, Lupe. You'll always find employment with me. I'll sponsor you somewhere, somehow. You'll be able to work here legally. I'll try to keep you out of a fight to get the company back but I can't guarantee you won't be pulled into it. I promise to let you know if I'm aware of anything that might hurt you or your family. Can you live with that?"

"I'm not sure I can."

William swallowed. "Will you help if I need you?"

"Depends. Maybe if there's no other way. Not if it means my family might suffer."

"Lupe."

"Best I can give you, William."

"Alice" left the check on the table and returned to the kitchen. William and Lupe hardly noticed.

"I could have destroyed those documents without telling anyone."

"I know Lupe. Thank you. Are we still friends?"

Lupe stared at the table. He looked at William. "Still friends."

"I'll pick up the check, Lupe."

They shook hands in the parking lot.

"Thanks. I won't forget this."

"I would have felt guilty if I didn't help."

"Does anybody else know about this? Has anyone else seen it?"

"No. Only you, me, the people who created and discussed it"

"I have a project running at the house in Mountain View. The lead is a brilliant engineer from Japan. He's creative. His ideas are good. You'd like him."

"I heard about this."

"I knew it would get out. I hope it doesn't cause trouble for VK."

"I don't think he cares. He and everybody else are fed up with LightSwitch."

"I hope I can do something about that."

"So do I."

"Why don't you talk to VK? See if you can help afterhours. We don't have any money. I can give you equity. Help us, Lupe. If we're successful we'll all have money."

"I'll talk to VK."

"Thanks, Lupe. Take care of yourself. If there's anything I can do for you I'd like to hear about it."

"The best thing you can do for me is get the company back without help from me."

"I promise to try. Goodbye Lupe."

"Goodbye William."

Forty-Five

William chose a window table at the general store. Natalie, Joshua and Liz-Beth joined him. William shared the business plan. Joshua's eyes widened. He didn't look surprised.

"Amazing, isn't it, Josh?"

"Don't mean to make you sound naïve, William. Writers want you to think brilliant investigators solve cases with Sherlock Holmes intellect. The truth is somebody usually leaves incriminating evidence. Somebody else discovers it and hands it off."

Joshua scanned the bookmarked pages. He shook his head.

"Where did you get this?"

"I'd rather not say."

"Did you steal it from the company?"

"No."

"You found it on a park bench."

"I'd tell you if I could."

"You might not be able to protect your source."

"I need to if it's possible."

"It's a smoking gun. We can guess who wrote it, but we have no proof. It's obvious to us but not to everyone we need to believe it. There's no date. There aren't any names on it. You need to be able to connect it to Dunn and Cousie and prove it was written before they terminated you. Can you do that?"

"What if we can't do that?"

"It doesn't make a case. We can try using it to pressure them. If I were their attorney, I'd make you prove it came from my client."

"I need to know how far we can go with it."

"Your source must be important to you."

"It is."

"Hold up guys. What are we talking about?" Liz-Beth asked.

"Page 12. They planned to manufacture a temporary financial crisis to force William out, buy his shares at a deep discount, reverse the crisis and sell the company for a profit. This is criminal fraud. They wrote the complaint for us."

"Can you believe somebody would put this in a business plan?" Natalie asked.

"I've seen it before. Whoever wrote it is terminally stupid or a serial white-collar criminal. Get away with this sort of thing enough times you think you're untouchable. I admire you for loyalty, William, but this could have come from a number of sources. You might be unsuccessful."

"It has Dunn and Cousie all over it. They have to be involved."

"How can you be sure?"

"There's a witness."

"You can't reveal who it is."

"I can't."

"Do they know you have it?"

"Dunn and Cousie? I don't think so."

Maggie left the counter after cashing out a customer. She pulled up a chair. Natalie passed the folder.

"Mason says Dunn & Cousie are overextended. The internet companies they invested in are bleeding red ink. They don't have the funds to keep them going."

"It doesn't surprise me, Liz-Beth. Internet companies are struggling all over the valley. Did you hear what Buffett said? 'When the tide goes out, you find out who's been swimming naked."

"Mace says the rumor is Dunn & Cousie are trying to roll LightSwitch into a portfolio and sell it off to a public company."

"I heard something like that from VK, Liz-Beth. They were shopping the company when they told me my shares were worthless. Those fuckers!"

"They might have an MOU that requires them to close by a specific date. If William sues them for fraud the buyer will back out. Dunn & Cousie have to tell them."

Everyone looked at each other.

"Couldn't they indemnify the buyer, Josh?"

"Not against criminal fraud, William. You couldn't hide that clause under Mt. Shasta. If the buyer can read they'll run like their hair's on fire. Dunn and Cousie have to avoid litigation. The strategy is settlement. All you need is the credible threat of filing."

"How do we put this on them?"

"Slow down, William. If we can't prove the documents originated with Dunn and Cousie before they sacked you we don't know if we can win in court. If you wreck their deal and you lose, they can sue you for damages."

"People, motive, circumstances. Who else could it be?"

"The defendant has the benefit of reasonable doubt, Liz-Beth. Criminal fraud is an aggressive claim with broad and severe consequences. It takes a strong case to convince twelve people to take a man's assets and his freedom. No matter how strong you think your case is, you never know what a jury will decide. You have to assume Dunn and Cousie know this or will be advised. If you can't tie them to this plan they can call your bluff."

"What if I lose in civil court?"

"The legal term is 'Tortious Interference in either a business expectancy or contract. They can accuse you of a malicious attack to inflict financial damage. The remedy can be severe, their losses plus multiples in punitive damages. It could have a lot of zeros in it. They could claim you sued them to kill their deal out of misplaced anger, frustration from thinking you sold out cheap. Your legal costs would be substantial even if you win. Think about who we're talking about, William. Two private equity investors we know aren't philanthropists. Don't expect mercy if you blow up their chance to dodge financial Armageddon."

The store went silent except for birdsong outside an open casement. Joshua continued.

"We could make these guys look greedy, dirty maybe, but if you can't prove they cheated you, if your claim appears specious, you're going to look like the dirtiest shirt in the hamper. This is huge William but we aren't quite there. I'll share this with Erik, tell him to keep digging, if that's OK with you, Liz-Beth. Let's keep this to ourselves. We don't want them to know we have this. We're dancing on the edge of a knife. Cousie already accused us of interference. If I were their attorney and I knew you had this, I'd accuse you of stealing company property. I'd file a cease and desist and have it on record. We would have to stop."

Maggie turned the documents over. "Somebody doodled all over it."

"Curious isn't it," Natalie said.

Joshua removed his glasses and looked at William. "Don't suppose you can tell me who did it, can you?"

"Nope. I don't know."

Forty-Six

"Will you walk me home, William?" Liz-Beth asked. "We can drop you with the car."

"Indulge me. I'd like to walk."

"I can go back with Josh and Maggie. I'll leave the car here for you" Natalie offered.

"That's okay, Nat. I'll walk home from Liz-Beth's."

Liz-Beth wrapped her arm around William's when they passed Duarte's and crossed the street.

"What is it, Liz-Beth? I know you have something to say."

"Why can't anyone know Lupe gave you the business plan?" She startled William.

"How did you know?"

"One day you get a message from Maria to call him. He can't talk on the phone. The next day you call a meeting and show us the business plan."

"Well done, Mrs. Holmes."

William shared his conversation with Lupe.

"What makes you think the plan is real?"

"What makes you think it isn't?"

"Stupid thing to write into a business plan and take it to a board meeting don't you think?"

"Joshua said it happens."

"What do you want to do if it's real, or if it's fake?"

"Proceed with caution. What else *can* we do? Ignore it? Duct tape Lupe to a chair and attach electrodes? Ask Dunn and Cousie?"

"Let's say it's fake."

"Dunn & Cousie planted it? For what reason?"

"To get us to use it so they can threaten to sue us for interference and IP theft."

"That's giving them too much credit, Liz-Beth. They're straight up thieves. I don't think they're devious enough to hatch that plot."

"If they did it's a trap."

"We can bluff them. If it doesn't work we put it back on the shelf."

"You'll expose yourself to IP theft. At a minimum receiving and using it when you know it was stolen. It will look like extortion."

"I know."

"What do you think about Lupe?"

"That he works for them? Not a chance. I hired him out of school. I can be fooled but I can't find it in me to suspect him. I don't think there's a dishonest bone in his body."

"Do they know him?"

"Not well."

"Less plausible it's a fake. They wouldn't leave it somewhere and hope somebody would find it and give it to you."

They paused at the post office while Liz-Beth checked her box. Empty. "I think it's real and Lupe's trying to help. What do we do?"

"Ask Mason to try to find another way to link them to it" Liz-Beth said.

"Why didn't you speak up at the store?"

"I wanted to ask you first."

"Thanks, Liz-Beth."

"It would help if you could get Lupe to step forward."

"I asked. He pushed back pretty hard. He's afraid of getting involved."

"Would you lose the company over it?"

"I can't force him. I promised to try to keep him out of it."

"Would he help if he was your last chance?"

"I dunno."

"He might be."

"Let's cross that bridge when we get to it. I promised him. Now I need you to promise me to keep the secret. Not even Josh can know. He might think he can trust Maggie and so it goes. Pretty soon the snowman knows, the man-in-the-moon knows and Dunn and Cousie know."

"Our secret William. You promise too. No more secrets between us. I tell you everything, you tell me everything. We make these decisions together. Deal?"

"Deal."

Forty-Seven

"I have Mr. Mace on the phone, Liz-Beth."

"I'll take it in here, Maria."

"News travels fast Mr. Mason."

"I thought we were on a first name basis."

"We are. This is business. Mason and Wiggins. I like the sound of it."

Mason chuckled. "I spoke with Joshua."

"What did he say?"

"He says the boy wonder has a smoking gun."

"He does but we can't link it to the shooter."

"Anyone I know?" Mason asked.

"Yep."

"What are you going to do with it?"

"Try to get a meeting; see what we can trade it for."

"When?"

"Couple of weeks."

"I just finished packing. I'm gonna have dinner with the Mrs. and head to the airport."

"What happened?"

"Nothing yet. I'm flying to the peninsula to see what I can find over there."

"About the plane?"

"Yeah. I did all I can with LightSwitch for now."

"It worked. Thank you. Let me know what you find."

"You bet. I won't be far if you need me."

"Godspeed, Erik."

"Godspeed, Liz-Beth."

Now let's see what I can come back with, Mason thought to himself. Mason went on a fishing trip, but not for fish.

Forty-Eight

The phone rang as Liz-Beth completed the Sunday Times crossword puzzle.

"Mr. Dunn," Maria called from the kitchen.

Isn't that interesting, Liz-Beth thought. *I wonder if he wants to ask me for a date. It's been so long, I'd accept if he didn't look so repulsive.*

"I'll take it in here, Maria."

"What a surprise, Mr. Dunn. What can I do for you?"

"Call me Osgood, Liz-Beth. We've known each other a long time."

"I'm afraid so."

"Hear me out, Liz-Beth. I didn't call to attack you."

"I've already spoken to your partner."

"I apologize for the way Robert spoke to you. I don't know why he's so torqued."

"He's always been such a charming fellow."

"He's been unusually abrasive. I told him it's just a business deal."

"Is it?"

"That's what I'd like to know. We don't have any business with you, Liz-Beth. Why are you involved in this?"

"What did you do to deserve my attention?"

"Let's not play games, Liz-Beth. I called you in good faith, not to pick a fight with you. I don't know what's motivating Robert. If he tells you, please share it with me. Do you want to have a business discussion or no?"

"Go on."

"You know we want you to end your investigation."

"Go on."

"We want to make a deal."

"How do you propose we arrive at terms?"

"Why don't you come to our office? We can talk through it there. Are you available a week from Thursday?"

"With Robert?"

"Yes, with Robert."

"Make it three weeks, conference room, Meyers, Cantrell, and Holmes, Pine and Montgomery."

"Your attorney's office?"

"I haven't retained them. They host federal mediation cases. Their facility, neutral mediator."

"We don't have anything to mediate."

"What are we meeting for?"

Osgood didn't answer.

"We can share an LOA, mail it back and forth, turn it into a contract."

"I'd rather do this face to face."

"Whatever you wish, Osgood. You have to give me something. Assuming I'm doing something, I'm not going to stop."

"Whatever you say, Liz-Beth. Can we make it 10:00AM, three weeks from Thursday?"

"I'll be there."

Liz-Beth smiled as she returned the handset to the receiver.

*　*　*

"Alright, Robert. We have our meeting. I expect you to be civilized whatever happens."

"Easy for you to say, Osgood. You have family money to fall back on."

"You weren't born poor, Robert. If you learn to be more careful with your money or you get along better with your family, they might help you. Oh, I forgot, you screwed them."

"No matter how much I made, Cindy would have spent me into the poorhouse."

"You had to have a trophy wife. You knew she was high maintenance."

"I don't like going out alone, and it's good for business."

"She could dent Trump's bank account. Why don't you introduce them? Maybe he'll take her off your hands."

"If we have to shutter all these dotbombs…You know I'm concentrated in them. I don't have the other interests you do."

"I'll have to take a loss too. You'd be better off if you diversified and made more friends than enemies."

"Water under the bridge, Osgood. I have to make it with the assets I have."

"Preserve what you can and live to fight another day."

"I'm not eating dirt, Osgood."

"Try humble pie."

"I worked hard for what I have. I'll fight to keep it. I won't be taken down by a kid and an old lady."

"When you find yourself in a hole, stop digging. I'll go along if it's what you want. You have more to lose than I do."

"I wish I could get this guy Mason off my back. He seems to be everywhere. He's looking in my trash bin."

"That's amusing. You're the dumpster diver. What haven't you told me?"

Cousie dodged the question.

"Liz-Beth and I go back a long way. She isn't gonna stop. If we can just get this guy Mason off our backs for a few weeks, we can close this transaction and be out of it."

"Pull yourself together, Robert. You need a survival plan. Did you dig up anything on Liz-Beth or William?"

"No."

"That's unusual. Everybody has something to hide."

"I'm trying. She's Mother Teresa, and he's a kid. He isn't old enough to be dirty."

Forty-Nine

"What do you think, Josh?"

"I'm not convinced we can accomplish anything, Liz-Beth."

"Let's throw the business plan in their face and demand the kitchen sink."

"Why would they fold when we can't implicate them?"

"They committed fraud. They know they *could* be implicated."

"What do you know that you aren't telling me?"

Liz-Beth didn't answer.

"As your attorney...."

"What attorney? You're retired, a consultant, a friend. Let me call the shots on this one. I'll take the responsibility."

"Liz-Beth."

"Sorry Joshua. I'll tell you more when I can."

"I advise against this meeting. Wait until we can link them to the plan."

"When will that be? What if they sell the company first? Dunn and Cousie will say the liability passed with the sale. It makes suing them much more complicated and they will have more resources. Do we have to sue CISCO, Lucent Technologies, Agilent, whoever they sell LightSwitch to, somebody who can keep us in court forever? We don't have anything we can bring against a public company and we don't have the resources for it. We have to take Dunn and Cousie down now."

"Who do you think William is protecting?"

"A LightSwitch employee."

"Did he tell you that?"

"Who else would come up with the business plan?"

"Do you think he would be willing to let the company slip away to protect this person?"

"Did you see the determination on his face?"

"I saw it."

"Do you have a better idea?"

"No."

"If they thought they had no exposure they wouldn't ask for a meeting. These guys are afraid of something. They might make an appealing offer."

"I still don't like it."

"Go with me on this one."

"It isn't you I'm worried about. We're a couple of geezers who don't give a crap what can happen to us, which is nothing. It's William and Natalie's lives we're playing with. William can walk away now. We can help him with his garage operation in Mountain View. If he's successful we'll forget about this. Why do we have to do it the hard way?"

"*Carpe diem*, Joshua. Let's see what they're willing to put on the table. We can always walk away."

"They can accuse us of trying to bust up a business deal."

"It's what we're trying to do, isn't it? Can they get anywhere?"

"Not without damages and proof we caused it. They can have a judge tell you to produce evidence that makes them look culpable or back off. They won't waste their time and money on that. They'll just tell us to go away."

"Why don't they do that now instead of asking for a meeting? Joshua, you're missing the point. For some reason they can't ignore us or they would. They don't even know we have the business plan. It'll be a shock, enough maybe to get what we want."

"What if it isn't their plan?"

"Of course, it's their plan."

"You really want to go up there and have a go at them, don't you?"

"Yes, I do."

"William is going to want to go. He has a right to be there."

"You said yourself it has to be between me and Dunn & Cousie. You know William is a distraction. If it spins out of control it can hurt him. If this blows up I want it on me alone."

"You really think you can pull this off, don't you?"

"What is there to lose?"

Joshua stretched his arms over his head.

"I hope you know what you're doing."

Liz-Beth laughed. "Haha, he's in."

Joshua sighed. "Who's going to tell William?"

"I'll take care of it. Who's going to tell Maggie?"

"I wonder if I have a decent suit that still fits and looks like I didn't buy it in 1950?"

Liz-Beth laughed. "You haven't gained a pound in fifty years. My dear; we aren't going to the most important meeting we're going to have for the rest of our lives in old clothes."

"Brooks Brothers' suits never go out of style."

"No matter, Mr. Retired Corporate Attorney. Nothing makes you more fearless than walking into a meeting looking at the top of your game, in new custom-tailored clothing like you left a trail of hundred-dollar bills on the tarmac when you walked off the steps of a Gulfstream and you don't need them enough to go back to pick them up. I'm going into that meeting looking like the queen of the business world, with the confidence of Maggie Thatcher. You're going looking like Ronald Reagan with the brains of Atticus Finch. My treat."

"Better make that Clarence Darrow. Finch lost."

"You better win."

"You don't have to do this, Liz-Beth."

"I reached an age and position in life where I can do any damn thing I want. I want to go to San Francisco and buy both of us encore ensembles. We're going in there power-suited."

"OK, Liz-Beth. You win. Save something for Dunn & Cousie. I don't think we should go ourselves."

"Why not?"

"They'll bring representation."

"You are representation."

"Not for this."

"Osgood didn't say anything about it."

"Did you tell him you're bringing me?"

"I see your point."

"Thank you, Mrs. Thatcher. We need an intimidator."

"Not G. Gordon Liddy, I hope. Who do you have in mind?"

"Irving Rothstein."

"Are you trying to bankrupt me?"

"Bankrupt who? You could bail out the republic."

"What does he charge? Five hundred an hour?"

"Oh, now you're worried about money. It would be worth every penny just to have him sit there. I don't think it will cost anything."

"Rothstein doesn't take pro-bono work for wealthy widows."

"It's for William. He returns favors for old friends and associates. I helped him out more than once. He's a successful, ethical man who doesn't need the money."

"I'll say he doesn't need the money. You know the mansion he lives in, top of the hill in Pacific Heights, next to the Presidio with the Bay view to die for."

"They *have* died for it. I've seen Rothstein do something noble, just to make something right. He knows Dunn and Cousie. He doesn't like either of them. He would enjoy making them squirm. If I can get him to agree would you let him join us?"

"I'll pay him for his time."

"Call it a no-charge preview. If you have to file a suit or this blows up you'll need him to represent you. I won't be doing that."

"Do you think it could happen?"

"No. You can back down. It's comforting to have Rothstein sitting there. It makes me brave. I can tell Maggie if it goes any further we're transitioning to a practicing attorney because we are. This has to bring it to the conclusion we want. I can go no further. Will that work for you, Liz-Beth?"

"I guess it has to. Natalie has a job interview in the city. Let's see if we can take go together."

"I like having Natalie around."

"You're a dirty old man."

"Not dirty, Liz-Beth. Just one who enjoys the company of beautiful young women. Do you know a man who doesn't?"

"I'm not young and beautiful enough?"

"Of course you are, but you *and* Natalie? Wow."

"Scuse me while I throw up."

"What's Erik doing you haven't told me about?"

"I'm going to have to ask you to let that go a while longer. We need to focus on what we have to do in San Francisco."

"It might help."

"It has nothing to do with LightSwitch or Dunn & Cousie."

"Does it have anything to do with William?"

"Let it go, Josh. We have work to do in San Francisco."

Fifty

"Didn't you say you're going to San Francisco, Natalie?"

"I have an interview next week."

"Will you move back there if you get the job?"

"If I get this one I can work from home. I'll go there once a week for meetings, or when I have a photo shoot."

"I'd be sad if you moved there full time."

"I wouldn't do that to you, Liz-Beth. You'd have to babysit William."

"That isn't so bad. I did it before you arrived. What about your apartment?"

"I sublet it to a friend. I can crash on the couch when I need to."

"Joshua and I need to go shopping in the city. Wanna go together?"

"Sure, sounds like fun. How are you getting there?"

"We can squeeze in the pickup."

"Let's not do that. I have a friend who lives in the city and owns a limo. I can have him pick us up and bring us back at the end of the day."

"You don't need to go to the expense. I wish I still had the Bentley. Sukie could drive us."

"Sukie resigned. I don't think he wants that job anymore."

"Yeah, I know. Seems like yesterday when he drove me around with Mr. Chuckles. I miss that."

"My treat. I'm sure my friend George would be happy to have the business. He likes to get out of town once in a while. He'll give us a good price."

"You shouldn't be spending money on limousines."

"It's OK, I have the money."

"I'll give him a generous gratuity."

"I'll let you know if he's available. What are you going to do with Mr. Chuckles?"

"I'll see if Sukie will take him for a day."

"They don't get along do they?"

"They need to work that out."

Liz-Beth called Sukie.

"Why do you do this to me, Liz-Beth? You know that bird doesn't like me and I can't say no to you."

"You and Mr. Chuckles need to learn how to get along. It's only for a day."

"I will drive you."

"In what car?"

"I will rent a car."

"You'd rather pay for a car rental than spend a day with Mr. Chuckles. That would hurt his feelings."

"Birds do not understand car rental. They have no feelings."

"This is why Mr. Chuckles doesn't like you, Sukie. You have no respect for him. You think he's just a dumb animal."

"Mr. Chuckles *is* a dumb animal."

"Shame on you Sukie. He understands being left alone. I haven't explained it to him."

"You are saying crazy things, Mrs. Wiggins."

"You know I don't like you to call me Mrs. Wiggins."

"You know I don't like to spend a day with Mr. Chuckles."

"If you drive us, who is going to stay with Mr. Chuckles?"

"We will take him."

"Mr. Chuckles, Joshua, Natalie, me, and you on an outing to San Francisco. I don't think so. Natalie already made arrangements. You're going to be a friend and take Mr. Chuckles. Maybe he'll warm up to you."

"He will warm up in my oven."

"Don't you touch a feather on that bird! He isn't an exotic dish you serve in China."

"Don't insult me Liz-Beth. You know I am Japanese! We eat sushi, not bad-mannered birds."

"Sure, Sukie. You don't look the least bit Chinese. You look Scandinavian. You're a racist, Sukie."

"So are you, Liz-Beth. You like to torture Japanese people."

"I am helping you learn to get along with birds."

"You can help me by not teaching this lesson. You are an exasperating person. I will take your bird for *one* day. You are going to owe me something very valuable for this."

"I'd rather owe you than cheat you. How much do I owe you now?"

"There are not enough rows on my abacus."

"The soroban was imported from China."

"Japanese make better use of it. Bring me the bird, Liz-Beth. It would make good soup. I promise not to eat it if this conversation can end."

"Him, Sukie. Mr. Chuckles is not an *it*."

Fifty-One

George Winston grew up an Indian fan in Cleveland. Six feet tall, he carried a heavy frame well. He had a round face with a walnut of a nose and small black eyes. His face pitted in his youth. It didn't make for a happy or popular teenager. He grew accustomed to it as he aged. He learned to compensate by being easy going and friendly. It took a lot of marbles to rattle George's can.

An average athlete, George plateaued with intermural sports. A solid "C" student in public school, he could have done better but he didn't have a plan or the ambition to carry one out. George attended community college, transferred to Ohio State, stayed in school because he didn't want to disappoint his parents. Neither did he want to serve his country in Vietnam. He thought if he didn't go to college, he would be drafted, sent there and returned in a body bag.

George drifted through university, majoring in one thing or another until accumulating enough credits to graduate with a BA in something. The best you can say for his time as an undergrad is unremarkable. Not a bad way to spend a few years, war or no, even though they were marred by political activism and war protests, not the idyllic college experience it could have been. George earned enough money working summers to feed himself, pay for books and tuition, rent half a two-bedroom apartment near campus, buy gas for a Volkswagen Beetle he bought with a down payment he saved and a car loan cosigned by his father. Unable or unwilling to dream up anything better, George floated down the education river, part of the flotsam and jetsam of a generation.

Not a Fortune 500 first round pick, George had to start somewhere. After graduation he went to work in his uncle's dry-cleaning business in Cincinnati. Two years later he drove the Beetle out to San Francisco, the most ambitious thing he did to date. He crashed with a college friend in the Bernal Heights neighborhood where he found work as a limo driver.

George looked substantial in a dark suit. The work suited his gentle nature. A quiet man who liked to serve, Wiggins would have approved. If he dreamed, driving a limo would not be George's chosen career. Easy money though, he earned enough to live in the city. He could pay rent, own a car, buy a drink at a bar, meet a girl and that satisfied him.

It's a short drive from George's apartment to North Beach and the Financial District where George earned his living. He'd live in North Beach but he wanted to go to bars, not live over one. Apartments in Bernal Heights are less expensive. It's quieter, less crowded, and the view of the Bay is captivating when the fog lifts. George loved San Francisco even though he had to give up cheering for the Indians.

Over the years, George saved enough money to acquire his own Lincoln Town Car, then another and another. Eventually he decided employees were not something he wanted. He cut the fleet to one and found enough customers from social interaction to keep himself going. He worked the North Beach night life, the young party crowd, the older raunchy-seedy clientele on Broad Street when he stumbled into it. He reserved mornings for sleeping in, afternoons for pool hopping and tanning. He worked nights when he needed money. George always needed money. For special assignments he rose early.

George picked Liz-Beth, Joshua and Natalie up in the morning and deposited them at Union Square. Natalie met a friend for brunch before walking to her interview. Liz-Beth went to a dress shop she hadn't visited in years. Joshua walked to a custom tailor on Pine Street.

"Have the bill sent to me, Joshua."

"OK, Liz-Beth."

"I want the best of everything, head to toe."

"OK, Liz-Beth."

"I want you to look like a cross between an industrialist and a gladiator - rich and powerful, tall and fit, terribly dangerous."

"What happened to Ronnie and Maggie?"

"Them too."

"OK, Liz-Beth."

"Don't be sarcastic, Joshua. I'll meet you for lunch at Max's on Market Street."

Liz-Beth faked an angry look followed by a wink. She stepped into the dress shop.

"Elizabeth Wiggins. I haven't seen you in years."

"Hello, Andrea. Sorry it's been so long. I have no use for fine clothes at the beach. I miss coming here though."

"Don't bullshit me, Liz-Beth. You have an account at every thrift shop in the Bay Area."

"You know me too well."

"Where's that crazy bird of yours?"

"Babysitting Sukie."

"Your Chinese chauffer?"

"Japanese. He'll lop your head off if you call him Chinese."

"I thought they didn't get along."

"Today they have to."

"It's good to see you, Liz-Beth. You look great."

"Thank you, Andrea. You always were a great liar. I look older than dirt. If anybody can make five feet, ten inches of old dirt look good, it would be you."

"That's the nicest a thing a customer ever said to me. What's the occasion?"

"Murder."

"Murdering or being murdered?"

"The former."

"Sounds serious."

"It cannot be overstated, Andrea. I need your best effort."

"You always get my best effort."

"That's why I came here. I need to look as stunning as Grace Kelly and as tough as Maggie Thatcher."

"With you, Liz-Beth, that would be easy. When do you need it?"

"Yesterday. Middle of next week, actually. I have to be wearing it when I return the week after. I need it a week early in case it needs alteration."

"There will be no need for alteration."

"I might go on a pastry binge."

"I've never seen you gain an ounce. Have they paved the road to Pescadero yet?"

"I love you, Andrea. Hitch your wagon, ride down to Duarte's on Wednesday night and do stand-up at open mike."

"I have you on file, but let's take measurements."

Fifty-Two

Liz-Beth and Joshua finished shopping and went for a walk along the Embarcadero. Natalie returned to Union Square. She thought her interview went well. She stopped in a coffee shop on Post Street near the corner of Post and Powell. Natalie stepped outside when the time came to meet Liz-Beth and Joshua. She turned left on Powell Street. When she reached the corner at Geary, a taxi driver honked a horn, hung his head out the window and yelled obscenities at an elderly woman absent-mindedly pushing a shopping cart into the intersection through a red light. The lady ignored it. Natalie rounded the corner distracted. She walked straight into someone and dropped her portfolio. It flipped open and tossed her illustrations across the sidewalk. She kneeled to retrieve them. A man in shiny black shoes and a grey business suit stood in front of her but did not offer assistance.

Why is he standing there? Why doesn't he walk away or help me? Natalie wondered. Natalie scooped up her drawings, stuffed them into the portfolio and froze when she stood up. Robert Cousie smiled at her.

"Well if it isn't my favorite niece."

"Every woman under forty with a pulse is your favorite niece, Robert. Do you still rent them by the hour?"

"That isn't nice, Natalie. Where did you get that mouth?"

"From your side of the family."

"Hey look Natalie, I don't want to pick a fight with you. You only have so many relatives. I know you don't like me, but I was married to William's mother. We *are* family."

"Too bad you can't choose your relatives."

"Be that way. I need to talk to you."

"We don't have anything to discuss, Robert."

"*I* do. Won't you have a word with your uncle? I haven't done anything to you."

"Not since you put one hand on my blouse and the other one on my ass at my 16th birthday party."

"That was a long time ago and I didn't mean anything by it."

"I was 16 years old, Robert. You were a grown man. Miriam's ex-husband. It meant something to *me*. What were you doing at my party? Anything to cause trouble for John and Miriam. You could ruin a perfect spring day, Robert."

"I'm offended, Natalie. I came to celebrate your birthday. I brought a gift."

"You never did get over Miriam, did you? Couldn't you let them have a life together without making a scene every time the family got together?"

"I told you I came to celebrate your birthday."

"Sure, you did. You go to birthday parties for all your 16-year-old nieces."

"You never told anybody about that did you?"

"It was too humiliating."

"Too bad the blouse was in the way."

"You asshole."

"Look Natalie, I don't think we should be hashing out things that happened a decade ago. Your boyfriend is causing me a lot of trouble. Could you speak to him about that? See if you can get him to lay off me, at least consider it? Maybe we can work something out."

"Are you fucking…***Fuck you*** Robert. I can't believe you have the nerve to ask me that. I'd rather ask him to kick your ass."

"Such a dirty mouth. Look, I don't expect him to like me. He's going out of his way to make my life difficult. I need him to lighten up."

"I know all about you, Robert Cohen. I know about the

philandering when you were married to Miriam. I know you changed your name because you got into trouble with the SEC and they banned you for life from the securities business. I know you stole William's company. Don't expect any help from me."

"Is that what you think? William was a dope. He ran his company into the ground, expanded right before the tech bubble burst. I took it over to avoid losing everything I invested in it. We took care of him. He didn't deserve to come out of it with anything."

"William started that company from nothing. He made it into one of the fastest growing companies in Silicon Valley. He didn't want your money. He wouldn't have taken it if knew where it came from."

"If not for me William would have been kicked out without a penny. If it didn't work out the way he expected it's his failure. This is wrong, Natalie. William and his friend, the witch of Pescadero, are trying to ruin me. I need your help. I'm your uncle and you need to help me."

"Are you serious? I couldn't help you if I wanted to. William isn't going to let this go. I don't want him to. I don't know how you took his company. I know you did it dishonestly. He didn't deserve to lose it the way he did."

"I invested in it to make a profit. I bought out William's equity when the company was failing."

"Your partner made the investment so William wouldn't know it was your money. You deceived him, kicked him out, and didn't pay him what his shares were worth."

"I gave him more than anybody else would have, not me actually, my softhearted partner did that. It was half my money. I didn't have to give him anything. I could have let the business fail. I could have bought it for nothing out of bankruptcy."

"You're pure evil, Robert. You stole the company out of revenge."

"That's a serious accusation, Natalie. You shouldn't say anything like that."

"I'm not a naïve 16-year-old you can fool, sweet talk, or intimidate. I know what you are. You're an evil freak. I don't want to have anything to do with you."

"You sound pretty tough in public, Natalie. I saw a scared little girl run to the neighbor's house when I had it out in the garden with William. You didn't look so brave then. Go crying to the neighbors, did you?"

Natalie hadn't been face-to-face with Cousie in years. She thought he looked like an old oak. A big tree still, but weathered, bent, battered from winds of ages. He didn't look the big confident man who molested her at her birthday party. His face sagged and wrinkled. His dark complexion turned an unhealthy color. Robert's eyes looked tired, red, alcoholic, like he hadn't slept well. Always well groomed, his hair was mussed and needed cutting. He was richly dressed, still a force but a shadow of the man he once was. For an instant she felt sorry for him, as a woman can for any man who aged and suffered. She also felt changed. She no longer feared Robert Cousie. For the first time in her life she felt mature, confident, a powerful woman. She pressed her lips together and shook her head at him.

"I'm not afraid of you anymore, Robert. You can't intimidate me. You're a hateful man. Mentally ill maybe, a misanthrope definitely, to be as cruel as you are. I don't ever want to see or have anything to do with you."

"Come on, Natalie. Look, I'm sorry. I didn't mean to hurt you. Let me make it up to you. I'll show you I'm not so bad."

Now he wants to be friends, Natalie thought. "I have to go, Robert."

"Just a minute," Cousie said in a harsh voice. He grabbed Natalie by the arm and squeezed. He was still a strong man, twice as big as Natalie. "Let's sit down and talk about this. We can be nice to each other."

Cousie pulled Natalie off balance.

"Let me go, Robert. You're hurting me." She couldn't break his grip.

Natalie noticed a shadow advance along the sidewalk from behind her.

"Is this man bothering you?"

Robert stared at George Winston. He released Natalie's arm. He growled.

"Stay out of this. It's family business. This is my niece."

"If you don't leave her alone you're gonna eat pavement."

Cousie backed off.

"Go find a 16-year-old to play with, Robert. Any girl or boy will do. You can buy one with all your money. You were an attractive man once. Now you're a repulsive old one."

"You're a nasty bitch like your aunt was."

"My aunt must have been temporally insane to have anything to do with you. Did you drug her to get her to marry you?"

"She wanted me and my money well enough."

"Get out of here Robert. I'll call the police and have you arrested."

"For what? Being your uncle? Asking for your help? You and William haven't heard the end of this."

"Are you threatening me, Robert? Do I need police protection?"

"You have all the protection you need, Natalie. Get lost, buddy."

Cousie and Winston stared each other down. Cousie gave in and walked away with a scowl.

"Have you been following me all day, George?"

"Not exactly. It's a nice day. I took the day off to hang around the city. The square is as good a place as any."

Natalie squinted at him. "I know a line of bullshit when I hear it. Do you have a crush on me?"

"Of course I have a crush on you. I don't drive halfway to Santa Cruz to pick up clients. I fell in love with you the night I drove you to Pescadero. You were a mess, every man's dream of a damsel in distress. I thought you would go to pieces on the drive. You have no idea how beautiful and vulnerable you looked that night. It broke my heart to drop you at your boyfriend's place. I wanted to keep driving down the coast and start a new life with you."

"Take me to your place for the night is more like it."

"More than that, Natalie. I have girlfriends."

"I could have been another notch on the bedpost." She smiled at George.

"I didn't watch you today because I thought I could sleep with you. I know there's no chance of that."

"You mean it, don't you?"

"Yes, I mean it. Did you ever look at yourself in the mirror? Watch yourself walk? Notice the way your upper lip curls? Those legs that night. One look was all I needed. Your boyfriend is one lucky guy. A fool to let you live in the city with hound dogs like me."

"You're no hound dog. You just proved it."

George blushed.

"You got it bad, George. You should have kept your eyes on the road."

"I couldn't."

"I'm glad you didn't."

Natalie grabbed George's arms, reached up and kissed him on the neck. George touched his hand to the spot. He thought he could never wash it. He thought Natalie smelled like a spring flower and her lips felt as soft as rose petals.

"You're a sweet man, George. You'll find someone to love. She'll love you back, too."

"If your boyfriend doesn't ask you to marry him he's an idiot."

"He *is* an idiot, but he's my idiot. Thank you, George, for running off my uncle."

"Is he really your uncle?"

"Yeah, he is, sort-of."

"I had a funny feeling about today, like you needed me. I parked the limo near the ferry terminal. You wanna wait here while I get it?"

"No, I'd like to walk. Will you walk with me?"

"Can I carry your homework?"

Natalie handed George her portfolio. George held out an arm. Natalie wrapped hers around it. They walked down Geary Street to Market, the dividing line between the financial district and South of Market; the neighborhood where Liz-Beth and Harold started and operated the Wiggins Trading Company. Natalie wondered how it felt to own a successful import/export business there, from the late 1940s through the 1970s. *Must have been pretty great*, she thought. She turned to watch a cable car roll down California Street. They crossed Davis.

"It's a great City, isn't it George?"

"It sure is."

"My uncle's a monster. I've been afraid of him since I was a little girl. Not anymore. I'll never be afraid of Robert Cousie again. Let's go find Liz-Beth and Joshua. I'm ready to go home."

Fifty-Three

Winston parked the limo near the corner when he returned from Pescadero. When he walked toward his apartment building he saw Cousie turn into the street from the opposite direction, park the Mercedes and walk menacingly in his direction. George stopped to light a cigarette. *Oh shit,* he thought. *I have to face this asshole. Maybe he'll pay me.*

Winston walked to the building entry and waited. Cousie looked angry.

"What the hell do you think you're doing?"

"I agreed to arrange a meeting, Mr. Cousie. I didn't agree to watch you twist her arm off."

"I didn't hurt her."

"Yes you did."

"You work for me. You do what I tell you to do. I do what I want. You don't interfere with it."

"If you have to get physical I'm out. I can't do this anymore."

"We're done with that. It didn't accomplish anything. The meeting is on. The next thing I need you to do is listen carefully if you drive them up here and call me after you drop them off. Do you understand?"

"Yes."

"I want you to tell me everything they say. Can you do that?"

"Yes, Mr. Cousie. Can we settle up? I have obligations."

"I'll pay you after the meeting."

"I did what you asked me to do."

"You stopped me from getting what I needed."

"She wouldn't have given you anything. You had to break her arm to get it."

"That's enough, George. Don't get in the way. Do what I ask. I'll pay you after the meeting with Liz-Beth."

"The other rides, it's been…"

"After the Liz-Beth meeting, not before."

Cousie swaggered to his car. George stood on the staircase and watched him drive off. *Shit, I'm in so much trouble,* he thought. He dropped the cigarette butt, stamped it out, and entered the building lobby.

On the short drive to the penthouse, Cousie wondered if his wife was home or practicing service and ground strokes at the tennis pro's apartment. Thirty years younger than Cousie, Cindy was the trophy he thought he needed. He loved what it did for his image and ego when he showed up at cocktail parties and expensive restaurants with Cindy on his arm. She loved designer clothing, expensive jewelry. She liked making an entrance, being ogled, flirting. She played the part well.

Robert did not love Cindy. Cindy did not love Robert. She was more escort than wife. They had a financial-social arrangement, not a marriage. Had he paid closer attention to credit card receipts, Robert would have noticed men's clothing he didn't have, that wouldn't fit him, from stores he never visited, a watch he had never seen, tickets to shows he hadn't attended, restaurants he never set foot in. It made no difference. He knew about Cindy's affairs. Letting her do what she wished was the easiest and least expensive solution. He let her buy what she wanted to keep her from moving on. For collecting things she didn't need, Cindy had a talent for spending money.

Cindy had a simple plan. She bought what she wanted. She filled several large units at 2nd Street Storage with antique furniture and designer clothing she wore once, twice, or never. She seemed to be on a first name basis with every clerk in every expensive boutique and department store in San Francisco. Robert thought the things Cindy bought on credit now may never be paid for, not if the meeting with Liz-Beth failed and he and Dunn couldn't sell LightSwitch. Robert thought it would be altogether fitting; revenge on nameless, faceless shop owners, parasites in his view, who took his money. The more Cindy spent from here on, the closer he came to even. *Maybe I won't pay them even if I can,* he thought. *I'll let Cindy explain it.*

Cindy woke between noon and three when she didn't have a tennis morning, a habit Robert detested. She could spend the morning with him if nothing else, he thought. He wanted a wife in the morning. A housekeeper would be an improvement and less expensive. He could neither make a housekeeper of Cindy, nor afford a divorce.

What am I going to do with her? Robert wondered. Her spending and living habits grinded on him, even while he could afford them. He had no interest in her kids, one each from two previous marriages. They too, always needed money.

Since the marriage, Robert could no longer afford a mistress. He thought Cindy's youthful cheerleader looks would satisfy him but she didn't like sex; not with him. Most of the time, he went without or bought it. Cindy preferred shopping binges, an occasional lover; often the tennis pro.

I have to fix this problem, Robert thought. He had no idea how.

Fifty-Four

Liz-Beth called Sukie when she returned from San Francisco.

"How did you and Mr. Chuckles get along?"

"He tried to bite my nose off."

Liz-Beth laughed at the imagery.

"What did you do to make him angry?"

"I tried to feed him. He flew out of his cage and dive-bombed me."

"How did you avoid destruction?"

"I practiced the ancient Japanese art of self-defense. I ran into the bedroom and slammed the door."

Liz-Beth couldn't suppress the laughter.

"After that?"

"He returned to his cage and ate his lunch in complete bliss, the ungrateful raptor. Akiko closed the cage door. He *likes* her. When I reentered the room, he cursed me. What a beak! That bird knows more curses than the honorable American Navy. Where did he learn such language?"

"The breeder must have been a sailor."

"I haven't seen such atrocious behavior since the outbreak of honorable dysentery on Iwo Jima."

"You were on Iwo Jima?"

"Yes. Fortification construction. I am lucky to have left before your army invaded. Had I remained, it is unlikely I would have survived. You would have had to eat Chinese cooking for more than fifty years. If you survived it."

"You're such a racist."

"You do not like Germans."

"I don't think they're inferior, just evil."

"That *is* racism."

"Let's not revisit this argument. I'm gonna hire a bird psychologist. You're going to therapy with Mr. Chuckles."

"I am not going."

"You are."

"No bird psychologist will take that bird as a patient. Mr. Chuckles will try to eat the doctor's nose. You need a bird strait jacket."

"You need a rubber room."

"Parrots should have joined dinosaurs in the great die off."

"What a terrible thing to say, Sukie. You're a mean little old Japanese man. No wonder Mr. Chuckles doesn't like you."

"*Me?* I am *not* mean. Mr. Chuckles is meaner than Ted Bundy, Hannibal Lector and George Patton."

"Oh, yeah? You're meaner than Sonny Liston, Ivan the Terrible, and Vlad the Impaler."

"Oh, Yeah? Mr. Chuckles is meaner than Sonny Barger, Whitey Bulger, and Jimmy Carter."

"Jimmy Carter! That's a low blow. I'm coming to get him right now."

"How fast can you get here?"

"You'll be sorry you said such things, Sukie."

"A day I wish for."

If she could carry him, a woman walking through Pescadero with a caged cockatoo would have made the Pescadero paper, if the village were big enough to print one. The weekly Pescadero news wouldn't fill the back of a #10 envelope. Liz-Beth needed a car. Natalie drove her in the MG to bring Mr. Chuckles home.

Akiko answered the door in a yellow kimono. Even though she grew up in Cupertino, she and Liz-Beth bowed.

"Hello, Liz-Beth. Sukie went to New Cotswolds to repair a leaky faucet. He told me to tell you everything he said about Mr. Chuckles is a lie. He was only joking."

Akiko covered her mouth with her hand and giggled.

"I knew it. The little bugger."

"He and Mr. Chuckles were uneasy for a while. After a few hours of glaring they ate lunch together. Now they are friends. Mr. Chuckles eats nuts out of Sukie's hand! You are welcome to bring him here anytime you wish. Do not expect my husband to say anything nice about it. He likes to tease you. It is Japanese culture to say one thing but mean another. You will not need a bird psychologist my husband says. Would you like to come in for tea?"

"I'd love too. Can we make it another time? We have to go home and make dinner."

"Why don't you stay for dinner? Sukie will be back soon. You can join us for traditional Japanese dinner. We have rice, home-made miso soup, fresh lingcod Sukie bought from a fisherman off his boat in the Half Moon Bay marina. Very delicious! We have fresh vegetables Sukie bought in the farmer's market this morning. You can invite William."

"That's unfair, Akiko. You know I can't turn down Chef Sukie's cooking. Can you join us, Natalie?"

"I'll ask William. I don't care what *he's* doing. I'm eating *here*. We have a couple of bottles of late harvest white wine we bought at the Bonny Doon winery. It's great with fish. I'll go home and get them."

"Wonderful, Natalie. We have a bottle of Sake. I hope you don't have morning appointments."

"We'll be back soon, Akiko."

On the way to the cottage Natalie told Liz-Beth she wanted a pet.

"You have all the fun!"

"William and a new job aren't enough for you?"

"Did you like having Bentley?"

"He was Bunny's dog. I enjoyed him. You care for them like a child that gets in trouble, can't speak and never grows up like parents wish their children didn't. They love you unconditionally. They're great companions. Bunny and Bentley were wonderful together. It's a good idea. I'll help you find the right one."

A Search Mission

Fifty-Five

Mason shared breakfast with Josh and Maggie before driving to Moffett Field.

Jason Stamback managed a Lockheed program for the Navy. He and Mason served together. Clean shaven, fit, six feet, salt and pepper hair, Jason retired with the rank of commander. They met in the Lockheed cafeteria.

"Good to see you, Jason."

"Good to see you, Mace. Can't tell you much about the Beckinsdale disappearance."

"Why is the plane missing?"

"Idonno."

"Any idea where it is?"

"Plane had a range, Mace. Could have flown anywhere between here and Denver, British Columbia, halfway to Hawaii without refueling. They could have almost reached La Paz. Pleasure flight. No idea which way they flew, where to look. It's a big ocean, a big mountain range to the east to lose a small plane in."

"No flight plan?"

"He didn't file one."

"Radar, air control records?"

"Nope."

"Come on, Jason. No flight plan, no radar or air control contact. They took off and just disappeared?"

Jason didn't answer.

"Some black ops test thing?"

"With his wife? No."

"Alright, a local low-level flight under radar. What was he doing up there?"

"Personal flight. It's a civilian plane. Like a company car, personal use on his own time as long as he paid expenses."

"What did you use the plane for?"

"Avionics, radar, aerial photography testing and development."

"That isn't much to go on."

"Wish I could offer more help. We all liked and respected John. You probably know his military record."

"Yeah, I do. Pretty impressive. The guy flew through the worst shit, came back from it."

"A virtuoso pilot. That's what makes it such a mystery."

"He didn't make a distress call. How do you explain that?"

"I can't."

"Was the plane well maintained?"

"You know better than to ask that."

"Was it?"

"Yeah, as good as it gets."

"Did he have enemies, anybody happy to see him gone?"

"Damn, Erik. Foul play? They queued up to claim they were friends. Nobody disliked him."

"Any kind of career rivalry? Business disputes you know of. Unpaid debts, gambling, affairs."

"That's going too far, Erik. I told you he was a standup guy. I'm not sure I would tell you if I knew different. Far as I know nothing like that. As program manager I interacted with him a lot, knew lots of people who knew him, socialized with him and Miriam. You turned down the wrong road here, Erik."

"Sorry, Jason. It's my job. I have to ask."

"Excuse me. He was my friend."

A middle-aged black man approached them from an adjacent table. Short hair, average height and build, he looked fit in flight line maintenance clothing.

"Hi, Eddie. Let me introduce you to Erik Mason. I served in the gulf with him. Eddie Johnson, Erik Mason."

"My friends call me Mace."

"I'll leave you two alone. I have to go to a meeting."

"Hope I didn't offend you, Jason."

"You did. I'll forgive you if you buy the beer."

"Meet you for happy hour in Sunnyvale. You know the place."

"Faultline Brewery. See you there."

"Mr. Mason."

"Mace."

"Mace….Sorry, I overheard you. My pop knew John in the South Pacific. I've been waiting a long time for this."

"Have a seat, Eddie."

Mason removed his aviators to look into Johnson's clear, intelligent eyes.

"How did you know him?"

"Pop introduced us when he brought me to work with him. Pop was a mechanic too. He started as a Navy cook in the South Pacific. They didn't let us Negros do much in those days."

Full of sarcasm, Johnson flashed a mouth full of bright white teeth when he smiled.

"The Navy was segregated then. We drove trucks and Jeeps. We moved the food, we cooked the food, we cleaned kitchens and latrines, moved the ammo, stored the ammo, that sort of thing. Pop met John in a cafeteria like this one, but under a tent in Guadalcanal."

Johnson chuckled.

"John sat down next to Pop. What do you think of that? A white

naval officer, a flier, sittin down to lunch with a black cook in the segregated navy. Pop thought he was in trouble, or gonna be. Just one guy to another guy, that's all."

"Color blind."

"Yeah; he was. John was a good man. Something bothered him, depressed him. He didn't say much, just he was transferring stateside, not gonna fly combat anymore. I guess he had too much of it. He wanted to know about Pop. What do you think of that? A white officer wants to know about a black cook. Pop told him he wanted to do something better. He was raised on a farm in North Carolina, a remote one where you had to know how to fix anything, keep the machinery running to get the crops in, keep the farm running. There wasn't any other way. John helped Pop get into aviation maintenance. The Navy didn't want to have nothin to do with that. No white pilot wanted to fly a plane maintained by a black man. John put Pop on the ground crew that serviced his plane. Pop said that was some sweet flyin' F4F. People noticed that. Some didn't like it. John didn't care. Pop didn't mind too much. Pop learned from that, proved he could do it. John made them look at him. They sent Pop to mechanic's school."

Johnson almost broke down.

"Pop said John was the finest man he ever knew. If not for him, Pop and I'd be sharecroppin in the Carolinas instead of livin the California dream."

"Pop still around?"

"No, he passed."

"I'm sorry."

"It's OK. Listen man, there's no way that plane went down from pilot error."

"How do you know that?"

"Come on man, you know who this guy was. John could fly a plane upside down through a drain pipe in a hurricane. He wasn't going to make some dumb mistake on a pleasure flight, take a plane down, get himself killed with his wife onboard. No way."

"What do you think happened?"

"I don't know, but I think I know where to look for it."

"How could you know that?"

"Come over here. Let me show you somethin'."

Mason followed to a wall with a poster-size print of the Farallon Islands.

"See this photo of the Farallons? No way you could take this photo with a camera you can buy in a camera store."

"Why not?"

"Look at the detail."

Mason moved closer to the photo. He practically put his nose in it. "You have to fly over the Farallons at altitude to take this. It's a wildlife preserve."

"That's right. It's one of ours. John told me he took this photo."

"It doesn't prove the plane went down there."

"It doesn't, but it proves he went there. He made a hobby of photographing those islands on his days off. He took dozens of these photos."

"It doesn't mean he went down there."

"Look man, you can't search the world even if you want too. If I were looking for that plane, I'd look there. I'll bet my black ass that's where it is."

"Why didn't you tell the people who were searching for it?"

"I tried. Nobody would listen to me. I'm just the guy who changes P3 engine oil."

"Son-of-a-bitch. I've got a Mooney at the San Carlos Airport. Wanna have a look?"

"Aren't you meetin' Jason?"

"If not this day, then someday. Let's go look for a plane."

Fifty-Six

They rotated out of San Carlos, flew up the coast a quarter mile off shore, five hundred feet over water. When they reached the Farallons, Mason took the plane up to thirty-five hundred feet. He handed Eddie a pair of binoculars and circled in a steep bank to give his passenger a clear view.

"What do you see, Eddie?"

"Nothin but rocks and grass."

"You're right about the camera. No consumer kit can take that photo on the cafeteria wall from this height."

"What do you think, Mason?"

"They could have flown along the coast under radar without filing a flight plan. They had to pop up to altitude like we did to fly over. Maybe they appeared on radar briefly and weren't noticed or were confused with another plane. Maybe they ran into trouble before they reached the altitude where radar would have picked them up."

"Could they be down there?"

"There isn't any place to land a fixed wing aircraft. I don't see any wreckage. Barren as these islands are we should see something if they crashed there."

"In the water?"

"That Cessna couldn't make it back to the coast from this height if they lost power out here. The water is the only place they could go if John had control of the plane."

"He had control."

"If they went down here they could be on the underwater shelf close to the islands. John would have gone there. If it sank further out and missed the shelf it's a long way down. It would take exotic gear and a lot of cash to find it."

"Do you think you could find it?"

"I dunno, Eddie. Let's go have that beer with Jason."

Mason flew back to San Carlos. They took the Taurus to the Faultline in Sunnyvale where Jason nursed a beer. They sat at a corner table and ordered a round.

"I think Eddie has a good idea, Jason."

"You aren't going to start this up again are you?"

"Why not?"

"It isn't going to bring them back, Eddie."

"Let's say I want to make it right."

"Come on Erik, how much cash is in this job?"

"Not a goddamned dollar, Jason. I won't take money for this."

"Patriot. You aren't thinking of doing what I *think* you are."

"Yup."

"Mason."

"I have a buddy with a salvage business in Alameda. He has a dive boat, a barge with a crane, balloons for raising boats."

"Shit, Mason," Jason shook his head.

"The crew is all ex-Navy. They'll volunteer for this, call it a long weekend fishing trip. The client will pay expenses. You want the plane back, don't you?"

"Not really. What's in it for Lockheed?"

"I thought you liked and respected the guy. Close the books. Do something useful instead of wasting taxpayer's money testing toys."

"Boy Scout."

"Not usually. I failed Samaritan badge. Kept me from making Eagle."

"Busy chasing Girl Scouts."

"One thing puzzles me about this, Jason. If they did go in there, why didn't somebody pick up a distress call?"

"We need the plane for that."

"Now you're thinking. You want it back if we find it don't you?"

"I have to take it back. It's ours."

"We'll need a forensics investigation."

"Eddie's the best we have for that."

"You must like this guy, Jason."

"Member of the family, Mace. You have to keep the peace in the family."

Jason smiled at Johnson.

"Gonna come along, Eddie?"

"Like to Mace. I don't dive."

"Don't worry about that. The divers we're gonna have can swim to Hawaii. We can use you on the boat. Jason?"

Jason sighed. "Sure, when are you going out?"

"Three-day weekend starts Friday."

"For how long?"

"Let's call it three days. That's long enough to search the shelf on the south side. If it's there we might find it. If not, we run out of time. Everybody has a day job."

"That isn't much. You can go back another time."

"Not likely. We have one shot at this. We get lucky or we don't. In or out Jason?"

"You mind telling me who the client is?"

"The Pelican Squadron."

"Who are they?"

"I'll tell you when I can, Jase. Hooyah."

"Hooyah Mace."

Fifty-Seven

Two divers and a boat owner pulled out of Alameda Friday morning O-dark thirty. They passed under the Golden Gate before sunrise. They ploughed through choppy water where the San Francisco Bay joins the Pacific Ocean in a seaworthy aluminum hull work boat, a 45-footer powered by twin diesels. The boat managed the transition easily. It would take 7-8 hours for a barge to reach them behind a tug if they found the plane. Mason, the third diver, sat in a deck chair in the stern with Jason and Eddie, first and second hands. The owner, Arlen Bishop, captained the boat. An old salt, a giant rough looking man, six foot seven, bald, dark brown wild beard grown to his chest, Arlen put on 100 lbs. since leaving the Navy. They called him *"Tonsey,"* a reference to his weight. Arlen looked like a human mountain. Deeply tanned, tattooed, scarred, he carried the marks of a rough life with a jovial disposition.

When they reached the Farallons, the sky teemed with birds circling for scraps. They rode the winds across a clear Northern California sky, disappearing briefly when they dove between the swells. Arlen drifted the boat. When the sun rose and warmed the morning, he removed his shirt exposing a back covered with a mass of burn tissue. Everyone noticed. Nobody said a word. Gouges on a forearm from some sort of trauma, jagged wounds healed over a shoulder and leg left him physically diminished but still imposing. Arlen didn't seem self-conscious from it. From a fishing family in Monterey, whatever he suffered he kept to himself. As a kid Arlen wanted to be a pirate. He never experienced that line of work but as a salvage captain he lived his dream of treasure hunting.

They came up empty on the first day. Air tanks exhausted again after a number of tries, the divers surfaced and sat on the transom.

"Call it a day, Arlen?"

"It's gettin late, Erik. You won't be able to see down there much longer. We oughta run the boat in before it gets dark, find a place for dinner. Pacifica's almost straight across."

"I prefer someplace more secluded. You mind runnin' down to Half Moon Bay? We can tie up at the pier, eat at *Sam's Chowder House*."

"It's a half mile walk, from the pier," Jason said. "You wanna do that? You've been in the sun and water all day. *Ketch Joanne's* is across from Pillar Point Harbor. There's a brewery down the street, the Inn at Mavericks down the road."

"That's a luxury waterfront hotel, Jason. It's a half mile walk from Ketch Joanne's. I'd rather sleep on the boat, get an early start in the morning."

"I've got a better idea, Mace, and its six miles closer. Ever hear of the *Moss Beach Distillery*?" "No, Arlen."

"Trust me, you'll like it."

They stowed the gear. Arlen ran the boat down the coast over friendly seas. The crew napped on the deck, sedated by rise and fall of gentle swells, droning engines, warm sun. They came inside the wheelhouse when the temperature dropped, as the sun hid behind a marine layer before reemerging in a sliver of clear sky between clouds and ocean. Arlen anchored the *Misty Seas* a few hundred yards off a secluded tree-lined cove that hid what looked from the boat like a mansion on a cliff. They dropped a Whaler over the side with the crane, boarded and beached it. They scrambled up the cliff onto a flagstone patio, stumbled into a dining room where they took a table and ordered dinner.

"Did you know about this place, Erik?" "No Arlen, I didn't."

"Used to be a speakeasy called Frank's Place. My grandfather lived in Vancouver, B.C. He smuggled booze into this cove during prohibition. Your politicians made us a nice family business, didn't stop anybody from drinking." Arlen laughed.

"We figured it out eventually."

"He gave the owner whiskey for lettin him use the cove and the restaurant basement for storage and distribution. Not the only bootlegger to do it. Frank made a fortune from an endless supply of free booze."

"I bet he could tell stories."

"I bet he did, Jase. I was too young. My daddy heard'im. Used to be a one-whore whore house in a place down the coast past Half Moon Bay called San Gregorio. Serviced the local farmers and fisherman. He said he wished it hadn't closed up. It would have made the trip more agreeable. Now it's a post office and a souvenir shop. What a waste."

"Look up her grandchildren, Tonsey. You might be related." That started a round of laughter.

"Didn't your parents live on the coast, Mace? I might be related to *you*."

"None of my relatives are that ugly."

Arlen punched Mason's shoulder with his good arm. Mason pretended the blow knocked him off his chair. "You should know better, Mason. My grandfather went with whores. He had better taste in women than yours did."

"You're Canadian."

"From there, Eddie. We're all from somewhere. Daddy moved down, started fishin' after prohibition ended, met mom and stayed here. She was a big boned woman. If Mason's father married a woman like her, he wouldn't be so puny."

"I wouldn't be this pretty."

"Daddy joined the merchant marine during the Second World War, sailed all over the South Pacific, chased the Navy wherever they chased the Japanese."

Arlen paused to think about that. His vacant eyes stared into space. "I came along after the war ended."

"Don't you wish you did a little bootlegging?"

"I did, sort of, Eddie. I tried bring'in' marijuana in here from Mexico in the 70s' to truck up to San Francisco. South coast dope. We called it Acapulco Gold."

"I didn't know they had brands back then."

"They had brands since they invented dirt. I got chased one night by the Coast Guard. Tried to run. They shot up the boat and set it on fire. That's how my arm and back got this way. We jumped overboard. They caught my mates. I got away. Had to find honest work after that. I went to work for daddy, ended up in the salvage business when the fishin' dried up. It's hard to make a livin' as a fisherman around here."

"You told me Arlen got hurt in Vietnam, Mace."

"I did, and he did, Jason. Depends on which story he's telling." Erik and Arlen winked at each other.

"How 'bout you, Erik? I bet you know a few tales."

"None as good as that one, Eddie. Let's go out on the deck. It's getting deep in here."

The wind kicked up after the sun went down. A marine layer floated onshore. Floodlights on the ocean side of the restaurant switched on. They lit the beach, the surf, the cliffs surrounding the cove, and a lonely Boston Whaler. Seagulls milled around the deck, hopeful for dessert. Mason ordered another round of drinks. The crew wrapped themselves in heavy woolen Mexican blankets the restaurant stored in footlockers on the deck. Erik avoided story-telling by leading a toast. "Captain John Beckinsdale, leader of the Pelican Squadron, Cactus Airforce, 1942, Guadalcanal Campaign. American Hero. We're here this evening, and America is America because of men like him, and what they did."

"Let's find the plane tomorrow," Eddie added, "if I have to learn how to dive and find it myself."

All of them dead tired by then, Erik picked up the check. They took the Whaler back to the *Misty Seas*. They crashed in their sleeping bags in the fog, wherever they found a bunk or a suitable surface to lay a weary head.

They found the plane on the second dive of the second day.

Fifty-Eight

Mason climbed onto the boat.

"Ten yards further out it would have sunk another 1,500 feet and been game over."

"How did you know, Mason?"

"I didn't, Eddie. We started from the middle and fanned out. Could have been any of us."

"Are they in there?"

"No, Jason. Doors unlatched. They got out."

"Any chance of finding them anywhere?"

"No, Eddie."

"How's the plane look?"

"In one piece, Jason. He set it down like a feather. We can raise it easy."

Arlen called for the barge.

An ocean-going tug arrived in the afternoon with the barge. They dove on the plane, found it again at one hundred and sixty-five feet. They stuffed a balloon in the cabin, one under each wing, and two under the fuselage. They pulled an air line down and blew the balloons up with a compressor. The plane gradually floated to the surface while two divers surfaced beside it. They slung two straps under the fuselage, gently lifted it out of the water with a crane, and placed it on the barge. A somber group circled.

"Up to you now, Eddie. Tell us what brought it down, why John didn't call."

"If the cause can be found, I'll find it."

"You have your plane back, Jason. Be gentle."

"I'll send a flatbed to Pillar Point Pier if it's OK with you, Tonsey."

"I'll run it down there, Jase, call you on the ship-to-shore when we're an hour out. Can you take Misty back to Alameda, Mace? I'll get myself back there."

"Sure. We need to keep this quiet, Jason."

"No worries, Mace. We'll take the wings off and throw canvas over it. Eddie can lock it up in an empty hanger on the east side of the Lockheed property near the bay. Nobody goes out there. Set up whatever you need, Eddie. Look it over until you figure it out."

"I'll find it."

"Listen, guys, we need to keep this between ourselves as long as possible. Only the six of us know. Let's keep it that way."

"I need help securing it in the hanger, and putting it up to inspect it."

"On a need-to-know basis, Eddie. OK?"

"Sure, Mace. We can store it tonight. I have plans with the family tomorrow. I'll get on it Monday morning."

"Jason, what are you obligated to do?"

"I have to call the FAA. Scrap it when they're done with it."

"Can you hold off on that?"

"Until Eddie has a look, yeah. After that, it's in their hands and it gets out. I won't be able to keep it a secret after they start investigating."

"Hold off as long as you can and let me know when you lose control. Are you OK with that?"

"Yeah, OK. I work for beer."

"Call me when you have something to look at, Eddie. I'll be chillin' in Pescadero. Let's go home, boys."

"Hooyah Mason."

"Hooyah Jase."

Fifty-Nine

The call came to Mason's cell phone Monday afternoon. It went straight to voice mail. "Come to Moffett" is all Eddie said.

Mason drove to the hanger from Pescadero. Going fishin' he told Joshua and Maggie. They knew he didn't mean it literally.

Eddie and Jason waited at the hangar door. The plane rested on sawhorses, wings installed, engine cover, cowl and doors off. Eddie walked them to the engine bay.

"See this pair of wires running through the firewall to the dashboard?"

Mason peered into the engine bay. "Yeah."

"Hooked up to the altimeter."

"What for?"

"They run across the engine bay to this relay, from there along the fuel line."

"Shit, the fuel line is shredded! What the hell could have done that?"

"See the burn marks on the intake?"

"Yeah."

"I want to say…small explosive device."

"Jesus Christ. It's a double murder. Jason, who would want to kill John and Miriam?"

"Maybe they didn't know Miriam would be on the flight. No idea why anybody would want to kill John. The company went into mourning when we lost him."

"The engine compartment burned. Had a full-on fire in here."

Eddie shined a flashlight under the exhaust manifold.

"There's a hole drilled all the way through. A small explosive device wired to the altimeter, set to go off when the plane reached a predetermined altitude. Shredded the fuel line. This hole in the manifold would have blown hot burning exhaust gasses on raw fuel, igniting it if the explosion didn't do it."

"It could have blown up the plane."

"No, Jason. Fuel pump would have quit. Not enough gas in the fuel line and carburetor for an explosion that big. It was a small charge, like an M80. It went bang, ripped the fuel line open. The fuel caught fire and burned up, engine quit and stopped the flow of fuel. That's all it could do."

"Okay, Eddie. Engine quit, fire burned out. Why didn't John make a distress call? If they were over the Farallons, or approaching them, he was probably above 3,000 feet. He didn't dive into the ocean. The plane would have broken up when it hit the water. He couldn't have reached the mainland, but a plane doesn't glide down that fast. Why didn't he call for help?"

"See these loose wires branching off the relay? They match the ones from the master switch. The explosion took them out. He had no power, Mace. The plane was electrically dead."

"Fuck... When and where was the plane's last service, Jason?"

"Here. Day before it went down."

"Where did it go from here?"

"Half Moon Bay. John took it home."

"Why didn't the charge go off on that flight? What altitude was it set to explode, Eddie?"

"Don't know, Mace, but look over here. See this switch in the line? This plane doesn't need a switch there. If somebody installed it to arm the charge the first time the plane went up, charge would blow on the second ascent."

"Shit, Eddie. Whoever did this knew John was going home. He set this up to go off when he left from there."

"Maybe, Mace. One thing we know for sure, it was set for the second flight. They didn't want the plane to go down on the flight from Moffett."

"Why not? What difference did that make?"

"No water between Moffett and Half Moon Bay. Plane goes down over water, no flight plan, no radar contact, no distress call, maybe never found. No wreckage, slim chance of survival, no bodies, no evidence."

"Somebody knew when and where John went, and didn't want to get caught. Who had access? Who serviced the plane, Jason?"

"I have to check the records."

"Those two crackers you transferred to C-130s."

"Are you sure, Eddie?"

"Pretty sure, Mason. Southern racist white boys from Alabama. I don't forget them."

"Tell me about them."

"White trash. Long stringy hair. Kinda skinny-ugly. Tattoos. Looked like a couple of stoners. Shared a trailer in San Jose."

"What kind of people do you hire, Jason?"

"They know how to maintain planes."

"And kill them. Trailer park means nothing. You know what it costs to live here. They weren't paid software engineering money, were they?"

"Didn't care much for personal hygiene either. I transferred them for sloppy work and bad attitude. Found a project lead to take them after John's plane went down. Never made the connection."

"Let's not jump to conclusions, Jason. Why would they do this?"

"I have no idea."

"What else can you tell me about them, Eddie?"

"They went to San Francisco on weekends. For kinky stuff, I think. Had a friend up there. Came down here once in a black limo. Didn't look as bad as these dudes, but creepy. I think he owns a titty bar. All I know, Mason. Don't spend much time around white trash racist dudes."

"I understand. Might be useful, though. Where are they now, Jason?"

"I don't know Mace. They left the company."

"Right after John's plane was lost?"

"Not sure. Maybe. Have to check employment records with HR. Jesus, this is ugly."

"When are you going to call the FAA?"

"Are you done Eddie?"

"Pretty much."

"I shouldn't wait. Some curious mind is going to wonder what's in here and why we are. The FAA needs to hear it from me. They won't be in a hurry though. It's an old case, not in the papers. No celebrity involved. We don't have to tell them everything we found."

"How long?"

"I don't know. Week or two maybe. They'll come out from Washington, take their time."

"Any way to slow it down?"

"Treachery and obfuscation. I can be hard to reach. Tell me why."

"Might be related to another case that needs to progress before this gets out."

"I'll do what I can. No promises."

"All I can ask. If you track them down, I'd like to know where they are."

"Sure."

"Think you might have current addresses and employment records?"

"Good question. If they skipped, the Sunnyvale PD might have to bring in the FBI. Think they'll find them?"

"Probably. Eventually."

"Mason."

"Yeah, Eddie."

"What do you think happened to them?"

Mason paused. "Hypothermia."

Eddie's chin quivered. He left the hangar in tears.

"I'm sorry we had to find out this way."

"We can bring it to closure, Jason."
"There are sharks out there."
"I'd rather believe that isn't how it ended."

Sixty

"The meeting's on for a week from Thursday, Erik."

"Good timing, Liz-Beth. The window is rapidly closing."

"What do you mean?"

"We found the plane."

"Oh, my God. Please tell me."

"Ditched in the ocean near the Farallon Islands. Nobody inside. They got out, Liz-Beth. I think they perished in the water."

"That's so sad. How did you find it?"

"Long story. Can we save it for later?"

"Sure. What happens next?"

"Lockheed has it. The FAA will examine it, issue a statement."

"How long before it gets out?"

"A week or two, maybe longer. It's an old case, nothing to gain from expediting it. The FAA won't be in a hurry but it won't take long to inspect a small plane."

"This is too much of a distraction. We need to have the meeting first."

"Can you move it up?"

"No."

"Can you slow the investigation down?"

"No, has a life of its own now. It will be in the papers."

"This isn't good."

"I know. I think I know which investment banker Dunn and Cousie are using to shop LightSwitch."

"Can you speak with them? We need to know when the M&A discussion started."

"They won't speak on the record. They can't. Banker/client

relationship issue. We have to depose them under oath, and threaten to subpoena their records. We have to file suit for that."

"That would be huge, Erik. I wish we had time for it."

"Nothing more I can do at my end. Is this still just between the two of us?"

"Yes."

"Sounds like you have to knock it out of the park at your meeting. What's Josh think your chances are?"

"Less than 50%. We have to bluff them."

"Bluff *those* guys? Your witness isn't cooperating?"

"William can't tell us who it is. He might be willing to lose the company."

"That would be too bad. Is he going to the meeting?"

"No, we don't want him there. It'll open Pandora's box."

"Doesn't sound promising."

"I know, but we're out of time. We have to go with what we have."

"Does William know he isn't going?"

"He doesn't know about it."

"He's gonna be pissed, especially if it doesn't go your way."

"I have to tell him. I dread the discussion."

"Best of luck, Liz-Beth. If anybody can pull it off, you and Josh can."

"Thanks Erik. You did great work for us. Amazing, considering the mountain you moved quickly and quietly. I don't know anyone else who could have done it."

Sixty-One

"William, aren't you taking Natalie to Pilates in Half Moon Bay?"

"We're leaving now. I'm going to take the class with her."

"Can you skip it tonight and drop by?"

"Sure. What's up?"

"I need to share something with you about Dunn & Cousie."

"Can you tell me what it's about?"

"I'd rather wait until you get here."

"Okay, I can be back in an hour."

"See you then."

"Who was that?"

"Liz-Beth. Did she say anything to you, Natalie?"

"Why do you ask?"

"She wants me to stop by the cottage."

"I thought you were taking the class tonight."

"Liz-Beth asked me to skip it."

"I can drive myself. I'll drop you off."

"Let's do that. I'll walk back if class hasn't ended."

Natalie dropped William off at Liz-Beth's and drove to Half Moon Bay. Liz-Beth put Mr. Chuckles to sleep. She waited in the great room.

"William, I have something to tell you. It's good. I don't think you're going to like all of it. Osgood Dunn called. He asked for a meeting."

"That's interesting. Was he civil?"

"Yeah, he was. He apologized for Robert's aggression."

"Hard to believe Robert can be reasonable without a gun to his head. Let's go talk to them."

"Joshua and I are going. He's bringing another attorney."

"Okay."

"I mean just the three of us."

"You mean I'm not going?"

"We're afraid the discussion will degenerate into an argument about your performance."

"I performed well. They wrecked the company."

"We know. It's a red herring. They could throw it at us and derail the meeting. How can I explain this? Look, we want this to be... Joshua and I want to threaten them with the business plan into giving up ownership in LightSwitch. We need to focus on that or we won't succeed."

"It doesn't involve me?"

"It does, but I want to force them to sell their shares in the company to me."

"What do you mean?"

"I want to buy it and bring you back to run it."

"You want me to let you use their business plan to buy my company? I'm not going to let you do that."

"I know this doesn't sound right. Please think about it and tell me you'll let me do it."

"Who else knows about this?"

"Joshua of course."

"You set up a meeting behind my back."

"Osgood called and asked me to a meeting. I agreed. Now I'm telling you."

"This is bullshit, Liz-Beth. I obtained the business plan. It's my company. I have to do it."

"With what money, William? You're going to accuse them of fraud and make them *give* you the company?"

"You can loan me the money. I'll sell some shares and pay you back. You can keep some equity if you want to."

"Do you think I want to own a failing technology company, *any* company at my age? I retired thirteen years ago. You'll get your company back. There's another reason. You know I have history with Cousie."

"An investment you made. Another friend of yours lost his business to Cousie. Natalie told me."

"His widow still suffers. I never forgave myself for failing to help him."

"You aren't responsible for that. Cousie did it. This is about avenging your friend for something that happened twenty years ago. It has nothing to do with me."

"It has everything to do with you. The same man is responsible."

"If we do this together you have your revenge."

"They could turn this around and sue us for blackmailing them. I don't want to expose you to that."

"I'll decide what risks I'm willing to take. You're using me to avenge your friends!"

"Please don't jump to conclusions, and don't raise your voice. Yes, I am using you. I'm doing it to help you too."

"If it doesn't work where does it leave me?"

"Safe."

"I'm sorry about your friends. I'm not giving you the business plan so you can use it to screw Cousie."

"What's the problem as long as you get your company back?"

"How do I get it back?"

"I'll make you CEO and recapitalize it."

"With your money?"

"There can be other investors."

"Whoa. Now you're buying my company, raising money, bringing in other people. That's how I lost it. Don't you think you should have discussed this with me?"

"I *am* discussing it with you. Do you think you can scare a couple of experienced investors who are also lawyers into believing you can win a civil fraud case against them? I have to call the meeting off if we can't do it this way. It's your decision, William. What do you want to do?"

William stood and paced the room.

"I'm tired of being manipulated."

"I don't want to help you blow the only chance you have to get your company back."

William sat down and folded his arms across his chest. An angry, stubborn expression spread across his face.

"Mason told me Cousie's back is against the wall. We're running out of time."

"What's going on with him?"

"That's all I know."

"How much time do we have?"

"I don't know. Not much."

"When's the meeting?"

"Next Thursday."

"Next Thursday! This is a goddamn ambush!"

"I've only known about it for a few days. I didn't have the courage to discuss it with you because I was afraid you would react this way."

"I have every reason to act this way!"

"We have to do this the only way we think it can work."

"No! I can't agree to this. You can't use the business plan without me."

"I'm pretty sure this is your last chance to get LightSwitch back in one piece."

"I don't care, Liz-Beth. If it's dead, it's dead. Nobody is going to do this without me. *Damn you, Liz-Beth!*"

"You don't trust me. That really hurts, William. You think I'm trying to cheat you."

"You're using me. You admitted it. Josh too. I didn't think he would do this. And Erik."

"You have to learn to trust somebody, William. We've all been trying to help you since the day you arrived in Pescadero."

"Sorry, Liz-Beth. I don't like this. I'm going home. I'll move on, do something else if I have to."

"You're going to let them win. I'm disappointed."

"So am I, Liz-Beth. Natalie will be expecting me. Good night."

"Don't go away angry. Say no if you need to, but don't storm out of here like you don't care about our friendship."

William stepped outside, slammed the door, and stormed back to the cottage, angry every step of the way.

Liz-Beth's stomach rose. She felt pain in her heart. That foolish, foolish boy, she thought. It's a little implausible. I thought he might agree to it. He doesn't trust me. That hurts. That really hurts.

The argument woke Mr. Chuckles. He shrieked for attention when William slammed the door. Liz-Beth entered the guest room and pulled the shroud off the cage. Chuckles paced back and forth on his perch. Liz-Beth opened the door and brought him out on her hand. Chuckles stared at her and cocked his head.

"You know I'm unhappy, don't you Mr. Chuckles?"

Liz-Beth swung her hand to her shoulder. Chuckles hopped on and started grooming her.

"I'm sad, Mr. Chuckles. So very sad."

Sixty-Two

Natalie braked the Alfa to a stop in front of the cottage.

"Hi, William, did you have a good talk with Liz-Beth?"

"You knew about this didn't you? Why didn't you tell me?"

Natalie sighed.

"Liz-Beth wanted to tell you one-on-one."

"Goddamn it, Natalie. Why did you go along with this?"

"Do you think we're out to get you?"

"You agree with her."

"I don't know what to believe, William. Josh and Liz-Beth think this is the best way. It sounds like they want to extort Dunn and Cousie. I don't think I want you involved in that."

"I knew you would say that. It's my company. She's using me to get even with Robert."

"So what if you get the company back? What did you tell her?"

"I said no."

"You said no! What could it hurt if they tried and failed? You wouldn't be any worse off than you are now."

"What if she buys the company and I don't like what she wants to do with it? That's what happened with Dunn & Cousie."

"What can you do with it now? Jesus, William. Do you think Liz-Beth wants to run a technology company? She will let you do whatever you want."

"You don't know that."

"You think they're trying to cheat you? Is that it? You don't trust Liz-Beth? You ass. You horse's ass. After everything she did for you. How could you think such a thing? Who recruited Josh and hired Mace, spent all this time and her own money? Her car is in our driveway!"

"She wants to get even for Edgar."

"So what? She wants to help you at the same time. What's wrong with that?"

William brooded.

"You know, William, I don't care if you get the company back. You can do something else. How did you leave it?"

"I told you I said no."

"And then you left?"

"Yeah, I walked home."

"In your usual tactful way? Do you know how Liz-Beth must feel about this? You must have cut her to the bone. Do you ever think about anybody's feelings but your own? What do you expect her to do? Tell Josh she was only kidding, fire Mace and walk away like nothing happened? After all this. Are you going to give her the money she spent on this?"

William didn't answer.

Natalie shook a fist.

"If you hurt that woman, I swear to God William, I'll knock your head off. I don't care if you change your mind or not. If you weren't nice about it, you need to get your ass over there and apologize. You can't leave it this way. I take that back. You need to apologize *AND* give her the goddamn business plan, and let her do whatever the hell she wants with it."

"You know what, William? If you get nothing out of this, you would still owe her for what she's done to help you. When I came here, she was your only friend! You were a wreck. You should be willing to let her do this just to help her get even with Robert if it would make her happy."

"I'm sorry, Natalie. I'm not going to do that."

"You selfish, self-centered jerk! Miriam spoiled you. You're blowing a chance to get your company back because your ego won't permit you to trust the best friend you ever had, the best friend *anybody* ever had.

What about me, William? I can't live with you in this shack like a couple of losers. This is a chance to change that. I could be in my apartment in the city. I can find somebody with a *career*. A normal guy. Not a geek in love with cars and computers, so fucking paranoid he can't trust his best friend.

You spend too much time with your goddamn microprocessors and not enough with people. I could be with somebody with social skills who acts like he loves me, who wants a comfortable home to live in and a family."

This woman you don't trust begged me to stick it out with you. She said you would come around with time and tenderness. That woman loves you like a son. She has a heart of gold. I haven't seen her do or say one mean or dishonest thing to anybody. How could you think she would take advantage of you? She helped you get back on your feet. Did she ask for anything but friendship?

The way you treated me in Mountain View. I went through all of it with you. You let me walk out. You know how much that hurt? You acted like I didn't matter at all to you. You didn't ask me to stay. You didn't call me for months. You never called me. We knew each other since we were kids, William. Was that the end? Did you care if you never saw me again?"

"Do we have to get into this now, Natalie? You know what happened to me."

"What happened to *us*! Remember the night I came here? What did you do when I came to the door? You stood there like a *dork!* I had to tell you to get my bags. Do you realize what it took for me to come here like that? To this shack in the middle of nowhere. At midnight. Without knowing if you were with someone. Without knowing how you would react. You aren't the only one with problems. I was so unhappy at work I quit my job. I was lonely. Do you know how much I needed you? Did you throw your arms around me and tell me you missed me? Did you kiss me? Did you ask me how I've been, where I lived, what I did, if I was seeing anybody? Did you give a shit if I never came back?"

"I was glad you came back, Natalie. You surprised me. It was dark. I didn't know your bags were out there."

"Right, I showed up on Friday, at midnight, with a hankie. You didn't have the sense to ask. You only wanted to fuck me and use me as a bed warmer."

"That's not fair and not true, Natalie. I was happy to see you. I wanted you to stay."

"Why didn't you tell me? Why didn't you call me for six months after I moved to the city? Why didn't you tell me you loved me and you wanted me to come here and stay with you? Did you just *assume* I wanted to stay here, or was it okay if I just fucked you and went back to San Francisco in the morning?"

"I wanted you to stay. You know I'm not very good at talking about this sort of thing."

"I'm not very good at living without it. Since we were teenagers, you never learned how to talk to me. You always took me for granted. That won't work anymore. We've been here for months. This place has no space. It's drafty. It barely has hot and cold running water. We have a closet for a bathroom. We have a cubicle for a kitchen. I need space of my own. I'm halfway living out of a suitcase. Can I have a freaking closet of my own? It's okay for you to live with nothing but a tooth brush, one clean T-shirt, and one dirty one. It isn't okay for me. I'm a *woman*. Do you get that? This is like camping. Okay for the summer. When winter returns, I want to be in a house I can make into a *home*. A *real* house, William. Not a goddamn shack. Are you such a fool you think I can live like this forever? You have a perfectly livable house in Mountain View. We were happy there. Why can't we *live* there instead of using it as a laboratory? Couldn't you ask me before you decided to do that? It was our *home,* William. Why do you leave me here when you stay overnight in Mountain View with your engineer buddies?"

"You know we pull all-nighters there. Do you want to be there for that?"

"I want you to ask me what I want."

"You can come with me."

"I can come… *No*… Not like that. Not like a mascot."

"I… thought you liked staying here when I'm working."

"Why the hell would you think that? Because I could go over to Liz-Beth's and soak in her tub? The house in Mountain View has a tub. I want a MAN in it. Are we a couple or not, or am I like, a part time rental? What do you think we are? I want you to tell me."

"We're a couple, Natalie. I'm working to build a product and create a company. It takes time."

"I need to be more important than the house, the engineers, *and* the company. I need you to need me *more*. You *idiot*. You have no idea what a woman needs. Do you think you just have to service me and feed me? Like a pet? A trophy?"

"That's not fair, Natalie. You know we don't have a lot of money. We have no income. I can't rent an office in Silicon Valley, maintain the house and this cottage, buy equipment and pay business expenses."

"You can sell the goddamn house and rent an apartment, or sell this shack so we can move into the house and you can rent an office."

"I can't sell this cottage. It's my parent's place. I spent summers here when I surfed Mavericks. The Mountain View house is a valuable asset. It would be a mistake to sell it."

"Is that what this is about? Assets? Then you should get a *JOB*. We need a comfortable place to live. If you want to continue this relationship you have to stop thinking and acting for both of us."

"If I can make a business out of what we're doing in Mountain View I can improve our living arrangements."

"I don't care about that. I need us to be partners, to make these decisions together. I need you to consider my needs, to care about what makes me happy."

"We're discussing it."

"Because I'm *making* us discuss it. You should know what I want by now. I don't need you to be a rich technology entrepreneur.

I just need us to have enough, for you to think the most important thing is to be with each other. I know you love me, William and you just aren't very good at expressing it. I need you to try. I don't want to feel a pet anymore, and I don't want to live in this goddamn dog house forever. I need to see a way forward."

"I get it, Natalie. As soon as we get the company funded, I'll rent office space and we can move back to the house."

"You *don't* get it William. This can't be dependent on the success of the company. It has to be no matter what. If we have to work for somebody, be average working people, I don't care. I only care that being together is the most important thing to you and you want me to be happy."

William put his hands on his thighs. He dropped his head and looked at the floor. He stood, approached Natalie, and tried to embrace her. She backed away.

"Not this time, William. You think you can melt me or I'm going to cry and we're going to make love and when you wake up you're going to be relieved that I forgot all about this. I don't want to hug you, William. I don't want to be kissed. I sure don't want to make love, and I'm too angry to cry. I don't think you're ready. I can't believe what you did to Liz-Beth. I know you were mean to her after she tried so hard to help you. I can see the guilt on your face. You can't just throw your arms around me and expect me to believe you're a changed man. You have to convince me."

"How do you expect me to do that?"

"You're going to Liz-Beth's. You're going to apologize for whatever you said to her, tell her you trust her with your company and your life, and thank her for everything she did for you. You're going to tell her she can do whatever she wants with the damn business plan. If she accepts your apology maybe *I'll* forgive you if you can convince me you're capable of being a partner who shares life instead of dragging somebody along with whatever you feel like doing. I need to believe making a life with me is the most important thing in your world."

"It's late, Natalie. Liz-Beth is probably asleep."

"Wake her up if you have to. Don't let her spend the night thinking about what you said. She would appreciate it if you woke her to tell her."

"I'm sorry. I'm not ready to do that. I have to think about this."

"You don't have to think about apologizing to Liz-Beth."

"I haven't changed my mind about the meeting."

Natalie lifted a jacket off the coat rack.

"William, I'm sure I love you as much as your mother loved your father. She loved him a great deal, and he could be as big a dork as you are. She told me when she wanted your father to propose to her, she told him she would follow him to Idaho to plant potatoes and spend the rest of her life watching them grow, as long as he watched them with her. Your mother, with the private university education, the New York banking family, the summers in the Hamptons; the Pulitzer Prize winner, war correspondent, world traveler, willing to give it all up to be with your father, the flying hick, to live in the middle of nowhere if he just asked her.

It isn't necessary for us to be rich, or for you to build the most successful tech company in history, or anything like it. It's only necessary for us to love each other enough so none of that matters. I need you to understand and believe this. I love you, William, but if you want me to stay with you, you have to do better."

A pang of fear gripped William like a fever of a hundred and four. He realized he could lose Natalie forever.

Natalie opened the door.

"I'm going to Liz-Beth's so you can be alone to think about this, and I can be with Liz-Beth who is no doubt terribly hurt about whatever stupid things you said to her. Damn you, William. Figure out what you want, and what you're willing to do to have it. Whatever you say, you better mean it."

Natalie walked through the door and left William standing alone in the cottage.

Sixty-Three

iz-Beth opened the door for Natalie. She looked disappointed, not as sad or hurt as Natalie feared.

"Hi, Liz-Beth. Hope you don't mind I just dropped in. Did I keep you from going to bed?"

"No, no. Thanks for stopping. Please come in."

"I really gave it to him tonight."

"For what?"

"For whatever he said to you."

"I didn't like it either."

"He jumps to conclusions, loses his temper, says things he shouldn't, expects everyone to overlook it. Not this time. I can't believe he won't let you take the meeting without him, that he thinks you're just using him, or trying to take advantage of him."

"He doesn't believe that. He'll let Joshua and I go without him."

"How do you know that?"

"He's been through a lot. He isn't over it yet. He feels helpless and manipulated. He'll get over it. He wants his company back, and he knows this is his only chance. I hope he gets over it quickly because we're out of time. We have to go now."

"What about your feelings?"

"I didn't expect that."

"I can't believe he would speak to you that way."

"It's his problem. I admit he got to me. I'm over it. Do you want to stay here tonight?"

"I'd like to."

"Do you have everything you need?"

337

"I left a few things in the guest room and bathroom. I let it all out, Liz-Beth. The shack we live in, the lab in the house, the insensitivity, taking me for granted. I feel a lot lighter. I was pretty harsh. I think I had the right to be."

"You should have discussed it sooner."

"I thought he needed to stay focused. I didn't think he would listen anyway. I thought it would work itself out. Now I think he's willing to live in that shack for the rest of his life. I think he likes it. He takes off up the coast in his father's car on Saturday morning, he drives home, we make love all day, make something to eat and he thinks life is wonderful."

"Doesn't sound too bad."

They giggled.

"Sure, okay. The rest of the time I'm left in that shack by myself unless I come here. There's nothing for me to do in Pescadero. I need a career and we need a livable home. He has to figure out how to do it, and we have to decide on it together."

"How did he take it?"

"He sat there like a sack of flour."

"A little lame at relationship talk, is he?"

"That's an understatement."

"Something inside of you changed, Natalie. I noticed it on the ride back from San Francisco."

"I ran into Robert before George and I met you."

Liz-Beth looked shocked. "What happened?"

"He was his usual nasty self. He wanted me to talk to William."

"What did you tell him?"

"I said *No*. We argued on the sidewalk."

"Why didn't you tell me?"

"George ran him off. It didn't seem like a big deal."

"You mustn't go near him, dear. He's desperate."

"I didn't go looking for him. We bumped into each other at Union Square."

"Did he hurt you?"

"What is it, Liz-Beth? Do you think he's a violent criminal?"

"I need to know what happened."

"He looked rough, not at all himself. I stood up to him Liz-Beth. For the first time in my life Robert Cousie didn't scare me. George saw us arguing and chased him away."

"You need to stay away from him, Natalie, at least until after the meeting."

"What's happening, Liz-Beth?"

"He came to your place Pescadero. He confronted William. He called me. He tried to intimidate you. Whatever his mental state is, it will probably worsen. It's coming to a climax, Natalie. It will be more stressful between now and then."

"Do you expect him to come here again?"

"I don't know what he'll do. If you run into him someplace, don't confront him."

Natalie looked alarmed.

"No wonder you were quiet on the return drive. I thought you were just tired."

"Something good came from this, Liz-Beth. I feel like a woman. I'm not a little girl anymore. I can stand up to anything and anybody."

"Don't get carried away."

"I won't. I just see things differently. I'm going to be more assertive about what I want."

"Good for you, Natalie."

"Maybe I should go back and live in the city."

"That would make me sad."

"I can work from here sometimes, be here on weekends. What am I talking about? I just walked out on William."

"No, you didn't."

"Our relationship has to change and so does our living situation. I'll move back to the city if we can't get through this. I'd like to come and visit if I do."

"Whatever you do, I hope we can spend lots of time together. I think you can work it out."

"I love you, Liz-Beth."

Natalie hugged her.

"What are you going to do about William?"

"Let him try to convince me to come back."

"I wouldn't be too hard on him."

"You're a bigger softie than I am, Liz-Beth."

"Let's have a party. I'll open a bottle of wine, we can get buzzed, laugh about the men we knew. I knew a few doozies."

"Tell me everything about Bunny and Bentley."

"And Sukie. I'd love to."

Sixty-Four

William sat in the great room with a shot glass and a bottle of bourbon. He rested his face in his hands and thought about the evening as he gazed out the picture window. His personal life, he realized, imploded in little more than an hour.

It took an hour after Natalie arrived at Liz-Beth's for the phone to ring.

"Do you want to guess who that is, Natalie?"

"I know who it is."

"Do you want to answer it?"

"No, Liz-Beth, you take it."

"Hello, William."

"Hello Liz-Beth. I know we need to talk in person. It's late. I thought it would be better to call. I didn't want you to go to sleep the way we...the way I left tonight. I'm sorry about the way I spoke to you. You were right about everything. I know you wouldn't do anything to hurt me."

"Thank you for calling. Let's not discuss this now. Just assume I'll accept your apology tomorrow. Do you want to talk to Natalie?"

"Yeah, if she wants to talk to me."

"Natalie?"

"What is it, William?"

"Look, I'll make it right with Liz-Beth. I already took back everything I said."

"You'll let her take the business plan, and have the meeting?"

"She can have the meeting anyway she wants it. I don't care

what happens to the company. I care about you and Liz-Beth. You said a lot of things tonight I need to think about. You were right."

Natalie glanced at Liz-Beth. She raised her eyebrows. Liz-Beth knew what William said without hearing it. She smiled.

"It's too much to get my arms around in an hour. Can we talk about it tomorrow?"

"What would you like to say tonight?"

"I felt terrible about what I said to Liz-Beth. I couldn't let her go to sleep without speaking to her. I don't think I could have slept well either, maybe not at all. I heard you, Natalie. I want to work this out."

"Great, see you tomorrow. I want to hear all about it."

"Wait. Can't you come back? I'll come and get you."

"Liz-Beth and I are having a party. Girls only."

"Don't be like that, Natalie. I'll come in the Alfa. I'll talk to Liz-Beth."

"No, William, that train left the station. It's girl's night. I'm going to do Liz-Beth's nails. She's going to do my hair. You know, girl stuff. We have lots of wine to drink."

Natalie smiled at Liz-Beth. Liz-Beth put her hand over her mouth to muffle a laugh.

"Oh, come on, Natalie, you know we're going to work this out. Don't punish me like this."

"I'm not punishing you, William. I want to spend the evening with my friend Liz-Beth. You stay in Mountain View with your friends when you work late don't you?"

"I stay there because I'm tired from working twelve hours straight. I can't drive back after that. I'd rather be here with you."

"Pretty good, William. You're learning. Not tonight, though. I'm tired of this. I need a break."

"Please, Natalie. Don't do this to me. I'll be up all night."

"Don't beg, William. It sounds pathetic. I need a night off."

"OK, can we spend the day together tomorrow? I'll take the day off. The guys can do without me. Hell, I'll give *them* a day off."

"How generous. You don't pay them."

"I buy the pizza."

"Sure, probably. I'll call you."

"You promise?"

"When I'm ready. We're going to stay up late and sleep in."

"You always sleep in."

"You have a problem with that?"

"No. Let's not fight anymore. We did enough fighting tonight to last a long time, more than we did in a year. Okay. I give up… have a good night."

"And what?"

"Goodnight to Liz-Beth."

"And what?"

"I love you, Natalie."

"I love you too, William. Goodnight."

Natalie hung up.

"What do you think, Liz-Beth?"

"Well done. Don't make a career of it."

"Did you do that with Bunny?"

"Are you kidding? The Germans shot him out of the sky. He had enough warfare for a lifetime. When he signed on with me, he was already house broken."

"Maybe I should put William in the Army. You know, send him to boot camp."

"You just put him through boot camp. Give him a graduation party. Let's skip the wine, pop a bottle of Champagne, and get on with it. We have men to make fun of."

Sixty-Five

William didn't sleep well. He rose before the sun, walked to the great room, sat by the picture window, and spoke to a stuffed pelican.

"I really screwed up last night, Dusty. I'm here by myself in the dog house. No offense, pal, you're good company for a dead pelican. Sorry about this dump. Natalie doesn't like it either. What am I going to do today? If I know her and Liz-Beth, they won't be up for hours. I bet they enjoyed every minute of me being here by myself. Probably had a good laugh about it. Yeah, I know, Dusty. You're stuck here too. Thanks for keeping me company. I can see Natalie's smiling face resting on a pillow. Women one, man zero. Why do I feel outnumbered ten to one when there are only two of them? Hmmm. Never asked if you were male or female."

William showered and threw down a cup of coffee. He decided to walk the trail by the marsh. A hundred yards from the cottage he wondered who was awake and not at work.

* * *

Sukie came to the doorway in a purple kimono, tabi socks and sandals. He wore the hair that circled his bald spot in a ponytail. His scruffy beard had grown wild. He looked like a rogue samurai.

"Come in, William. It is good to see you. I am grooming the garden. Do you mind if I continue?"

"No, please do."

William removed his sneakers and stepped into the house.

"Mrs. Nakajima will prepare tea."

Sukie passed through sliding doors to the bedroom where Akiko wrote haiku. She sat in a light green kimono on a tatami mat at a small table. Akiko smiled at William as she glided into the kitchen on wooden sandals. He returned the smile. Even though Akiko was native American, William bowed politely. *Interesting that they wear traditional Japanese clothing at home,* William thought. *It looks comfortable.* When Sukie returned, they walked to the Zen garden.

Akiko carried tea service for two, a cast iron kettle call *tetsubin,* and a bottle of cold filtered water to the tea room. She set the service on a tatami mat and used a piece of tatami and a match to light charcoal in a pit. The roof of the room has a vent to let the smoke out and a cover to prevent rain from entering. Akiko placed the kettle in the pit and poured cold water in it from the bottle.

"Where's Charles today, Sukie?"

"He is with his girlfriend. She is very *hot.*"

"He hasn't spent much time at the lab this month."

"Ichiro has responsibilities. He must keep his girlfriend happy."

I should take a lesson, William thought.

"Your rake is leaning on the wall behind you."

Did I think I could avoid it? William asked himself. He began working the opposite side of the garden. Already groomed to perfection, it needed only the *act* of grooming.

"You have more trouble with women, William."

"How did you know that?"

"I know everything."

You can't keep a secret in this place for an hour, William thought. He went down the list of people who probably knew what happened last night. *Liz-Beth and Natalie, Joshua and Maggie, Maria and her family, Sukie, Akiko.* Everyone he cared about and would not want to know. *I wonder if Charles and Lupe know? If they do, everybody who works at the lab knows, everybody at LightSwitch knows, everybody in Silicon Valley knows. Ridiculous. I'm not that important. I don't want to think about this*, William told himself.

"In your dreams, were you a kamikaze?"

"What?...What do you mean, Sukie?"

"You act as if you wish to disrespect your friends and destroy yourself. Would you like to borrow my ceremonial knife?" Sukie lifted a *tanto* from a shelf, wrapped the blade in white linen, and pointed it at his belly.

"Cut here and pull the knife in this direction. It is the honorable way."

"A little extreme isn't it?"

Sukie lowered his hand.

"Liz-Beth and I have been friends for many years. I will not permit anyone to speak to her in a disrespectful way."

William saw anger in Sukie's eyes, though he spoke in a calm and steady voice. William continued grooming.

"I'm ashamed of myself."

"What will you do about it?"

"When Natalie calls, I'll go to Liz-Beth's and apologize. Please don't be angry with me. I already feel bad about this."

"I am disappointed in you, William. You should learn to trust. You should not assume everyone is trying to cheat you because some men did. If you become too defensive, you will shut out people you need, and who need you. You must speak carefully. Hold your thoughts until they can be shared. Do not project anger or frustration on people who care about you."

Sukie paused. William did not respond.

"You do not have to hold your thoughts *now*! I want to know if you *agree*!" Sukie spoke in a deep angry voice.

Sukie startled William. William held the rake parallel to the ground, palms up and offered it to Sukie. He bowed his head in a gesture of surrender.

"I agree."

"I want to know if you will do as I ask."

"I'll try."

"NO, William!" Sukie raised his voice. "It is not good enough to try. I want to know if you will do as I ask in your conversations with Liz-Beth."

Sukie's eyes were menacing, unforgiving; the eyes of a Japanese Army officer who had seen terrible things and perhaps, William wondered, had done some of them. William wondered if Sukie had killed anyone. At that moment, he believed Sukie could. He knew Sukie wouldn't hurt him, but the anger in his voice and eyes surprised William. The little man scared him.

"I'll be careful about the way I speak, and what I say to Liz-Beth."

"Then you will not need my tanto today."

William swallowed.

Sukie placed the knife on the shelf. He walked to the other side of the garden and took the rake from William. He placed a hand on a shoulder level with the top of Sukie's head. His eyes were now consoling, but his voice still deep and firm.

"I will forgive you *one time*. You must never speak to Liz-Beth disrespectfully again. If you do, I will be very angry. You will not like it if I am angry with you."

The fury of the angry samurai subsided, the tone of his voice now somber.

Sukie led William to the tea room. They sat on mats on opposite sides of a low teak table, stretching their legs in the pit made for the purpose to wait for the water to heat.

"This is how we speak man-to-man in Japan, when matters of importance are discussed."

"I would like to go to Japan someday."

"Maybe Ichiro will go with you. I am old now. I do not have happy memories of life in Japan. I have decided I do not wish to return.

"When you go to Liz-Beth's today, say only what you need to say. Make no excuses. Let her say what she wishes. Do not argue and do not disagree. Do not ask about things she cannot tell you.

Let her accept your apology if she chooses to, and accept what she tells you. Sit quietly as you are sitting now.

Something happened a long time ago, William. It left Liz-Beth with a great guilt that haunts her. This guilt wished to be freed since she learned what happened to you and your company. I know you have heard this. You know little of it, or how much Liz-Beth needs to be free of it. She may share more of it with you now, or, she may never. You need to know it is a millstone she carried for many years since we lived in San Francisco. She needs to shed this stone now.

Your arrival here in Pescadero, makes it possible for her to atone for a tragedy for which she blames herself. She does not deserve this blame. She punishes herself for something she wishes she had done but could not. It is this regret which she now wishes to cast off to end her torment. You can help her do this. After it is done, she will be free of a memory that made her unhappy for many years."

"You mean at the meeting in San Francisco?"

"Yes."

"For what happened to Edgar?"

"Yes."

"Is it really better if I don't go?"

"Yes. Liz-Beth wishes to conduct this meeting in her own way. It is true. It will be easier for her to succeed if you are not present. If she is successful, you can only benefit. If you can believe anything I tell you, believe what Liz-Beth said. Let her do this."

"Thank you for telling me."

"You would have realized this if you were not so quick to anger. You would have realized it on your own today. You must consider who Liz-Beth is, who you are to her. These things place her motives above suspicion. Why would Liz-Beth take advantage of you? For money? She gives it away. For power? She has no interest in such a thing. Foolish thoughts, William. You must know she would never do anything that would harm you."

William lowered his head. He felt ashamed.

Akiko returned with a ceramic teapot filled with whole tea leaves. She poured hot water into it from the kettle.

"Your company seems very important to you, William. It is not. A successful career does not depend on any single adventure. It depends on how we manage our failures. You are young. You can start another company. People you care for, who care for you, cannot be replaced so easily. Some can never be replaced.

You lost your parents when they were young and strong. You did not experience them as old people. We seem strong and wise to you. We are old, Elizabeth and I. Our experiences have aged us. We will not be here for you forever. You are lucky to have a friend like Liz-Beth who cares so much for you. You must treasure this and honor her with kindness and respect, always."

William felt his stomach contract. His eyes teared. He swallowed. Sukie poured tea for William and himself. They sipped together quietly until Sukie broke the silence.

"You are very important to Liz-Beth, William. You brought her great happiness. In a careless moment, you can take this happiness away. Words can hurt deeply, even more than casting stones."

A pang of fear pierced William's heart.

"Is Liz-Beth sick?"

"No, no. She is well. You must understand it is because she cares so much for you, that you can hurt her easily. You are a *man*, William. You must stop acting like a spoiled boy."

"I can do this Sukie."

"Good, now you must walk home. Liz-Beth will call you soon."

"How do you know that?"

"I know everything."

"Her cottage is right here. I can walk…"

"*NO*, William. You are thinking like a boy. Liz-Beth is sensei. She will lead you. Go home. Wait for her call. Let her decide when she wants to see you. It will not be long. Wait here."

Sukie walked to the bedroom. He removed an envelope from

a drawer. He and Akiko exchanged glances when she saw it in his hand. Sukie rejoined William.

"Give this to Liz-Beth when you see her. Do not open it. I have kept it for her for many years. She is not aware of its existence. She needs it now. It is a gift you can give her at an appropriate time."

"Thank you, Sukie."

"Go *now*, William. I will walk you to the door. Remember what I told you. If Liz-Beth wants to share something with you, listen patiently. You will understand a great deal more than you do now. If she does not, wait as long as it takes, if necessary, forever. Please do not pressure her to take you to the meeting in San Francisco. Let her do this as she needs to."

William pulled his sneakers on, tied the laces and bowed. Sukie bowed.

"Thank you, Sukie."

"You are foolish sometimes, William. You know Mrs. Nakajima and I adopted Charles. We love him, but if I had a son of my own genes, I would wish him to be like you.

Good luck, William."

Sixty-Six

William found a message on his answering service when he arrived home. Natalie hadn't returned. Liz-Beth invited him to her cottage. He checked his watch. Eleven AM. He left a message at the lab. He wouldn't be there today or tonight, maybe not tomorrow. He took the Alfa to Liz-Beth's.

Liz-Beth answered the door. She smiled as if nothing had happened. Natalie stood behind her with arms folded and a face of stone. Mr. Chuckles glared from his perch. William slouched like a wounded teenager. *God,* he thought. *Even Chuckles is angry with me.*

When she realized William would have stood there like a frozen popsicle forever, Liz-Beth held her arms out and stepped forward to hug him. She buried the side of her head in his chest and squeezed. He wrapped his arms around her. *Wimpy hug,* Liz-Beth thought. She didn't care. She knew he felt bad about what he said. Good enough.

"Come in and sit down."

Liz-Beth and Natalie sat in adjacent chairs. William sat across from them on the sofa. Natalie looked like she wanted another go at him. William slouched.

"I…"

Liz-Beth cut him off. "I don't want to make a big deal out of this. I accept your apology. I have no time for drivel."

"I feel very bad about this. I should never have spoken to you that way, or doubted you for a second. I won't do it again."

"That's enough. I want to forget this ever happened. Every-thing is as it was."

William handed Liz-Beth a large manila envelope.

"Take the plan, go to the meeting, do it any way you want. Just tell me what I can do to help."

"Do you have anything to say to your girlfriend?"

William's head hung like a hound dog's. He looked twice as sad.

"Natalie, I apologize for everything. I need you to come home and stay with me. I want to talk about living arrangements. I don't have any solutions now. I'm sure we can make something work for both of us. We can plan it together."

Natalie thought William's words sounded prepared. She sat expressionless and silent. Her arms remained crossed.

"Natalie, if it would make you happy, I'll quit everything and move to Idaho to grow potatoes. I just need you to stay with me."

Natalie's expression changed from scorn to surprise. William had never spoken to her with so much passion. He convinced her. Her eyes sprung open. She leaned forward. She unfolded her arms and rested them on the arms of the chair.

A smile of satisfaction spread across Liz-Beth's face.

"You are the most important thing in my life, Natalie. I'll do anything to keep you."

Natalie jumped off the chair, threw herself into William's arms, and showered him with kisses.

Liz-Beth cleared her throat. "It's getting warm in here." She walked to a casement window and cranked it open. "Can you wait till you get home, or do you need a room?"

William and Natalie smiled.

Natalie sat next to William. She wrapped an arm around his waist and leaned against him. William put an arm over her shoulder. Liz-Beth sat across from them. She sighed, "Oh brother."

"We only have a few days before the meeting. Can you speak to someone at LightSwitch and get an update, William?"

"I'll talk to VK. What do you need to know?"

"Morale, sales trends, financials, projects, inventory. Everything you can pass on in summary. Tell me what you need to make the company successful if we get it back. Put it in a term sheet with a sum on it so I can speak from it."

"I can do that."

"I need to figure out the company value, be informed enough to negotiate effectively with Osgood and Robert. Otherwise it's just a game of wills."

"I understand. Will you call me from the meeting?"

"Of course."

"I'll go crazy if I have to wait until you get back here."

"I'll let you know."

"I hope you can make this work, Liz-Beth."

"I do too, William. If it's too expensive I'll help you with the business in Mountain View."

Natalie interrupted. "William, I have someone to introduced to you. I'll be right back."

William's eyes followed Natalie with curiosity as she disappeared into the spare bedroom. She returned cradling a female Springer Spaniel puppy. William approached them.

"Liz-Beth has a new puppy. That's nice, Liz-Beth. Cute doggie."

"She's ours William. We picked her up this morning."

William blanched.

"Now you live with two females." Natalie said. Liz-Beth grinned.

"What are we going to do with this?"

"With her, William. Her name is Bernice. We're going to love her."

"Ah… didn't we agree to discuss these things?"

"You hadn't agreed yet. I consulted Liz-Beth. We think it's a marvelous idea."

"Thanks, Natalie," Liz-Beth said sarcastically.

William frowned. "Thanks, Liz-Beth."

"Look at her tail wag. Isn't she sweet? You're busy, William. I need something else in my life. She's a dog like Bunny and Liz-Beth had. We can walk her. You can take her hiking. You need to get out more, get some exercise, stop spending all your time in the lab playing with transistors. Look how sweet she is."

William bent down. "Bernie" licked his nose.

"She likes you."

"What do we do with her when I have to go to Mountain View and you have to go to the city?"

"Liz-Beth will help out. Liz-Beth?"

"I like having a dog in the house."

"It's a conspiracy. She's going to grow into a big dog, forty, fifty pounds. She's going to need space. How are the three of us going to live in the cottage?"

"That's what you have to figure out."

Liz-Beth chuckled. "Y'all have a big time. I'm going for a walk."

William removed the envelope Sukie gave him from the breast pocket of his jacket. He handed it to Liz-Beth.

"Where did you get this?"

"Sukie."

Addressed to Liz-Beth in longhand, written with a fountain pen, the return address a simple signature; "Harold Bunny Wiggins." Liz-Beth gave it a pensive look. She placed the letter on the coffee table. She left William, Natalie, Bernie, Mr. Chuckles, and walked to the trailhead at end of the street.

Redemption

Sixty-Seven

When Liz-Beth returned she found Mr. Chuckles perched in his cage. William, Natalie and Bernie were gone. She sat on the sofa, opened the envelope, and removed a letter.

Dearest Liz-Beth,

You are reading this because I have gone without saying every-thing I wished to. Do not mourn me. I had the most wonderful life a man could have, and in you my love, the best wife ever. I hope in some small measure I helped make you happy. If I have fallen short, failure is mine alone. I regret any pain I may have caused you. I never intended any.

Take care of Bentley until he joins me. Be kind to Sukie. I know you had your differences. He has grown to love you and will be loyal to the end. I'm sorry I could not remain in this life to comfort you in old age, as you have for me. For your love I am eternally grateful. My only regret is I left you no children. Perhaps you have met someone from a younger generation who provides companionship. I hope you have.

The death of our dear friend Edgar is the one event that marred our near-perfect lives. I know it hurts and you punish yourself still for his death, but dearest, please believe there is nothing we could have done to help him. Edgar's pain ended long ago. You and Evelyn suffer still. Forgive yourself, Eliz-abeth. Find time to be Evelyn's friend. We did not visit her enough after moving to Pescadero. I'm certain she misses you.

Be well and live a long and wonderful life, Liz-Beth.

Until we meet again,

Yours and forever,

Bunny

Sixty-Eight

A knock on Liz-Beth's door announced William's arrival.

"Come and sit down, William. How did your meeting go with VK?"

"He told me what we need to know."

"How's it looking?"

"Revenue declining, forecast down, morale low, cash on hand for two more payrolls if they don't pay all the current bills. They're down to 30 days, Liz-Beth. Credit hold with suppliers, parts inventory low, two months behind in rent. I wouldn't worry about the rent. Business is imploding in the South Bay. Nobody's queuing for space. The order book looks like a black hole, like the sales force has been on vacation. They can do better than that. They probably sense they'll be laid off soon, are spending their time interviewing."

"Do you think you can keep them?"

"If they have product to sell and we can pay them, sure. They'll smell the money. The whisper number is two hundred thousand jobs will be lost in the South Bay before unemployment peaks. Anybody who has a job wants to keep it."

"Maybe Dunn and Cousie stashed money away. Did you ask VK to speak with the CFO?"

"They let him go. Somebody from Osgood's staff is acting CFO."

"Great," Liz-Beth remarked with sarcasm. "Maybe they moved cash off the books in case they can't sell the company. The creditors would get it. Are you sure you want this company back?"

"It sounds worse than it is, Liz-Beth. The team's intact. The critical people are still there. They need operating capital, new products, leadership. We have an exciting prototype running in the Mountain View lab. Customers need it. We can leapfrog competitors."

"I'm retiring from engineering, Liz-Beth. I'm gonna let Charles do it. He's better than I am. If I take his creation to the office and show it around, it will generate excitement. VK's team can make a solid product out of it. We have to be able to pay everyone until it starts producing revenue. If we can, they'll get behind this like they did when we were the hottest networking company in the valley."

William captured Liz-Beth's attention.

"We need money to build beta systems. We have to deliver them to our best customers, let them try them out, help us make them production ready and provide references. We always took care of them. They'll give us a shot."

"With business in recession, why would anybody buy new equipment?"

"We can save them money. Customers always need faster and less expensive. That's how they compete. We need to spend money on marketing, go to a couple of trade shows, schmooze the analysts, the technology editors, create a buzz. It's the fastest way to place new products with customers."

"It sounds like you thought this through."

"Nothing to think about. I've done it."

"How long do you think it will take?"

"If we start now, in twelve to eighteen months we'll be growing again and making money."

"Why not just grow a company from the Mountain View lab?"

"It'll take three to five years to get where LightSwitch is if I have to start from a living room. The industry moves too fast for that."

"It will be expensive to buy LightSwitch and re-capitalize it. Are you sure it's worth it?"

"To start with a fully functioning company and an industry leading product line? You bet it is."

"OK, William, give me a budget and let me think about it."

"Here you go."

William tore two sheets of paper out of a notebook and handed them to Liz-Beth.

"One page with talking points, and budget numbers, the other with summary proforma, and funding requirements."

Liz-Beth looked at the capital requirements.

"Those are big numbers."

"We have fixed engineering and manufacturing costs. We can't run a business without facilities and people. We have to get off credit hold with suppliers so we don't scare away the customers. Look what we can do."

William pointed to revenue numbers.

"Looks good if you can do it. I'm just a trader. I don't know anything about this business."

"We did it before; from my dorm room. This is a functioning company with customers. I *know* we can do it."

William pointed to the bottom line.

"Are you sure you can do that?"

"Pretty sure."

"I'd rather not lose my life savings if I can avoid it."

"You're too smart to risk that much. Tell you what, you risk your savings, I'll throw in Natalie. If I don't make this work, she'll murder me."

"What do you think, Mr. Chuckles?"

Chuckles raised his wings and bobbed his head. He chatted approval.

"Wow, William! He *really* likes it. He's displaying his crest!"

"Dusty likes it too."

"Still need to keep Lupe out of this?"

"Yeah, I do."

"Let's find out what we have to spend to buy the company. I'll call George, round Joshua up and tell him it's on. Before you go, I'd like to share how I feel about this."

"Sure."

"I know you're excited about the possibility of getting the company back and executing this plan. You have to realize it may not happen."

"I know."

"If we aren't successful, I don't want you to be so disappointed that you give up what you're doing in Mountain View."

"I started that because I thought I lost LightSwitch forever. I'll keep it going."

"William, it's important to be successful in your career. It isn't who you are. I had a friend who killed himself because he lost his money. He left a young wife in debt. He shouldn't have done that. She never got over it. If he never owned a successful business, if they never had money, it didn't matter to her. She thought life could be good if he collected rubbish. She only cared that they had each other."

"There is no circumstance I can imagine which would cause me to consider suicide. I'll always have Natalie. I can always find some way to earn a living."

"That's what I want to hear. Don't assume Natalie will always know this. Never stop telling her you love her. Make her believe it. Living together will be so much easier. Your friends Joshua and Maggie, Sukie and me, Chuckles, Bernie. We all need you and want you to succeed. I'm sure you will have a great career. Only Steve Jobs can be Steve Jobs. Don't give up anything to be like him. Be yourself. See your future - Make your future."

"You saw *Caddie Shack.*"

"I watched it with Sukie. We laughed through it together. Chevy Chase was a clever man."

"I want you to know about Edgar and Evelyn, why what happened to them is so difficult for me. They were close friends. Edgar didn't need to die. Bunny and I tried to help. We would have done anything for him. He wouldn't let us. I felt like I failed them. I can't let that happen again.

Robert drove Edgar to suicide. He has no remorse. He profited from it. That's all he cares about. After all these years of living with the memory, I have this chance, probably the only chance to make Cousie pay. Helping you is more important. If I had to choose, I would help you. I have this possibility of doing both. I need to try. Can you understand?"

"I do and it's okay."

"Thank you for the information. Joshua and I will do our best. If we fail, will you let me help you with your new company?"

"Absolutely."

Sixty-Nine

George left his apartment at 7:00AM. He chose Highway 280 for the drive down the peninsula. Morning traffic is light in that direction, a reverse commute southbound out of San Francisco. After passing the first few cities, there are no commercial properties, no billboards, just greenspace overlooking the bay to the east, trees and hills to the west, until you reach the San Andreas Lake System west of the airport, and the Crystal Springs Reservoir near San Mateo.

George turned onto the westbound ramp on Highway 92. He drove across the coastal mountains to Half Moon Bay, then south along the coast to Pescadero. Liz-Beth and Joshua waited in the general store. George thought they looked great in the business clothing they bought in San Francisco.

"Would you like coffee and a bagel, George" Maggie asked.

"No thanks, I had something before I left the house."

"We have plenty of time, George" Liz-Beth asked. "Can you drive up Highway 1? I haven't been on it north of Half Moon Bay in a long time. I'd like to drive along the ocean."

"Sure Mrs. Wiggins."

Gazing at the ocean induces daydreams. Liz-Beth remembered driving the route with Bunny in the Bentley. They were happy memories. She thought about the last ride in the Bentley from the dealership after seeing Sukie off to Japan, a melancholy memory. So long ago, so many experiences since, it seemed to have happened in another lifetime. Liz-Beth's link to her life before Bunny died, returned with Sukie to New Cotswolds. Now events caused her to revisit it all.

George and Joshua sensed Liz-Beth wanted to be alone with her thoughts. They passed through Half Moon Bay, El Granada, Moss Beach, Montara, without disturbing her until George asked which route she wanted to take from Pacifica.

"Do you want to drive along San Francisco Beach through Lincoln Park and the Presidio?"

"No, George. Driving through the city is tedious. Why don't you take Sharp Park by the golf course to 280?"

George turned onto Sharp Park Road at Pacifica. It wound east up a steep hill, over the ridge past Skyline Drive. He picked up 280 north to drive into San Francisco.

"Do you want to go over the notes William shared with me, Josh?"

"Just in summary, Liz-Beth. You handle the business issues. I'll focus on legal matters."

"Mason says it's rumored they're trying to close by the end of the month. If they can't, creditors could start bankruptcy proceedings. If they can't stop it, the assets will be scattered. We can buy the remains, but we won't be able to keep the employees together. William needs them. We have to have terms we can live with now, or we walk away."

"Just so we understand each other, we can throw the business plan at them, but if they call our bluff it ends there."

"Right, I'm willing to pay a premium. I can value the company based on what William thinks he can do with it. If it costs more than that, we stop there. Under no circumstances am I going to back a civil fraud suit. The company will be dissected before it gets started. I'd rather use the money to help William with his new venture."

"I think that's wise, Liz-Beth."

"Mason says Dunn & Cousie invested in a bunch of worthless dotbombs. If they found a company that will acquire the portfolio, they can exit all of them with one transaction. They may want too much for LightSwitch by itself because the dotbombs are bleeding cash and aren't worth anything. I hope they buy this business plan bluff. If they don't, we made this trip for nothing."

Route 280 ends at the San Francisco Caltrans Station. George continued on the arterial until he reached 2nd Street where he turned left. When they crossed Townsend, Liz-Beth powered the window down. She felt saddened first, then determined when she remembered Edgar's office in the middle of the block to the south. Somebody turned it into condos. *Baldwin Audio might have still been there,* she thought. She wondered if they were following the route he walked one evening twenty years before to the Montgomery Street BART Station.

Hold yourself together, Liz-Beth told herself. *"Rest in peace, Edgar. This is for you,"* she whispered. Joshua heard her. He turned his head but couldn't see Liz-Beth's face. It pointed down Townsend Street through the open window. Liz-Beth wiped an eye with a handkerchief. Her anger rose when George turned right on Market Street one block northeast of the entrance to the Montgomery Street BART Station. George turned left at Fremont, left on Pine to make a circular route through one way downtown streets. The limo continued to Montgomery where George rolled to the curb and stopped at the corner.

"I have a couple of rides lined up in the city this morning, Mrs. Wiggins. What time do you think you need to return?"

"I'm not sure, George. If the meeting is short, we could be done by lunch. If it runs longer, 2:00 PM, maybe later. What works for you?"

"As long as you let me know before lunchtime I can look for afternoon work."

"I'll call you when I can. You know I'll take care of you."

"You've been generous. I'll work the morning and wait to hear from you."

"Can I pay you when we return to Pescadero?"

"Sure."

George opened the driver's door but Joshua stopped him, stepped out, walked around the limo, and opened the door for

Liz-Beth. They walked diagonally through the intersection of Pine and Montgomery, through traffic lights shining red in all directions.

Liz-Beth smiled. "This is the crossing that scares people from Manhattan. New Yorkers think they'll be run over."

"Only if we know they're New Yorkers," Joshua added.

They passed through the door of Max's deli. The smell of fresh baked breads, pickles and cold cuts hung in the air. The breakfast crowd had gone to the office leaving it almost empty.

Short, stocky, middle age, Irving Rothstein stood from a table by the window to greet them. Dressed conservatively in a nondescript single breasted grey suit and a red tie you couldn't guess the ability of the man who wore it. Physically unassuming, one hundred percent mental, you couldn't miss the intelligence in his eyes. Known for a sharp wit, a quick tongue, the timing of a standup comic, Rothstein never backs down. He remembers everything and focuses like a laser on points that matter. He can be terrifying to someone on the wrong side of a contest.

"Rothstein!"

"Hello, Joshua. Nice clothes! Did you rob a bank, or are you ripping off orphans and widows?"

"Widows are too smart for me. Let me introduce you to one."

"This must be the famous Elizabeth, and the rest of the long name, Wiggins. Sorry I could never remember it all."

"If you haven't gone mad from litigation, you know it. Liz-Beth," Joshua said, "Mr. Rothstein here, has more kills than a Marine sniper. He's top gun legal."

"Joshua exaggerates. I don't win them all."

"We called him Oy-Ving. Like oy-vey in Yiddish. The literal translation is Ouch! Pain!"

"Mr. Irving Seymour Rothstein, may I present Mrs. Elizabeth Victoria Simpson Harold Bentley-Wiggins, dame extraordinaire of Pescadero Village, Queen of New Cotswolds Castle, slayer of business dragons."

"I'm delighted to meet you, Mrs. Wiggins."

"The pleasure is mine Mr. Rothstein. Please call me Liz-Beth."

"My friends call me Irv, or just Rothstein."

"New Cotswolds is hardly a castle," Liz-Beth said.

"I visited. It's impressive. I admire modesty."

They chose a booth by a window. Liz-Beth shared the condition of LightSwitch, background, goals of the meeting.

"I read the business plan Josh sent me. With a credible witness or a date and name on the business plan, you have a case. With none of them it's a bluff."

"We know, Irv. I wanted the opinion of somebody who's still practicing. Do you want to skip this?"

"Not a chance. I'll go just to watch them squirm. If this is their plan they will. I hope we can do better, though. I knew Edgar too."

Liz-Beth raised an eyebrow. "You told him about that, Joshua?"

Joshua didn't answer.

"My wife and I went to a dinner party at Edgar and Evelyn's. I know what happened. Edgar spoke about Harry. What a character your late husband was. I wish I'd known him."

"Thank you, Irv. How did you know them?"

"Edgar was a roommate, a squash partner at Stanford. I went to their wedding."

"I thought you looked familiar."

"I was fit then, had black hair, and more of it. I saw you with Evelyn at the funeral."

"Did you know about this, Joshua?"

"Yeah, I knew."

Liz-Beth sighed and stood. "Gentleman, it's show time."

They walked diagonally back through the intersection, and into the 505 Montgomery Street building.

Seventy

"We're ten minutes late," Liz-Beth said when they stepped off the elevator on the 25th floor.

Reception escorted them to the northeast corner of the building, to the offices of Meyers, Cantrell, and Holmes.

Osgood Dunn and Robert Cousie sat in high back padded leather chairs at a long table in a posh conference room across from a spectacular view of the North Bay. The morning sun warmed the room. The fog had taken a day off. Patrick Sullivan, their long-time counsel, sat between them.

A slender man, middle aged, six feet tall, Sullivan had a narrow face on a head shaped like a hatchet. Piercing blue eyes straddled a long narrow nose that flared at the end like a trowel. Known in legal circles as "The Hawk," he dressed in a tailored herringbone suit, white shirt, red tie. Crevassed cheeks pincered a small mouth above a pointed chin. He combed his thinning jet-black hair straight back. Sullivan looked like an evil character right out of Dickens but his eyes, expression, mannerisms were deceptively friendly. A big smile exposed a full set of chemically whitened teeth big enough to fill the mouth of a quarter horse but everyone knew him as a meat eater. Aggressive when he fought for his client's money and the assets of their victims, "The Hawk" stood, extended a smile and a hand across the table.

"Hello Rothstein, didn't expect to see you today."

Oy-Ving and the "The Hawk" shook hands.

"Hello, Sully."

"Why are we always on opposite sides of the table, Irv?"

"Because your clients are always screwing my clients."

Sullivan laughed. "It's going to be that kind of morning."

"What the hell's he doing here, Osgood? Did you know about this?"

"We brought Sullivan, didn't we? Did you expect them to show up naked?"

"This country lawyer Wertheimer's a nobody. *Rothstein*'s a gunslinger. Why is *he* here?"

"Don't worry about it, Robert. They have nothing on us."

Myron Meyers brewed a cup of tea on a side table at the end of the conference room. He turned around for the greeting. "Lady and Gentleman; *Wow*, you look great Liz-Beth. You're back in circulation."

"Ask me out, Myron. You might get lucky."

A tall man, Myron looked academic. With narrow shoulders, a large head on a weak neck, poor posture, a pouch, but a full head of salt and pepper hair and handsome features, he was good looking from the chin up. In oversized black horn rimmed glasses he looked like a wimpy Cary Grant. Divorced, quite a bit younger than Liz-Beth, she meant it. *A date*, she thought, *that could be fun! I haven't been on one since 1945.*

Myron wore red suspenders over the shoulders of a white long sleeve button down shirt with a red and black striped bow-tie. He looked every bit the college law professor he was.

Everyone took a seat.

"From what Liz-Beth tells me," Myron began, "we don't need introductions. We do need ground rules. Why don't we proceed unless one of us needs refreshment."

No one did.

"We can have pastries brought in later, lunch if we go past twelve o'clock. Is everyone prepared to move forward?"

Everyone nodded.

"This is not mediation. It is not arbitration. It's a negotiation meeting at a neutral location agreed on by both parties. No recording is being made. I may offer opinion or suggestion. I may not. Nothing I say is binding on either party, nor is any agreement made here today without supporting documentation. We're all professionals. I don't expect to referee, but I'd appreciate it if you keep it civil. Yell and scream if you must. I can't have chairs flying through windows from the 25th floor. If it gets too hot in here, I'll call security and have all of you escorted out of the building. I don't care who starts it. Understood?"

"That isn't necessary."

"Your client's visit to Pescadero makes me think it is, Patrick. Would you like to discuss it with him?"

Patrick looked at Robert. "Anything you haven't told me?"

"It's bullshit. Don't worry about it. Let's get on with it, Myron." Couse loosened his tie and opened his collar.

"Rooms are reserved through the afternoon for private discussion at opposite ends of the hallway. I'll remain here in the conference room. Reception is available if we need to come and get you or for something you need.

I understand Mr. Dunn and Mr. Cousie object to the inquiry Mrs. Wiggins is making into their business affairs concerning ownership and management of the LightSwitch Company. Mrs. Wiggins is willing to end this activity for consideration. Is this correct?"

Liz-Beth and Osgood agreed that it is.

"It's your meeting, people. Resolve your differences."

"What's it going to take, Liz-Beth?"

"It's pretty simple, Osgood. All you have to do is sell LightSwitch to me. Do you have an idea what you want for the company?"

Three startled men stared at her across the table.

"I didn't expect you to say that, Liz-Beth. Why not? Indeed, we do," Osgood said.

Robert tore a sheet from a yellow pad, wrote a number on it, folded the paper in half and passed it across the table.

Liz-Beth's eyes widened. Her brow furrowed when she unfolded the paper, read the number, and handed it to Joshua.

"You must be kidding. Is this a starting number?"

"No. That's what you have to pay us if you want the company."

"This is ridiculous. It's a great deal higher than you valued it when you bought William's shares."

"We didn't have to give him anything."

"If this is a good number you should have given him a lot more. Maybe you shouldn't have forced him out."

"*Liz-Beth*, we agreed not to get into that. It doesn't matter."

"Okay, Joshua."

Liz-Beth opened a briefcase and removed the documents William gave her.

"There are a few things we should discuss about the condition of the company. Declining revenue and forecast, employee morale, credit hold, cash on hand, back rent. I can go over it point by point, but you already know it."

"Sounds like you have information you're not privileged to, Liz-Beth," Osgood said.

"We have a mole, Osgood."

"It doesn't matter, Robert."

"What makes you think the business is worth more than twice what you valued it for less than a year ago? What value have you added?"

"We found a buyer that will pay the amount we just shared with you," Osgood said. "We buy them for low value, sell them for high value. It's what we do."

"It isn't what you usually learn about a failing company that has one foot in the grave," Liz-Beth responded.

"The condition of the company hardly matters. We have an offer on the table and a closing date we agreed to. Due diligence is complete. I don't see why we should entertain anything less."

"They didn't agree to this price."

"We threw in something."

"A bundle of worthless dotcoms with no cash, no business plan, no revenue, no idea how to generate any? I want to meet your buyer. I have marsh land for sale if he's that stupid."

"I'll introduce you after we conclude our business."

Cousie smirked.

"I don't believe you. They have to know the dotcom companies aren't worth anything" Liz-Beth said.

"I'm not lying. The buyer is a LightSwitch customer with a pending order. They have a lot of our equipment in-house, in need of an upgrade. They can buy part of the company with the money they have to spend refreshing their infrastructure. Buy LightSwitch and you can pick up this order. One of their business units builds and sells networking equipment. They can merge product lines, save cost by eliminating duplicate accounting, marketing, and sales positions and consolidate facilities. LightSwitch is worth a lot more to them than it is as a standalone company. That's value we uncovered and showed them. We earned the valuation, Liz-Beth. Why should we give it to you?"

"Could this be true Joshua? I don't know anything about this business."

"How do I know? I'm a grocery store clerk."

"I screwed up. We need William here."

Irving leaned toward Liz-Beth. "I'm not an industry expert. I have industry clients. It sounds like the buyer is one of the big telecom companies. It's possible."

"Thanks, Irv. Would you mind telling us when you discovered this opportunity, Osgood?"

"You know I'm not going to tell you that."

"I don't suppose you care to tell me who the buyer is."

"I can't. It's a public company. Why would I anyway?"

"To convince me this is what I have to pay."

"No to anything less should be sufficient."

"Joshua?"

"The smoking gun; may I have it?"

Liz-Beth reached into her case, pulled out a copy of the business plan and handed it to Joshua. He positioned his reading glasses on the end of his nose.

"Gentlemen, I'd like to read some of this to you if I may, to see if it sounds familiar."

No one objected.

"On page twelve of this document it states; 'By holding back a tranche of funds and delaying order bookings and shipments into the next quarter, the company will experience a short-term cash crisis and a monthly dip in revenue enabling purchase of the outstanding shares at a deep discount to their intrinsic value.'"

Joshua paused to observe the shock on Dunn and Cousie's faces. He continued, "Seems to me this is why the perceived company valuation declined precipitously, just before you terminated William and bought his shares. Do you know anything about this?"

Osgood grimaced. He closed his eyes and turned away. "What is this?" Sullivan asked. Unable to answer, Osgood froze. Robert turned scarlet.

Joshua continued. "Billings will decline, payment for goods sold will be delayed."

"There's no need to read anymore of it."

"You seem to be familiar with this, Osgood. How could that be?"

"That's the goddamned LightSwitch business plan!" Robert yelled. "It's company property and you have no right to have it."

"Shut up Robert!" Osgood admonished. Sullivan frowned.

"My clients are unfamiliar with this particular draft. It sounds related to the company. If you wish, go ahead and finish."

Joshua continued. "Hmmm. Your clients recognize it. 'As funds are later released, the cash crisis will be remedied. When delayed orders are booked and shipped in the following quarter, the P&L statement will improve dramatically. LightSwitch can be sold as an independent company or sold as part of a portfolio to a large telecom enterprise. Discussions are ongoing with potential buyers through investment banking and advisory services.'"

The room went silent. Liz-Beth and Joshua waited for someone to speak. Rothstein wore a poker face. Myron stared at Dunn and Cousie in disbelief as he assimilated what he heard. Osgood and Robert sat speechless. Sullivan, "The Hawk," shook his head and stared at the ceiling.

"Did you share this with William before you fired him?" Liz-Beth asked.

Joshua scratched his head. "Good question, Liz-Beth. I have several more. Did Dunn & Cousie control the tranche of funds? Was it in the accounts of Dunn & Cousie? Did you make the decision to delay order bookings, product shipments, billing? Did you enter into discussions with an advisory company or a buyer to sell LightSwitch before you dismissed William? At what valuation? Do we need to ask your investment banker?"

Robert started to speak. Patrick held him back with a forearm and a stern stare.

"My clients had nothing to do with the substance of this document, not the part you read. Anything that sounds like they have, must be purely coincidental, circumstantial, immaterial."

"Really?" Joshua continued. "Mr. Cousie is right, of course. This *is* the LightSwitch business plan. Printed right here on the cover."

Joshua held the plan up and pointed to it. "If not Mr. Dunn and Mr. Cousie, who else had the means and the motive to write and execute such a plan?"

"Let me see it."

Joshua passed it across the table. Sullivan handed it to Robert.

"This is a copy. Where's the original?"

"Isn't it in your possession?" Joshua asked. "You're the chairman, Osgood. Do *you* have it?"

Osgood didn't answer.

"You have the original, Liz-Beth. Where is it? How did you get it?" Robert asked.

"What makes you think we have an original? Is yours missing?"

Cousie didn't answer.

"Do you have the original, Joshua?"

"I don't have it, Liz-Beth. I thought Robert had it."

"Do you have it Irv?"

"I've only seen this copy." He winked at Liz-Beth.

Patrick, "The Hawk" glared at Dunn and Cousie. "I want fifteen minutes" he said to Myron. "Let's go have a talk, gentlemen."

The three of them walked down the hall and entered a meeting room.

Rothstein, Liz-Beth and Joshua joined Myron at the refreshment table after Cousie, Dunn, and Sullivan left the room.

"I don't teach this in tort class, Irv. I've never seen anything like it."

"You should spend more time in private practice, Myron."

Seventy-One

"Have you guys lost your minds? What were you thinking when you wrote this into a business plan?"

"What *were* you thinking, Robert?"

"I didn't write it, Osgood. It came from notes of the previous board meeting. Your secretary put in it there and distributed it."

"Who told her to do that?"

"We needed all the board member's votes for a majority."

"They already agreed to it. We didn't need to put this in writing. I don't have a copy."

"I put one on your desk in a manila folder with the rest of the material for the board meeting. If you went to the office sometimes, you might have seen it."

"Where's your copy, Robert?"

"I don't know Patrick. I wonder if I left it in the conference room."

"You left it in the conference room at LightSwitch? Jesus! You guys are making an ass out of me. Call LightSwitch, get somebody to grab Osgood's copy, find your copy and bring it to me. Is there anybody there you can trust?"

"What are you getting at, Patrick?"

"Somebody in the company gave them the business plan. You have a *rat* Osgood, somebody who hates your guts and wants to bury you. Do you have any idea who it is?"

"They all hate us."

Sullivan put a hand on his head.

"Where does this leave us?"

"Do the other board members know you wrote this, Robert?"

"No. They received it in the mail."

"They know where it came from. Where did you compose and print it?"

"LightSwitch. I printed at Dunn & Cousie. It was mailed from there."

"From Dunn & Cousie! It could be on both systems. Its proof you had it. Maybe proof you wrote it. The envelopes have a Dunn & Cousie return address. It won't help to retrieve the copies board members have. You need to get it off the Dunn & Cousie computer systems and out of LightSwitch and Dunn and Cousie offices; every copy. Get it off the LightSwitch system *fast*."

"I gave the thing to reception to print, the one with the boobs."

"Bonny. That's all you think about. On a thumb drive?"

"Yeah."

"Where's the thumb drive?"

"I don't know, Patrick. My desk drawer? Maybe she deleted it after she copied and printed it."

"Deleted documents can be retrieved from disc drives. You have to get the thumb drive and have the computer drives backed up without the business plan, then the ones that had it magnetically erased or removed from the office and destroyed."

"How does that help us? They already have it."

"I thought you were a lawyer, Robert. Did you buy your degree at Walmart?"

"I haven't practiced in forty, I...never practiced, actually. I didn't graduate or take the bar exam."

"That explains a few things."

"None of that matters, Sully. Let's argue about it later. How much trouble are we in?"

"If a prosecutor can't prove this is your business plan a criminal complaint is hard to win. He has to convince a jury beyond a reasonable doubt. It's difficult, but not impossible given the strength of the circumstantial evidence. A civil complaint though, a tort, that only needs preponderance of evidence. Plaintiff's attorney, in this case Rothstein, only has to convince a jury you *probably* committed fraud. I beat Rothstein in the past. Never when a client gave him this much to work with."

Sullivan gnashed his horse teeth.

"Assuming you aren't in prison for criminal fraud I can delay Rothstein for a while if you want to spend the money. We still have to settle on the courthouse steps. You can't let him take you to trial."

"Shit." Robert shook himself.

"You have to sell the company to Liz-Beth. If you sell it to the telecom guys, you open a Pandora's Box of coyote ugly with unlimited possibilities for damages if they get dragged into a civil suit. Rothstein will murder you in civil court. A jury award for something this egregious will have a lot of zeros and a couple of commas in it. My advice to you is get back in there, sell this company for the best price you can get and pray they leave happy."

"What do we need to get out of this, Robert? If we get what we paid William for his shares will it make us whole?"

"Almost, Osgood. What do we do with the internet companies?"

"Shut them down. They aren't worth anything."

"You're forgetting the deal termination fee and the fees for due diligence and investment advisory services. If we sell the company to Liz-Beth we owe the telecom guys a million dollars."

"*What!* Why did you agree to that?"

"To get the sale!"

"We can't lose another million dollars. What would you do, Sully?"

"Your tort exposure is more than a million dollars. I'd take what I could get, pay my share of the termination fee or find a bottomless well to hide in."

"I hate this, but I can cover it. Half a million dollars. Shit!"

"I can't, Osgood. I have to sell everything I have including the furniture. That might not do it. All my liquid assets went into those companies. I'll be living out of a shopping cart in the Tenderloin District. Those internet assholes. They don't know what they're doing."

"You didn't think they were assholes when you thought they were gonna make you a billionaire."

"Shut up Sully and think of a way out of this. We aren't paying you to tell us we fucked up. We're paying you to keep us out of trouble."

"If you told me you were gonna put this bonehead plan in writing I would have fired the client."

"This isn't getting us anywhere" Osgood said. Let's see what Liz-Beth is willing to pay for the damn thing. I can live with losing a lot of money, not with blowing a lot more fighting a lost cause with Rothstein, trying to stay out of prison, or both. Don't let them figure out we know how much trouble we got ourselves into."

"Play it cool, Osgood? Do you think they don't know?"

"They aren't coming after you for fraud, Robert. They're bluffing."

"How do you know that Sully?"

"Did you defraud Liz-Beth?"

Sully paused to let it sink in. Robert and Osgood glanced at each other.

"What are we worried about?" Robert asked.

"The guy you defrauded."

"What's Liz-Beth doing here?"

"She's buying the company back for William. They don't want revenge or money. They want the company. Make a deal, Robert. If she buys LightSwitch, no harm, no foul. You might get out of it."

"How do you know that?"

"Liz-Beth's been retired for twenty years. Joshua runs a general store. Both of them are in their seventies. What do they want a broke network equipment company for?"

Osgood and Robert made eye contact.

"You guys are making me look bad. I'll help you as much as I can. You have to do the rest. You're my clients today, maybe not tomorrow. I'll see you back there."

Sullivan, "The Hawk," returned to the conference room. Rothstein stood by the refreshment table spreading cream cheese on a bagel.

"Want half, Sully? Need to keep your energy level up."

"No danger of falling asleep this morning, Irv."

"Couple of nice guys, your clients. Representing them must be lots of laughs."

"Do you ever feel like firing your clients?"

"Sure. I send them to you."

Sullivan chuckled. "Buy you a beer later, Irv. Maybe you can introduce me to a scout troop that lost their lunch money to bullies."

"Take you up on that, Sully. Not sure about the scouts. I like beer."

"We need a new attorney, Robert."

"We need a new life, Osgood."

"You want to jump off the roof, Robert? I'll hold the door for you. Sully's right. We can't sell it to the telecom guys. Let's see if we can negotiate our way out of this. The dotcoms may be a total loss, but we can get more for our LightSwitch shares than we paid for them. Let's find out how bad Liz-Beth wants LightSwitch."

Osgood and Robert returned to the conference room.

Seventy-Two

"Under the circumstances, we're willing to make accommodation. We aren't admitting we had anything to do with this business plan. This is extortion, Liz-Beth but we'd rather discount the company than waste time and money fighting you."

"I love that you can say that with a straight face, Osgood. I'm prepared to give you the price per share you paid William. The business has deteriorated. It isn't worth as much now, but I'll do this to get on with it."

"That won't work for us. We tied a lot of capital up in it for a long time, invested more to keep it going, managed the company. We'll take 150% of the price per share we paid William. That's more than fair. It's a lot less than where we started."

"Your management expertise didn't add any value. If your management skills and capital didn't stabilize the business, it's worth less."

"Tell you what; we'll throw in the internet companies. You can do something with them."

Liz-Beth laughed. "Pay the shutdown costs. Bet you'd like me to do that. Deduct that from what those dogs are worth and you have to pay somebody to take them."

Osgood ran a hand through his hair.

"Leave the internet companies out but add the cash we put into LightSwitch this year to the price we paid William for his shares for keeping it alive for you."

"It's alive in spite of you."

"Let's get out of here, Osgood," Robert said. "She can't do

anything to us. By the time we shut down the internet companies we'll have nothing left but a bowl of mice nuts."

Cousie stood, lifted his case off the floor, started for the conference room door.

"Gentleman, may I speak?"

Myron jumped in. "Mr. Rothstein."

"You bozos are lucky Mrs. Wiggins wants to buy your LightSwitch shares. Liz-Beth, if you don't get everything you want today I'd like you to tell Mr. Beckinsdale I'd be happy to represent him in this matter on contingency. I'll even pick up the court and discovery costs. The district attorney is a personal friend though we're sometimes on opposite sides of a contest. If he became interested in this matter he could use his vast budget and investigative powers to prove you authored and executed this business plan, if for example, a LightSwitch board member chooses to implicate and testify against you to save his own ass. If you were able to make a deal to stay out of prison, assuming the prosecutor doesn't think it's in *his* interest to put you there, it will cost you dearly. At a minimum, he will make you sell William's shares, maybe for less than Liz-Beth will pay you. A judge might order you to *forfeit* them. I would not want your legal bills. Make a deal this morning, gentlemen. It will save you so much money."

Rothstein paused to let his comments sink in. "Selling LightSwitch to another company is problematic. With a criminal fraud judgment in hand, William will take you to civil court for the amount you receive from the sale, plus triple damages. The buyer will sue you for damages when we name them as co-conspirators, and we make them give the company to William. If you don't get this, maybe Mr. Sullivan will explain it to you. Gentlemen, I suggest you make Liz-Beth happy."

"You can't threaten us, Rothstein! That's extortion!"

"Is it Robert? I have nothing to gain. If you take my advice, I'll lose a case. Should LightSwitch be sold to anyone except Liz-Beth I'll feel the need to do my civic duty."

Rothstein's words hung in the air.

"Mr. Sullivan?" Myron asked.

"Five minutes in the hallway."

"We might have sold the company for a profit. Why the hell did you push so hard you brought Rothstein into it? If I were Liz-Beth I'd cut my offer in half. You just torpedoed us."

"I don't give a shit, Osgood. If we give her what she wants I'm dead broke and starting over. I'll take my chances, sell the dotcom portfolio, collect the cash and worry about it later. I don't think Beckinsdale is gonna sue anybody. What if he does? If we don't get enough money from Liz-Beth I'm screwed anyway."

"You're the architect of this cluster-fuck" Osgood said. "You should pay for all of it. I was stupid enough to be your partner. I'll take my medicine and move on. I'm not going to quadruple down on financial losses and I'm not going to risk going to jail for you. You can't sell our LightSwitch shares without my signature. Nobody else on the board will support you. Rothstein will come after all of us."

"I have nothing to lose, Osgood. Loan me enough to cover my share of the termination fee. We can make it back on the next deal."

"*What!* Loan you your share of the losses? Sure, Robert. If you don't help me sell LightSwitch to Liz-Beth for whatever we can get in the next 10 minutes I'm going to the prosecutor's office with Rothstein to beg for mercy. You can fend for yourself. It isn't my fault you're so wadded up. You did that to yourself. If you want to go down in flames, flame yourself. You better follow me back in there, keep your mouth shut, and sign anything and everything I sign. I'll do the best I can, but at the end of this meeting, I'm leaving clear of this mess no matter what it costs me. Sully, will you try to talk sense into him?"

Osgood returned to the conference room. He asked for a few more minutes.

Cousie paced the hallway; obstinate, defiant, angry. Sullivan folded his arms across his chest, stared at the floor with a look of disdain on his face, crossed his legs and leaned in a slouch on a corridor wall. Cousie returned to the conference room followed by his attorney. He sat down next to his partner and looked him in the face. "Do your worst."

"Let's get this over with, Liz-Beth. It's close to lunch time" Osgood said.

The hog wants to visit the trough, Liz-Beth thought. "I'm willing to buy the company for the valuation you set when you bought the shares from William."

Osgood folded his hands in front of him and leaned his elbows on the table. He took a deep breath.

"We'll sell it to you for 25% above that, and believe me, at that number we're losing our shirts. If it gives you any satisfaction, we have to eat our investment in the internet companies too."

"No." Liz-Beth shook her head.

"15%."

"No."

"10%. Our last offer."

"No."

Joshua leaned over and whispered in Liz-Beth's ear. "*Liz-Beth*; you can end this."

"A 10% premium, Joshua? Why should I give them more than they paid William?"

"Did you forget what you came here for? In the big picture, it doesn't matter. It's worth more than they paid William to close this out."

"Whose side are you on?"

"William's side; I've never seen you this stubborn, Liz-Beth. Get the company."

Liz-Beth turned to Rothstein. Rothstein nodded. "You won, Liz-Beth. Take your prize home."

"What you paid William, Osgood, and we have a deal. If no, I'm leaving."

Cousie turned scowling into an art form. Osgood grimaced.

"OK, Liz-Beth, I'll go back and draw up the papers."

"I have an agreement right here. All we have to do is fill in the numbers and dates and sign the originals."

Liz-Beth pulled two copies out of her case.

"We have to go over this, Liz-Beth. Surely you don't think we can cover everything in two pages. Do you want to turn this into a term sheet?"

"I'd love to accommodate you for my own protection. We have to take a risk. This agreement spells out what you have to do to transfer ownership and what the price is. Hand me the shares, I'll hand you the money. I'm prepared to transfer funds into escrow and complete the transaction today. You're in the conference room of an escrow agent."

"Liz-Beth," Osgood started to speak.

She cut him off.

"I'm done with this. We do this now or I leave you to William and Rothstein."

Osgood looked around the room. He rocked back in his chair.

"Fill in the blanks and pass it to me."

Liz-Beth filled in and slid two originals across the table. Osgood scanned them, picked up his pen, clenched his jaw, and added his signature.

Cousie's cell phone rang as Osgood handed him the two originals. He glanced at caller ID. "I have to take this."

"Robert, sign the goddamn thing."

Cousie dropped the agreements on the table and left the conference room. "Just a minute," he said into the cell phone as he passed through the doorway. The oxygen followed him out of the room.

"It's almost twelve o'clock, George. Where the hell have you been?"

"I had clients. I worked all morning."

"I pay you for information when I need it."

"I called as soon as I could, Mr. Cousie. How's it going?"

"I don't have time for this shit, what the hell do you have for me?"

"On the way up, they discussed the company business plan."

"We know about that. They just creamed me with it. What else do you have?"

"They were talking about law suits."

"What about them?"

"They agreed there's no way, under any circumstances, they would sue you."

"*What?* Repeat that."

"Under no circumstances will they sue you. If they can't buy the company today they quit. They walk away."

"What about William?"

"They'll help him with his new business."

"You heard this?"

"Yeah, they were in the back seat right behind me."

"You're absolutely sure this includes William?"

"Yes."

"What exactly did they say?"

"If they can't make a deal with you today, they want to invest the money they were going to buy LightSwitch with in a company William started in Mountain View. They don't want William to sue you."

"I'll be goddamned. Are you sure that's what you heard?"

"Yes, I'm sure. Look, I need to see you."

"Not right now. Call tomorrow."

Cousie hung up.

George looked at his phone. "That son-of-a-bitch. He owes me money and he's ducking me. Where the hell is Liz-Beth?"

Seventy-Three

Cousie paced the hallway while tension skyrocketed in the conference room. He ducked into the men's room. He relieved himself, walked to a sink and washed his hands. Cousie contemplated what he heard. *If George is wrong, I'm fucked if don't agree to sell LightSwitch. I'm fucked if I do. Would Osgood go to the prosecutor with Rothstein if I refuse to sign? He might. They don't know George told me what they said in the limo. Did they fake that story about funding William's company? No way! George is right! Rothstein is bluffing. William will take the money to fund his new company.*

Cousie splashed water on his face. He toweled it dry, looked in the mirror and said, "You aren't dead yet, you son-of-a-bitch."

Cousie swaggered into the conference room, necktie loosened, collar open, wearing an inexplicable look of confidence on his face. He sat down next to Osgood. Everyone waited in silence and suspense.

"Have a nice time? Didn't piss yourself, did you?"

Cousie glared at Osgood. A round of smirks circled the room.

Cousie tore the agreement of sale out of Osgood's hands and picked up a pen. He crossed out one of the lines, wrote a number above it and signed both originals. He passed it across the table to Liz-Beth.

Liz-Beth picked it up and leaned back in her chair. She held the agreement at an angle so Joshua and Rothstein couldn't see it. Liz-Beth looked angry enough to chew the legs off a table. She stormed out of the conference room, down the hall, into one of the meeting rooms.

Joshua and Rothstein looked at each other.

Rothstein looked at Myron. "Excuse us. We need ten minutes."

"It's almost noon, Irv. Should I order in lunch?"

"Wait till we return Myron."

"What did you do Robert?" Osgood looked mortified.

"I crossed out the amount, wrote in the number we started with this morning, plus one million."

"You *WHAT?* Are you out of your fucking mind? Why did you do that?"

"Take it easy. We're going to get it."

"What the hell makes you think that? She already said she won't go there. She'll throw it back at us and walk out."

"One million isn't much for six internet companies. We put six million in them."

"She doesn't want them."

"It doesn't matter."

"What do you mean it doesn't matter?"

"The call was from George. He told me they'll either pay our price or leave and drop everything. There'll be no criminal complaint, no civil suit They'll invest the money in a company William started. We get our price for the entire portfolio with enough to pay the termination fee, or they go away and we sell the portfolio to the telecom suckers. We win either way."

"You trust that dumbass limo driver?"

"Not his judgment. He heard them agree to it on the ride up."

"How do you know what William wants to do? Liz-Beth can buy the company and he can sue us anyway."

"She doesn't want William to sue us. She wants to buy LightSwitch back for him or help him with his new company."

"He can still go to a prosecutor with Rothstein."

"With what damages?"

Osgood looked at Patrick.

"He's right, Osgood. If she buys LightSwitch and gives him his shares he has no loss. You offered to sell your shares. If she declines and funds his new company you can still claim no harm no foul. You screwed him but if he comes out of this in good shape there's no guarantee he will win an award by suing you. If he were my client, I'd advise him to take Liz-Beth's money and get on with his new business venture. It might be easier and better than suing you and fixing LightSwitch."

"Just wait until they come back," Robert added.

Joshua and Rothstein followed Liz-Beth into the meeting room.

"What happened, Liz-Beth?" Joshua asked.

Liz-Beth showed them.

"Why the hell did he do that?"

"The man has balls."

Liz-Beth circled the conference room table while Joshua and Rothstein leaned on the backs of high-back chairs. She walked deliberately, deep in thought, chin in her hand. She stopped after completing a circle.

"Remember when you read from the business plan? Didn't it seem odd the way Robert reacted? Angry, not surprised like Osgood and Sullivan. Why do you think it didn't surprise him, Joshua?"

"I don't know."

"His copy is missing. He realized we had it. Who else knows we had it?"

"You, me, Irv, William; whoever gave it to William. Natalie, Maggie, Mason."

"Who else?"

"I'm drawing a blank."

"Did we discuss this in front of anyone else?"

"Ah…The limo. We discussed it in the lim…..Oh, shit!"

"George knows Cousie. Natalie ran into Cousie at Union Square. They had an argument. Did you know about that?"

"No."

"George set it up. He followed her all over San Francisco while we went clothes shopping. He pretended to chase Cousie off when Natalie tried to get away from him. It was an act. Jesus. We've been taken by a limo driver."

Joshua rubbed the back of his neck. "Osgood didn't seem to know we have a copy of the business plan. Why didn't Robert tell him?"

"He didn't want Osgood to know how stupid he was to lose it. That call Robert just took. It came from George. Cousie would have signed the agreement without changing the amount if George hadn't told him we were bluffing."

"Jesus."

"Cousie jacked the price back up, probably above what they have LightSwitch sold for to cover the shutdown costs for the zombie internet companies, maybe a deal termination fee to the acquiring company. Robert doesn't care if we buy LightSwitch or not as long as he knows we won't sue him or go to the district attorney. If we give him his price, he gets enough money to shut the internet companies and terminate the acquisition. If we don't, he knows we go away. They do have LightSwitch sold, the internet companies with it, or for enough money to shut them down and be rid of them."

"Shit, Liz-Beth, how long has George been working for Cousie?"

"Guys, Guys," Rothstein interrupted. "We don't have time for forensics. It's all very interesting but right now they think they can walk out. If you want to buy the company or negotiate further you need to get back in there."

"Let me think a minute." Liz-Beth started another lap around the table, stopped part way, rested her hands on the back of a chair.

"I understand your thinking now, Joshua. I cared too much for William and Evelyn to be rational about this. I wanted to make it right for both of them. Sorry I dragged you into this, Irv. I have every confidence you can win in court, but it isn't worth it to any of us."

"I wish all my clients could see what matters as clearly as you do" Rothstein said. "I'd love to argue this one, but only you and William know the best course. Whatever you decide, I'm in your corner."

"Thank you, Irv. I promised to call William and I need to call that SOB George."

"Why don't you let me call George?"

"Play dumb, Josh. Let him drive you back. There's no reason to make him or Cousie aware you know they're working together."

"That's a good idea, Irv. As much as I'd like to hold him accountable, it might be better to keep him coming back like a dog for another bone."

"Call him in the conference room, Joshua" Liz-Beth said. Make sure Cousie hears you. Do you have his number?"

"I have it."

I could ask Sukie to lop George's head off, Liz-Beth thought, "*but he might do it.*"

"We better get back there before they leave."

"They aren't going anywhere, Joshua said. "They need to see if you take their offer. Come on, Irv. Let's keep them busy while Liz-Beth calls William."

Seventy-Four

William took the call on his cellphone.

"It's almost twelve thirty, Liz-Beth. I'm going insane."

"Sorry William. I had nothing to tell you."

"What's the news?"

"We threw everything we had at them. Joshua was magnificent. Rothstein was awesome. I could kiss them. We almost pulled it off but they acquired inside information."

"What do you mean?"

"If you speak to George don't say anything about this. Not a word. I'll tell you more when I see you. Do you understand?"

"You mean George told Dunn and Cousie something? What could he know? How could he know them?"

"I don't know but I think he does and he did. Assume anything you say to George or he hears you say, will go straight to Cousie. Tell Natalie, OK?"

"Sure, Liz-Beth. My head's spinning."

"If you were here this morning it might have exploded. Look William, I'm really sorry. They want too much for the company. We have to let it go. Can you accept this?"

"Maybe."

"I'm very disappointed. The thing that hurts the most is I have nothing to tell Evelyn. I can't bring Edgar back but God knows I tried to do something…I'm so tired of this, William. I did my best. We all did."

"You're totally done with this?"

"Yes. We'll help you get your Mountain View business going. Can we put this behind us?

"There's nothing left for you to try?"

"No."

"What are you going to do?"

"I'm going to say no thanks and come home."

"Don't do that."

"Why not?"

"I'm coming up there."

"*No*, William."

"I have a surprise."

"What kind of surprise?"

"I've no time to explain. I have to get on the road."

"You won't be here for more than an hour."

"I'll be there in *half* an hour. Make sure they don't leave."

"You can't…where are you?"

"I'm on a 101 ramp, in Santa Clara."

"You can't be here in half an hour. You have to park. You'll kill yourself on the freeway."

"Natalie will meet me at the curb. She can park the car. I'll go right in the building."

"What are you driving?"

"Dad's car."

"Oh my God, William. Don't do this!"

"What do we have to lose?"

"*YOU!* I'm leaving now. They won't be here."

"I'll call the law firm and tell them I'm coming."

"William, *please*."

"I don't have time to explain, Liz-Beth. Please go along. This is what *I* need to do…Liz-Beth? Are you there?"

"Not again. Not twice in one lifetime."

"I'm not Edgar, Liz-Beth. I'm not going to die on the highway. It's a depression down here. The freeway's empty. I have it all to myself all the way to the city. Now please go and buy me enough time to get there before they leave. It's the 505 Montgomery building isn't it?…Liz-Beth? What floor?"

"Twenty five."

"I'm hanging up now. I'll get there as close to one o'clock as I can. Ask for a lunch break, whatever you have to do. Just keep them there. I'll see you soon, Liz-Beth."

"William. William!"

William disconnected.

Seventy-Five

"Tighten your seatbelt, Lupe. It's gonna be a hell of a ride."

William latched his five-point harness and hit the starter button. The engine exploded into life. He positioned the gearshift lever in first, nudged the gas petal and eased the clutch out. When the car began rolling he punched it. The rear wheels broke free and spun up a white cloud of tire smoke as the car lurched diagonally forward. Lupe screamed *"Holy Shit!"* and grabbed the lap belt with both hands. William turned the steering wheel to point the front tires in the direction of the slide. The car struggled to go where the front wheels pointed. When it straightened out, the rear tires found grip. The car catapulted onto the freeway, rapidly overtaking vehicles that passed them while they accelerated through the ramp. Lupe grimaced and gripped the lap belt like he wanted to rip it out of the frame. William went through the gears with the motor screaming. *Give me all you got*, he said to himself. They rocketed past 100 miles an hour like the *Millennium Falcon* shifting into hyper drive, and shot up Highway 101.

William really did have no traffic. *I hope the cops are on vacation,* he thought. He weaved past a handful of cars and trucks like they were motoring backwards. He flashed his headlights at vehicles lumbering in the left guardrail lane with no idea of the sports car rapidly overtaking them. Lupe calmed down and thought if they weren't killed, this might be fun.

Liz-Beth's blood pressure soared. Her mind filled with visions of flashing red lights and ambulances. A pang of fear gripped her like a vise across her chest. She thought about the afternoon she let

Edgar leave the Wiggins Trading Company, despondent, alone. It almost brought her to tears. She held the back of her hand against her forehead. *How foolish of me,* she thought. *I should have let him come with us. I need to pull myself together. What do I tell them?*

Liz-Beth composed herself and returned to the conference room. Robert sat in a slouch with his arms folded, a smug look on his face. Osgood looked terrified. His brow glistened. Patrick, "The Hawk," looked like he wanted to jump out a window. His luck held. They don't open.

Joshua and Irving sat calmly. Myron rested his elbows on the table, chin in his hands wondering what in the world just happened. When Liz-Beth entered the room he sat at attention as if a curtain had just risen on the last act of a tragicomedy.

Liz-Beth took her seat and shrugged her shoulders. She took a deep breath. "You win, Robert. I have to have it. It's been a long morning. I'm tired and hungry. Why don't we take a lunch break and return at 1:15 to wrap this up?"

Robert looked self-satisfied, Osgood surprised. Patrick looked amazed. Myron's mind twisted into a pretzel.

"All you have to do is sign it, Liz-Beth."

"I can't exactly, Robert. I didn't expect it to cost this much. I didn't arrange enough financing. I don't know how long it's going to take to put that much cash together."

"Are you screwing with us, Liz-Beth?"

"Would I do that, Robert?"

What a piece of work, Joshua thought. He and Rothstein smiled at each other. They wondered what Liz-Beth was up to.

"Oh, fuck off, Liz-Beth. You're so full of shit."

"I'm not screwing with you, Robert. I can't write a check in that amount."

"Sign the agreement. Get the money to us later. We'll give you 72 hours. Okay with you, Osgood?"

"No, Robert," Liz-Beth insisted. "I want this completed today before you change the price again."

"How can I do that if we all sign?"

"I don't know, Robert. You're a tricky guy. Half an hour ago I could have bought LightSwitch for a million dollars less than I have to pay now. What suddenly made you so brave?"

Cousie didn't answer.

Osgood shifted his legs. He gazed out the window. "She's playing you like a piano, Robert," he whispered.

"Do you have the LightSwitch shares in your office, Osgood?"

"No, Liz-Beth. The transfer agent is the Bank of California. They have them."

"What are the chances you can get them over here today?"

"It's possible if the right people are in."

"I'm leaving with them, or I'm leaving. You've done a lot of business with them over the years, haven't you? I'm confident you can find a way."

"Shit, Liz-Beth," Osgood muttered.

"Here's what I'm willing to do. I'll buy the company at your price if we can complete the transaction today. I have to go talk to a man about converting assets into cash or getting a line of credit against them so I can pay you. I think I can do it. If we can't transact the business this afternoon I'm done with this and LightSwitch is yours to do with what you want."

"Five minutes, Liz-Beth," Osgood said.

Osgood, Cousie and Patrick huddled in the hallway.

"What are you doing, Liz-Beth? I thought you decided not to buy the company."

"I'm not gonna buy it, Josh."

"You're gonna give me a stroke."

"Please don't have one. I can't lose any more friends."

Osgood confronted Robert in the hallway.

"What the fuck is she doing?"

"Whoa, Osgood. Such language."

"Something's wrong with this, Robert. Let's get the hell out of here."

"Sounds good to me. I still have time for nine holes."

"We aren't interested in helping you with your fucking hand-icap, Patrick. A bird-in-hand, Osgood. The other sale can fall through. We can get enough out of her to cover all of it. You can spare an hour to see if we can close and leave with our money."

"Don't be a sucker, Robert. We're free to sell the portfolio. We'll get it done."

"Osgood! We'll get enough to cover the breakup fee. They might take half. We'll come out a half a million ahead. All I'm asking is to get the shares to see if we can close the transaction. What could happen?"

"Had a client hit by an asteroid. On his birthday."

Cousie scowled at Sullivan, "The Hawk."

"Osgood?"

Osgood left for the Bank of California, three blocks away.

Rothstein offered to make a run to the corner *Subway*. "Come downstairs with me, Sully? Walk you out, Liz-Beth?"

"Thank you, Irv. I need a two-lawyer escort with all the barra-cudas swimming around here. Oh, you're one of them Sully." Liz-Beth winked at him. Not one to think of adversaries as enemies, "The Hawk" grinned back.

"I need to stop by the men's room. Can you wait a minute, Irv?"

"In the hallway, Patrick."

"Would you mind telling me, Liz-Beth?"

"I'd like to, Irv. I don't know what's gonna happen."

"Is somebody joining us?"

"William. I don't know what he's up to. I hope this doesn't turn into a bigger catastrophe than it already is. I'm going for a stroll."

Liz-Beth took the elevator to the lobby. She left the building, turned east on Pine Street toward the ferry terminal, in the oppo-site direction of the Bank of California.

Seventy-Six

The speedometer hovered somewhere near 130 when William merged onto Highway 280, slowed the car to eighty-five and continued down the hill to the end of the freeway at the Caltrans Station. When he reached a red light he slowed down and called Natalie as he looked for cross-traffic and police cruisers, saw none and rolled through the intersection without waiting for the light to turn green. Natalie rushed out of her office and ran down the sidewalk. William said, "Get to Pine and Montgomery as fast as you can, Liz-Beth needs me, I'm a few minutes away, I love you."

Liz-Beth returned to the conference room as Rothstein and Sullivan dug into the meatball subs Rothstein bought in honor of "The Hawk's" clients. Rothstein winked at Joshua and handed him a half. Myron absently chewed on a jelly doughnut, eyes pinned from a sugar fix. Cousie fidgeted in his chair.

"Are you finished playing games, Liz-Beth?"

"Osgood isn't back yet, Robert."

"When he gets here, I expect you to sign and give us our money."

Osgood returned with the LightSwitch shares.

"The bank will send a fax confirming transfer of ownership by close of business tomorrow if you get instructions to them by the morning. Did you get what you need, Liz-Beth?"

"It's taken care of."

"Can you sign now and give us a check?"

"As soon as it arrives."

William called Natalie again when he rolled to a curb. He left a message on her cell phone.

"The car's parked on Pine Street east of Montgomery. I left the key under the mat. Please park it legally for me. I love you, Natalie. Call you later."

William left the car in a loading zone near the corner with the four-way flashers on. He and Lupe jumped out, ran into the building and took the elevator to the 25th floor. Lupe ducked into the men's room. William paused to catch his breath in the hallway before stepping through the conference room doorway.

"Look what the janitor swept in," Cousie said.

"Why do I feel like asteroid bait?" Osgood asked him.

Patrick looked puzzled. "Who's this, Osgood?"

"William Beckinsdale."

"You need asteroid repellent," Patrick said.

Joshua winked at Rothstein.

Myron's head took another lap around his neck.

Liz-Beth smiled and waved at William. He nodded.

"Come here to kick our asses, wonder boy?" Robert asked.

"I'm here to buy back my shares in LightSwitch."

Robert laughed. "You're too late. Liz-Beth just bought them."

"Do you have a signed agreement of sale?"

"Almost."

"Make you a better offer."

"You want to throw in your shack in Pescadero?"

"Better than that. First, I want to introduce you to someone."

Lupe followed William into the conference room. They sat next to Liz-Beth. William winked. Liz-Beth contorted her face to suppress a smile. She wanted to get up and breakdance.

Joshua looked puzzled.

Rothstein's eyebrows rose to his hairline.

Patrick, "The Hawk" wondered if he could slide under the table and slither under the door.

"Who's this Osgood?" Cousie asked.

"Don't you recognize him, you *moron*? He works at LightSwitch."

"The rat," Patrick said.

Dunn and Cousie turned as white as sheets of linen drying on a clothes line on a sunny summer day.

Patrick choked on a meatball.

William gestured to Lupe. "I'd like to introduce everyone to Guadalupe Garcia. He's an engineer at LightSwitch."

Lupe nodded at Liz-Beth.

No longer able to contain herself, Liz-Beth leaned back and broke into the biggest smile that ever lit a face.

"Holy crap," Joshua said. Lupe's entrance caught him by complete surprise.

Rothstein allowed himself a satisfied grin.

"Lupe," William asked, "Is there something you'd like to say?"

Lupe looked at Dunn and Cousie.

"The day of the board meeting, the day you terminated William, I arrived early for an engineering meeting in the conference room. I found the door open. I sat in a chair against the wall as the board meeting ended. I saw Mr. Cousie place a folder on a refreshment table where he picked up a pastry on the way out. A few minutes later when I went for coffee I noticed the folder was still there. I picked it up and looked down the hallway. Mr. Cousie was gone. I put the folder in my laptop bag with the intent of giving it to him later. When the engineering meeting began I forgot about it. I reached in the bag for writing paper and accidently pulled out the folder. I removed a document and realized I had the LightSwitch business plan. After the engineering meeting I tried to give this to you, Mr. Cousie. You already left the building. Later I thought you must have copies. Probably you didn't need it.

Dunn and Cousie's mouths dried out like the Mojave Desert in August. Patrick "The Hawk" ran his hands through thinning hair above an expression of complete disgust.

"Where is it now, Lupe?" William asked.

Lupe held up a folder. "I brought it with me."

"Oh shit, Robert."

"Sorry Osgood."

"I bet your fingerprints are on the folder, Robert," William said.

"Somebody else brought it to the meeting. I might have handled it there. I didn't know what was inside."

"What do the initials RC stand for? Radio Controlled?"

Lupe continued. "Before the engineering meeting ended I heard Mr. Dunn and Mr. Cousie talking to the other board members. They said they had a buyer for LightSwitch, they were selling the company."

Osgood gaped in horror. Cousie's forehead could have boiled an egg. Patrick wondered if he could make it to the fire escape before the meeting ended.

Cousie stood and yelled at Lupe. "His word against Osgood, myself, the entire board. What's William paying you?"

"He pays me nothing," Lupe answered in a resentful voice. Cousie couldn't rattle him. "I'm just a dumb Mexican. I'm too dumb to think up a lie."

"You are lying! You goddamn wetback," Cousie yelled.

"VK was there."

"Why isn't he here?" Cousie asked.

"He's picking his daughter up at the airport. He can join us if we need him."

Lupe pulled the business plan out of the folder and pointed to it. "These are your initials, Mr. Cousie. RC. Robert Cousie. I saw you doodle on it."

Lupe sucked the energy out of room. When Cousie sat down the conference room went silent. He and Dunn were drained. Patrick, "The Hawk" leaned back in his chair. A silly smile spread across his face. He clasped his hands behind his head, stared at the ceiling and daydreamed a Pebble Beach birdie. *Nothing more I can do here,* he thought.

William stood. "Gentlemen, in light of this development, I'd like to make an offer to buy my shares back. Is there a term sheet?"

Liz-Beth handed William the sheet of yellow paper Cousie

wrote his offer on. He crossed out Cousie's writing, wrote something above it, folded it and passed it across the table. Cousie picked it up with shaky hands.

"Do you have an agreement, Liz-Beth?"

She handed both copies to William. William replaced her name with his, changed the amount, made a cross, and added his initials in one of the quadrants. Liz-Beth initialed it. "I brought the funds with me," William said.

William walked around the conference table. He dropped two signed agreements and the folded yellow paper in front of Cousie. Cousie unfolded the sheet of yellow paper. Osgood stared at it expressionless. Cousie turned a pale shade of green. "The Hawk's" daydream of a Pebble Beach birdie turned into a double bogey.

William had written on the yellow paper:

"For the purchase of all of their LightSwitch shares, I offer the firm of Dunn & Cousie the sum of One Dollar."

William pulled his wallet out of a back pocket and removed a crisp new one-dollar bill. He snapped the bill, placed it on top of the agreement and declared, "Paid in full. Sign the agreements and hand back one of them with the shares."

"Fuck you, William. You'll never get them," Robert glared.

William nodded confidently. Yes, he would. He glanced at Rothstein.

"William," Rothstein said, "If they don't sell you the shares right now, I'll escort you to the district attorney's office to help you file a complaint. Perhaps Mr. Garcia will join us."

Osgood stared at Cousie. Cousie looked at Patrick.

"I can't save you this time," Patrick said.

Osgood pulled the agreements in front of him, signed both copies, added his initials, pushed it back to Cousie.

"Sign and initial, Robert."

Cousie glanced back and forth between the agreement and the yellow term sheet. The words *One Dollar* reached out for him like a giant, red, flashing, three-dimensional neon sign, obliterating his self-image of a successful life in the business world, now in ruins. He never imagined it could end this badly. At that moment, if any living human felt lower than whale poop, his name was Robert Cousie. Cousie glanced at Rothstein and looked up at William. His eyes returned to the agreement. He added the initials "RC," and signed.

Cousie stood up from the table and walked by William as if William wasn't there. William stared at him as he passed. Cousie's knees weakened when he reached the doorway. He held the doorjamb to steady himself. He stumbled out of the conference room, and across the hall. He stopped halfway, dropped to his knees and vomited. They heard him retching through the conference room doorway. No one uttered a word. Cousie staggered to the water fountain next to the men's room. He levered on the water, ran a finger through the flow and used it to wash his mouth. He walked unsteadily down the hallway, bent over, one arm holding his briefcase against a hollow abdomen, the other sliding down a wall. He pressed the elevator button. It seemed to take forever to cable to the ground. He felt like a fall leaf, detached, dying, helplessly floating down to decompose in the compost bin. It felt like the ride to Hades. When the elevator landed he walked across the lobby, out of the building, diagonally through the intersection, west on Montgomery Street. A few minutes later, he could no longer be seen from the 505 Montgomery Street building through windows on the 25th floor.

Osgood stood. "I guess you bought your company back, William. "I'll have the shares transferred into your name. Do I have to meet the district attorney?"

William glanced at Rothstein. Rothstein shook his head no.

"Ask me after the shares are transferred, Osgood."

"Do we have a deal?"

"Yes, for the shares. There isn't anything further to discuss until they're in my name."

Osgood grimaced. "I have to go back to the bank."

"Before you leave Osgood, I want my office back. As the

soon to be majority shareholder and new CEO, you're evicted. Your security card will be disabled, your email and voicemail passwords deleted before you cross the street. I'll have the office packed and your personal belongings shipped to Dunn & Cousie. Everything else is mine."

"I guess you won this one, Liz-Beth."

"There is no next one, Osgood."

Osgood left the room.

William texted VK, "It's done."

"BRAVO!" VK texted back.

"How about that beer, Rothstein? I need it now."

"Meet you at the bar at Broadway, Sully."

Patrick, "The Hawk" left the room.

Liz-Beth couldn't remember a happier ending since VE day, 1945. William walked around the table and hugged her. Joshua called George and told him he and Liz-Beth were ready to leave and would wait for him in the lobby.

"Don't you want to hang around and celebrate, Liz-Beth? Patrick's buying."

"No thanks, Irv. I just had the most exhilarating and exhausting day in fifty-six years. I want to go home and soak in the tub."

"How about you, Joshua?"

"Thanks, Irv. I'm going home with Liz-Beth. Why don't we all get together for dinner one night? I'll call ya."

"You two were amazing." Liz-Beth kissed Rothstein and Joshua.

"Lupe." Liz-Beth grabbed him by the arms. "What made you decide to help us?"

"I couldn't let the bad guys win. I've been fighting injustice all my life. Maria, the whole family; we're here because it's a country of opportunity, of fairness, of rule of law. If I didn't help and you lost, it would have erased everything we came here for. I'd be like them. I'm glad you won, Liz-Beth. I'm glad I could help you."

"You're a good man, Lupe. Thank you."

Liz-Beth held William's hands, leaned back and beamed with

a mother's pride. "You magnificent young man. You were out of this world."

William thanked Joshua and Rothstein. He pointed to the table. "Osgood left the dollar. Not counting Dunn and Cousie, there are four other board members. You suppose they can split the dollar six ways?"

Rothstein chuckled. "It's a tip. He left it for Myron."

The room busted into laughter.

"Let me know the next time you feel like driving like that so I can jump out before you start the car."

"Sounds like you want to choose the moment and method of your demise, Lupe. VK said he didn't know anything about the business plan."

Lupe smiled. "He doesn't. I only said he was there."

William laughed. He put his arm over Lupe's shoulder. "Let's take a walk, Lupe. Dinner at Natalie's, maybe you'll like her roommate."

"What do you think about that, Myron?" Liz-Beth asked.

"Ah…bit more exciting than tort class."

"Come and see me sometime."

Myron swallowed hard. His slouch appeared more pronounced than in the morning. He raised a timid hand in a wave as Liz-Beth passed through the doorway.

"You could have knocked him over with a feather, Liz-Beth."

* * *

Liz-Beth and Joshua shared a quiet limo ride back to Pescadero.

George glanced in the mirror for clues. "How was your meeting?"

"Oh, uneventful. What did you think Joshua?"

"Kind of boring."

George returned his eyes to the road. He felt surprised and confused. "Where you successful, Liz-Beth?"

"You might say so."

Seventy-Seven

George dropped Liz-Beth and Joshua in Pescadero. He returned to San Francisco in frustration. Cousie didn't' take his call.

Liz-Beth spent the last of the afternoon holding and feeding Mr. Chuckles. The bird sensed her relief and shared her contentment. One dollar, she thought behind a satisfied smile. He bought the company back for a dollar! Liz-Beth threw her head back and laughed out loud.

Maggie knew the outcome from the expression on Joshua's face when he walked in the door. They embraced in the living room for the longest, most satisfying hug they had in a long while.

Recent years were more stressful than any Liz-Beth experienced since the war. Results of the day wildly exceeded her expectations. Liz-Beth drew a bath. Immersion in hot water put her body on idle but not her mind.

The world seems to lurch forward every fifty years, Liz-Beth thought, *most of the productive life of a human being. As if we are born on the first day of the fifty first year, to push the world forward until we tire and pass the work to the next generation. Every generation has a defining event. Bunny, Sukie and I, we had the Second World War. Our generation created the world of the second half of the twentieth century and everything in it. The internet will be William and Natalie's event. They will use it to create the first half of the twenty first century. What sort of world will they make?*

Liz-Beth joined Joshua and Maggie for a quiet dinner. She slept that night as well as any in her long, productive life. The following morning she visited Sukie. *All those years,* he thought. *Liz-Beth finally defeated and cast off the dragon.* That afternoon, Akiko found him performing traditional Japanese dance routines on their flagstone patio. She had never seen him do this. *My husband has gone crazy,* Akiko thought. When asked what he was doing and why, Sukie answered, "I have never been so happy."

Mason waited patiently. The events of Thursday were a day in the life in his line of work. Liz-Beth called him at noon.

"I'm going to spend the weekend with Evelyn in San Francisco."

"Let me drive you up. I'm flying in this morning."

"Oh? You want to drive all the way to San Francisco after flying here from Las Vegas?"

"I can share more about what happened to John and Miriam, tell Josh and Maggie if you don't have to leave in the morning. Where are William and Natalie?"

"They stayed over in the city. They're driving down the coast tomorrow."

"Why don't you call your limo guy. Have him meet us downtown tomorrow evening, drive us to Evelyn's. I'll have a talk with him on the way back to my car."

"Just talk?"

"Yeah, just talk. Do you have a way to get home?"

"I can stay with Evelyn as long as I like. Natalie will bring me back."

Seventy-Eight

When Cousie left the offices of Meyers, Cantrell, and Holmes, he did something he had never done as an adult. He walked home. Only a half mile to the entrance of his building, the last three blocks inclined steeply. Now in his mid-seventy's, not in the best condition of his life, not on the best day of his life, Robert found the climb onerous.

Cousie wanted time to himself. He needed to avoid George. He owed the man money he didn't have and didn't want to give him if he had it. Cousie was stripped, his fortune reduced to the value of a bowl of oatmeal. Lifestyle change would be radical and forthcoming. He couldn't pay his monthly expenses.

Robert's career in corporate financial engineering just ended. Evil deeds and professional mediocrity caught up with him. He survived reverses. He could move on, to what? He knew Osgood would have his name off the door and his desk pushed into the hallway by morning. It didn't matter. Robert didn't know how to be a partner or a friend. He measured people by how much money he made by associating with them. When the sum totaled zero, he discarded them. As transparent as optical Schott glass, associates gave him equal consideration. Osgood could clean up the mess, Robert thought. He still had a business to run. Robert didn't.

Cousie nodded to the doorman and took the elevator to the penthouse. He stepped inside and threw his jacket on a sofa. When he reached the kitchen he found a note from Cindy. She didn't have to tell him she went shopping. If not that it would have been the spa, the tennis club, or all three.

Robert thought if he delayed paying some bills, made minimum payments on others, they could live for a while off credit cards and cash advances until they reached their credit limit. Cindy won't suspect anything until purchases are denied and memberships cancelled. Robert found the vision of her humiliated at checkout, turned away from spa and tennis club amusing. *Almost worth it*, he thought. He wondered how long after that he could con her into believing they weren't broke, or if he wanted to. A smile spread across his face when he realized he only had to find a way to keep her shopping.

Cousie thought he could hold off the mortgage company, the HOA, the car payments and go to Europe for a couple of months. He thought Cindy might contribute by falling off a boat and drowning. He could collect the insurance money and disappear into Croatia.

Robert took the elevator to the lobby, bought a copy of the Wall Street Journal in a convenience store and returned to read it on the balcony with a martini. *I'm not broke,* he said to himself, *not when I can still kick back in the sun with a newspaper and a cocktail.*

Robert absently shuffled the pages of the Journal without reading them. He reflected on the disaster created by the internet bubble. He couldn't admit to himself some people profited from it honestly. In Robert's calculus, he succeeded from personal genius, failed only when somebody let him down or cheated him. He admitted he sometimes made unfortunate choices. In his twisted logic, it isn't the same as being wrong.

Cousie thought he had Liz-Beth checkmated. He never imagined the business plan would escape, William would show up with a witness at the last minute and make him face down Rothstein with four aces to a straight flush. He knew life would never be the same, but Cousie being Cousie, he thought he could land on his feet somehow.

The following morning, Robert did a second thing he never did. He slept in on a weekday. He rolled over and looked at Cindy. They were out late the night before. They had a lot to eat and drink. At ten in the morning, she was out cold or pretending. *If the former she would sleep*, he thought, *into early afternoon. If the latter it made no difference. If I left before she rose she wouldn't miss me.*"

Robert showered and shaved. He dressed in a tailor-made charcoal suit, white shirt, black Gucci's, no socks, no tie, open collar. He took the elevator to the lobby, ordered steak and eggs in the café across the street and left to tour the city. It felt like farewell.

Robert left the garage in the Mercedes, a leased car he could drive a while longer. He drove to the South of Market neighborhood. He parked on Embarcadero and walked the waterfront past the marina, admiring progress the city made since the earthquake opened water views to the east bay when it took the elevated highway down in '89. He thought the property near the Bay Bridge would make a good location for a stadium.

Robert wondered if he could hold a garage sale at his storage space on 2nd Street, pocket the cash before anyone noticed, remove the lock, leave the door open, report the contents stolen and collect insurance money. The thought of Cindy finding it empty amused him. *Insurance is a racket*, he thought. *You can't steal from thieves.* Her stuff, bought with his money, hardly used if ever. She didn't need any of it. She just wanted it. Now Robert needed money but Cindy would never agree to part with her booty.

Robert returned to the car, drove north on Embarcadero, past the ferry terminal, the piers along San Francisco Bay, past Fisherman's Wharf, to the Marina Green. He parked to admire the boats that hadn't left the St. Francis Marina in years. Moored there to boost egos he thought, finance the yacht club, hold the slips for current and future generations of owners. Floating cocktail platforms for trust-fund babies. Did they deserve them? Did they earn them? It didn't matter. Robert approved of decadence. He wondered how many were seaworthy, if their motors would turn over, if their batteries were dead. He looked across the water to Alcatraz and couldn't imagine he belonged there if it was still an active prison. *That was for criminals,* he thought. *A better place for condos. Why should they have had that view?*

He strolled through Crissy Field, a base where he might have been stationed when the Army used it as an airfield. He stood on the beach south of the Golden Gate, dreamed of the time a pilot could take off from the grass and fly a biplane under the bridge. He drove across it to the Marin Headlands to gaze at the postcard view of the city across the bay, framed between the bridge towers. He made out the building he lived in, for a little longer. Robert re-crossed the bridge and wondered if the day would arrive when he didn't have three dollars for the toll.

He drove through the Presidio. The post and barracks were Army Spartan but classic in their simple design, color, material, in their red brick and white wooden trim, under red roofs of terracotta. He parked and gazed at the city and the ocean, the bay and the bridge, the beach and surf, from a grassy hill beneath trees that shaded the ground before the colonies declared independence. A magnificent property he thought, one of the world's finest. He wished he could have acquired the rights to develop it when he had the resources. *What a shame,* he thought. *It can never be done.*

He drove to the end of Marine Drive, parked at the base of the Golden Gate Bridge, stood on the walkway by the seawall. He watched the windsurfers sail the deep water across the bay, long boarders catching breakers. He let the spray hit him in the face and salt an expensive suit as the wind drove waves against the seawall. They soaked his shoes and wet his feet. He didn't care. Compared with the coming tsunami, a splash of surf hardly mattered. The scent of the bay, the sight of the bridge and waterfront cleansed his sinuses and sharpened his senses. A feeling of foreboding enveloped him. He could think of no solution. Robert enjoyed many good years in San Francisco. He knew this is the probably the last one. In two or three months, life would descend into hell. He felt like a wall fell on him. He stiffened himself, determined to hold up under it.

Robert wound down Lombard Street on the return drive. He passed Mel's Drive-In and wondered if he someday had to work in a place like it, just to survive. Could it become that bad? Could he descend from financial elite to nameless, homeless, penniless? As strong as Robert was despicable, even a man with a heart of stone has a limit.

Seventy-Nine

Josh and Maggie closed the store for the day. Liz-Beth joined them at Duarte's to wait for Mason.

"Hello everyone."

Mason kissed Liz-Beth and Maggie. Joshua ordered him a beer.

"How was the flight?"

"Champagne flight, Josh. Rush hour on 101 is tougher, more dangerous, and the view isn't nearly as nice. Congratulations on what happened in San Francisco. It turned out well didn't it?"

"Exceeded expectations. Thanks for your help."

"You're welcome. You and Josh did the heavy lifting. I wish I could make a better ending for John and Miriam. Sorry I couldn't bring them back."

"You did the best that could be done. Better than anyone else did. I'm grateful for that. If not for your efforts, we would never know what happened to them. I brought Josh and Maggie up to speed on what you've done."

"Thanks, Liz-Beth. You know I've been looking for John and Miriam's plane."

Josh and Maggie nodded.

"Somebody at Lockheed had a pretty good idea where it was. We located and salvaged it."

"How did Lockheed get involved in this?" Joshua asked.

"It's Lockheed's plane."

"John and Miriam didn't own it?"

"No Maggie. I know they did pretty well, but a Cessna 210

Turbo is an expensive airplane, a doctor's plane. They didn't need one of those. Did you ever wonder about that, Josh?"

"No."

"A simple, light civilian plane is all they needed for personal use. John needed something bigger and more powerful to test avionics and camera systems, part of his work for Lockheed."

"John was a spook?" Maggie asked.

"No" Mason chuckled. "He helped develop classified communications, navigation, systems displays and camera systems on government contracts. He kept the plane at Half Moon Bay for convenience, commuted in it when he stayed in Pescadero. Lockheed let him use it for pleasure flying."

"What brought it down?"

"He had an engine compartment fire that took out the electrical system."

"That's why they couldn't find them."

"No radio, Josh. He couldn't call for help."

"Go on."

"Does it matter Josh?"

"John and Miriam were our friends. We need to know."

"They left from Half Moon Bay, flew up the coast over water, probably at low altitude along the beaches. They vectored west near San Francisco. The fire started when John took the plane up to pass over the Farallon Islands. The Farallons are a local flight from Half Moon Bay. John didn't have to file a flight plan. He must have flown under radar. Nobody knew they were out there and in trouble."

"Why couldn't he find a safe place to land?"

"Did you fly much with them, Josh?"

"No, we didn't. I don't know much about flying."

"The Farallons are a pile of rocks. There's one small, rough, grassy area and a couple of buildings, no place there to land a plane. They were twenty miles out, not high enough to glide to shore. If they were near the coast John could have set it down in the swells, close enough to swim in, in a flat level field, on a road. If they crashed somebody would have seen it. They had to be in the water. Nobody realized they were missing until the following morning when the plane hadn't returned to the Half Moon Bay airport."

"Oh my God. They could have been rescued."

"No Liz-Beth. The average year-round water temperature near the Farallons is fifty-five degrees. They were gone by then."

"Why didn't a rescue team find them?" Maggie asked.

"The Coast Guard ran helicopters up and down the coast. The plane went under before they arrived if they searched the Farallons. Did they keep a raft in the plane?"

"I don't know," Joshua said.

Mason paused to swallow.

"They had a chance with a raft. It might have been seen from the air by a boat or ship. They could have had flares. Without one, it would have been pretty hard to spot two people bobbing up and down in the water, even if rescuers knew where to look."

"All that war experience, all the testing. He dies on a pleasure flight."

"The flight was doomed, Josh. If there was any way to survive this, John would have found it. I thought we could dive on a few shallow areas where the plane could be recovered. It was the only chance we had without a comprehensive bottom search. Some of the waters they flew over are very deep, unsearchable without exotic equipment we didn't have, a lot of time, a government size budget. I put our chances about fifteen percent."

"I wanted them to try" Liz-Beth said.

"We were lucky. A Lockheed employee knew John well enough to guess where they went. We found it on the edge of an underwater shelf. A few yards in the wrong direction, it would have sunk in an underwater canyon, out of reach of everything but equipment used to locate shipwrecks and rescue submariners in deep water. It would have taken Captain Nemo and the Nautilus."

"Light planes float for a while from air in the wings. We found it intact with the doors open. They climbed out before it sank. I wish we could give them a proper burial. If it means anything, the Navy commits their dead to the sea. I want to say hypothermia isn't a bad way. I'm not trying to spin this into something good. Thinking about leaving William alone, friends like yourselves behind, that was probably the worst of it. I'm sorry I can't give you more than that or tell you something better."

"Give me the bill. Whatever the cost, it was worth it."

"It didn't cost anything, Liz-Beth. I asked experienced divers I knew for help. One of them owns a dive boat and scuba gear. He had access to a commercial barge with a crane. They wouldn't let me compensate them. They volunteered, brought their own equipment, paid their own expenses. I turned men away, could have had a hundred of them. John was a combat airman. A legend and a hero who survived a terrible time and helped other fliers through it. They knew what he did in the war. I wish I had a chance to meet and hear about it from him. There was no way we were gonna leave them on the bottom of the ocean if we had any chance of finding them and no way anybody would accept money for trying. It was an honor. If William has a memorial service you'll be surprised how many will attend. Loyalty in the business world doesn't compare with bonds you make in the military, in wartime when your lives depend on each other."

Four pair of moist eyes met across the table.

"I need to pay you for this."

"Not a chance, Liz-Beth. Not for this one. Pay me for helping you with LightSwitch."

"It's all work, Erik."

"How can I accept money for this when nobody else will? I'm Navy too. Make a contribution to a disabled vet organization in John and Miriam's names. That will be appreciated."

"I'm glad we know how it ended. What about the plane?" Joshua asked.

"Lockheed will show it to the FAA and scrap it."

"When are you going to tell William?"

"Not just yet, Liz-Beth."

"When?"

"Can we see how this plays out? They have a way of turning into surprise endings."

"Under what circumstances would you tell him or not tell him?" Liz-Beth asked.

"I can't say until circumstances present themselves. I know we don't have to tell him yet and I think we should wait until we do."

"Erik has a point" Joshua said. "William and Natalie are having a big time right now. Why don't we let him enjoy it?"

"Josh."

"Do we want to put William through this now? For what benefit? What do you think, Maggie?"

"I think we should wait. What harm can it do as long as Erik keeps us in the loop?"

"Are we all agreed then?" Mason asked.

They were.

"Did the kids head down the coast, Liz-Beth?"

"They drove down with Bernie in the Alfa. They're spending the weekend in a cabin at Carmel River Lodge, driving down to Big Sur Saturday. William makes his triumphant return to LightSwitch Monday morning."

"Like Caesar entered Alexandria," Maggie said.

"I hope his head doesn't swell to Caesar's helmet size," Liz-Beth answered.

"How did the limo driver get involved with Cousie?"

"That's what I'm going to find out tonight, Josh."

"Have you got a minute" Joshua asked.

"Sure. Meet you at the car, Liz-Beth."

Liz-Beth and Maggie left Duarte's. Erik and Joshua stayed behind and Joshua picked up the check.

"What's going on, Erik? I know you haven't told us everything."

"There's something I'm uncomfortable with."

"What is it?"

"I'm not sure. It has to play out a little bit."

"You can tell me" Joshua said.

"I can't." Mason answered. "I need you to go with me on this for a little while."

"Something to do with waiting to tell William and Natalie?"

"Indirectly, yes. With the plane. I'm not sure yet. It's better for me to tell you when I am."

Eighty

iz-Beth called George and asked him to meet her at the San Francisco Caltrans station at 7PM. Mason dropped Liz-Beth off at the entrance. He parked fifty yards down and across the street, and walked back to join her. George arrived minutes later. He knew who Mason was. They never met. Liz-Beth shocked him when she made the introduction.

Mason hadn't shaved in two days. He wore a heavy bulky black leather jacket over tan kaki straight leg military style pants tucked into black lace-up combat boots. George thought Mason looked menacing and his jacket might conceal a canon. It unnerved him. George knew he couldn't handle Mason. He thought he had the same chance of winning a heavyweight boxing title. None. Shaking hands with Mason felt like grasping a steel beam hinged to a boulder. He flinched at the strength behind Mason's grip and the toughness and callouses of the palms of his hand. Mason smiled and spoke politely, but he stared at George with unfriendly eyes. Clinging to the hope he wasn't busted when he knew he was, George drove Liz-Beth and Mason to Evelyn's. Evelyn smiled and waved from the building entrance. Mason exited the limo, opened the door for Liz-Beth, gave her a goodnight peck on the cheek. He returned to the back seat and pulled the door closed. Liz-Beth paid George through the driver's window for a round trip from the Caltrans Station and told him she wouldn't need him the rest of the evening. George knew he'd been had. Realizing he could have driven off while Liz-Beth and Mason stood outside the car, he wished he had thought of it in time. Lacking a better plan he continued the charade.

George felt safe as long as the limo rolled in traffic. The two men didn't exchange a word on the drive. When he glanced in the mirror, George saw Mason gazing out the window, expressionless, watching the city glide by on a damp moonless night. When they reached the Caltrans Station George's false sense of security dissolved like a sugar lump in coffee. He couldn't think of an escape. He could only hope Mason's appearance had nothing to do with him, that Mason would exit the limo and board the next train.

Mason sat quietly after the limo braked to a stop. George waited in the driver's seat for something to happen. He froze when his eyes met Mason's in the mirror. They looked mercenary, his face an angry frown.

George thought about reaching for his 9mm. He knew he wouldn't make it. He scanned the sidewalks, the train station looking for people milling around, a policeman, a cruiser, any witness that would deter Mason. The neighborhood looked abandoned under dark overcast skies adding to his sense of dread. The streets were still wet and the air humid from a late afternoon shower. Warm, damp, and stale air hung ominously in the car. Mason ran the window down. He raised the tension by waiting in silence.

"Is there something else I can do for you?"

"You know who I am, don't you?"

"Yeah."

"I just wanna talk. Clients pay me to talk to creeps so they don't have to. How did Cousie learn you know Natalie?"

"He's a regular customer. I've known him since I took him to a strip club on Broadway a few years ago."

"Good answer. Not to the question I asked. I know you know Cousie. How does Cousie know you know Natalie?"

"We started talking about women one night when I drove him to meet one at a hotel. I told him about the night I drove her to Pescadero. He knew William lived there. He asked me her name. How many Natalie's take a limo to Pescadero that aren't William's girlfriend?"

"Why did you tell him you dropped a woman off in Pescadero?"

"Did you ever meet her? She's the most beautiful girl I've ever seen. An amazing fare to take somebody down there, single girl like her. A dream fare. I told everyone I saw for a week."

"Why did you tell him she would be in San Francisco?"

"He said he knew her and wanted to see her if she came in the city. I didn't know they'd get into an argument."

"That was quite an act you put on at Union Square."

"They told you about that?"

"I watched it from across the street."

Shit, Winston thought. *He knows everything.* "How did you know we would be there?"

"See the brown Taurus parked down the street? Would you notice if you were followed in it, if the car trailed back in traffic?"

George broke into a sweat. He swallowed and ground his teeth. *Jesus, the guy's been following me. Where and for how long?*

"Look, that wasn't an act. If he hurt her, I would have *killed* him."

Mason thought Winston only half-faked the anger.

"It wouldn't have been necessary. Why would you want to protect somebody you stabbed in the back?"

"I fell in love with her on the ride to Pescadero."

"Love at first sight, huh? Let me understand this. You used the woman you were infatuated with to help your client try to screw her boyfriend, but if the client who paid you to set her up hurt her, you would have killed him."

"I didn't want anyone to be hurt. You gotta believe that."

"Turn around slowly and look at me."

George's eyes were moist. Mason saw fear and remorse.

"You *do* have a crush on her."

"I can't stop thinking about her."

"You can stop now. You dug a pretty deep hole for yourself in Reno. Got yourself so upside down I almost feel sorry for you."

"How did you know about that?"

"What did Cousie pay you?"

"Nothing. He owes me money and I can't find the son-of-a-bitch."

"He offered to pay off your gambling debts."

"That's right."

"He won't."

"How do you know that?"

Mason didn't answer.

"What do I do now? Skip town and hide out in Montana?"

"Talk to those guys. Work your butt off. Give them what you can, when you can. You'll be living on Mac & Cheese for a while. They won't break your legs if they think they can get their money."

"How am I gonna work around here?"

"You think Natalie and William are gonna call half the city and tell everybody not to hire you? Nobody knows about this. Go to work and pay your debt. I meet unusual people in my line of work. I never met anyone like Liz-Beth. That woman has the capacity to do things nobody would do. When I tell her why you did it she might forgive you, but if you ever do or say anything that might hurt her, or William or Natalie again and you meet a little Japanese guy with a sword, you better run faster than Halley's Comet. If he isn't around I'm never far. You know anything about a missing airplane?"

"No."

"You sure? If you're hiding something you're in a lot more trouble than you know."

"I don't know anything about an airplane."

"Cousie never mentioned it in reference to anything?"

"No."

"Look at me."

George turned around again.

"Know anyone who works at Moffett field?"

"No, what's there?"

"Pigeons… How did you meet Cousie?"

"Through another client."

"How'd you meet the client?"

"Referral. Drove him back from Sunnyvale one afternoon. He lives up here, partner in a strip club. We picked Cousie up one night on the way to Broadway. Kind of a rough guy."

"When was that?"

"A few years back."

"You owe him the money, don't you?"

"Yeah."

"He told you if you did what Cousie asked you to do, he would pay off the debt."

"Yeah."

"What was he doing on the Peninsula?"

"He knows a couple of guys at Lockheed. Went to visit them."

"Ever meet them?"

"Just when I picked this guy up to bring him to the city."

"What do they do there?"

"Airplane mechanics."

"This guy have a name?"

"Stanley."

"Last name?"

"He never said."

"Just Stanley."

"Yeah." George nodded.

What's his real name? Mason wondered?

"Pays in cash?"

"Yeah."

"This guy go out with Cousie much?"

"Once a month."

"Where do they go?"

"Strip joints, hotels."

Mason paused to ponder that. Cousie knows somebody who knows two airplane mechanics that work for Lockheed, Moffett

Field. Goes by a fake name, pays in cash, strip club owner, loan shark, tells George if he does something for Cousie he'll forgive George's gambling debt.

"Are you gonna put the police on me?"

"For conspiracy to commit fraud? Don't flatter yourself. I need you to disappear. Don't speak to anybody about this so we don't have to have any more talks. Pretend you don't know anything or anybody, no matter what you see or hear. Can you do that?... Answer me."

"Yeah, I can do that. I'm a limo driver."

"Act like one. You aren't the worst guy I know, George. You were willing to stand up for Natalie. You're lucky it turned out the way it did. If not, your gambling debt would feel like a minor irritation. In the unlikely event you hear from Liz-Beth or Natalie, I wouldn't take the call, not for a while."

"What happened yesterday?"

"Didn't I tell you not to discuss it?"

George didn't answer.

"Don't be a schmuck, George. You aren't a very good criminal. You have to be remorseless for that. If you screw around with guys like Stanley and Cousie they'll use you and get you in trouble. Driving a limo isn't the worst job in the world. Do it well. Here's my card. Call if you hear something you think I should know."

Mason stepped out of the limo, walked down the street and crossed to the Taurus. He looked back once from the median, started the car, and drove off with one eye on the rear-view mirror. When he reached the corner he saw the limo door open. George stepped out, leaned on a fender, lit a cigarette, and took a long pull with unsteady hands. He leaned his head back and exhaled a big cloud of smoke.

Mason punched in a number. He called his nephew on the cell phone.

Eighty-One

Mason turned right on Fifth Street and right at Brannon. He drove to the Embarcadero, parked the Taurus and stepped into his favorite eatery in San Francisco. They knew him well at Delancey Place, a public restaurant in a half-way house for model inmates from the California state correction system. Located in the gentrifying neighborhood of South of Market, Mason often ate at the bar when he visited the city. On this particular night, as he finished an entrée, he ordered a single malt scotch and took a call to a booth to speak in private.

Mason's nephew, police detective Andrew Riley, logged five years in uniform. Promoted to plain clothes, on his first assignment, Andrew and his partner, veteran detective Thomas Riehley, were the criminal investigation team of Riley and Riehley.

Thomas is as tall and black as Andrew is short and white. Not yet a week working together, known in the precinct as Mutt and Jeff, salt and pepper, ebony and ivory, the keyboard brothers, the Riley twins, Andrew found it amusing. Thomas didn't. He didn't like breaking in rookie detectives but he warmed in a week to naturally likable "Andy the Kid."

Mason served with Thomas in Special Forces, had great respect for him. After Andrew's promotion to plain clothes, Mason made the introduction.

Mason sipped a dram of Aberlour while he listened to his nephew describe his first plainclothes assignment.

The doorman let Riehley and Riley into the building when they flashed their badges. At their request he didn't call ahead.

Cindy answered the door for two conservatively dressed men in medium grey single-breasted suits and narrow dark ties.

"Mrs. Cousie?"

"Yes."

"I'm Lieutenant Thomas Riehley. This is detective Andrew Riley of the San Francisco Police Department."

"Is this a prank?"

They presented their badges.

"We'd like to have a word with your husband. May we come in?"

"I'll get Robert."

The officers stepped into the doorway.

Strange, she thought, the doorman didn't call. What would the police want with Robert? Dressed in evening clothes of a high-priced call girl, Cindy had been prepping for her mirror. She called Robert to the door and returned to her dressing room.

The building lobby impressed. Not as much as Cousie's penthouse. Andrew peered around Thomas into an expansive living room with sixteen-foot ceilings beyond a broad entry. Framed in floor-to-ceiling glass spanning the outside wall, Andrew saw the Bay Bridge lit for the evening, arcing across the water toward Treasure Island. A living work of art, headlights of cars crossing the bridge resembled a firefly army on the march. Frank Sinatra crooned "My Way" on a Bang and Olufsen. A mélange of perfume and aftershave wafted through the air above opulent furnishings. Roche Bobois, an original Jackson Pollack. *Like a movie set*, Andrew thought. He had never seen anything like it. Thomas had been in the finest high-rises. He had.

Robert walked down the corridor concerned that someone made their way past a doorman who didn't notify him. He wore dark gabardine slacks and Marco Bruno loafers with no socks. Bare from the waist up except for a towel around his neck and a few shaving cream remnants clinging to his face, he held a gold-plated razor. Robert prepped for a rendezvous after Cindy went to bed.

"What can I do for you gentlemen?"

Thomas took the lead.

"Robert Cousie?"

"Yes, and you are?"

"Lieutenant Riehley and Detective Riley from the San Francisco Police Department."

They showed him their badges.

"Is this a gag?"

"It's no gag, sir. Can we speak with you?"

"You come to my home Friday night to discuss business fraud? Can't the DA wait until Monday?"

Two puzzled officers exchanged glances.

"I'm sorry?" Thomas asked.

"We resolved that business two days ago."

"I don't know anything about a business fraud, Mr. Cousie. We're from homicide. We're here to ask you about the death of John and Miriam Beckinsdale. It occurred a number of years ago. We have reason to believe it was a murder."

Robert blanched. His knees buckled. His razor fell to the floor. He slew to the side, threw out a hand to steady himself against a wall. Fuck, he mouthed. I never imagined…

"Mr. Cousie, can we sit down? We need to ask you a few questions."

"Yes, yes of course. Sorry, I…was married to Miriam."

"We know."

Robert led them into the living room.

"Ah, make yourself comfortable. I, yeah, um, is it OK if I put on a shirt?"

"Yes, of course. Go with him, Andrew."

Cindy glided by on her way to the kitchen. In an evening gown even more immodest than the already immodest dress she wore when the detectives arrived, she shot a flirtatious look at Thomas as she swayed down the hall leaving little to the imagination.

"What is it, Robert?"

"Nothing, Cindy. I'll talk to you later."

Robert walked slowly and methodically down the corridor to

the master bedroom. Andrew trailed a few steps behind. Robert's shoulders slumped as he sat on the edge of the bed and dug his toes into luxurious carpet.

"Mr. Cousie."

"A moment please."

Cousie stood and walked to a chest of drawers. He opened a middle drawer, removed a freshly laundered shirt and placed it on the bed. He pulled the towel off his shoulder, opened the top drawer, and groped for a faded photo under a neatly folded stack of handkerchiefs in the left rear corner. Miriam stood in the sand on a Long Island beach, a young woman in a white sundress and a large sunhat. Youthful, smiling, beautiful. Robert held the photo in a shaking hand. He wiped a moist eye. Cindy knew where he hid it and didn't care. Robert slid the photo into a pocket and closed the drawer.

Robert turned his head and saw Andrew admiring a bust of Alexander the Great on a dresser across the room. He opened another drawer, reached in with the towel, removed a dark metal object with it, folded and placed the towel under an arm. Andrew watched him walk into the bathroom. Robert tried to close the door behind him. Andrew rushed the room, threw out a hand on the edge of the door to prevent Robert from closing it.

"You wanna shake it for me?"

Andrew backed off. "Leave it open."

"May I have a little privacy?"

"Close it part way."

Robert positioned the door to block part of the view of the bathroom. He sat out of sight on the commode. Andrew waited outside.

A man's life can be based on lies. Robert lied to himself that the world treated him unfairly. He lied for a time that Miriam loved him, not John. He lied that he could be faithful. He believed misery licensed him to inflict pain and punishment, to seek revenge on anyone he thought had cheated him or wronged him, or might if they had the chance.

Now with everything lost, Robert viewed with clarity, so much he believed, and thought, and did, had been wrong. He admitted to himself he had been wrong, about everything.

Robert's mind raced through his experiences, a swirling collage of images funneling back to Miriam. He reached into his pocket for the photo. His eyes moistened, his chin trembled. For the first time, as far back as he could remember, he cried.

"I loved you Miriam," Robert whispered, more tenderly to her photo, than he ever did to her. "Why did you have to fall in love with John? I'm sorry I was unfaithful. I didn't want to hurt you. God help me, I didn't. I couldn't live with you and John together. John was my best friend."

Robert's mind numbed as he stood, reached across the vanity, and leaned the photo against the mirror. His head pounded. The room turned slowly on an axis. Grout lines deflected into chevrons as his eyes went out of focus when he stared at the travertine.

Always a schemer, Robert leaned on the vanity and faced the mirror on unsteady legs. *I could shoot my way out of here, make a run to the airport, disappear into hiding,* he thought. He had a passport and a shoebox stuffed with hundred-dollar bills hidden behind the drywall in the master closet. It would be enough for a start. He knew it wouldn't work. He'd never reach the airport gate. His half-baked vision of escape to Croatia, an opportunity lost by a day, he knew he had to spend the rest of his life in courtrooms and prisons. A long stay in a place he thought most resembled hell. San Quentin probably, with a view through prison bars of a life that used to be. He knew he would never leave on his feet. Robert survived a short stay in a country club prison in upstate New York. He didn't think he could navigate maximum security with violent criminals, not for long. A few hours ago, he didn't think he belonged there with people like them. Now he admitted to himself that he did. The best he could hope for was death in prison of natural causes.

Life ends for everyone. Its better when you can choose the time and place, when family and friends provide comfort, and last words give meaning to life. Not for Robert. A tired old man, alone, with no future, no goodness to remember, nothing to be proud of to leave behind, Robert had only his reflection in a mirror, an image that evening, he came to despise.

"Mr. Cousie? Mr. Cousie. Is everything alright?"

Robert didn't answer. He placed the towel to the side of his head, gripped the .380 auto concealed inside, and shot himself in the temple.

Andrew rushed into the bathroom as Robert collapsed to the floor. Thomas drew his side arm. He reached the doorway in time to see a pitiful look on the rookie detective's face as he stood over the body.

Cindy heard the shot from the kitchen as she leaned into the refrigerator trying to decide between salad and yogurt. The open door threw enough light to see through everything she wore. She looked up, paused for a moment, chose and casually bit into an apple before closing the door and calmly swaying down the corridor. An expression of disgust crossed her face as she looked down at Robert, bleeding out on the bathroom floor.

"What did you do?"

Cindy was a cold one.

Eighty-Two

"Why didn't you cuff and arrest him, Andy?"

"He was a person of interest, Uncle Mace. Cousie knew somebody in San Francisco, who knew the suspects. We could only question him."

"Okay kid. I understand police work."

"He hired them to do it, didn't he?"

"Yeah, he did."

"I feel like a jackass. My first plain clothes assignment and I let the suspect shoot himself."

"Don't feel bad about it. Cousie's life was over. He would have spent the rest of it behind bars. You saved taxpayer's money from years of incarceration and legal maneuvers."

"How much trouble is this going to cause us?"

"I wouldn't worry about it. They'll ask you how he got his hands on the gun. What if he turned it on you? Thomas sent you in there to prevent it. What did he say about it?"

"He told me not to worry. He says he knows I realize I screwed up, that he should have made sure I didn't."

"It's his problem too. He can manage it."

"What about the limo driver?"

"Don't waste your time. He doesn't know anything. If they catch the suspects he might be able to identify them. Can you sandbag this when reporters call?"

"We can say we're investigating. There isn't much to share."

"Thanks, kid."

"I have to go to the station after they clean this mess up. Wanna meet for a nightcap?"

"Sorry Andy, gotta tell a man about a suicide. I'm staying at Josh and Maggie's tonight. It's getting late. It's a long drive. Catch you on the next visit. Give me a call if you wanna talk, okay?"

"Sure, Uncle Mace. Thanks."

Mason called Joshua and told him to expect him in two hours. He sat in the booth at Delancey Place, sipped his scotch, thought about what to tell Liz-Beth, Josh and Maggie, and what if anything to tell William and Natalie.

Eighty-Three

Cousie's suicide shocked Josh and Maggie. They listened with grim faces and sad eyes. An evil man, a tragic life, less though, than the tragedy he rained on others. The predator died by his own hand but no satisfaction could be found in it.

"It's late, Josh. Wanna save the rest until morning?"

"I'll be up all night, Erik. What did you learn from George?"

"He had a gambling debt. Cousie promised to pay it off. He didn't. George didn't get anything. He's a limo driver trying to get through life. Forget him."

"Does Liz-Beth know?"

"No, Josh. I wanted her to enjoy the evening with Evelyn. I have to call soon. It'll be in the morning paper. Better if she hears it from me. Are the kids in Carmel?"

"Yeah, they called. They sounded happy. If they get out of bed tomorrow they'll go to Big Sur. I wouldn't bet on it. What are you going to tell them?"

"I don't know."

"You have to tell them."

"Why? It's just a suicide in the city. That's how it will be reported. A few lines, column three, page four, local business news. Depressed from disastrous internet investments, businessman kills himself, leaves wife and two grown children from previous marriage. Stories about losses from the internet bubble collapse are everywhere. This one will be dead by the time they return from Carmel. If they don't see it in the paper this weekend they'll miss it."

"They'll find out," Joshua said.

"We agreed to give them a few days of peace."

"What do you think, Maggie?"

"I agree."

"OK, Mace. We can go with it."

Mason called Liz-Beth.

"I don't know what to say, Erik. I wanted him stopped. I didn't want him dead."

"You didn't kill him, Liz-Beth. He made the decision to exit whatever hell he lived in. It's over for you and your friends. Thanks to you it's gonna be better for everyone. Can I bring you back from the city?"

"I'll wait for Natalie. I want to spend a few more days with Evelyn. When are you going home?"

"I'm gonna spend the weekend with Josh and Maggie. I hate leaving Pescadero. It's so exciting."

"What do you have planned?"

"Store inventory. Maggie has me counting cereal boxes."

"Wish I could join you."

"We could use your math skills. You are one great lady, Mrs. Wiggins. I'd love to visit with you when I visit Josh and Maggie."

"I'll look forward to that, Erik. Thank you for all your help. We couldn't have done it without you."

Eighty-Four

No one but Cindy and the building doorman she paid to accompany her to the cemetery witnessed Robert Cousie's ignominious end. She paid the doorman in cash, the funeral home and cemetery by credit card. Only the doorman could be certain of undisputed compensation. Credit cards are reported lost or stolen. Card holders disappear. Funds would be credited, eventually.

At the gravesite, "You moron," is all Cindy said.

Cindy removed her clothing and jewelry from the penthouse when she arrived home and stuffed it in the back of her Mercedes SUV. She cleaned out the contents of the storage units on 2nd Street, had it loaded on a truck and shipped to parts unknown. She hired an auction company to pick up and sell the furnishings and art from the penthouse and deposit her share of the proceeds in a numbered account. A clean-out company would remove the remains.

Cindy was gone. In her escape, she erased the life of Robert Cousie from the penthouse he lived in, and schemed in, as if he never existed. Victim of the pursuit of everything at any cost; people to use, someone to own rather than cherish, Cousie's life would well be forgotten by everyone who knew him, of everything he did, before the new owners of the penthouse moved in.

Late in the day, Thomas returned to the building to search for anything he may have missed. He found the front door ajar, the penthouse cleaned out. Furnishings and artwork gone. Closets open and empty. He discovered two steaks in the freezer, unfinished salad in a serving bowl, an apple and two dirty place settings on the kitchen island. He found a photograph of Miriam leaning against a mirror in the master bathroom and a jagged hole in the sheetrock, in an inside master closet wall.

Eighty-Five

On the way back to Las Vegas, thoughts that interrupted Mason's sleep the last few nights made him feel like driving past the San Carlos Airport. He exited the freeway anyway, drove through the airport gate, parked in front of the terminal. He sat in the Taurus while the motor idled until his thoughts coalesced into what he needed to do before flying home.

Mason backed the car out, left the airport and returned to the freeway. He drove south and exited in Menlo Park. He continued south on Middlefield, through Palo Alto, to Mountain View, where he stopped in a coffee shop and ordered a latte. *How will William and Natalie take this?* he wondered? *What can I do to help them? Perfect humans are only found in cartoons and comic books,* Mason thought. *The rest of us, we're all flawed.*

Mason finished his latte, left the coffee shop and drove to the Lockheed facility at Moffett Field. He found Eddie Johnson rebuilding a P3 Orion engine in one of the hangers.

"Hi, Eddie. Can we have another look at the plane?"

"Sure, Mace. What's up?"

"Let's have a look, then I'll tell you."

They walked to hangar #2 on the east side of the property. Eddie unlocked the door. Mason walked to the nose of the plane with Eddie following behind him. He lingered over the engine bay.

"Anybody been in here?"

"Except for the master in a maintenance locker, I have the only key. Nobody can get in without me."

"What if the shredded fuel line was replaced with an old one that's heavily oxidized but undamaged?"

"Like it was underwater?"

"Yeah. With a loose rusty hose clamp that might have allowed it to leak onto the exhaust manifold or disconnect and fall on it."

"What are you talking about, Mason?"

"What if the relay and the arming switch were removed, if the wiring to the altimeter and master switch were gone? The hole in the exhaust manifold filled in or…forced into a crack?"

"It would look like mechanical failure."

"It would, wouldn't it?"

"That's evidence tampering, Erik. I can't do that."

"Do you know what a Mitzvah is, Eddie?"

"A Mitzvah? No."

"It's a Hebrew word, technically a commandment from God. It has a secondary meaning. A religious duty to perform a moral deed, a selfless act of kindness, to help someone with no benefit to yourself. God isn't always around but we are. We all break the law" Mason said. "We choose the time and purpose."

"Why do you want to do this, Mason?"

"To save nice people a lot of pain."

"The scumbags will get away with it."

"The guys who did this are missing and long gone. The plane's been underwater for years. No witnesses. No motive. All the evidence is circumstantial. Can they find them and prove they did it? It's an old case. A cold case. Who would make the effort?"

Eddie's face contorted.

"Ever been on a jury, Eddie?"

"I've been called, not selected."

"First time you sit in a jury box in a capital case you discover how much power a judge has, how much power a jury has, how helpless a defendant is. You think about what it means to take a man's freedom, to take his life. It's a hard thing to do. You have to be sure. We think we know what happened but we don't have to make that decision. We don't have to look human beings in the eyes when we decide if we want to put them in prison for life or send them to death row. We don't have to live with the consequences. We don't have to listen to a skilled attorney advocating against it. No matter how certain you and I feel about this we can never know what a jury will decide. They may never be caught. They might catch them and a jury might let them go. Either way, John's son will learn his father and mother were murdered. It will pile a lot more pain on top of what he's gonna feel when he learns we found the plane, maybe for nothing. It would be better for him and for John's memory if he never knows."

"Jason will know."

"Jase and I go back a long way. I'll have a talk with him. If he says no I'll tell you. If he agrees, only you, Jason, and I will ever know."

"Where's the justice for John?"

"Justice is for the living, Eddie. It does nothing for the dead. Do you want to punish the guilty more than you want to help John and his son? The murder of your parents can scar you for life. John's son, William, he's recovering from a devastating business disaster. Why not shield him from another kick in the gut? For the sake of John and his son, Eddie, why don't we help them?"

"Have you ever done anything like this?"

"Yeah, I have."

Mason shocked Eddie.

"Don't be surprised, Eddie. Worse things happen. Innocent people are harmed. I'm sort of in law enforcement. Is that it? I'm really not. I want the best result for my client."

"I can't do this."

"I need to tell you what William's been through, Eddie. You might think it's what John would want you to do. We don't have time for that now. Go with me on this. I'll owe you a big one."

Mason thought Eddie was softening. He couldn't be sure.

"If you witnessed a hit and run accident would you chase after the driver or stop to help the victim?"

Eddie swallowed.

"I'm going to leave it with you, Eddie. Whatever you decide, it's okay with me. Either way, this conversation never happened."

Mason held out a hand. Eddie hesitated. He took it. When their eyes met, Mason couldn't know what Eddie would decide. Satisfied with the effort to convince him, Mason left.

Eighty-Six

After a day of exploring Big Sur and dinner at the Rocky Point Restaurant, William, Natalie and Bernie returned to the cabin they rented in Carmel. Tired from all the hiking, Natalie went straight to bed. William stayed up with a glass of wine in the living room and Bernie snuggled on his lap. She looked at him with unconditional love.

William thought about all the things that happened in the last few months until his thoughts landed on his parents. The vision of them flying along the coast in the Cessna came to him, as it sometimes did in a dream that returned when he thought of them doing things they loved to do together. A tear came to William's eye as he wished they had lived to see him succeed as a founder and leader of a business, now thinking of starting a family of his own. He toasted them. *Mom, Dad, I wish you could be here to see Natalie, Bernie and me starting a life together.* He carried Bernie with him to the bedroom.

William and Natalie rose for brunch in Carmel. The restaurant provided a stainless water bowl to set on the sidewalk. Natalie brought the treats. She hated leaving Bernie outside. Bernie didn't understand why she couldn't be inside. A dog has to learn her limitations.

William and Natalie were too busy enjoying themselves to read the weekend paper. After burying so much baggage they only had time for themselves, for Bernie, and the future.

They checked out of the cabin and drove to Pescadero, stopping along the way to explore the coast. They made dinner at the cottage and turned in early.

Lupe told VK what happened in San Francisco, that William and Natalie went to Carmel for the weekend, that William would come to the office Monday morning for an all-hands meeting to announce his return and share how he wanted to move the company forward.

The Monday morning San Jose Mercury News reported no investor suicides, no discovery of missing airplanes. The FAA wouldn't be notified for another day. If Cousie rated a few lines in the back pages, William and Natalie would have missed them.

Life began to normalize. Moving back to Mountain View, William's return to his company, would bring the adventure full circle. After all the pain, Natalie had what she wanted, from events she set in motion with a midnight visit to Pescadero.

After breakfast, William reached for the Alfa keys. Natalie suggested he take his father's car. She reminded him to take Dusty.

"I want to go too. Let's take Bernie."

"How can you take a day off from a new job?"

"I'll tell them I had a death in the family."

"I'll ask Josh if we can leave Bernie with him and Maggie."

"She can sit on my lap. She likes riding with us in cars. Isn't LightSwitch dog friendly? You're the CEO. If it isn't, fix it. Wow! I'm living with a CEO again!"

The marine layer retreated overnight, clearing the skies before the sun rose over the coastal mountains. They left in full sun, meandered up Rt. 84. The engine turned over lazily, exhaust note deep and mellow. Bernie sat on Natalie's lap, front paws on the car door, leaning her head outside the windscreen, face in the wind. Dusty napped in the boot. Not many people commuted from the coast on Highway 84, to work in Silicon Valley. They didn't see another traveler until they passed La Honda.

They turned south at Alice's when they reached Skyline Drive. South of Sky Londa, Skyline Drive winds along a ridge on the top of the Santa Cruz Mountains. It passes through open spaces near several wineries, a performing arts center, a school for foreign students striving for acceptance to the best American universities.

Fog lingered on the ridge line. A mist from the marine layer saturated the trees like a light rain. Droplets fell from the canopy as they passed underneath, spotting the windshield, sailing over car, and man, woman and dog, and Dusty, the intrepid pelican. Bernie threw out her tongue and snapped her jaws to capture a rain forest shower. Excited and happy, she begged for attention and received it, expressing joy as only puppies do. Like a child, every experience a new adventure.

They drove along the crest of the Santa Cruz Mountains past Portola Valley. They turned off Skyline Drive onto Big Basin Way where the sun burned patches of blue in the fog as the street name changed to Saratoga Avenue. The route dropped them into the heart of Silicon Valley.

Layoffs and bankruptcies from the bursting internet bubble reduced rush hour traffic to a trickle. An eerie morning commute seemed more like weekend than weekday. As prospects for quick recovery faded, it felt like nuclear winter descended on the northern California technology industry. William had a mission. Recapitalized, debt reduced or eliminated, product line revitalized, with any luck at all, LightSwitch could survive.

They drove through Santa Clara, reached San Tomas Expressway, crossed Highway 101 where William and Lupe waited on the ramp to hear from Liz-Beth and began their mad dash to San Francisco to ambush Dunn & Cousie. When they reached Montague they were minutes away.

William turned into the car park. Anxious to greet employees he hadn't seen in months, he idled past rows of cars until he reached the isle that lined up with the LightSwitch entry. Lupe stood next to VK in front of employees arrayed across the front steps.

"Did you know about this, Natalie?"

"Of course. VK called this morning when you were walking Bernie. I wouldn't miss it for anything."

William knew how to make an entry. He crept to the end of the aisle, turned the car at an angle to the building and braked to a stop in front of the crowd. He stood on the driver's seat and waved. LightSwitch employees led by VK and Lupe erupted in cheers and applause. The windows of the office building filled with curious faces. William and Natalie shared a smile. William stepped out, walked behind the car, opened the boot and held the old pelican up in triumph. The crowd responded with a second round of cheers.

"Dusty," William said, "We're back."

Dusty was speechless.

VK and Lupe shook William's hand and hugged him. The rest of the employees queued for a turn. With everyone greeted, the celebration subsided. William, Natalie, Bernie and Dusty climbed the front stairs and stood at the entry. William addressed LightSwitch employees with the wave of an arm and a one sentence speech.

"We have a company to run!"

When they entered the building, the mission of the Pelican Squadron was complete.

About the Author

Harvey Sherman has a Bachelor's Degree in Communications from Penn State University. He is a retired computer industry executive in the process of reinventing himself in pursuit of the elusive second act in American life.

After spending twenty-three years in the computer industry, ending thirteen years of it working as a software executive in Silicon Valley, Harvey retired and returned to the Seattle area to decompress. Having always enjoyed spinning a tale since his teenage years, he began writing a novel centered around lessons in life learned by playing the game of baseball. The story is set in New York City in the 1950s and 1960s, most of it around the time the old Yankee Stadium was about to be replaced.

After completing a draft of the novel, Harvey decided his writing skills needed polishing before he could fashion it into something worth reading. He began by writing what was intended to be an 8- to 12-page character study of a few inhabitants of the small coastal town of Pescadero, located between San Francisco and San Jose, which he visited on weekends while he lived in Silicon Valley during the years straddling the Internet Bubble of 2000.

The study unintentionally blossomed into a short story of some 60 pages which Harvey felt had so sad an ending. Rather than change the ending as Hemingway would have done, (Papa is said to have written 49 ending to A Farewell to Arms before choosing one), Harvey decided to write another story, this one beginning in the town of Mountain View in Silicon Valley. Upon sharing the two stories, a friend remarked, "Interesting, but what does one have to do with the other?" Not a bad idea, Harvey thought. It could make a novel.

Having both stories coincidentally ending on a beach in Pescadero, though with decades separating the time they arrived there, Harvey thought, why not have the characters meet there?

A novel was born. Far too many years, too many drafts, and thousands of hours later, the novel was completed.

Harvey resides in Kirkland, Washington, near where some of *The Pelican Squadron* takes place. He is looking forward to writing out the origin story—the prequel, and the sequel, and moving on to the next chapter in his life . . . whatever it will become.

Harvey's hobbies include stock portfolio management, amateur vintage car racing, home remodeling, motorsports and wildlife journalism, and photography. He enjoys the state of Washington's great geography: the Cascade Mountains, the Skagit Valley, the Olympic Peninsula and the Pacific Coast, the lakes and the high country desert of Eastern Washington, the Columbia Gorge, and the Palouse. He likes driving to Northern Nevada to visit friends, to Northern California, and flying to Florida for vintage car events.

Reach out to Harvey. He can be found at harveysherman@frontier.com. He loves to hear about and discuss readers' thoughts about *The Pelican Squadron,* their contributions of which added greatly to the development and quality of the book.